THE UNRAVELING OF MICHAEL GALLER

THE UNRAVELING OF MICHAEL GALLER

A NOVEL

STEVEN M. RUBIN

spark press

Published in 2026 by
SparkPress, an imprint of The Stable Book Group

1569 Solano Ave #546
Berkeley, CA 94707
https://shewritespress.com
Library of Congress Control Number: 2026904164
ISBN: 979-8-89636-374-3
eISBN: 979-8-89636-375-0

Interior Designer: Andrea Reider

Printed in the United States

To my mother,
the bravest person I know to face death.
To my father,
the bravest person I know to face life.

CHAPTER 1

1994

Massachusetts

Through a weary squint, Michael watched his house come into view and settle into the frame of the back seat window. It confirmed the end of a long weekend stay at his Aunt Ellen's.

He peered curiously out the window and saw the street was teeming with parked cars, which was unusual for this suburban neighborhood of abundant driveways and garages. But the most peculiar part of the scene was the available space directly in front that seemed reserved for their arrival.

The transmission bumped into reverse, and when his aunt twisted herself around to back into the space at the curb he caught her eyes with an inquisitive gaze. She hesitated when she saw he was awake and looked at him longer than necessary, as if she had something important to say but not the authority to say it. Instead, she tendered an unconvincing smile that seemed strangely laden at the corners.

The car idled an instant longer until her attention moved to the parking task at hand: back, forward, back again, forward again, stop.

Michael unbuckled the restraint and stepped out onto the sidewalk, dragging the heavy suitcase off the seat with him. Its contents seemed excessive for such a short visit, and his aunt came around quickly to relieve him of a burden she clearly recognized as beyond his means.

"I can do it," he declared as both hands struggled to clench the handle. "You can take Daniel."

She acquiesced, went around to the other door, and hoisted Michael's younger brother out of the seat without waking him. The two years that separated Michael and his six-year-old brother warranted a significant difference in their need for sleep.

Michael labored up the walkway with short, lumbering strides, feeling diminutive against the three-story home beset by a darkening sky that hadn't yet fully claimed the day. The first floor had long since been converted to a small income-generating apartment that his father had once explained was helpful in paying the mortgage, but this updated configuration created a first-floor foyer with a wide stairway that climbed to his family's living area on the upper two floors.

He dragged the suitcase through the doorway and to the foot of the stairs, where he crooked his neck up at the mountain of steps, crowned by a large stained glass window, and acknowledged defeat.

"It's okay," his aunt said, peeking from behind the sleeping Daniel, whom she held draped over her shoulder. "You go on ahead."

Michael released the suitcase and plodded up the first flight of stairs. When he turned the landing banister, he quickly saw the familiar faces of a family gathering. From behind him now, the stained glass window seeped the light of somber colors up the final rack of steps onto equally somber faces.

He wanted to continue his flight all the way to the third floor, where his aunt was now on her way to lay Daniel into bed, but instead he found himself floating from room to room. He quickly realized this gathering included not just family but also friends and neighbors. Some were sitting, some standing, some engaged in quiet conversation, and others just mulling in each other's presence amid a constant and awkward murmuring.

Nobody yet had spoken to Michael. They weren't ignoring him—they had acknowledged him with their stifled glances—but it seemed as if they all knew something he did not and they weren't allowed to speak to him until he also knew.

He puzzled over how he could learn the secret without someone engaging him. His aunt had accepted greetings and muted conversation upon her entry; she obviously knew the secret, had known before they got to the house, and had refrained from telling him. So he set out in search of his mother, who he was sure would speak to him. She would be in the kitchen; moms were always in the kitchen.

Instead, he found his father there, seated in his usual place at the table head and staring somewhat detachedly at the empty chair beside him. The side chair was where Michael's mother would sit during meals because it was easier to reach all the appliances, cabinets, and drawers from there. If Daniel dropped a fork, his mother would pick it up, place it in the sink, and return with a clean one from a drawer. If Michael wanted juice instead of milk, she would go to the refrigerator and ask him what kind he wanted. When Michael's father was ready for a second helping of dinner, she would always anticipate the exact moment and serve him again without him needing to ask. In the kitchen, she would gladly wait on her family. But no one would ever dare take advantage of that, because outside the kitchen each family member was responsible for their own "messies," as she called them: promptly putting away clothes and toys, as well as weekly chores commensurate with their ages. Even at eight and six, the boys knew that if they took advantage of their mother within the kitchen, conditions that existed outside of it could easily be implemented there as well.

In front of Michael's father was a full mug of black coffee with no straw of steam twirling out of it. On the side of the mug was a dark, watery bead that slid like a teardrop down a child's face. Michael's eyes followed the drop down to the table, where it coalesced with a small, wet stain.

A helping hand reached for a sponge at the sink and wiped the table dry.

That's Mom's job! Michael mentally protested.

"Welcome back, Michael," his father said blandly. Michael didn't associate the blandness with indifference; rather, it implied that his father had more to say and that the salutation was unimportant. "Where's Daniel?"

"Asleep. Aunt Ellen carried him up to bed."

His father paused in thought and then rose up out of the chair, bumping the table and spilling more coffee as he did. He was average height, not quite six feet, so he did not have to bend to reach his thick-lensed glasses from the table. When he put them on, the deep squint that occupied his face did not erase as it usually did.

"Would you join me in my study."

It wasn't really a question and he didn't wait for a response, just put his hand on the back of Michael's neck and guided him out of the kitchen and down the hallway to his study.

The room had only four pieces of furniture: a large mahogany desk, a gray spring-back chair that had needed oiling for as long as Michael could remember, a bookcase housing nothing but novels on its many shelves, and a gray leather sofa that faced the desk. His father had lobbied for matching coffee and end tables but his mother had felt that the more surface area in his study, the more places there would be for messies to accumulate. This was a valid notion, considering the desktop was strewn with papers, files, and binders. A green banker's lamp rose above the only allowed messy in the house like an oil derrick towering above a tempestuous and mottled sea.

Michael sat on the sofa and stared out beyond the desk into the void created by the now-black sky and the brightly lit room meeting on the window's surface. He watched the reflected image of his father slowly closing the door. His knees were short of the sofa's edge, so his legs protruded straight out, obliging his father to crouch beside him instead of in front of him as he brought himself down to Michael's eye level.

"Your mother passed away this weekend," his father said with an inflection that sounded practiced and a quiver that did not.

Michael knew his father was a man of few words and that they were never subsequently modified because they were always well thought out and always accurately reflected what he wanted to say. It was clear he must have spent a unique eternity in front of a mirror repeating that sentence like a mantra before finally deploying it to Michael.

With the words finally launched and floating between them, his father appeared ready to recite another practiced line—likely something to skillfully guide the tragedy into a safe berth. But something made him wait. He studied Michael's broadened eyes like they were windows into his mind, seemingly unaware that his own eyes equally betrayed the thoughts that lay behind them.

Michael's mind immediately came alive with activity as he began to dissect his father's statement. He recognized the phrase "passed away" as how adults stated someone had died, and he knew that meant he would never see his mother again. He had been fully aware of her illness—she was always returning from lengthy hospital stays, she always looked exhausted when home, and his father was always apprehensive whenever he saw her active—but his father had always obscured the technical details of her experiences, discreetly harboring them behind hopeful smiles and avoided stares.

So Michael had stood by in silent observation. He had witnessed from respectful distances the conversations with a multitude of doctors, he had perceived the efforts of sophisticated treatment plans, and he had noted the helpless aftermath of aggressive surgical procedures that never seemed to achieve promising results. He recalled the first time she'd come back from the hospital, when her every movement was accompanied by a grimace and a hand placed quickly near her abdomen. A scar once had scowled at him when her shirt had pulled out of her waistband. The second time she'd returned from an extended stay, she'd done so with a deep hollow beneath the left side of her blouse that was subsequently balanced on the right side by a third visit. Although the hugs never stopped, the places he could nestle had slowly been carved away, and he had secretly pined to be pulled tightly into a bosom that no longer existed.

He'd never really known what was specifically wrong with her, however, and not until now had it ever occurred to him to ask. It wasn't that he'd never cared; he'd just felt he wouldn't understand the answer completely. But today he would.

"How did she die?" he asked.

"She had cancer." His father's voice shuddered once again as he named his wife's killer, but this time his body quavered with it too.

The word itself seemed to assault Michael, clanging against his eardrums before draining slowly into his brain, where it dislodged an unfamiliar breed of anger. *Cancer* was what had drained thirty pounds of her body weight in the last year. *Cancer* was what had forced her to sit silently, alone, behind closed doors. *Cancer* was the evil that had mercilessly deteriorated her body, crawled through her insides in indiscriminate places, gnawed at her, and devoured her. *Cancer* was what had stolen his mother's life. A shotgun could have shredded the life coursing through her to the same effect and the same autopsy result: *Cancer.*

Michael's eyes started to well up and his nose began to run. He was displaying all the symptoms of crying without actually sobbing. But as his eyes began to dampen, his picture became more focused rather than blurred. He realized he was now looking directly into his father's eyes, and what he saw made him want to cry as much as what he felt. He saw his father on the outside—his face taut with the seriousness of the moment, his eyes weary from lack of sleep, his skin pale from the drain of his emotions. But he also somehow saw his father on the inside, suppressing an overwhelming fear that Michael could not measure. His father's expression was that of a child who desperately wanted to run away and find a place to hide.

It was the same expression Michael had observed as he was loaded into his aunt's car before the weekend. After more than two years of helping his wife outrun cancer's pursuit, his father had apparently recognized the time had finally come when she would stumble, fall, and be consumed. And although he must have wanted to be oceans away from the scene, he would be no farther away than a clenched handhold. A suitcase had been overpacked and the boys had been sent away instead.

Michael could only imagine the swift bedside vigil his father had endured. A deep night, maybe two. Her placid repose secretly struggling with a hidden enemy that had grown frustrated of stealing away only pieces and now had come to claim its prize in full. The light in his mother's face fading . . . her head sliding down the pillow. Gone.

And now, in his father's study, he was looked at by eyes that wanted to be compressed into the innocence of a small boy's body. But at the same time, Michael was trying to come from under the camouflage of his youth into the body of an adult. He wanted to be mature in a situation that required it by showing his father strength, even though he sensed frailty would suffice.

After this extended pause, Michael said the one thing that would relieve the building tension. "I understand."

The rush of air that left his father's lungs sounded like a sigh, but when he immediately afterward inhaled, it became clear he had been holding his breath.

Michael welcomed his father's reach over the armrest and around the back of his neck; he leaned forward, and they drew close together. They hugged for a long moment, avoiding the remainder of whatever other words might have been prepared. The time spent was clearly shorter than anticipated but the results greater, perhaps, than expected.

His father stood up, pulling away from Michael. "I'm going to check on Daniel. I'll leave you alone for a bit." He wiped his cheeks below his glasses with an instinctive stroke of his fingers, then studied the wetness as if it would tell him from whose face it had originated.

As Michael looked up he saw the bright shine around his father's withered eyes and knew they were his father's tears. While studying him further, he observed the length of the unshaven beard stubble that had claimed his face, almost masking its pallor, and how his shirt was awkwardly disrupted at the collar and baggy and buckled at the waist. No belt. One hip pocket almost pulled out. He clearly had been wearing these clothes for more than a day.

His father was a mess—a living, breathing messy. But it was the look of fear that concerned Michael most. A fear not of what had just happened but of what was to happen *next*. His father seemed to want to run again, this time from an inescapable responsibility, half of which sat directly in front of him and the other of which was sleeping just one floor above.

"Dad." Michael interrupted his father's reach for the doorknob. "Can I ask you a question?"

"Anything at all."

"What part of heaven is Mom in?"

His father turned slowly toward the window, but Michael could not tell if he was looking out into the sky or at the reflection of him on the sofa.

"The best part," he replied before continuing his escape.

Michael again watched the reflected image of his father closing the door—only this time, he disappeared behind it.

CHAPTER 2

Avery Thomas stepped off the elevator on the fifth floor and paused until the doors closed behind him. Each time he came to this floor he did this to remind himself that he should make the trip more times each day. After all, his department responsibilities included managing the thirty draftsmen drawing the complicated networks of pipes, platforms, and reactors that constituted the chemical processing plants Alosa Engineering designed and constructed.

But Avery was usually on the tenth floor with the model builders. He enjoyed watching a crew of adults play with color-coded pieces of plastic tubing, glue, and a set of instructions the fifth floor referred to as blueprints. Before Alosa actually built anything, it had to be constructed as a model first. This would ensure that all pipelines, valves, and walkways represented on the blueprints could actually be produced in the final construction. Too often, a valve would be found butting up against a handrail or a pipeline intersecting with a steel beam. By first building it on the tenth floor in miniature, these problems could be identified and resolved in the home office instead of at the job site, which could be in Korea, Singapore, or the Middle East.

As computer hardware and software advanced, model building was being replaced by three-dimensional Computer Aided Design software. Draftsmen were now trained on CAD computers, which had led to a decline in the need for models. As a result, Avery needed to be spending more time with the CAD operators on the fifth floor than with the model builders on the tenth—but he could not tear himself away from watching the tangible results of colorful plastic tubes cultivated into a complicated matrix of pathways. To him, they expressed purpose and direction, and he was fascinated by the patience and meticulous attention to detail that characterized a good model builder. He often found himself standing in front of hobby shops at the mall, envisioning himself walking out with large, colorful boxes filled with disassembled cars, planes, and ships, only to be interrupted by his wife reminding him he still had not fixed his son's bicycle or completed some other uninteresting chore.

He meandered to the end of the long hallway, which yielded to rows of computer workstations and specialized desks for mechanical drawing, each one's angled top blocking the view of the workstation in front of it. No door or sign announced this was the CAD room, and nothing announced that Avery had entered.

As he patrolled the rows of workstations, he noticed the hairless head of Jack Galler glinting over the top of the desk behind him like the sun scraping the edge of the horizon.

It was fifteen minutes after five, and the only people remaining were those behind on a project and a few younger, more determined employees trying to get ahead on projects to garner favor with Avery. Jack Galler fell into neither category, and Avery wondered why he was still here.

Jack always completed his work on time. He even regularly found time to assist on other projects or job segments that were not his responsibility. But he never worked one minute past five o'clock.

Avery knew Jack's history. When his wife died, whatever he was likely to become in life had apparently died with her. He'd once been a young, ambitious engineer with a bright future who was willing to put in the time needed to climb the corporate ladder into management. But without the safety net of his wife to share the workload of raising a family, bringing in a second income, and maintaining the household, he'd had to decide between bettering himself or bettering his children. It must have been both the easiest and most difficult decision he had ever made. It was as if he had jumped into the street to push his two boys out of the way of a runaway bus: The decision to save his children would have been easy, but absorbing the impact of the oncoming bus himself would have been difficult. Even Avery didn't see a gray area there.

Everyone Jack worked with at Alosa had continuously moved up and around him, either earning promotions or finding better jobs with other firms. But for either of these to happen to Jack, he would have to provide a greater commitment to his career, which would take away from the commitment he had made to his children. From what Avery knew of the man, he would likely never want to say to his children, "I have to work late tonight" or "I have to go into the office this weekend." Jack Galler would always be there for his children, and always on time.

Avery had started as a CAD operator for Alosa five years ago, just after Jack's wife died. He'd worked with Jack on many projects and gained great respect for his work ethic. Where almost everyone else beheld Jack as a "clock puncher" for leaving at five o'clock sharp each day, Avery recognized the true commitments the man had preserved, and without ever abandoning the responsibilities of his employment. For years he'd watched Jack subtly pass off ideas and completed work to others, including Avery himself, so that he would never be recognized as promotion material. He never wanted to be tempted away from his family obligations.

Avery was about to tap Jack on the back of the shoulder but decided to walk past his desk, turn, and face him directly instead.

"Your computer is using electricity that hasn't been budgeted for," he jested in reference to his staying late.

Jack's eyes lurched to his watch. "Damn!" he said, and instinctively began collecting his desk items to leave.

"What are you so engrossed in that has you pushing for overtime?" Avery asked.

"I've discovered something else you haven't budgeted for," Jack said.

Avery listened for sarcasm in Jack's response but found it absent. While he looked at the name of the open folder on Jack's desk in a search of answers, Jack stored away pencils and slips of paper that had accumulated on the blueprints unscrolled atop his desk.

Torque-Wrench Specifications and Procedures was scrawled across the top of the folder. The torque wrench was an industry tool used to tighten rivets and break off the excess material when the proper torsion was attained. Jack would have had to search diligently for this file; the wrench's operation processes had been developed years earlier.

Avery's eyes now moved to the title on the blueprints. Jack, timing it perfectly, gave him just enough occasion to take in the project name before rolling up the specifications for the Gateway Desalinization Plant being constructed in Kuwait.

"We have five tons of rivets already waiting in the Middle East, Jack. Did someone forget to bring a torque wrench?"

"You should have six tons if they're galvanized."

"You're right, and we do," Avery admitted. This was the first time Alosa was using galvanized rivets on a job; he'd forgotten to add the weight increase of the zinc coating in his calculation, and Jack had caught him on his error. "Keith already determined we don't need to recalibrate the wrench for galvanized," he fished. "Did you discover something different?"

Jack's leg was jittery as he checked his watch again. "I can't imagine there'd be a problem with the *specifications*," he volleyed back.

Usually, Jack would make Avery earn the information he supplied him. Sometimes he would draw these conversations out for hours, and sometimes days. He would let Avery brew over the hints he provided and the reports he presented. He didn't want to make it so easy that Avery was insulted. But today he was clearly anxious about getting somewhere quickly, so Avery suspected this interaction would be quick.

He did catch the blatant hint about the discovered problem: If Jack's budget discovery wasn't in the *specifications*, then it must be with the *procedure*. It was the only other option written on the folder he had out on the desk.

"There can't be a problem with the process," Avery protested. "These steelworkers are too well trained. They secure rivets like an Indy pit crew changes tires."

Avery was jiggling his line, trying to make the bait look interesting, but Jack would not bite so easily. His sport coat was wrapped over the back of his chair and he somehow, without standing up, managed to writhe directly into it as he continued preparation of his exit.

"My son, Michael, cut his finger yesterday . . . you know how kids can be." He shook his head. "Anyway, I went to put a bandage on it and he stopped me. 'You need iodine,' he said. 'It has to be protected on the inside, not just on the outside.' Of course, I didn't have iodine in the house. I had to go out and buy some before he would allow me to put a bandage on it."

"That's all very interesting, but . . ."

After observing a diminutive squint seize Jack's eyes, Avery halted himself to continue listening.

"So I'm sitting here this afternoon, and it occurs to me that we didn't price out any paint for Gateway."

"Let me understand this," Avery summarized. "I have five . . . no, *six* tons of galvanized rivets and a work crew of three hundred ready to start assembling Gateway tomorrow, and you're working late to tell me you want iodine covered under the company medical plan?"

Jack checked his watch again and his patience evaporated. "You have a galvanized rivet, protected on the outside," he said brusquely. "The torque wrench snaps off the end and exposes a part of the rivet that is not galvanized. Adding the paint protects it from rusting. *From the inside*," he emphasized. "Look, I'm very late. You can have Keith work up the estimated cost of the paint tomorrow. Would you be kind enough to return this folder for me?"

Not waiting for an answer, Jack stood, handed Avery the torque-wrench folder, and started striding for the elevator bank at a tempered pace that implied he knew Avery would be in tow.

The walk to the elevator passed without words. Jack had never been so terse with Avery before, and he never completely provided a solution for a problem that was someone else's responsibility, even when he knew the answer. There had to be more, otherwise Avery would not be holding this file. It would take him longer to figure out where it came from than for Jack to simply return it to where he found it. Costing out the paint was irrelevant. It would require a couple of hundred gallons of paint to cover the tips of over one million rivets, sure, but this would pale in comparison to the $350 million cost of the entire project.

Jack wasn't concerned about the cost of the paint. He'd had his nose in the *Procedures* file.

They arrived at the elevators, where Jack pressed a call button immediately. The down button lit up with a coinciding *ding* that seemed to emanate from nowhere.

Avery let the folder rest by his side and regarded Jack closely. He was in a hurry today—but he was always in a hurry. He was either rushing home or racing to the store or dashing to the bank. He was buying groceries or he was clothes shopping for his kids. Hurrying to the ball field, or maybe to a school play. It was as if he was always trying to outrun that speeding bus, convinced he could do it if he just kept moving.

Yet with all the things he had to do, and with the short time span he had to do them in, he never seemed to forget or neglect to do any of them. He might not arrive in the office until nine and he might always be gone by five, but he was always where he was supposed to be, exactly when he was supposed to be there.

Avery pressed the up arrow and the *ding* repeated, but with a higher-pitched tone.

"If I review this procedure file, Jack, I'll realize that no one has advised the construction crew that they need to stop after each installed rivet and put on a dab of paint, won't I?"

"I don't know, I hadn't gotten that far into the file."

Of course he had.

"We'll either have rusting rivets or spend months sending people around with a paint bucket and brush in search of each and every one of them," Avery presupposed.

"Like finding a million needles in a haystack," Jack confirmed.

"And in some places, that haystack is over two hundred feet high." Avery looked up at the ceiling, envisioning one of the higher towers.

It was a simple tool and a simple process, thought Avery. But no one had considered reviewing it. No one but Jack, and it wasn't even his responsibility. But even so, he'd brought it to light, and he'd done so while trying as hard as possible not to take the credit.

Tonight, Avery would spend hours on the phone trying to reach Kuwait and the construction manager to review the new procedures, as well as get the paint and other materials to the job site.

There was an awkward silence as the two of them stared at the lit arrows on the wall that signified their respective directions.

"How is Michael?" Avery asked in an attempt to personalize the exchange.

"It's all I can do to protect him from the elements of the outside world, and now he wants to be protected from the inside."

The lower-pitched *ding* resounded and Jack moved impatiently closer to the doors as if the tone had been personally assigned to him.

"Good night, Avery."

"Good night, Jack."

The elevator opened and swallowed Jack whole to be regurgitated into the lobby, where he would slip through the revolving door like a well-oiled cog.

When Avery's elevator arrived, he paused before stepping in. "I must come down here more often," he said aloud to no one.

Even though he was two floors up, Michael still heard the door swing open in the downstairs hall. He did not need to check his watch to know it was six thirty; he had been checking it almost every five minutes for the last hour.

What followed was an orchestra of sounds that had become especially familiar to him over the last few years. It began with the short squeak in the hinge just before the front door thumped closed. This triggered a vibration that rattled through the entire house, shaking a loose windowpane in Michael's bedroom. Next, his father's shoes scuffed and thumped up the hardwood steps. In the kitchen, the shopping bags were dropped onto the table with a thud and their rustling joined in chorus. The bags were emptied and folded, which led to a crescendo of refrigerator and cabinet doors opening and closing as his father distributed the groceries to their proper locations.

Next came the long pause, as if he were waiting for applause. But none ever came.

Tonight, however, something different happened. Instead of beginning his next composition of washing dishes or peeling potatoes at the kitchen sink, his footsteps retreated back down the stairs and out of the house. He returned two minutes later and started up the stairs again, but this time he was ascending more slowly.

He was either exhausted or carrying something heavy. Michael's pulse quickened as he resolved it to be a birthday present—a *big* birthday present.

He closed the book he was reading, leaped off his bed, and jaunted down the stairs to the second floor to meet his father climbing up from the first.

They both were traveling the same number of steps, but Michael arrived first.

He turned the corner at the banister and looked down the next flight and saw the frame of his father, idle in front of the stained glass window. He was resting awkwardly with a large box cradled in both arms, except it didn't seem to be the box that was making him uncomfortable. His mouth hung lazily open and his tongue poked out as if it was trying to remove itself from the much-needed airway.

"Where's your brother?" he called up the steps.

"Watching TV. I'll get him to help with the box." Michael purposely did not offer to help with the gift-wrapped box because it was clearly a present for him. Taking it from his father on the landing would have diminished the presentation.

He went to the next room, where Daniel was lying on the floor, facing the television, elbows propped up and head resting on his hands. Michael had no idea what he was watching; all he heard was a loud, continuous laugh track with no accompanying dialogue.

He went over and stood by the set, facing Daniel. This was the stance that indicated he would turn the TV off if his brother ignored him.

"Go help Dad on the stairway. He asked for you."

Daniel hesitated for a moment, but upon observing Michael's commanding pose he did a push-up to his feet and went out to the stairwell. It had become clear over time that he understood the value that the shelter of an older brother provided but also that it came at a cost. He had become very good at taking direction and following instructions quickly.

Michael followed him to the top of the steps to monitor the gift's chain of custody.

"Bring this into my study . . . and place it carefully on the floor," Jack instructed Daniel with a pause in the middle for an extra breath. He looked up and saw Michael. "Michael, go down to the car. There's a cake . . . on . . . the front seat."

Michael wanted to be excited for his birthday and his unknown booty, but his father's lack of composure concerned him. He went down the stairs, and as he passed within inches of his father's sweat-soaked shirt at the landing, he thought he felt heat emanating from his father's body.

When he returned, the stairway landing was vacant.

"Hurry, Michael, we're in the study!" Daniel yelled from upstairs. "Hurry up and open your present!"

He went up the stairs, taking them two at a time, and deposited the cake in the kitchen before racing into the study.

His dad was on the sofa and Daniel was on the floor appraising the box, almost ready to open it himself.

"Hurry," he cried, "something is moving inside!"

Michael looked to his dad for approval to open the gift. His father nodded consent, but Michael knew the protocol of opening gifts. "Is there a card, Dad?"

His father acknowledged there was with a second nod and reached into his suit coat with his left hand. When he raised it off the armrest, Michael saw a sweat stain that remained there like a disobedient shadow.

The card got halfway to Michael before it subtly retracted for just an instant and with an accompanying wince in his father's jowls, as if a sharp pain had just hit him so quickly that he thought maybe it actually had not happened at all.

Michael grasped the card and read it aloud, but he quickly realized that no one was paying attention. Daniel wanted the box open to free whatever was inside, and his father seemed to want to free himself from some unidentifiable yet threatening burden.

After reading the card, Michael went over to his father and thanked him with an enveloping hug. This time, he was sure he felt the heat from his father's body. He pulled back, wiping his father's sweat from his own face.

"Are you okay, Dad?" he said—softly, so as not to attract Daniel's attention.

His father's eyes closed. "I'm fine. Just open your present so I can go make dinner."

Michael kneeled on the floor next to his animated brother and the intriguing box. He stuck his finger in one of several holes and was about to rip the paper when his father abruptly said, "You can ease up on that hug now."

"I'm down here, Dad."

"Of course," his father said, but when he opened his eyes they betrayed his disorientation.

Michael slowly tore the paper while keeping a watchful eye on his father. When he lifted the lid, it was Daniel who exploded with excitement.

"A puppy!"

Out jumped an impatient yellow Labrador retriever with wide eyes, a smooth coat, and a pink ribbon around its neck. It went straight to Michael, jumping into his arms, then out, then back again. It could have only been in the box for a few minutes, but given the excitement it was showing, it must have seemed like an eternity. It was as if it had been once again released from the womb, this time into a new world: the Galler world.

Michael was now as excited as Daniel as they frolicked on the floor with the puppy jumping and licking all over them.

"Thank you, Dad! This is the best present ever!" he gushed without ever taking his eyes off the new member of the family.

When he did finally get up to hug his father again, he found him now stretched across the sofa with clenching pain on his face. He was trying to clutch his chest but only succeeding in squeezing a fistful of his shirt. His breathing was raspy and erratic.

Michael took immediate control of the situation. He went over to Daniel, who was still playing with the puppy, and picked it up into one arm. With his other hand, he took Daniel by the shoulder and led him over to the sofa.

"Dad is not feeling well. Quickly, go into the bathroom and soak a towel in cold water. Wring it out in the tub and then bring it to me." He made sure his instructions were clear and concise, so eleven-year-old Daniel would follow them immediately and exactly.

Daniel observed his father's condition, and the joy of the birthday present went right out of his face. He opened his mouth to speak, but no words escaped. When Michael released his shoulder, he seemed to remember he had been given an assignment and he rushed out of the room.

Michael rummaged quickly among the clutter on his father's desk for the telephone and dialed 911. While it rang, he walked it back to the sofa and crowded his body onto the edge. With the dog in one arm, the phone squeezed into his neck, and his other hand now squeezing his father's, a voice on the other end asked him the nature of the emergency.

"My name is Michael Galler and I am thirteen years old. I think my father is having a heart attack. I live at 18 Franklin Street. My brother will be waiting outside in front of our house, and I won't hang up the phone until you tell me I can."

The ambulance arrived in six minutes.

Daniel led two female paramedics up to the second floor. The taller of the two attended to Michael's father, whose condition had improved, and began taking vital signs and starting an intravenous drip. He could only stand helplessly watching in the doorway.

The shorter one began questioning Michael. She was only about five feet tall, with blond hair and a ponytail pulled through the back of her hat. She wore a blue uniform with authoritative emblems on the shoulders and looked to be in her late twenties. When she smiled for him she revealed perfect teeth. The nameplate on her breast pocket read *P. Bailey.*

She had a calming effect on Michael; her feminine warmth was something he had not felt in years. It had a feeling of tenderness that seemed to supersede their age difference and the seriousness of the moment.

Under her comforting influence, Michael shared that his father had been doing nothing out of the ordinary, as far as he could tell, before things took a scary turn. After conferring with her partner, P. Bailey relayed to the boys that their father's condition was stable and that they would prepare to take him to a hospital.

"Where's your mother?" asked P.

"She passed away five years ago."

"Oh . . . I'm sorry." Pause. "Well, we're going to take real good care of your dad. He seems to be comfortable now. If he had a heart attack, and we won't know for sure until the hospital runs some tests, it doesn't appear it was very bad. Is there someone who can take care of you while we transport him?"

"My aunt will be here in an hour. I've already called her. We'll be fine until she gets here."

She regarded Michael with what seemed like a startled appreciation. She looked around the room and down the hallway, as if suggesting another adult should be in the house to have managed the situation so well. Then she looked back to Michael with the sincerity of a parent.

"I've had to come into many people's homes, as well as movie theaters, sporting events, and even city parks, and I typically find frightened and frantic family members shouting or crying for me to help them. You made the emergency call?"

"Yes."

"You saw to the comfort of your father, kept your brother's emotions in check, arranged for the ambulance to easily find the house, arranged for someone to come and take care of you?"

"Yes."

"All in six minutes?"

Michael didn't respond.

"You're a very conscientious and courageous young man," she offered. "And that is a very pretty puppy you have there. What's her name?"

"Her?" Michael looked away from the paramedic's reassuring eyes and then down into the dog's curious eyes.

"Yes, she seems to be a girl," P. said with a smile, fondling the pink ribbon.

Michael stroked her small back in careful thought and then responded with a smile of his own. "Bailey," he said. "Her name is Bailey."

CHAPTER 3

Michael hadn't been inside a hospital since his mother's surgeries. During her illness, he had visited her whenever his father thought it was appropriate, or whenever his mother felt she had the strength to give him and Daniel the attention small children required. Sometimes he'd only been allowed to watch her sleep, his father demanding absolute silence. The three of them would sometimes fall asleep nestled together in the accompanying chairs while his mother either watched them rest or was sound asleep herself.

But this was the first time he had been in an emergency room, and he found the atmosphere very different. Upstairs, among the semiprivate rooms, there was a sense of stability, balance, and harmony. Patients rested, nurses dispensed medication, and doctors perused charts. Heart monitors beeped at steady pulse rates, IV solutions dripped at steady intervals, meal carts circled at meal times with their blended smells wafting through the ward. Patients were rehabilitated with specific treatment programs before being released on scheduled discharge dates.

Sitting in the waiting room of the ER today, Michael sensed none of this. This was a place of confusion and fear, a place with more questions than answers. Patients waited to see doctors, doctors waited to run tests, and family members waited for news. Sounds were erratic and random. Patients entered unexpectedly through the rear of the building, bringing with them the foul smells of the unsanitary world and commingling them with the smell of sterility. If the hospital were a living entity, he thought, its survival would be a strange digestive reversal with nastiness fed into its bowels, restored, and expelled out its jaws in a more pleasing form.

As he further regarded his surroundings, Michael spied a boy about his age sobbing incessantly into his mother's bosom while he cradled one of his arms. A man dressed in dirty overalls and a tool belt unwrapped a blood-spattered towel from his hand and then, seemingly repulsed by what he saw, rewrapped it. An older woman with no apparent illness or injury sat alone and returned his stare.

This was a place Michael did not want to be, and it was most certainly a place he did not want his father to be. His aunt had vanished with a nurse behind a door an hour ago, and no one had since returned to check on them. He sat patiently with Daniel, trusting that someone eventually would.

Finally, his aunt returned to the waiting area with another woman he had not seen before. They both wore the same expression on their faces: apprehension, but not distress. They guided the boys to an area where they could speak more privately.

Their aunt sat them down and spoke in an eager tone. "This is Dr. Prendergast. She'll speak with you directly to explain what's happened to your father." She looked to Dr. Prendergast as if passing an imaginary baton.

The doctor, who remained standing before the three of them, hesitated. Michael thought maybe she was preparing a translation of her more technical conversation with Aunt Ellen to a lower intensity for him and Daniel to comprehend. But before she had a chance to speak, he expressed a simple observation that seemed to take her by surprise. “You don’t look like a doctor,” he said.

Aunt Ellen leaned forward to offer an embarrassed apology, but Dr. Prendergast held up an easy hand to prevent her. She would address Michael’s concern herself.

“Michael, women today have many different important careers, such as doctors, lawyers, accountants, and police officers. I can assure you I have all the skills and knowledge a doctor needs.”

“That’s not what I meant. I meant you don’t *look* like a doctor.”

Dr. Prendergast glanced down at her appearance as if to take inventory of herself and then seemed to understand that Michael’s comments were not reflective of her gender but rather her lack of a lab coat, scrubs, and stethoscope.

“You’re right, I guess I don’t look like any doctor you may have seen on TV.” She smiled. “And you look too young to have handled this situation so well. I guess looks can be deceiving, which is why I always prefer to judge people by what they have on the inside.”

Michael liked her immediately. She had fielded his comment honestly and directly, and he now knew she would not hold anything back when providing him with the assessment of his father’s situation.

“Will you tell me what’s inside my father?” he asked, using her response to segue.

“Your father has two things inside of him right now,” Dr. Prendergast said. “One is very bad, and the other is very good.”

She held up a fist in front of him as a prop and he stared at it intently. Daniel did what he usually did, which was to sit quiet and still and study his older brother.

"The heart is a muscle about the size of your fist and it acts like a pump, pumping blood through the arteries." She squeezed and opened her fist repeatedly. "The arteries are like pipes. As long as they aren't obstructed, the blood will flow freely through them, carrying oxygen throughout the body. But if the arteries clog, it prevents the oxygen from getting where it needs to go."

She paused to leave opportunity for a question, but none came, so she continued.

"There are several factors that can cause this—bad diet and lack of exercise, to name a couple. Fatty deposits, called plaque, build up inside the arteries and make it difficult for the blood to pass. It takes a long time, many years, before it becomes difficult for the blood to bring oxygen to the heart."

"So what happened today was caused by something that was growing inside him for years?"

"That's exactly what I'm telling you." She nodded approvingly. "It's a very slow process. It's like hair in a drain clogging your sink. As the plaque grows and grows, the opening of the pipe gets smaller. The heart has to work harder until eventually it gives out, like it did today."

This explanation sounded very familiar to Michael, and he knew exactly from where.

"You said there was something else inside my father, something very good . . ."

"Yes." She held up her fist again. "Your father has a very strong heart. Surprisingly strong. We think more than a few of your father's arteries surrounding his heart have blockage. Many people would have died tonight had this happened to them. But we believe your father's heart suffered relatively little damage from this event."

Way to go, Dad! Michael mentally cheered. But it was a cheer from the upper deck of an empty stadium.

Daniel seemed prodded by this enthusiastic nuance in Michael's demeanor to contribute to the dialogue. "What happens now?"

Michael cast a sideways glance of approval at his brother.

The doctor's tone became more upbeat as she described the process of coronary bypass surgery. She explained with great clarity how she would take an artery out of their father's leg and use it to go around the blockage and reroute the flow of blood like a traffic detour. She exuded confidence at the prospects of success and their father leading a normal life again. The boys expressed fascination by the procedure and the capabilities of modern medical science, and the mood became more relaxed and unhindered.

As Dr. Prendergast prepared to hand the imaginary baton back to Aunt Ellen and excuse herself, one thing still concerned Michael. He was confident his father would fully recover, but the future now concerned him.

"You're leaving the hair in the drain?" He wanted the answer to the question, but he continued the doctor's analogy for Daniel's benefit.

"Well, yes," replied Dr. Prendergast.

"So it's not a cure?"

"It is possible that plaque could continue to build up in his arteries, or in other arteries that are clear now. That's why he'll need to make dramatic changes in his lifestyle, which I've already reviewed with your aunt. It's not unheard of for people to undergo bypass surgery a second time."

Michael felt some comfort in the fact his father had two legs, each with a spare artery, but hadn't his mother's body been shaved away over the years before yielding to death? He was beginning to have a problem with this concept.

"This plaque in my father's body . . . how is it different from cancer?"

She reflected for a moment before answering, as if first trying to determine the source of the question in the hopes of providing the answer in the clearest language. "There's a tremendous difference. But to keep it simple, cancer is made up of living cells that grow inside the body. Cancer is alive."

"Yes," Michael responded with all the emotion of a vigilant sentry. "It is."

Michael left his father at the hospital with unfettered confidence he would completely recover.

It was Friday evening; the boys didn't have school the next day. Aunt Ellen would spend the night with them at their house, and in the morning they would, again, overpack a bag and drive back to her house.

Michael intimately recalled the events that had followed his visit to her house five years earlier. He began to reminisce about his mother, but he had few memories because he'd been so young when she died. In fact, the more he tried to remember, the more he realized he had *no* memories of her. Even mental images of her actual profile had disappeared, replaced by images of photographs he had seen. It nettled him that he could not force an image of his mother into the forefront of his mind. Each time he came close, it was replaced by the memory of a photograph he recalled—pictures his father cherished, or grainy pictures his aunt had dug up from a little-used drawer.

Bailey was elated to see them return. Michael felt negligent for having left her alone for so long, and so quickly after releasing her from her box. She'd likely paced for hours and wondered, as best a toddling puppy could wonder, whether this recent change in living conditions was a good thing or a bad thing.

Aunt Ellen began cleaning up the soiled messes Bailey had made, simpering at the thought of the puppy fitting right in with the family—already making her own messies. She seemed to feel, as Michael did, that it made no sense for anyone to discipline the dog over these first transgressions.

"I know it's late, but I think I should take Bailey for a walk," Michael offered. "I'll use my belt and we can buy a leash tomorrow."

He was happy to take his new friend for a walk, but what he really wanted was to just go for a walk himself and collect his thoughts. He looped the belt around Bailey's neck and secured it like a noose.

"Don't let her get away," Daniel said.

"I won't lose her," Michael responded, already starting down the stairs.

Outside, a crescent moon shared its light with the polished sky. Michael cast his eyes upward and tried to find the best part of heaven. Then he just tried to find heaven. Then he stopped looking up.

The moon hung over him like a squinting, watchful eye as he started down the graded street. He allowed Bailey the opportunity to sniff out her new territory along the way, and she clearly smelled the scent of many other dogs that had made this outing before her. Each bush, each tree, every shrub, and every flower bed she approached and sniffed all contained the odor of claimed territory. There didn't seem to be anyplace she could call her own, beyond the carpet in the house.

"It will take some time and patience," Michael empathized. "Someday your scent will claim this whole neighborhood."

Time and patience, he further reflected. Like the time and patience it had taken for his father's arteries to be claimed and threaten his life. Like the time and forbearance it had taken for cancer to infect and deteriorate his mother's body to claim her life. Both his parents were threatened by an evil they could not see, did not even know was there, until it was too late.

It was hard enough growing up evading the evils that could be seen. But at least there were instructions for that:

Look both ways before crossing the street.
Don't talk to strangers.
Watch your step.
Say no to drugs.
Beware of dog.
High voltage.
Keep out.

How could anybody be expected to evade the evils that lurked *inside* the body? Neither his mother nor his father could do it. They'd spent so much time and effort trying to protect their children that they'd failed to protect themselves.

His pace quickened, his stride lengthened, and his arms swung like synchronized pendulums, creating a jolting action on the makeshift leash. Bailey was no longer trying to explore the neighborhood; she was just trying to keep pace with her tether.

He wondered what these evils were that lurked inside the body. Evils so powerful and so dangerous that sane people would allow parts of their body to be removed or rerouted. Evils so vile that the mere mention of their name could impale with fear all those who heard it colliding in the same sentence with their own name.

The answer disturbed him.

Cancer is alive.

The doctor's words banged inside his head and echoed like a gong, re-emanating the initial strike into a washed-out vibration only to be struck again.

Michael was jogging now. His pace was steady and measured. He could feel the blood moving through his veins, as if a highway accident had been cleared and traffic was beginning to move freely. He passed trees and telephone poles so quickly that it seemed they were stepping out of his way.

That hot summer day of five years ago was apparently not the day Cancer had left the Galler household. Michael could now see that it was attempting to reach out and destroy more of his family.

But Cancer had many weapons in its arsenal for destroying its prey. Malignant cellular growth had slowly and finally stolen Michael's mother; now it seemed to be employing a new disguise in pursuit of his father.

Dr. Prendergast had explained that his father's condition had been caused by a high-cholesterol diet and lack of exercise. But Michael knew better. Cancer had invaded his father's body and was trying to force his heart to stop pumping.

Cancer was smart, he thought. It knew his father had too strong of a heart to attack it directly. He had to have a strong heart to have been with his wife through her hardest times, to have survived her loss, to have raised two children from such an early age, held his job, and maintained a happy household. So it had decided to leave the heart alone and destroy the plumbing, knowing that this would render the pump useless. But because it also knew Jack Galler's heart would be difficult to choke the life out of, Cancer had attempted to block not one, not two, but several main arteries. Only then could it bring down a man as solid as him.

Michael was running now. He could feel his heart thumping in his chest. He could hear his own breathing. His body moved swiftly and smoothly, slicing through the thick night air. He pumped one arm and trailed the one holding the leash to prevent jerking Bailey's neck. The puppy was running hard to keep up, but the belt choked her and it seemed she could not pull in the necessary amount of air to maintain the pace.

When his father returned home from the hospital, Michael would help protect him. He'd make sure he ate the right foods, participated in abundant exercise, and saw his doctor on a regular basis.

But the poison was still in his father. The doctor was not removing it, only bypassing it. And if it ever did claim his father, Michael surmised he would be next. Which meant he would also have to proactively protect himself.

He didn't know how to do this against something he could not see or sense. But he would find a way. As a start, he would follow the doctor's instructions himself. This would keep him healthy. He had to stay strong to stay protected.

But it wasn't enough to just protect himself. He had to protect Daniel as well. His little brother wasn't keen enough to sense the danger, never mind defend himself against it. He would be Daniel's firewall, and nothing would get past him.

Michael was sprinting now. He stole more of the sidewalk with every stride he took. Bailey was now fighting his progress, as he was practically dragging her. But he would not stop. He felt good. He felt great. He released the belt from his hand.

He was running faster than he had ever run before. His arms pumped like pistons. Each leg raced the other to be in front. He began blowing the air out of his lungs so he could inhale fresh new oxygen faster. Sweat beaded up on his forehead and dripped down his face. Even his hands threw off sweat as they swung high and low.

The blood coursed through his veins and he could feel the friction of the corpuscles heating their pathways. And as they cooked, he ran faster. His heart beat like a war drum. Faster and faster. Louder and louder. Both his lungs and heart began to compete for space to expand within his small chest cavity.

His body was redlining and pleaded to shut down, but he continued to run. He needed to get stronger on the inside; each muscle, each organ, each bone had to be strong and formidable.

He passed houses and trees and hydrants and parked cars as if they were planets in his universe and he were an asteroid searing through space, unaffected by their gravitational pulls.

Reaching the end of the street, he leapt like a long jumper to cross over to the next sidewalk. He planted his left foot and threw his right one out in front of him like a sail ready to catch the wind. But his left foot had no spring remaining, and it collapsed. Gravity became suddenly evident after all;

he fell to the ground and slid across the macadam, scouring his palms as he braced against his fall.

When the driver of the minivan saw the shadow vault into his headlights, he stomped his brakes. With the additional ability of steering, he swerved away from it into its wake and was jolted as the van ran over something that felt like a log. The front right tire popped flat but the shadow he'd seen, which now registered as a person, had already passed across the left side of the van. He must have hit something else.

The van was still moving but skidding to a stop as another object, this one smaller, also pierced his headlights. He swerved again, this time to the left, and again he felt as if he'd run over something. The van began to slide sideways, with the passenger side grinding toward a parked car. There was no crash or scraping of metal, just a solid thud that somehow evoked a safe landing.

Michael didn't see the van until it was already past him. At that point he was too busy tempering his own fall to be concerned with the driver avoiding his own disaster.

His body rolled to a stop and began heaving for oxygen. It was numb from the sprinting, and his clothes were pasted against his body by sweat. The only thing he felt was the stinging, burning sensation of his abraded hands.

When he regained control of his body, the first thought into his mind was Bailey. He had let go of the leash and had not paused to see how she'd reacted to her freedom. Had she stopped running? Taken off in a different direction? Followed behind him?

The shaken driver stepped out of the van, assessed his health, found it adequate, and then searched for what he'd hit before striking the parked car. Standing next to his open door, he squinted into the shadows and searched the street like a submarine commander scanning the horizon at periscope depth.

Something brushed his leg and he jumped back. His eyes caught sight of the jaunting dog and followed it to the middle of the street, where it stopped next to a boy who lay gasping for air. Resolving the van had simply bounced up the curbstone and then down, he went to the boy's aid.

Bailey ran up to Michael and began slurping the sweat off his skin, surely not understanding how grave of a situation had just been avoided. Michael raised up his hands to protect his face so he could continue drawing in all the air possible. Bailey smelled his wounds and began cleaning them with quick, wet swipes of her granular tongue.

As his breathing and heart rate abated to normal levels, Michael chided himself for not also adhering to the forewarnings of the outside world.

Look both ways before crossing the street, he reprimanded himself.

CHAPTER 4

"Where is it?"

"I don't know what you're looking for."

"You know damn well what I'm looking for."

Tremont knew exactly what his mother was looking for, and he usually would help her find it. But today he had different intentions.

"I suppose I do, sort of. But I don't know if you're looking for the cocaine or the marijuana or the pills . . ."

"Don't get smart with me, you little shit!" Her tone changed to desperation a little more quickly than usual.

She was mechanically picking clothes up off the floor and searching the pockets: front left, front right, back left, back right. She discarded an empty pair of jeans and picked up another.

"These drugs are killing you, Ma."

"These drugs are keeping me alive!" she snapped.

"I could help you look for it."

"You *will* help me look for it!" She wasn't speaking with the authority of a mother to her son. She was speaking with the fervor of a strung-out, drug-addicted failure. What she needed, she needed now. But she was already high on something, so Tremont could not figure out her panic.

"I *could* help you look for it," he repeated, this time with a different emphasis.

She looked at the wall clock and her tone became even more urgent. "Help me look for it, Tremont?" It was more of a plea than a request.

"Ten dollars."

"What?" she asked incredulously.

"You heard me."

"You want me to give you ten dollars to help me find *my* shit?"

"I *expect* you to give me ten dollars to help you."

"You'll help me look or I'll kick your ass into every corner of this apartment until I kick you into the corner that has my coke," she growled. "It'll be a nice little mother-son activity."

The government-assisted tenement had only two rooms attached to a small kitchen. The kitchen had barely enough room for a table and three chairs. Even the small laminate cabinets seemed crowded for space. The bedroom had two twin beds pushed together, one tall dresser, and one nightstand. The other room served as a living room in the daytime and Tremont's bedroom at night. The foldout sofa bed was currently open, forcing their beleaguered coffee table to sit agreeably by the rusted radiator. With so few "corners" in the apartment, Tremont was not overly concerned by his mother's threat.

"Ten dollars," he repeated.

She reached out her hand, but there was no money in it. The hand kept coming until it reached around him and struck his backside. "How about ten of those?" she demanded.

He snickered. At fourteen years old, he was past the age where spanking had any effect. But she did like to start her floggings with one good spank. Maybe it was for sentimental reasons.

He didn't respond. He just continued to watch her agitate.

She turned away from him in frustration, went into the bedroom, and began searching in the drawers again. "I'll find it myself."

"No, you won't." His calm voice easily carried through the small rooms.

She was beginning to get frantic. She was searching clothes in the drawers, tossing them out onto the floor, then picking them up and searching them again. Then she stopped, and Tremont knew his words had finally begun to register in what was left of the functioning part of her brain.

She turned slowly, her eyes tilted and her mouth hanging lazily open. Tremont was standing in the doorway like a shadow.

"Do you know where it is?" she asked.

No response.

"You do know where it is."

No response.

"You little fucker. You took it!"

"Ten dollars."

He was beginning to feel uneasy. Maybe this wasn't a good idea. But he had already started down this path and couldn't reverse course now. His certitude was wavering, but he wouldn't allow his demeanor to reveal it.

"That coke is worth five hundred dollars, you idiot. And you're asking for ten?"

Tremont hadn't known how much it was worth until now. But ten dollars seemed like enough money for this risky venture, so he'd tried for ten. Of course he would have asked for more if he'd known its exact worth. But he didn't want to increase his price now. He needed to maintain an air of confidence. She had to believe he knew what he was doing and that he was serious. Wavering or renegotiating now would soil the opportunity.

"You're getting a bargain," he said, hiding the thought of all that lost money.

She walked straight at him and walloped him on the side of his face with an open hand. His head cocked sideways with the force of the blow, but he didn't fall. He'd learned to keep his balance during these episodes. He felt a thick driblet of blood trickle from above his eyebrow but resisted the urge to wipe it.

His mother again looked up at the wall clock and sighed, as if resigned to resolving it his way for now. She now began looking for money but seemed to be looking in all the places she would hope to find the cocaine. On her knees, her head buried in the bedroom closet, she shouted out to her son, "I don't get my paycheck until Wednesday!"

Tremont hated when she referred to her state welfare check as a paycheck. It implied that she worked, which he could not ever recall her doing. His grandmother worked a full-time job as an office assistant in a nearby accountant's office. *She* received a real paycheck.

He had seen both types of checks from time to time. His mother's was cut from large check stock with a computerized typeface. The food stamps looked like play money with their large denominations printed in various bright colors, attached together in a coupon book. They seemed more like a worn-out obligation rather than compensation for hard work. His grandmother's check, in contrast, was simple and unassuming, like the modest way a proud person would earn a living.

But neither had the appeal of cash. And that was what Tremont was after.

His mother came from out of the closet, stumbling through the debris she had tossed out of it. This time she grabbed each of his shoulders and shook him uncontrollably. "This is not a good time, Tree. I need that coke."

When she stopped shaking him, she continued to cling to his shoulders. He stared piercingly into her bloodshot, teary eyes and sensed a different kind of urgency from how she usually acted. He was getting an ill feeling about his plan, and he looked for a way to step out of it with a benevolent poise. But he had already committed himself. If he didn't stand up to her now, he would forever be subjected to her abuse and humiliation.

"And I need that money," he replied.

She shook him again. This time she shook him so hard that even her own body was rocking feverishly, as if she were trying to shake herself out of this nightmare that was her life.

They were at a standoff. She could not give him what she did not have, and he could not surrender a strategic position he had risked so much to achieve.

One other thing gave him an uneasy feeling: She seemed to know something that he did not. She knew something and was uncomfortable with the knowledge, and Tremont did not know it and was uncomfortable with the lack of knowledge.

He saw only one resolution. He needed to find a new source for the money. But first he needed to find out what had his mother so distraught.

Both questions were answered simultaneously when a steady knock sounded at the front door.

His mother redirected her anger at the wall clock, as if that were the problem.

"Shit—he's early," she whispered, as if the man on the other side of the door had his ear pressed against it. She continued whispering. "You've got to give me that coke. Now. It doesn't belong to me."

Tremont was just piecing that together himself before she enlightened him. But he had already decided he was committed to taking this as far as it would go—until he had ten dollars crumpled in his clenched fist.

There was another knock at the door, this time firmer.

Tremont felt like a matador standing in the middle of a bullring awaiting the release of the bull. He looked toward the protective door and directed his mother, "Go ahead, let him in."

His mother stood leaning weakly on the kitchen table, motionless. She looked at Tremont, the clock, the door, then surveilled the room one last time, seeming bewildered by her options. She ran a hand through her hair as if she could rake an idea out of the knotted mess.

"I can't control what happens when he comes in," she warned.

Tremont pushed out his chest, cracked his neck, and dug his fingernails into his palms. "Could you ever? Let him in."

The door was being pounded with the fleshy part of a fist by the time Tremont's mother succumbed to her helplessness. She turned the dead bolt, unhooked the chain, glided the slide lock, turned the knob, and swung the door open wide.

Barry's frame engulfed the doorway, letting in very little light from the hall lamp. He was dressed in washed-out gray jeans, a plain blue collared dress shirt, and a blue denim jacket. His lips clasped a freshly lit cigarette that blazed as he inhaled. The color of his eyes was taken from the same red swatch as the tip of the cigarette, with one seemingly trained on Tremont and the other on his mother.

Rolling the cigarette between his lips like a third eye casing the apartment, he kept the two eyes in his forehead leveled on the apartment's two occupants. "Problem?" he asked before stepping in. His voice was deep and smooth but stung like hard alcohol.

"No . . . no problem at all . . . of course not . . . I've been waiting for you . . . come in . . . can I get you a beer?" Tremont's mother went into the refrigerator, removed a can of beer, and presented it to Barry with one hand while fumbling a cigarette in the other.

"No time," he said, still in the doorway. "You know why I'm here."

She looked at Tremont with begging eyes. She was over her head without a life jacket.

This was not working out the way he had expected. Even he was over his head trying to interact with Barry. Now that Tremont was maturing, Barry had started using fists on occasion, making his mother's open-hand smacks refreshing by comparison. But Tremont had a life jacket: a plastic bag filled with white crystal sheltered in the crotch of his pants.

Barry seemed to sense the awkwardness of the silence. Tremont's mother could not look directly at him. She started scrabbling to get the cigarette in her mouth. Tremont, who usually disappeared into the bedroom when Barry arrived, stood curiously only as far as the bedroom doorway.

Barry took one step into the apartment, closed the door behind him, and cast both eyes on Tremont.

"What's up, Tree?" he asked with a provoking smirk.

I might as well pick up where I left off, Tremont decided. "I need ten dollars."

"So?"

"You need your drugs."

Barry looked over at Tremont's mother. He watched for a moment as she opened the beer for herself and held the can in a trembling hand that kept time with an incessant mutter that was released between heaving breaths on the now-lit cigarette.

As if acknowledging no path to his purpose with her, he went straight to Tremont, grabbed a fistful of hair, and dragged him over to the unfolded sofa bed. Pushing down on his head, he forced him to sit on the edge, as if aggressively training a dog to sit.

"Okay, little man. You and I are going to have a discussion." Barry remained standing and glowered down at his prey. He took a long draw on his cigarette and exhaled the excessive smoke down into Tremont's face.

Tremont inhaled the unappetizing blend of tobacco and breath, exhaled quickly, and spoke first to attain control. "Let's keep it simple. I—"

Whap! Barry's open hand struck without allowing Tremont to finish his thought.

"Don't hurt him! It's my fault! I'll get it for you!" his mother pleaded.

She ran up to Barry and grabbed his arm by hooking it in hers. Barry cast her off like a winter overcoat, sending her crashing to the floor under the kitchen table.

Barry's attention returned to Tremont, he reached down, again grabbed a muss of hair, and pulled Tremont's head back so he was looking up at him. "You're fucking with me, and I don't like to be fucked with. You're going to give me my dope, and after you do, I'll hit you one more time. It doesn't get any simpler than that."

A hatred seethed within Tremont as he confronted the man responsible for his birth. Barry was his father by genetic definition only; his presence in Tremont's life was as fleeting as his mother's sobriety. The apartment was nothing more than Barry's spare closet. The door was only opened to either stow things he wanted hidden or hoard things to be used at an opportune time. Tremont and his mother were merely additional contents of this sordid storage facility. His mother was a simple vessel he used for sexual and hostile release, and Tremont was just something that had accidently spilled out of the closet one day, only to be shoved back in for long-term storage.

He looked up into Barry's giant, hairy nostrils and felt that freedom could be won from this now—freedom from abuse, freedom from humiliation, freedom from the bonds of hatred. He was a boy maturing to a man, a butterfly peeling back its cocoon, a new country being born. And his flag would be a ten-dollar bill.

"Ten dollars," he repeated.

Barry picked him up off the bed by his hair and held his face up to his. They stared viciously into each other's eyes until the stares became clouded by smoking, burning flesh as Barry's teeth pushed the cigarette tip against Tremont's nose.

Tremont was clutching Barry's wrist with both hands above his head while his feet kicked in a hopeless search for the floor. When he felt the hot ash branding his flesh, he reacted by taking one hand away and driving a fist up into Barry's chin.

Barry bit the filter off the cigarette so the rest fell to the floor and released his grip on Tremont, dropping him to the floor with it. "You little shit!" he barked. "You feel like being a man today? Did you wake up this morning with your first erection? Did it give you a little dose of power?" Barry's voice dropped a few decibels. "Let me show you power . . ."

He disappeared into the bedroom. Tremont heard the same rustling sounds his mother had made fifteen minutes earlier during her frantic search for Barry's cocaine. But this time the noise halted after just a moment, because Barry had found what he was looking for.

He emerged with a gun. "This is power, little man. And you're on the wrong end of it."

Tremont was still on the floor, now at eye level with his mother, who cowered under the table with vacant eyes. He gave her a disbelieving glare for keeping a gun in the house, but she was useless. He was in this alone. Somehow, the intensity of this realization was empowering.

As Tremont tried to push himself up, Barry again grabbed his hair and propped him up on the coffee table so his back was pressed up against the radiator's ribcage. The heat was on and it burned into his back muscles.

Barry continued to pull on his hair as he pressed the gun up against his face. "Now, why don't you tell me what's going to happen next."

Tremont's eye was half closed, the entire top of his head felt as if it would peel away like a sheet of Velcro, his back was searing as it pressed into the iron grate, and the flesh of his nose continued to smolder. With every fragment of courage he could summon from the hidden places within his body, he told Barry what would happen next.

"Twenty dollars."

The last thing Tremont expected to see was Barry cock his head in puzzlement. And he thought it would be the last thing he would ever see as he squeezed his eyes shut and waited for the blast of the gun, waited for the explosion of his head spattering the walls. The seconds ticked by as if in dramatic pause of the inevitable. *What is he waiting for?* he pondered with what he believed to be his final thought.

Instead, he felt the gun move away from his face, and then Barry grabbing his arm and twisting it. As Tremont resisted, Barry compensated by applying more torque. Tremont combated with opposing pressure, but Barry was simply too strong for him.

With his palm turned up, Tremont prepared to let out a scream, but he resolved to hold it inside for as long as he could. The room would echo with the sound of his snapping ulna before it would be drowned out with his piercing shrill of pain.

Contrary to his expectations, the pain did not increase. Instead, he felt a small, folded piece of paper pushed into his palm. It had the unique, coarse texture of American currency. The pressure on his arm subsided.

Tremont hesitated before releasing the tension in his body. He heard his mother's soft cries over his heavy breathing.

He didn't need to check the bill's denomination to know it was a twenty.

Barry stood up, took a step back, and regarded his son. "I want you to come and work for me, Tree."

He tossed the gun through the bedroom doorway and onto the bed, then paced over to Tremont's mother. "You and I are going to have our own discussion later," he said without looking directly at her.

He turned back to Tremont, who was slouched on the coffee table, breathing erratically.

"Are we done here?" Barry asked.

"No," came an empowered response.

"Are you shitting me?"

Tremont paused to get some strength. Then he unzipped his pants, reached in, pulled out a cloudy white plastic bag, and pitched it to Barry. “Now we’re done.”

Barry caught it, tossed it gently in the air to test its weight, put it in his front pants pocket, and left.

That’s how Tremont Williams completed his first drug deal.

CHAPTER 5

Michael walked down the hallway of his high school after the last bell of the day with all the authority of a graduating senior that was his right. He could coast through this last semester if he chose, but he did enjoy most of the classes he was taking, so he continued to complete his assignments with vigor. He excelled in math and physics courses, finding comfort in the idea that everything that happened did so for a calculated reason.

He toiled, however, through English and literature classes, as they were too open for interpretation. He deliberately challenged widely held interpretations of famous works to prove his point. His most prominent argument took up a full class as he tried unsuccessfully to argue that Hamlet's well-known soliloquy, "To be or not to be," was a contemplation not of suicide but of murder.

There was one class, however, in which he found a distinctive delight, and as he entered the school's computer lab, he found her sitting in a wheeled desk chair facing the front of the first row of computers the way a gambler would sit before a row of casino slot machines.

Before she looked up at him, he raised half of his shirt collar in a bid to appear just a bit unkempt.

"Hi, Ms. Cavanaugh. You look like you're in Vegas trying to play several slots at once."

"Not me, Michael." She chuckled. "I never understood how people could lose a quarter on every pull of the handle, expecting to make it up on volume."

Michael relished her intelligent wit. He also enjoyed her teaching ability and style, her lessons and assignments. But mostly he enjoyed her long, sinewy legs that she always made available for public viewing with skirts that never draped below her knees.

Ms. Cavanaugh—or Ms. Calves of Awe, as she was warmly known to the male student body—was wheeling back and forth between computers, using her legs as gracefully as a gondolier navigating the canals of Venice.

"What are you doing?"

"One of the school's computers was infected with a virus. I'm scanning the drives to see if any of the lab's computers have been exposed."

"Whose computer was affected?"

"Mr. Burnell's. Apparently, while he was printing out final grades, the computer wiped out his entire hard drive, including the operating system. We have some people looking at it now."

"Was it introduced accidentally or was it sabotage?"

"Like I said, some people are looking at it."

"It's interesting," Michael posed, "that under certain conditions, a computer can be programmed to terminate itself."

She tilted her head at the existential thought but reframed the idea through the lens of a programming instructor. "Like I teach my students, computers only do what they're told."

Michael approached and could hear the whirring of the disk drives as they searched for rogue programs. "Any luck?"

"That depends on how you define luck. I'm searching for viruses hoping I don't find any; I could be lucky if I don't find any . . . or lucky that I did find them. Every scan I've completed so far has come back clean. I'm just waiting for these last three to finish."

The three computers scanned themselves independently, with their disk drives emitting random grinding sounds. Michael waited with his teacher for them to conclude. After a couple of minutes, the noise stopped and the monitors displayed the same summary message: "SCAN COMPLETE. NO VIRUSES FOUND."

Michael stood by patiently, enjoying Ms. Cavanaugh's graceful movements as she shut down the last three computers, until she turned her attention to him. "What can I help you with?"

Shaken out of his adolescent trance, he provided a lagging response: "I need some help with your final assignment."

"Why don't you pull out your disk and we'll pop it in and see if we can work out the bugs."

Michael ignored the unintended juvenile innuendoes, but he did register them. "It's more of a conceptual problem," he said. "I don't think we'll need to look at a screen."

"What type of project did you choose?"

"I'm simulating a dice game."

"That seems relatively simple." She tilted her head. "Where are you running into trouble?"

"I'm having difficulty generating a random roll of a die. The programming language's random number generator can only generate a value between zero and one. I can easily multiply that by ten and round it off to establish a number between one and ten, but I need a random number between one and six. I'm here for some guidance."

"That's an interesting little problem; let me think for a minute."

Michael savored being in Ms. Cavanaugh's presence. He always asked questions in class just to hear her voice being directed at him. Sometimes he made his programs more difficult than they needed to be so he could spend time with her after class for additional instruction. He was sure she saw through his intentions; it had to be evident that the loss of his mother had left him yearning for a matriarchal influence. But he often felt she tried to provide an acceptable, subtle tenderness without overstepping the boundaries of the student-teacher relationship. She seemed to take particular interest in his work, and from time to time she questioned him about his activities outside the classroom. Sometimes she even ventured a compassionate smile in his direction that seemed meant for only him.

After a moment of looking up at the ceiling tiles in a thoughtful pose, Ms. Cavanaugh continued her thinking aloud. "It seems each number has a one-sixth chance of being rolled. What is one-sixth expressed as a percentage?" she asked rhetorically as she reached for her calculator.

"It's 16.7 percent," Michael responded before she could tap even one of the calculator's buttons.

She raised her eyes from the calculator display and caught Michael's gaze. He immediately worked to suppress any betraying signs of guilt for knowing the answer already.

"Hmm . . ." she said faintly, as she was seemingly now contemplating both the programming problem and the reason for Michael's visit. But she continued, "If we generate a random number between zero and .167, that could equate to a roll of one. If we generate a random number between .168 and"—she paused to see if Michael would inject the answer, but he was silent—“and .334, that would equate to a roll of two. And so on. In other words, divide the possible random numbers into six different buckets.”

Michael cast his eyes upward, pretending to think. “Yes, I see what you’re doing. I can program that.”

She was wearing a gray-and-white herringbone skirt that started above the knee. Her white silk blouse was finely pressed and draped casually over her breasts, making it difficult to determine their size and shape. Even though Michael tried not to stare into her bosom, he couldn’t help but think of resting his head there. Not in a sexual way; it was more a feeling born out of a desire to feel secure, and he only became aware of it as he pondered her shape beneath the blouse.

“Thanks for your help,” he said, but he didn’t leave; he still hadn’t done what he came to do. He usually had no difficulty controlling a conversation, but with her it was different—difficult the way it is sometimes difficult to talk to a parent. He felt awkward around her now and knew he was at risk of saying or doing something he hadn’t prepared for.

A silence developed; he had to do something before she sensed his immaturity.

He stood quickly, jammed his hand in his pocket, and clutched the ticket—but the opportunity was lost. He backed toward the door. “I’m late for practice. Thanks again for your time.”

He turned away, but he heard the wheels of her chair squeak as she pushed it away from the workstation and stood. “Are you competing on Saturday?”

He stopped his charge for the door and turned back to her. “Yes, the state championships are at Boston University.”

“What event are you entered in?” She moved toward him.

He was calmed by this new tone and her smooth, silky stride. "Two-mile run. I think my chances are good."

She walked right up to him and straightened his collar. Not just the side that was folded up; she went around his neck with both hands and smoothed it in its entirety. As she removed some lint from his neckline, she said in a comforting voice, "I'm sure you'll do your very best."

Michael waited for a kiss on his forehead but, of course, it never came.

He did, however, see an opportunity to complete his purpose. "The coaches give all the competitors tickets for parents and friends; I have an extra one if you're interested in coming." He took his hand out of his pocket and presented the ticket to her.

"I'll give it some thought." She was noticeably careful not to brush his hand as she took it from him.

She regarded the ticket in her hand, then considered the student in front of her. Her expression was the same one she affected when laboring to decipher a student's tangled programming code. *What's the intended outcome?* she would inevitably ask. But all she mustered now was, "Hmm . . ."

The second call for runners bellowed over the stadium loudspeakers: "ATTENTION TWO-MILERS. RUNNERS MUST REPORT TO THE INFIELD NEXT TO THE LONG JUMP PIT. THE EVENT WILL START IN TEN MINUTES."

"I think I need to answer this one, Dad."

Michael stood on the outside lane of the straightaway against the chain-link fence that separated the running track from the grandstand, wearing loose-fitting shorts and a singlet embroidered with gold and brown, his high school's colors. The number twenty was pinned to the front of his singlet, hiding the image of a lion poised to attack.

His father stood beyond the fence with a 35-millimeter camera hanging from his neck. The fence was six feet high and so required them to speak through the links like a prisoner and a visitor from the outside world, although unclear who was who.

"Before I go," Michael asked, "do you have any inspirational words?"

"Run fast," his father said. "Run very, very fast."

"Gee, thanks," he said sarcastically. He had hoped for something a little more emotive.

But his father did try again. "I wish you luck. Daniel and I will be up in the top row of the stands, and with you every step of the way."

A bright sun shone above the stadium and its rays seemed to fight off some distant clouds. His father's sunglasses covered most of his face, and the features that were visible were cast in shadow from the visor of his baseball cap.

Excitement bubbled through Michael. This was to be his last meet before graduating, and he was roused by his father's presence, as he always was. But he was also curious about something, and he was compelled to find out about it now.

"Dad, can I ask you something?"

"Anything at all."

His question needed a preface. "I'm very grateful you've made it to all my meets, *all* my meets, and have gotten the chance to see me compete. It means a lot to me."

His father nodded. "It makes me feel proud to watch you."

"But everyone else's dad is always down on the infield . . . helping the kids stretch, giving last-minute advice, and cheering for them along the track during the race. You always sit up in the stands, as high up as you can get. Don't you want to be down here with me?"

His father pursed his lips and his jowls tightened and then loosened. He removed his sunglasses, and Michael saw a glint of pain in his eyes as he stepped forward and curled the fingers of both hands around the thin metal links.

Choosing his words carefully, as he always did, he responded to his son's question of devotion. "Michael, I can't help you to run fast—that's what your coaches are for. I can only teach you to listen to your coaches and teach you to work hard to achieve success. The other side of this fence is your arena, not mine. It's where you take everything you've learned and everything you've practiced, and perform. It's those other fathers who don't belong in there." He peered into his son's eyes. "The reason I sit in the stands is because it's the best place to watch you run. And I love to watch you run. I've watched you win every conference race this year, and I've been both exhilarated and proud each time. I'm your fan, Michael, and fans belong here in the stands."

Michael's eyes began to well up and he wiped his dampened nose across his bare arm. He was both sorry and glad he'd asked.

"LAST CALL FOR ALL TWO-MILERS. REPORT TO THE INFIELD NEXT TO THE LONG JUMP PIT."

"Your nose is running." His father grinned. "I think it should have its own race number."

"I love you, Dad."

"You'd better get going."

Michael turned and started toward the long jump pit, only to stop and turn back to his father. "Why the top row?"

"To be closer to your mother."

The starter's pistol sounded and twenty of the state's fastest high school runners bounded into action. Like a swarm of psychedelic bees with their varying school colors, they sprinted for position down the straightaway to the first long, wide turn, where they unraveled into a single file.

Emerging out of the first turn, Michael found himself in the middle of the procession.

The track was a quarter mile around. The first runner to complete eight laps would be crowned this year's state champion.

They progressed around the oval, hugging the inside lane. Other athletes continued to participate in the interior field events, and the runners passed the high jump bar on the first turn, paralleled the long jump runway down the back straight, circled the shot-putters around the far turn, and passed the coaches and fathers on the final straightaway to the start/finish line. After seven more laps a white tape would be stretched across the lanes, waiting to be sliced by the winner.

After the second lap, the runners segregated into two distinct groups. The first group had four runners and was about twenty yards ahead of Michael, who led the second group.

The pace of the lead runners was fast, but he was still close enough to hear their coaches yell out split times as they completed each lap. It was still early in the race and he was comfortable with both his pace and position. He was extending a tether on the lead pack, but not so far ahead that he could not reel them in. After maintaining this position for the third lap without losing any distance on the lead pack, he looked back over his shoulder and saw he had pulled about ten yards ahead of the other runners. What was behind him now was unimportant.

Michael liked it here, isolated between the two packs, because here he was unaffected by the pace of the other runners. He felt no obligation to lead and no obligation to follow. He was running the race as he had trained: in solitude.

About four thousand spectators dotted the stadium seats. Most were parents and other family members, or school contingents that had come to cheer on their fellow classmates. Each group had a different judgment of what the best vantage point was, which caused large occupied areas and equally large unoccupied areas.

Jack and Daniel sat high up in the grandstand, beneath the press box. They looked down over the many empty seats, across the groups of spectators, and surveyed the full expanse of the track.

"He's staying too far back," Daniel submitted without taking his eyes off the race.

"These runners are at a much higher caliber than what he's used to," Jack said. "By keeping the race in front of him, he can assess his competition. He knows what he's doing."

"I hope so," replied Daniel.

I hope so, too, thought Jack.

Michael approached his halfway split time, passing the gaggle of fathers. He would usually study their faces to see if this would be the day his father would join them. Today, he ignored them, as he should have always done. They were quiet as he passed by in solitude with his steady breathing and flapping feet.

He looked ahead and began to size up the lead pack. Unlike a lion trying to identify the weakest member of the herd, he sought out the strongest. That would be his target.

By the fifth lap the buffer between Michael and the lead group had grown to thirty yards. He maintained this distance as he classified each of the four lead runners and projected their outcome. They each wore a different color, making it easy for him to assign them an identity without the benefit of faces. White had already fallen back five yards from the leaders. His pace was slowing arithmetically, but by the next turn he would slow geometrically and maybe even drop out. Blue was a runner Michael had raced and beaten in a conference matchup earlier in the season, so Michael knew the pace was too fast for him; he should fall off the pace by the next lap. Black's calves appeared too taut, so even if he could maintain the pace, he would not be able to sprint through the finish. Red led the charge, challenging the others to try an outside berth to pass. No one contested, and this left Red as the runner to beat, and Michael was now triggered to start his move to the front.

White's pace had seized as predicted and Michael was now close enough to reach out and touch him. He took one last look back, saw no one challenging him, and then cruised around White like he was a harbor buoy.

Red increased his speed, sensing the finish, and pulled away from both Blue and Black. Michael increased his speed to match the leader as if attached by a towline. Although he did not close the gap on Red, he did overcome the other two—first Black, and then Blue.

While being overtaken, Blue looked to his right, recognized Michael, and offered encouragement—"Go get him, Galler." As Michael settled in ahead of him and began pulling away, he heard one last inspiring gasp from him: "You can do it!"

The bell sounded the last lap. As if veering off formation on a bombing run, Michael accelerated his advance.

He had trained arduously all season. Bailey was his running partner during his longer training runs, and at the track she chased him back and forth while he did his wind sprints. Every practice was a chance to improve his conditioning, his stamina, and his endurance. He followed his coaches' workout schedules diligently, he did weight training for strength, and he maintained a proper diet to keep his body well stocked with energy.

Each conference meet was an opportunity to test his progress and his vulnerability. He'd won his event repeatedly this season and now felt confident that if ever Cancer attempted to challenge his mettle in any of its forms, he would defeat it. He was turning his body into an impenetrable fortress, capable of withstanding any onslaught Cancer could conjure. But today was his toughest challenge to date, as the pool of competition had been expanded statewide.

The race had now been reduced to one lap and Michael needed to make up a thirty-yard deficit. His pace was now faster than it had been in any other race he had participated in and he was sure he would set a personal record. But that was unimportant to him. All he cared about was *winning*, and in doing so demonstrating to himself that he was invincible. Beating Red would allow him to maintain this self-defined immortality.

As Michael taxied out of the first turn and onto the backstretch, he began his acceleration. A long jumper concurrently began his controlled jaunt down the runway, running parallel with Michael. Michael continued to accelerate and synchronized his stride with the jumper's. As the long jumper reached the end of the runway, he planted his foot and leaped high above the sandpit. Michael simultaneously reached his maximum speed, catalyzing a euphoric charge.

Entering the final turn, he began to close the gap.

Looking down the track, Michael saw two officials stretch a finishing tape across five lanes, holding it chest high. As he came off the turn, he was now only ten yards behind Red. He knew he could catch him; it was now merely a question of whether he would run out of track first.

The crowd pulsated with eager cheers that exposed no favorite toward the boy in brown or the boy in red. But as Michael continued to close the gap, the insistent clamoring became palpable support for him, the underdog.

The distance between them closed faster with each step Michael took. He was sprinting as the distance between them and the finish line exhausted itself like a fuse racing toward an explosive.

Michael pulled right up behind Red, then glided over to the second lane to gain room to pass. With just steps to go, his body started to lean forward in a last-ditch effort to outdistance his opponent. As he started to fall forward, he leaped like a caped superhero with outstretched arms. His eyes were now fixated on the finish tape, his hands clawing forward in a last desperate attempt to clutch the ribbon.

While falling to the ground, his eyes closed, his head dropped, and his fists clenched. His body fell flat to the track. He dared not use his hands to temper his fall for fear of letting go of the tape. He turned his head and his jaw slammed into the track; as he slid forward, his elbows scraped, his jersey tore, and his knees abraded. If he had been a matchstick, he would have ignited as his body juddered to a stop.

He lay on the ground, afraid to open his eyes and afraid to open his hands. He had no idea whether he had snatched the tape or not.

Slowly, he opened his eyes. Light seeped in at first, then drenched his retinas. He saw the track, the lane marker, and his arms. He followed his arms to his wrists and then to his hands. And there, stretched between his two fists, was . . . nothing.

Michael continued to lie on the ground as other runners crossed the finish line, sidestepping him as if he were cow dung. Judges and coaches came to his aid and helped him up. The entire front of his body was scraped and scuffed like an old work boot; he looked like he had just been cast out of a car on the highway.

The sweat on his face dissolved into tears.

He was sobbing through a muted bawl and everyone sympathized, acknowledging the pain from his wounds and the defeat of his effort.

But Michael wasn't suffering the pain of his injuries. He wasn't even suffering the loss of the championship. He was suffering the anguish of having been beaten. His body had failed to overcome the challenge, and this meant it was vulnerable to his fears.

He hobbled to the crowded infield grass, found a spot clear of flying discuses and shot puts, and collapsed in pain and exhaustion. He lay on his back and stared into the sky, trying to ignore the stinging sensation that emanated from every exposed area of skin.

The sky was filling with thick white clouds that took on the shape of vultures, pushing the sun farther down the horizon.

Suddenly, his view was obscured by the familiar outline of his father's silhouette. Without seeing the details of his face, he heard the familiar voice say, "That was the most spectacular effort I have ever seen, Michael."

Michael continued to stare upward, but now he was looking right through his father, into a void that he had never sensed before. "I lost," was all he could reply.

"If only the race were five or ten feet longer, you would have passed him and won."

"No, Dad. I made my move too late."

"Did anyone tell you that you broke the state record?"

No one had told him. But hearing it now didn't make any difference to how he felt. It didn't matter that he would have had to run a personal best by almost ten seconds to break the record; he'd still lost.

"When I crossed the finish line, the record had already been broken," he said in a low voice. "Only one thing happened today: I lost. I'm sorry, Dad. I let you down."

"Let me down? How could you say that? I'm beaming at what you did today. You gave everything you had at the finish. You'll always know that you gave it your best, and you'll never have to look back and think you could have tried harder. You didn't let me down, Michael—just the opposite."

Michael was too exhausted, mentally and physically, to talk anymore. He just wanted to lie there, alone, and pass into oblivion. "Somebody went to get a trainer for me, to clean and bandage this mess," he muttered. He was too tired to even gesture to his wounds. "I'll meet you in the parking lot after I get cleaned up."

"Are you sure?"

"Yes."

Michael's father reached down and wiped his face dry with a towel he had somehow acquired, but then there was nowhere else he could wipe that wasn't scraped and raw.

"I'll see you in the parking lot," he said. "Remember, I'm very proud of you."

His outline disappeared, revealing a darker, more threatening sky.

Michael continued to lie on the ground. He replayed the race in his mind, wondering if he could have started his thrust to the finish earlier; if he had, maybe he could have won. Or maybe he could have run harder to the finish. Or maybe his body just wasn't strong enough, wasn't capable of fending off every foe. This thought depressed him terribly. He had won every conference competition this year, but when it really mattered, the state championship, he could not post the victory. He disappointed his father and his brother and was ashamed to let them see him in this wrecked condition.

As he lay there with his open, festering wounds exposing his body to the world and all its harmful influences, he had never felt more vulnerable.

An unfamiliar female voice interrupted his internalized self-deprecation.

"There you are. I've been looking for you."

Michael could not see where the voice was coming from without sitting up but he was still too tired to move, so he remained supine and conversed with this new entity sight unseen. "You found me."

The pause that followed asked the question of who she was and why she was here.

"I heard you have open wounds that need attention. I'm here to take care of you."

Finally he sat up, trying to suppress a grotesque grimace as he was stung by the abrasions on his arms and legs.

When he laid eyes on the owner of the voice, he was captured by the perfection of her figure. She wore athletic shoes with socks pushed down around her ankles, revealing silky smooth shins. Her thighs were perfectly proportioned to the rest of her legs, and her red cuffed shorts fit the curve of her hips as if tailored. A white crew neck shirt fit comfortably over her modest breasts, evoking the image of apples tucked firmly into a homemade pie.

He studied her face and found it familiar, although he knew he had never met her before. It seemed to contain the characteristics of many people he might have met, and yet the combination of all these common features made her somehow unique.

For all the comfortable familiar features of her face, however, he found her eyes somewhat disquieting. They seemed to slope toward the bridge of her nose—or maybe her eyebrows were shaped to provide this sinister effect? Regardless, Michael found them captivating.

Boston University: Staff Trainer was imprinted on her breast pocket and revealed her function. He also noticed she was carrying a zippered canvas bag, which he was sure contained her medical supplies.

She surveyed Michael's damaged condition. "Did you win?"

"No." Michael did not want to start the conversation by indicating he was a loser, but what could he do; that was the correct answer.

She knelt next to him, inspected his wounds, and then began unpacking her bag. She removed a small stack of gauze pads, a roll of white medical tape, several rolled elastic bandages, a pair of scissors, and a clear plastic bottle holding a brownish liquid. She tore open a gauze package, squirted some of the liquid onto the pad, and directed her attention to Michael.

"This is going to sting," she warned. "I have to scrub everything clean."

"It couldn't get any worse," he replied.

"Ready?"

Without waiting for a response, she began scrubbing with the soaked gauze.

He was wrong; it did get worse. It felt like a branding iron was pressing into his arm. She continued to scrub even after the sting of the antiseptic subsided, like she was sanding furniture to a smooth finish. But Michael was not made of wood, and the pain continued.

Finally satisfied that the wound was clean, she tore open three more squares of gauze and pressed them over the wound. They held in place while she returned to the bag and removed a rolled wrap made from a thin, spongy material.

"This will keep your hair from pulling when you remove the dressing," she explained as she unrolled the sponge around his arm. After making several loops, she tore it and then repeated the same motions with a two-inch-wide roll of white medical tape. Ignoring the scissors, she used her teeth to tear the tape and pressed down the loose end.

"Three more limbs to go," she said.

Satisfied she could competently dress his injuries, Michael began scanning the infield and the grandstand for Ms.

Cavanaugh. He hoped she had attended to see him compete, but more importantly, he wanted to introduce her to his father.

His attention was returned to his injuries as the trainer began scrubbing his other arm.

At first Michael thought she was trying to hurt him purposely, but as he studied her efforts he saw she was making careful, gentle preparations before imparting the pain. He again watched her unwrap the gauze, clean, scrub, cover, wrap, and tape. It was as if she were trying to prepare and wrap the perfect gift.

She kept at least one hand always touching him, even when she reached for any of the many items she had available on the turf. This gave Michael a sense of comfort and security that he took as an opportunity to initiate a conversation.

"I'm Michael."

"Julie."

"I appreciate you doing this."

"That's what I'm here for." She smiled and shrugged. "I go to school here at BU and I'm working my way to medical school."

"What year are you?"

"Sophomore."

"You still have a long way to go."

She finished taping the second arm, looked up, and caught Michael's eyes. "I'm prepared for that," she said sternly, her tone almost offended.

Judging from the way she'd laid out her equipment and supplies, Michael agreed she was a very prepared person. Her words revealed the deep commitment to her task.

Talking reminded him that his jaw ached from the fall, but the pain was manageable, so he did not see the need to mention it.

As Julie began working on his knees, he continued searching the stands for Ms. Cavanaugh. He scanned each row, starting from the top and working his way down.

When he reached the bottom row and came up empty, he examined the fence line. Scrutinizing from left to right, he inventoried each face there.

Three-quarters of the way down the fence line, he spotted her. She was waving in an attempt to get his attention, which she now had.

Michael lifted a bandaged arm and returned the wave in eager acknowledgment, as if to say, *Yes, yes.*

Ms. Cavanaugh gave Michael a thumbs-up, saluting his competitive effort.

"Your girlfriend?" Julie asked without checking to see who he was waving to.

"One of my teachers."

Ms. Cavanaugh pointed to her watch, indicating she had to leave. When Michael altered his wave to communicate, *No, no*, her expression suggested that she would try to wait.

Julie's work on Michael's legs seemed a bit gentler than her work on his arms had been—maybe even intimate. Her pace had slowed and he was struggling with deciding whether to hurry her up so he could catch Ms. Cavanaugh, walk with her to the parking lot, and introduce her to his father, or to stay here and spend more time with Julie. He was starting to feel an attraction toward the trainer, which made the decision difficult.

Michael sat still and observed Julie's patience and Ms. Cavanaugh's impatience. He raised two fingers to Ms. Cavanaugh to ask her to wait two more minutes. She responded by raising the same two fingers, indicating no more than two minutes.

He had gotten used to the burning pain and more readily accepted the ensuing sting as she nursed his knees until it appeared she had completed her treatment.

"You're finished," she said. "You should change these wraps in a day or two and put on some fresh bandages." She grabbed a handful of gauze and a roll of tape and laid them aside for him to take with him. "Next time you take a dive, make sure there's a swimming pool underneath you."

"I'll try to remember that."

"Is there anything else I can do for you?" she asked suggestively.

Michael struggled with his response. He took one last look at Ms. Cavanaugh, then looked again at Julie. He had managed to get his teacher to come to the meet and did not want to let the opportunity slip away. But at the same time, he had not expected to meet someone himself that interested him. He had to decide now between a woman for himself and a woman for his father.

He took one more look into Julie's arresting eyes and answered her question.

"I hit my jaw on the track when I fell. Maybe you could take a look at it."

She moved closer to him and held his jaw the way one would line up an intimate kiss.

"Move it up and down," she instructed.

He obeyed.

"Now side to side."

He obeyed again. He closed his eyes while she continued to manipulate his head.

"It feels okay to me. I could tape your head to protect it," she said with a smile. "But then you'd look like a mummy."

They both laughed, which made Michael's jaw ache.

"I'd want you to be there for the unveiling," he quipped.

She tilted her head. "Are you asking me out?"

Michael hesitated, wondering for a moment who'd actually just initiated the invitation—then, "Yes," he said. "Could I have your phone number?"

"I don't think that's a good idea . . ."

Michael's heart sank into his shorts. Suddenly, the pain throughout his body became more evident than before.

"I'll get in touch with you," she finished.

His face ignited with surprise. "That's great!"

She packed up her satchel and started to rise. "I'm glad we met."

Michael sensed the deal was not yet closed. "How will you get in touch with me?"

She leaned down and brought her face close to his again, taunting him with her eyes. She took hold of his racing bib and tore it loose from the safety pins as if ripping the heart out of his chest. "I've got your number," she said.

She stood tall and walked away. Michael's eyes didn't leave her as she crossed the infield until she melted into a crowd.

He turned back toward the fence and, without surprise, saw that Ms. Cavanaugh had been removed from the landscape as if she had been airbrushed out of a photograph.

CHAPTER 6

Michael stood in front of the bathroom sink but was too small to reach the medicine cabinet. He stepped up onto the toilet seat and leaned on the sink with one hand for balance. He used the other hand to pull the cabinet door open. When his hand came into view, he saw it was holding a small piece of paper. He stood tall on the toilet and unfolded the paper with both hands.

Look in the bathroom, behind the mirror.

He recognized the handwriting as his mother's, but it was freshly written. He refolded the paper and obeyed the instruction: Continuing to lean carefully against the sink, he pulled the cabinet door toward him to open it.

As it opened, the new angle exposed his reflection, revealing a face he had not seen in many years. The face of a small boy stared back at him. His hair was cut short, betraying the innocent facial features of an undeveloped face. The eyes gave away no hints of sorrow, and the cheekbones brandished the rosiness of youth.

He continued to draw open the small door until the full contents of the cabinet were in clear view. His eyes took in white bottles of aspirin, cough syrup, tweezers, and other assorted items that could be found in any neighborhood convenience store. But there was no need to take inventory, because what he was looking for was in plain view on the bottom shelf.

He took the folded piece of paper—it looked similar to the one already in his hand—closed the mirrored door, and hopped off the toilet. He unfolded the paper and read it aloud to himself.

"Look in your baseball hat."

Somehow he knew he had to follow the instructions in each note. If he did, something good would happen. His enthusiasm elevated as he tried to recollect where his hat was.

On the first floor, there was a closet that held coats, boots, shoes, umbrellas, and, of course, hats. He hurried down the steps, flung open the closet door, and saw his hat hanging on a hook. He reached up and pulled the hat off its perch, causing another folded piece of paper to flutter to the closet floor like a newborn finch making its first attempt at flight. It landed in one of his father's old work boots.

He pulled it out and again read aloud to himself: "Look under your pillow."

He felt like he was getting closer, which excited him more. He ran up the flight of stairs to his bedroom and cast aside the pillow at the head of the bed. Underneath was another clue.

"Look in my hair."

"Look in my hair?" he repeated aloud as a question.

The handwriting was his mother's so he assumed he should look in his mother's hair. But where would he find his mother?

The kitchen! His heart began to palpitate as he raced down to the kitchen.

He slid to a stop on the linoleum floor—and there she was! Sitting right where she should be. She was at the kitchen table in her usual chair, having coffee with Aunt Ellen. On the table he saw two coffee cups, steaming with warmth, and a vase of tulips with bright petals sitting high atop firm stems.

They were talking to each other but Michael could not hear their words.

He studied her face. It seemed so real, not like any photograph he had ever seen. The skin seemed softer, more fluid. Her lips moved and her eyes blinked. He sensed emotion in her words as she spoke across the table. Her hair jostled as her head moved.

And then he saw it. Awkwardly nestled in her hair was a small, folded piece of paper. He wanted to take it, remove it from her, but he was immobilized.

He stood next to his mother with his eyes fixated on the note. It didn't belong in her hair. Nobody's mother had paper in her hair. But there it was, and he'd been instructed to remove it. Yet all he could do was stand there helplessly, paralyzed by bewilderment.

Suddenly, he heard his name being called from a distance.

"Michael! Michael!"

He could not place its source, but it seemed to originate from a far-off place. It was calling him away, but he could not go until he liberated the paper from his mother's hair—or was he trying to rescue his mother from the paper? He felt himself drifting away, but he could not leave until he fulfilled his quest. The paper had final instructions for him and he needed to access them. But he could not step closer, he could not lift his arms, and he could not speak.

He wanted to shout. He tried to scream out, but he choked on his own voice.

"Michael!"

It continued to call him away, and then someone seized his arm.

"Michael!"

Michael grabbed the thing holding his arm and jolted forward in his bed. He was awake and adjusting to a new vision, this one of reality.

He was face-to-face with Daniel, who was grasping his arm.

"Get up already, you have a phone call," Daniel said in an annoyed tone.

Michael's eyes were forced open wide, absorbing all the real objects and colors surrounding him. "Who is it?"

"I don't know, some girl."

"Who?" Michael asked, a little more interested now.

"I don't know. She didn't say."

Michael swung his legs over the side of the bed and sat up. The blood rushed to his head, and he had to take a moment before getting up. He headed out of the room but not without a parting shot: "Next time, *ask*."

He decided on the phone in the kitchen as he reached the bottom step, then changed his mind and went to his father's study and lifted the handset at his father's desk, assuming that Daniel was likely somewhere in the house on a different phone, listening.

He cleared his throat. "Hello?"

The line felt vacuous.

"Hello?" he repeated.

Still no response. All he heard was the empty hiss of a terminated connection.

"Daniel? . . . Daniel? . . . Daniel, I know you're there. Are you sure it was for me?"

Daniel hesitated and then responded guiltily, "Yeah. She asked for you."

"Are you sure you didn't know who it was? Did you recognize the voice?"

"No."

"Well, she's gone."

"I tried to get you up. You took too long to get to the phone. No wonder she hung up." Daniel was clearly trying to keep the blame on Michael to divert the attention from his eavesdropping.

"Hang up," Michael said angrily.

He heard a click and then, with a headful of curiosity, returned his handset to the phone's cradle.

CHAPTER 7

Michael twisted the plastic ice cube tray, loosening the cubes from their compartments, then shook the tray, causing five cubes to jump out and land on the tops of the other cubes. He put these in a tall glass, refilled the tray with tap water, and replaced it in the freezer. Then he filled the glass with orange juice and returned the carton to the refrigerator.

Michael drank only juice or spring water, no soda or other sugary drinks, and he preferred to use a lot of ice cubes to dilute the acidity of the juices.

He gathered up the glass, along with his father's coffee mug, which he'd prepared moments earlier, and a stack of envelopes—all addressed to Michael Galler—and deposited them on the kitchen table.

"Have you made a decision yet?" his father asked him as he sorted the envelopes into two piles.

Instead of a left and right pile, Michael moved the three thick envelopes closest to him and pushed the two thin envelopes farther away. He then separated the three thick envelopes in front of him so their return addresses were clearly displayed.

The envelopes had already been torn open, although the contents could have been determined by examining their size. The thin ones were rejection letters and the thick ones contained acceptance materials for the universities Michael had applied to.

"Not yet," he responded. "I really like Princeton's engineering program, but the school is in the middle of New Jersey. Columbia's engineering school is equally impressive, but New York City may be too overwhelming."

"So you've ruled out the Wentworth Institute right here in Boston?"

"Of course. You know I only applied there as a safety."

Michael knew his father was struggling with the two opposing issues of tuition and educational opportunity. He'd seen his illuminated face when the Ivy League acceptance letters arrived and had heard his boastings to neighbors. He also had seen him sitting under the dim light of his desk lamp in the late hours, surely calculating scenario after financial scenario.

"I plan on working hard in the summers and getting a job on campus," Michael said. "I've applied for several student loans and a few scholarships. Dad, I'm not helping you pay for my education, you're helping me."

His father smiled. "If it's between Princeton and Columbia, I don't think you can make a wrong decision."

"Thanks, Dad."

"Will you try out for the track team?"

"No, I'll be too busy."

His dad's eyebrows lifted. "Too busy with what?"

"Remember how you said I lost the state championship because the race just wasn't long enough?"

"Yes," his dad responded cautiously.

"Well, that won't happen again," he announced. "I'm going to train for a marathon."

"A marathon?" his dad asked incredulously.

"That's right."

"That's twenty-six miles!"

"Plus 385 yards. If I can complete that distance, my body can conquer anything."

Michael tilted back his glass one last time, draining the last of the juice. The clinking sound of the ice cubes was drowned out by the ringing of the telephone.

"I have it." Michael reached behind him and pulled the phone off the wall.

A marathon, his father mouthed inaudibly, his eyes still on his son.

"Hello?" Michael said into the handset.

"Is this Michael?" asked the voice on the other end.

He recognized it immediately for two reasons: one, because the first time he'd heard it there had also been no face associated with it, and two, because he had been waiting almost two weeks to hear it again, playing it repeatedly in his mind.

"Julie?" he gushed.

"Hi."

"I didn't think you'd call. Will you hold for a minute while I switch phones?" Not waiting for an answer, he darted out of the kitchen, calling over his shoulder at his dad, "Will you hang up when I pick up in the study?"

He closed the door behind him for privacy and instructed his dad through the phone line to hang up the kitchen handset. This accomplished, he spoke freely with Julie, having the comfort of knowing no one was listening in on his conversation.

"How did you get my phone number?" he asked.

"I could have checked the race results for your name and town and then looked it up—but instead I just looked on the back of your racing number where you completed the section on who to notify in case of an emergency."

There was no sarcasm in her tone, but Michael still felt foolish for not thinking of either option.

"I'm really glad you called. I didn't think you would, me being in high school and you in college." He was eager to feel her out on the age issue.

"Believe it or not, you seem a lot more mature than any of the guys I've met in college. Besides, you really fell for me, so I thought I'd give it a chance," she jested.

"I'm sure I'm not the first guy to ever fall for you," he shot back.

"No, but you may be the first to get terribly wounded in the process."

They both shared a light laugh as Michael inspected his healed wounds, and he was warmed by a sense of unique comfort—one he felt could last a long time, one he hoped would last a long time.

"Did you call before and hang up before I got to the phone?"

"No," she said. "It must have been one of your other girlfriends."

He wasn't sure if it was the denial or the reference to other girls, but her answer carried a weight to it that he found difficult to measure, which erased a small degree of that comfort. Maybe she was embarrassed to admit she'd called, or maybe it really was someone else who had called. Regardless, she was someone he wanted to spend more time with.

They spoke for half an hour before agreeing to meet the following Saturday. Michael would meet her at her apartment in the city, and they would spend the day exploring the Boston University campus and the city itself. Michael liked this idea because it would give him an opportunity to get a sense of college life; perhaps, he thought, this would help him finalize a decision about where to matriculate next year.

After hanging up, he could not contain his eagerness or his energy. He could not sit still and felt confined in the house. He put on his running gear and double-knotted his running shoes, then raised his chin and shouted through the house, "Bailey!"

When he did this, she normally immediately escaped from whatever room she was in and gamboled straight to Michael—but this time, there was nothing.

"Bailey?!" he called again. This time she did emerge from the living room, but she was lacking her usual enthusiasm.

"There you are." He kneeled in front of her and rubbed vigorously behind her ears while she rolled her head in enjoyment. He stared into her brown eyes as he ruffled her mane and playfully flopped her ears. He loved Bailey and spent a lot of time with her. He'd trained her to be obedient: She did not need the restraint of a leash during their runs, as she always stayed on his heels. She also shared his zest for activity.

Michael led her down the stairs and outside, where he stretched and limbered his muscles while she sniffed around the bushes. He was in a celebratory mood and felt like running a mile or two more than usual. He also wanted to alter the scenery from the drudgery of his typical route. So he started running down the street in the opposite direction from his usual course.

"Here we go, girl," Michael said to her as he started pacing himself. But he did not hear the jingle of her dog tags following at his footsteps. He stopped and turned.

Bailey was sitting diligently at the curb, looking reluctant to follow him.

"Bailey!" he called, but she did not respond.

She looked almost apologetic, but she didn't move an inch even when he called to her again.

He scanned the neighborhood for anything that might be discouraging her from following him. It was dusk, and the red glow of the sky still provided plenty of light. Most of the neighbors' cars were in driveways or garages, providing few lairs for lurking demons. Traffic was nonexistent on the quiet suburban street.

He marched back to her, scrubbed her neck, and began running in his usual direction, thinking it was the change in routine that was biasing her attitude.

Again, she did not follow.

He stood about twenty yards from her with his hands on his hips, wishing he could ask her what the problem was. Bailey had turned her body around to face Michael in his reversed direction but continued to sit utterly still with a compunctious look on her furry face.

He went back to her and pulled her by the collar with a frustrated jerking motion. She came forward three paces and then resisted against his tugging.

He resolved that his friend would not join him, regardless of the direction he embarked on.

"You're becoming an old mule!" he berated her. "You'd better be sitting right there when I get back."

The sun fell behind the horizon, the streetlights enkindled, and Michael ran off in the direction he'd originally chosen. When he looked back, Bailey was crouching down on her stomach, her head resting between her front paws.

Perched at the third-floor bedroom window, Daniel watched over the scene, observing Bailey's defiance and Michael's irritation. He could hear Michael scolding the dog, even though his voice was muted by the closed window.

And a few minutes earlier, he had also recognized Julie's voice on the phone as the same voice that had hung up two weeks earlier.

CHAPTER 8

The rain splashed onto the windshield in sheets. Just as quickly as the wipers could push it aside, the view was again obstructed and distorted.

Barry drove the car slowly, checking the numbers on the buildings. It was night and most of the streetlights were either broken or burned out. The rain added to the difficulty of the task, but Barry's squint exuded confidence he would find the correct building.

Tremont hadn't been told what number they were looking for, so he sat patiently, but curiously, in the passenger seat. He looked forward over the dashboard, pretending he could see what was ahead of him.

The street was lined with brick-faced apartment buildings four stories high, each one attached to the one next to it in a union that had begun over a century earlier. The front doors were half a story up, and each facade was adorned with a flight of exterior stairs. From the street, they looked like giant heads with their tongues hanging out.

"There it is," Barry said—aloud, but to himself.

He pulled the car to the side of the road, engaged the parking brake, and silenced the engine. The wipers stopped dead center on the windshield and the rain continued to beat down on the glass. What little that had been visible with the wipers employed was now a permanent blur.

Barry lit a cigarette with the car's lighter and drew hard on the filter. The cabin began to fill with smoke and Tremont stole some deep, quiet breaths, tasting the tobacco.

After three long draws and extended silence, Barry lowered the driver's side window and flicked the wasted butt onto the street. The rain extinguished the glowing tip immediately and the window returned to its closed position.

He turned to Tremont. "Listen to me carefully, and do exactly what I tell you to do. No different."

Tremont nodded.

Barry reached into his coat, pulled out a white envelope, and held it at Tremont's eye level. "There's one thousand dollars in here. I want you to deliver it for me."

Tremont reached for the envelope.

Barry swiped him in the head with it and then returned it to the space between them. "Don't touch it until I tell you to. I want you to go into this building and up to the second floor. Don't talk to anybody—don't even look at anyone. When you get there, you'll see some apartment doors. One of those doors won't have a number on it. Take this envelope and slide it under that door, then come back. You think you can do that?"

Tremont thought about how easy it would be—almost too easy. "Am I picking up anything in return?"

"Did I tell you to do anything else?" Barry boomed, so loudly that it even seemed like the rain stopped pelting the car for a moment before starting up again.

Tremont cowered. "No, you said just slide it under the door and come back."

"That's all you do. If you can do that for me, I'll give you fifty dollars."

Suddenly, Tremont didn't care what the envelope was for or why Barry wasn't just delivering it himself. In and out for fifty dollars? Simple.

Barry shook the envelope. Just as Tremont was about to take it, he pulled it back, just out of reach. Tremont looked into Barry's eyes to see what he was going to add.

In a voice that sounded like the rumbling of distant thunder from a storm one hoped would pass, Barry said, "Tree, prove to me that I can trust you."

"I'll be right back." He snatched the envelope, opened the door, and stepped out of the car.

He immediately felt the rain jumping on his head and dripping down his face. Still, he walked calmly up the steps to the door.

Standing close to the building provided some protection, so before entering he took one look around.

From the top of the steps he could see the street was empty of cars and people. Puddles reflected light from unknown sources and a lone tree stood in the distance as if watching him. He looked down at Barry's car and through the side window saw the red glow of a new cigarette.

He tested the doorknob and found it unlocked. He pushed the door open and stepped inside, away from the harshness of the rain.

The first thing he noticed was that he was alone. A bare bulb at the end of the hallway provided a weak glow and cast no shadows. In front of him to his left, there was a stairwell; to his right, a corridor with three doors. He stayed to the right of the staircase, to the first raised-panel door, which bore a peephole and two screwed-in brass digits, identifying apartment number eleven. As he progressed down the hallway, he read off numbers twelve and thirteen.

He walked back to the foot of the stairwell with a good indication of what to expect when he climbed to the second floor. Each door had a set of brass numbers that could be bought in any hardware store; each set was positioned just above a peephole.

He looked down at the contents of his hand and saw nothing but a plain white standard business-size envelope, firmly sealed. It wasn't very thick for containing $1,000, so he assumed it had ten one hundred–dollar bills inside.

He walked back to door eleven and bent down to test the width of the envelope and the space between the floor and the door. The envelope would fit.

He suddenly realized he had been inside the building now for almost three minutes and still hadn't even gotten to the second floor. He stashed the envelope in his jacket pocket and began his ascension to the next level.

The wooden stairs creaked under his weight, so he moved his path against the wall and walked on the lesser-traveled section of the boards.

When he arrived at the top of the steps, he turned around the banister to his right and looked down the hallway. On the ceiling, halfway to the end, was a bare bulb emitting the same dim light as the one downstairs. It highlighted the three doors on what was now his left. At the end of the hallway, a haggard double-hung window had been left open, inviting in the rain and the splashing noise of a passing car.

Adjacent to the window was the foot of the next flight of stairs leading to the third floor.

He started forward, hoping the first door would have no number and he'd be spared the chore of walking the length of the corridor. When he got there, he was disappointed to see the number twenty-three screwed into the door panel.

He continued to the next door, which was cast fully in the light from the bulb above, and he saw something he did not expect: The door had no brass digits, but the number twenty-two was sloppily painted on the door where the brass numbers should have been.

The first two doors on this floor were numbered; therefore, the door by the window had to be his destination. Keeping his eyes on the stairwell as he approached to be sure no one was stalking him from behind the rail, he stepped out of the light and walked toward the window.

Reaching the end of the corridor, feeling confident the stairs were unoccupied, he turned to the last door. He was disappointed to see the number twenty-one installed with brass hardware.

Tremont stood on the wet floor next to the window. He looked out and saw an iron fire escape that he had not noted when entering the building. Peering through the bars, he spied the roof of Barry's car. As he noticed this, a cigarette was discharged from the driver's side window and again immediately extinguished by the rain. Barry had smoked an entire cigarette and Tremont was still in the building.

He walked back to the door with the painted number on it and assessed his situation. *Slide it under the door with no number.* The door had no number on it, but it *was* numbered. Tremont presumed that this was the door Barry meant, but he wasn't completely sure. One thousand dollars was a lot of money to slide under the wrong door.

He didn't know what to do. The wind blew more rain into the corridor and he decided to stall by closing the window.

He walked back over to the window and attempted to push it down from the base, but it was stuck, so he reached higher for better leverage. As he pulled down it started to move—and then, with a sudden grunt, the window broke loose from its obstruction and it came down with a crash. He heard the counterweights inside the casing banging against the inside walls. He felt a deep twinge and squeezed his eyes closed, somehow believing that if he could not see, then no one else could have heard the noise.

The corridor was suddenly quiet again. He walked back to the center door, stood directly under the bulb, and stared at the painted twenty-two. He put his hand in his coat pocket and felt the envelope.

"Shit," he said under his breath. This had to be the door. He was in the right building, on the right floor, standing in front of a door that was not marked like the others. It was simple. *Slide the envelope under the door and get the fuck out*, he told himself.

But something didn't feel right about this whole situation. He was paralyzed in front of the door, unable to do one simple thing. If he screwed this up, Barry would not be pleased, and Tremont did not like the way Barry expressed his displeasure. He thought about returning to the car and confirming the correct door with Barry, but that would be no different than opening the car door and saying, "Hey, Barry, I'm stupid and I'm still holding one thousand dollars of your money."

The hallway was completely empty, but he did not feel alone. He felt like he was being watched and it made him uncomfortable standing under the light. Then he realized he was staring directly into the peephole. He had no idea if anyone was staring back at him, but he felt like there was another presence nearby. He strained to see what was on the other side of the hole, despite knowing the effort was futile.

He looked at the floor to visually measure the space under the door. He narrowed his eyes and saw small, barely noticeable scratches at its base. It looked as though it was a common delivery slot, which gave him some confidence that he should continue with his assignment.

He looked at the painted number, then the peephole, and then the floor again. Squeezing the envelope within his pocket, he looked at the doorknob and saw it start to turn.

As soon as Tremont had left the car, Barry lit another cigarette. He wasn't sure how long Tremont would be inside, but Barry would spend the minutes in tranquility, and nothing eased his thoughts as much as a cigarette.

This was the first time he'd ever been with Tremont outside of his mother's apartment. He had wanted nothing to do with being a father when Tremont was born—still didn't—and had never felt a stitch of guilt about it. Just because a farmer plants the seeds doesn't make him obligated to harvest the land. But Tremont was growing and maturing now, and Barry was starting to see a fierceness and intensity in him that he could put to good use.

The risks of dealing drugs were rising due to undercover narcotics police and aggressive competition. He could use Tremont to front some necessary activity and protect himself from most of those occupational hazards. But first he had to establish if Tremont could be trusted—not just with money and product but also with common sense and judgment.

Barry had been in this building two weeks ago to pay a visit to Reggie Gaines, one of his least creditworthy customers. Barry hadn't expected to get paid, but then again, Reggie hadn't expected to be walking with a limp for the next week. While in the building, he'd taken note of the surroundings and thought it would be a good proving ground for Tremont.

By the end of tonight, Tremont would understand his role very clearly.

The knob turned a full revolution and Tremont heard it click. Slowly, cautiously, the door opened.

Tremont froze where he stood. Options darted through his mind: leave now with the envelope, slide it under the door and run, wait to see who appears from behind the door, hide until they close the door. But he was paralyzed by the combination of his fear and his curiosity.

He heard the unmistakable sound of Barry's engine coming to life, signaling that time was running out quickly.

The door opened about three inches, revealing two chain locks that had been pulled taut. In the open space below the chain, the face of a meek old woman appeared.

"I thought I heard someone out here," she said in a jittery voice.

"Yes, I . . . I'm looking for apartment twenty-four," Tremont replied in an attempt not to frighten her, even though he was unnerved himself.

"Well then, you're lost. Because there are only three apartments on this floor." The only hint of her identity that she revealed was her graying hair. The rest of her body remained hidden behind the protection of the door.

"No other doors?"

"Nope. Just that window, which I heard slam shut. You need to open that back up so Pat can get back in."

"Pat?" Maybe Pat was the intended recipient of the envelope.

"Pat the Cat. He comes in and out through the fire escape, so I have to keep the window open. It's too difficult for me to open and close it all the time, so I just leave it open."

"I'm sorry," Tremont said. "I was trying to keep out the rain. Maybe he already came in?"

"If he had he would have scratched at the door until I let him in. He's such an impatient little shit."

Something about her amiable tone reminded him of his grandmother, and he felt obliged to mind her request. He went to the window and lifted it with difficulty and the rain wasted no time pouring in onto his shoes. He saw the car and the headlights were on, their beams revealing the intensity of the falling rain.

The car door opened and a soggy Tremont plopped himself on the seat and closed the door.

"What took you so long?" Barry asked impatiently.

"It was dark, I had trouble seeing."

"Is it taken care of?"

"I did exactly what you told me."

"You did? Well, there's another envelope in the glove compartment. Pull it out."

Tremont thought maybe it contained his fifty dollars, or maybe it was for another delivery. He pulled back on the latch and saw a pile of papers but no envelope. "Are you sure?"

"Yeah, it's under some of that shit."

Tremont reached in to rifle through the papers. Barry simultaneously reached over and smashed the compartment door shut on his hand, crushing his bones.

Tremont let out a horrified scream and tried to wrestle his hand loose, but it was caught on the latch.

"Do you feel that pain, Tree? That's the pain of me being busted and going to jail. Or maybe it's the pain of me getting a bullet in my gut from a deal gone bad. I want you to remember this pain, because you're going to do everything you can to keep me from feeling it."

Tremont was barely registering any of Barry's tirade. He was squirming to release his hand from the grip of the latch. He continued to groan as tears started to roll down his face. The latch had deeply pierced his hand and wedged itself between two of his knuckles. As he struggled, it scratched harshly against the bones. It was the single most enduring pain he had ever experienced—worse than any thrashing he had ever received.

He pawed at the latch and started to leverage the compartment open but Barry slammed it closed again, increasing his pain to even more excruciating levels.

"If you're going to work with me moving drugs and money, then you need to remember one thing: If something doesn't look right or feel right then you don't go through with the deal. It means you're getting set up by cops or by some other asshole who wants to take you down. And I'm not going down with you." The pressure in his voice coincided with the pressure he applied to Tremont's hand. As he emphasized certain words, he pressed harder on the glove box, sending bolts of pain through Tremont's whole body.

Deal. Cops. Asshole.

"All the doors had numbers," he finished. "You should have gotten out of there and brought the money back."

Tremont finally spoke. "You set me up, you asshole!" he shrilled, writhing in agony. The movement only magnified the pain. "Let me go!" he squealed.

"Let you go? You're stuck with me now. You just threw away a thousand dollars of my money, sliding it under some stranger's door. You owe me that money, and you'll work for me until you pay back every cent. I wanted to see if I could trust you to do the right thing, but you didn't think about the situation. If it was a real situation, you would have fucked it up."

Numbness set in, veiling the pain in Tremont's hand. He stopped struggling and sat motionless, looking at the closed jaw of the glove box that was gnawing on his hand. In a calm, subdued voice, he said, "Give me back my hand."

Acknowledging he had made his point, Barry abruptly leaned back behind the wheel and left Tremont to wrestle himself free from the trap.

Tremont tried to pull his hand out of the mouth of the glove box, but it was caught on the latch like a limb caught on a shark's tooth. He pushed his hand forward, then down off the hook of the latch, which freed him. He closed the compartment with his other hand before Barry got any ideas about continuing this ritual.

He stared into his hand and felt for the hole between his knuckles. He didn't care that he was bleeding all over the car because it was Barry's car.

Still fingering the hole in his hand, he said evenly, "I did exactly like you told me to do. I looked for a door without any number, but I couldn't find one." Tremont had already decided not to mention the old woman. "Let's make a few things clear today: First, the only person who can't be trusted here is you." He slowly reached up and put the envelope on the dashboard with his good hand. It was torn open. "Second, I do not owe you one goddamn penny." He accompanied the envelope with its previous contents: cut-up pieces of paper the size of currency. "And last, if you ever touch me again . . ."

He paused, because he didn't know how to complete the threat.

"You'll do what, little man?" Barry retorted in an amused tone.

"I honestly don't know. But I can promise you it will be very, very bad."

Tremont continued to stare into his wound as if the very bad thing were in his hand.

CHAPTER 9

The neighborhood was not what Michael expected.

The elevated Southeast Expressway perpetually flatulated on the streets of South Boston. If the wind was blowing south, an invisible cloud of exhaust would permeate the buildings. If the wind was blowing north, the area was spared the toxic fumes of automobile waste, only to be rained down upon by spent jet fuel from altered flight paths implemented at nearby Logan International Airport.

To his right was a six-foot-high chain-link fence separating the street from a parking lot. The lot was occupied with large blue trucks branded BOSTON SANITATION DEPARTMENT on the door panels. To his left was one long residential building that stretched the entirety of the block and rose to three stories. Every forty or so feet, a Palladian alcove protected a door to the inside of the building.

Michael peered into each alcove for the door number the way a dentist would inspect a gaping mouth, unsure what he would find.

Just like Julie had said, number eighty-one was two alcoves from the end. With no sidewalk to his right, Michael parked the car right up against the fence to protect it from the street. He heard the crunching of shattered glass beneath his tires as he slowed to a stop. After he turned the key back in the ignition, the engine rattled several times before coughing itself into silence.

He stepped out of the car and, trying to avoid the remains of someone's smashed car window at his feet, regarded the apartment building. It was made of red brick, but each alcove was constructed of pine boards. Some were weathered and dilapidated, while others were well-kept, painted, and adorned with flowerpots. Five doors down to his left, two contractors carried a panel of sheetrock from the back of their pickup truck into an alcove, where they disappeared. A car was double-parked with hazard lights flashing. Three youths stood on the corner smoking cigarettes, one of them drinking from a brown paper bag. A tall older woman walking by with a bag of groceries eyed Michael suspiciously while the sound of expressway traffic roared nearby.

He was nowhere near the Boston University campus, and nobody in his view resembled a student. He turned back to the car and pulled on the door handle to assure himself it was locked, even though the broken glass suggested that it did not matter.

Not knowing if he was about to see rotted gums or well-flossed teeth, Michael approached the alcove of number eighty-one.

He was comforted to find it freshly painted and well-kept. He placed his finger on the button next to J. MYERS and pressed it anxiously.

"Hello," came a voice from the intercom.

He recognized the willowy voice as the one he had played over and over in his mind since meeting Julie. The image of her had faded, however, and only his imagination reminded him how striking she had been to him. The longer he had spent away from her, the more he had ached to see her.

"It's Michael," he answered.

"Come on up," she answered. "Third floor."

The door emitted an extended buzzing, indicating it would be temporarily unlocked. He pushed it open and rushed up the stairs, taking them two at a time. On one of his strides between the second and third floor, he cleared three steps without issue.

He did not have to guess which door was hers because she was standing in the hallway when he arrived to her floor, cast in the glow pouring out of her bright apartment. Her hair was pulled back in a ponytail, revealing all the soft features of her face. Her eyes rendered a welcome tilt.

"It's not what you expected, is it?" she asked, clearly alluding to the neighborhood.

"Not at all," he admitted, already intent on absorbing the contents of the apartment. "I was a little uncomfortable driving down some of these streets."

Her furniture was modest; most of it looked pre-owned. But the apartment had subtle elements to make it warm and bright. The curtains matched the throw pillows on the sofa. Two large floor plants lived near the windows as if protecting the smaller ones on the sill. Framed posters of impressionist paintings hung perfectly straight and at eye level. A computer and printer, shrouded with dust covers, were on a worktable in the corner. A small purple candle released the heady smell of lilac from its burning tip.

"Why do you live so far from campus?" he asked.

"To be near the university hospital," she said. "I'm assisting in some medical research there."

"I saw the hospital when I came off the expressway. It took me ten minutes to get through all the traffic lights." Michael was studying her now. She wore tight jeans with flat shoes and a soft pink shirt that hung down to her braided leather belt, just covering her midriff. Somehow, he felt as if she had dressed for him. "What kind of research?"

"The effects of concussions in sports-related injuries."

"I hope you're not a subject," he said with an awkward smile.

"Hardly," she responded. "I do testing for one of the sports medicine physicians." Then, "Can I get you anything?"

"Water would be fine," he responded. "With lots of ice?"

He followed her into the small efficiency kitchen so he could remain close to her, watch her every movement, and maybe even sample her scent.

The galley kitchen was small and immaculate. It was white with a border of flowered wallpaper running along the edge of the ceiling. Assorted baskets sat atop the wall cabinets, adding a country feel. A dishtowel matching the border hung, perfectly folded, on the door handle below the sink. There were no visible dishes, clean or dirty. The stovetop was so clean it looked new, though its design revealed its antiquity.

"You don't cook much?" Michael asked, referring to the cleanliness of the stove.

"Actually, I cook all the time. Always on the weekends, and as much as I can during the week." She pulled a baking pan from the refrigerator, covered in tinfoil that was perfectly sealed around the pan's edges. "Try this, I made it yesterday."

She withdrew a fork from the drawer next to the sink and pulled back the tinfoil cover, unveiling lasagna that had yet to be sliced into. She then reached up into a cabinet to retrieve two glasses. This caused her shirt to gently lift and expose her flat stomach. Michael was glad he'd followed her into the kitchen.

"You're shorter than I remember," he said as he watched her push up on her toes.

Julie pulled down the glasses and looked up into his eyes. "You're taller than I remember."

He sat down on the kitchen floor, reminiscent of when he'd met her on the stadium infield grass. "This is exactly how I remember you."

"Then let me take care of you again." She pressed her palm to his forehead, indicating she wanted him to stay on the floor, then went to the freezer, stole three ice cubes, and clunked them down into one of the glasses. Not satisfied on his behalf, she took two more and placed them in the same glass before filling both glasses from a jug of spring water taken from the refrigerator.

She bent down in front of him and handed him the glass. When he took it, he noticed her hand also held a paper napkin for him. It was a small gesture, but it struck a chord so low that he felt it was from a lost part of his scale. He could not determine what it was about this gesture that captured his attention, and it nagged him momentarily before he dismissed it.

He took a deep breath, inhaling all the air that enveloped her body. He smelled the fresh, clean scent of an ocean breeze that had blown miles inland, as if taunting him to make his way to the sea. He held it in his lungs until his heart pumped its newly enriched blood to every remote capillary in his body.

"Thank you," he said.

She accepted it as gratitude for delivering a cold drink to him, even though it was proffered for being a tender, beautiful, mature, intelligent woman willing to spend an entire day out of her life with a young, molting teenager with no sense of how to reciprocate the warmth she offered.

She sat down on the floor across from him and presented him with the fork, which she had speared through a perfectly carved taste of the lasagna. He went to take the fork from her, but she resisted and held it up to his mouth as if serving him medicine. He passed his nose over it and closed his eyes as if he were about to taste a fine wine. When he opened them, she was smiling genially in response to his playacting.

He bit the end of the fork and savored the blend of pasta, tomato sauce, mozzarella, and ricotta cheese. But there was more than that. His father had made uncounted lasagnas that had never tasted like anything more than any of the major ingredients. But Julie's lasagna had a flavor unlike any he could remember having tasted in the longest time. There were undetermined spices and blends of cheeses dancing on his tongue and melting into a satisfying serum. He swallowed it into the cavern of his stomach, where it settled into a void he hadn't known existed until a satiated smile formed on his lips.

They both continued sitting on the floor. Julie had her back up against the refrigerator and Michael's back was pressed up against a cabinet door. Their legs interlocked in the small floor space. Michael felt as natural with her as a knife and spoon at a place setting. He looked into her face and could almost sense she knew what he was thinking, or she somehow felt his flow of emotions. He felt comfortable enough at this very point in time and space to extend forward and kiss her as if it were the end of their first date. But it was only the beginning, so he restrained himself.

"I have the day all planned out," Julie said. "I thought we could head over to Commonwealth Ave. and I could show you the BU campus. We could check out the bookstore and then grab a bite to eat. There's a place in Kenmore Square that serves the biggest, sloppiest, greasiest cheeseburgers you've ever laid your hands on."

Thinking it was not the right time to tell her he didn't eat red meat or any greasy food, he replied, "I think that's a great idea." He gulped down some water and found it cold and refreshing. "I have my dad's car. We can drive over from here. I definitely don't feel comfortable walking through this neighborhood."

"Sure," she said.

"Why do you live here?" he asked again, for some reason expecting to get a different answer than before.

"I told you. I wanted to be close to the hospital. I didn't want to live in a dorm with a bunch of kids right out of high school, and the rent is a little cheaper out here."

Her words suggested that she felt she was more mature than others her own age—and yet she had still decided to pursue Michael, who was only a high school senior. This gave him a sense of confidence that she found him exceptionally mature for his age. She had apparently seen something in him that she felt compelled to pursue, and now he was the subject of her attention. This attention was giving him an odd sensation of comfort that he could not interpret, and he wanted to more clearly define it. He clutched the napkin she'd given him as if it were a clue.

He watched her now as she washed, towel-dried, and put away the two glasses and the fork, and then replaced the tinfoil on the lasagna pan with nary a wrinkle and returned it to the refrigerator. In minutes, the kitchen had no visible signs it had ever been used.

She slipped back into the bedroom and returned with two heavy sweatshirts, each one neatly folded so the university logo on them was clearly visible. Only one of them had a hood.

"You might want to wear this," she said. "It's going to be chilly today." She handed him the one without the protective hood and he unfolded it to examine the size for fit.

It was a large sweatshirt; he could tell it would fit comfortably. He tried to refold it so he could carry it until they were outside walking the campus, but he was unsuccessful in returning it to its impeccably symmetrical package. When he looked at Julie with a twinge of embarrassment, she took it from him and held it up by the shoulders. Like a magician doing a sleight of hand illusion, she folded it effortlessly in midair and handed it back to him.

Michael stood there with the sweatshirt under his left arm, looking at Julie. Their eyes connected for a long time. He was mesmerized by the sinister tilt of her brow, which had a bewitching effect. It was coupled with the comfortable features of her face, which created an interesting beauty unlike any he had ever seen before.

Julie seemed occupied with something beyond Michael's eyes, as if she were looking through them to see something else, to see what was behind them. She didn't seem interested so much in his physical features as she was in his thoughts and emotions.

And she seemed to have captured them both. All Michael could think about was that he had experienced her with all his senses. He had listened to her voice through the intercom with no associated visual, he had seen how clean and tidy she was, he had felt the warmth of her hand pressed up against his forehead, he had smelled her scent and absorbed it into his body, and he had tasted her through a recipe of her own preparation. All these things pulled at him, because he could not identify why they had such an impact on his psyche.

He dabbed at the corners of his mouth with the napkin to be sure there was no sauce hiding in the crevices. Then, afraid to destroy the harmony of the newly restored kitchen with his refuse, he placed it secretly in his pocket and forgot about it.

Before leaving, Michael took another look around the apartment and found everything as undisturbed as when he had entered.

Even from inside the house, Bailey could still recognize the sound of the car coming into the driveway. Her ears perked up and her tail wagged uncontrollably. In her excitement, she jumped up onto all four legs and was immediately reminded why her running days with Michael were over.

Checking her balance, she moved cautiously down the steps from the upstairs bedroom down to the kitchen, where she knew Michael would arrive first.

Michael greeted his father in the kitchen with the car keys, but it was Jack who spoke first.

"How was your day?"

"It was the best day I've ever had," Michael said.

"Tell me about it," his father inquired with solicitous anticipation.

"We walked all over the Boston University campus. We went from Kenmore Square all the way up to the stadium where we met, and then we came all the way back. I saw the dorms, the classrooms, the BU Beach along Storrow Drive—there were college students everywhere."

"There's a beach?"

"Not exactly, but that's what they call it."

Bailey shuffled into the kitchen and nestled up against Michael's leg, which prompted him to rub her neck.

"I'm sure it gave you a hint of what to expect for the next four years," his father said.

He nodded. "It did. Now all I have to do is decide where to spend them."

"Tell me more about Julie," his father prompted, as if the two subjects were somehow related.

"She's very pretty, very intelligent. We hit it off really well." Michael could not contain his enthusiasm for both the day and Julie. "She seems really interested in me as a person; I've never experienced that with anyone before."

He was telling the truth but hiding the fact that he was uncomfortable exposing his thoughts and feelings to anyone outside of the family. It was rare for him to open up even to his family, in fact, and he'd tried to stay sealed with Julie, but throughout the day he had sensed that this secretly irritated her.

"Will you see her again?" his father asked.

"We made plans for next week." Michael gave Bailey one last, vigorous rub, indicating the massage was finished. He was also finished telling his father about his day. "I'm going for a run."

His father looked down at the dog. "Are you bringing Bailey?"

"I don't think she'll go." Michael sighed. "I think she needs some time to rest, or maybe she's just too old now."

"Why don't I make an appointment with the vet?" his father proposed.

"I don't think that's necessary. Let's just give her some time, she'll be fine."

His father exhibited a curious frown. "Do you think that's fair?"

"What do you mean?" Michael asked, taken aback by the question.

"You're more familiar with our family doctors than I am," his father said. "Every time you sneeze, it costs me a co-payment at the doctor's office. Don't you think Bailey deserves the same attention?"

Michael bowed his head. "You're right. Let's get an appointment this week."

He climbed the stairs to his bedroom to change into his running gear while also deliberating the changes that were taking place in his life. He was scheduled to run six miles today, but because he'd spent the whole day with Julie he had lost the daylight and would have to be satisfied with a fast-paced two miles. If he was going to spend time with her on the weekends, he would have to alter his running schedule, particularly once he advanced to higher-mileage runs that could take two or three hours, not including recovery time.

He also needed to settle on a college to attend. His father was pressuring him to decide soon because the deadlines were fast approaching, not only for acceptance but also for financial aid, scholarships, and campus job applications. Although Michael was excited for the opportunity to continue maturing, a welcome change to be sure, he still held some anxiety regarding the unknown, and that was stalling his decision.

He pulled his jersey up over his head and was about to toss it into the laundry pile on his closet floor but instead held it up by the shoulders. He made one feeble attempt to fold it into a perfect square, but the sleeves fell limply out of place. Instead of a square, he resorted to a ball—the simplest and most perfect of all the geometric shapes and the one most easily suited for dirty laundry.

He examined his exposed torso. His body was starting to physically change and soon would change even more. Not only was it still developing; his marathon training would make it thinner and more resilient. His heart and lungs would strengthen to sustain up to four hours of continuous running. His legs would strengthen to tolerate a seemingly never-ending pounding on pavement. All his other bodily systems would learn to work in unison to overcome pain and injury, fend off cramps, stay properly hydrated, and burn calories more efficiently.

This was a welcome change. He was still emotionally wounded from being defeated in the state championship. The suit of armor he was building for his body had been exposed as flawed. He would have to work harder to ward off not only the trials of completing a marathon but also the evils of Cancer and whatever form in which it would choose to reveal itself to him. Whether it be disguised as a tumor, heart disease, or some other physical ailment not yet unmasked, he would be prepared because he knew that once a person was diagnosed with its infiltration, it was too late. He was witness to the knowledge that Cancer never revealed itself until it already had its manacles securely gripping its prey. Once you received the diagnosis, the contract with time had already been consummated, and payment was your life.

He molted out of his pants like a lobster shedding its shell and revealing a softer, more vulnerable new exterior. Before tossing them into his laundry pile, he relieved the back pocket of his wallet and dug deep into his right front pocket to excavate any loose change. He also reached into his left front pocket, more out of an impulse to complete his inspection than out of an expectation there would be anything in it. But there was something in it. He pulled out the napkin he'd stealthily hidden at Julie's apartment.

Anyone else would have thrown that napkin away without a second thought, but not Michael. He sat on the bed and stared at it as if it were a talisman. As he studied the crumpled paper, he saw a red smudge of sauce and recalled the strange sensation that had briefly overcome him when Julie had initially handed it to him.

It was then that it occurred to him what was so foreign about the entire scene: He had been stimulated by the way she'd waited on him, yes, but what he'd found more intriguing was the realization that he had not been handed a napkin in almost ten years. He had been raised in a house with a man and another boy, and in their home napkins were taken *after* something had spilled. Only a woman would deliver a napkin as a preventive measure. It was a casual, insignificant observation, but it rained down on him the understanding that it had been too long since he had been in the care of a woman. And this meant so much more than being handed a napkin or perfectly folded clothes—it meant greetings with hugs, affection with kisses, and firesides with cuddling. None of the few girls he had dated in high school had ever cared for him at this level.

He lay back on the pillow and replayed the day: the apartment, the drive through the city, the walk across campus, the lunch, and the drive back. He spent all of one minute remembering those activities but spent over ten minutes cherishing the memory of the kiss.

They had gone briefly back upstairs to her apartment, where Michael had removed the sweatshirt and returned it to her, not bothering to attempt folding it. They had chatted and made plans for the following weekend—and then, as he'd stood in the doorway ready to exit, it was Julie who had advanced subtly forward.

"I've noticed that all day, whenever you've talked about your family, you've only mentioned your father," she'd said. "Where's your mother?"

She'd been probing him, and it had made him feel a bit uncomfortable. "She died when I was young," he'd responded hesitantly.

"Do you remember her?" she'd pressed.

Michael had sifted quickly through his memories, as he had done so many times before. But again, he'd come up with the same result: He could barely even remember her face, never mind any day or moment. He'd wanted to share this with Julie but had found it difficult to express. He'd continued to ponder the question.

"Can you describe her for me?" she had tried again. "I'll make it easy for you. Just use one word."

They had stared connectively at each other. Michael had wanted to answer the question but could not find the word, and he wasn't sure he could share it with her even if he did. He had looked away from her eyes and over her shoulder, as if the answer were floating in the air behind her, but there was nothing there. This nothingness that he had begun to associate with his mother became his answer.

"Gone," he had finally said.

Looking oddly satisfied by this, she had tried one more advance, this one both physical and emotional. She'd moved one of her hands forward and found Michael's by his side. Leaving it there, she'd interlocked her fingers with his and asked another question: "Can you describe me in one word?"

Michael had found the moment both provocative and intriguing. He hadn't needed to look behind her for the answer this time because she was the answer, standing there right in front of him.

"Here," he had responded.

Seemingly deeply affected by his response, she'd closed her eyes halfway and gradually extended her jaw for Michael to receive it. Their lips had touched lightly and then pressed firmly against each other. It had seemed to Michael that Julie's lips had parted first, and simultaneously their tongues had begun softly massaging each other. Their free hands had sought each other out to partake in the union their two bodies were creating, had found each other and clasped together.

It had lasted only for a moment of reality, but it had stayed with him for the entire ride home. And now, as he lay on his bed as naked as the day he'd spilled out of his mother's womb, he relived it, allowing it to last far longer than it actually had.

He had never experienced this type of physical contact so tightly wound with emotional discharge. It produced some discomfort in him, but Julie had seemingly thrived on it and had done everything she could to alleviate this unpleasantness.

Michael rose from his bed with renewed vigor and donned his running apparel and running shoes. He twisted his torso like a windmill to loosen his muscles. Next, he bent over, keeping his knees straight and allowing his calf and hamstring muscles to stretch. Still stretching, he lifted his leg and placed the heel of his foot onto the nightstand beside the bed. He bent over again, bringing his nose down to his kneecap, bouncing gently as his muscles burned from the extension. He squinted, his eyes closed, absorbing the mild, stinging pain.

When he opened them, he noticed his foot was resting on a stack of envelopes, the top one showing the Princeton coat of arms. When he pulled his foot off the nightstand to return it to the floor he accidentally dragged the envelopes with it, toppling them to the floor. He collected them in no particular order and returned them to the nightstand.

After stretching a few more minutes, he slipped undetected down the steps and out the door. Without Bailey at his heels, he ran off down the street alone, under the intermittent glare of the widely spaced streetlights.

CHAPTER 10

Michael sat restlessly in the waiting room of the local veterinarian. He clutched the leash tightly even though Bailey rested comfortably at his feet.

Daniel was circling the room, becoming friendly with all the other pets held in check by their owners. He had already stroked a small poodle, poked his finger into a cockatoo's cage, and playfully teased a Siamese cat and was now occupied with a mutt that endeavored to be a German shepherd but had mutated into something indeterminable. Its hind leg was bandaged and a plastic cone enveloped its head like an open space suit helmet.

Michael's father stood at the reception window, completing paperwork with a credit card in one hand and a pen in the other.

A cloaked speaker spilled out the lyrics to a popular rock ballad while Michael tried to identify it. In his mind, he tried to fast-forward to the chorus, which would betray its title, but each time he got close to recognizing it he was swept back into the verse, as if caught in an eddy while swimming.

His concentration was interrupted by a jingling bell; the entry door had just opened. All eyes directed themselves to a stocky man in his late twenties guiding a Doberman pinscher into the reception area. The man's bloodshot eyes advertised his hangover, while the exposed teeth of his dog expressed the man's displeasure at having to keep this early appointment. The poodle jumped up into its owner's arms and the mutt cowered under the seat, but Bailey was unimpressed and emitted a gaping yawn, disavowing the big dog's presence. The Doberman reacted to this with displeasure and the owner reined him in closer to his heel.

"Easy, Ulysses," he cooed.

As the man approached the reception window, Michael's father passed a clipboard back to the receptionist, sidestepped the Doberman, and returned to the empty seat next to Michael. Bailey rose and backed into the space between Michael's legs so Michael could massage her haunches. He rubbed gently, having learned many times before not to rub this part of her too vigorously, as it caused her to squeal.

Daniel finished playing with the mutt and turned to the Doberman, clearly considering a visit, but after witnessing its uninviting grimace he instead returned to the solace of his father and brother.

The three of them sat together for several minutes. Ulysses attempted to engage Bailey on several occasions by baring his teeth and raising the hair on his back, but Bailey was uninterested. Michael and Daniel, however, looked to each other and shared an expression of irritation at the lack of discipline the animal was exhibiting.

"Do you have any of those doggie treats left?" Daniel whispered to Michael.

"Yeah," he replied, handing him only one.

"Give me a few more; I'm going to piss off that dog."

"You're getting awfully daring lately." Michael raised an eyebrow.

"You just worry about yourself, I'll be fine," Daniel bounced back in a tone that seemed to hint at greater meaning than the words themselves suggested.

Michael gave his brother a handful of treats. Usually it was Daniel who observed Michael, but now Michael watched him for a change. As Daniel matured he was becoming more participatory and daring. But his actions seemed to drag a shadow of spite, the source of which Michael could not detect.

He knew he was a good big brother to Daniel, even though his actions might sometimes appear to exceed that obligation. Daniel always got help with his homework and chores, transportation, and even intervention when being bullied at school. But it was also Michael who had guided him into a healthy diet, sneaking the bag of potato chips out of his lunch bag and replacing it with an apple or banana. It was Michael who had crushed Daniel's first pack of cigarettes before one was ever lit. It was Michael who scheduled physicals every year for each family member. It was Michael who'd talked Daniel out of signing up for the football team for fear of injury. But now Michael could see that his little brother felt like a caged bird who needed to be let out to spread his wings, fly among the treetops, and feel the sun heating his feathers.

Daniel had shown Michael this change by making repeated attempts to show off his ability to fend for himself. These efforts were clearly directed toward Michael's eyes rather than his father's, because it was Michael who continued to hold an umbrella over his life. Because the ominous cloud threatening him was one that only Michael could see, Daniel continued to dance outside of its reach, testing for rain—and, continuously finding none, he was becoming increasingly temerarious in his ventures.

Daniel fed several of the bone-shaped biscuits to Bailey but not all of them, while likely considering what mischief he could instigate. Then he walked over to the poodle and, with the owner's approval, fed it some. He then went to the mutt and, reaching his hand into the cone, fed some treats to it. Then he approached Ulysses as the big dog looked on, licking its floppy lips with anticipation.

Daniel maneuvered very close to Ulysses, as if to feed him, but then walked past him to the reception window, passing his now-empty hand as close to Ulysses's nose as he could without touching it, projecting confidence that the fierce dog would not snap at him. Ulysses snorted at Daniel's hand and swallowed a mouthful of saliva.

Michael took this private moment with his father to seek out what the thorn was between Daniel's toes. "Did I do something wrong?" he asked in a hushed tone.

"No," his father answered back quietly.

"Then what's his problem?"

"He might be a little envious."

"Of what?"

"Your accomplishments. Your successes on the track and in school."

"He's been holding his own."

"You don't know how lucky you are, Michael. You have the opportunity to attend your choice of elite colleges. I can understand how he feels, because I'm a little envious too."

"What do you mean?" It occurred to Michael that his father was not so much answering his question about Daniel as he was offering some of his own hidden feelings.

"I've been proud watching you grow up, especially this last year. You have opportunities in front of you now that I never had. Being accepted to an Ivy League school is a remarkable accomplishment, and yet you have your choice of more than one. That would make a lot of people envious."

Daniel approached the receptionist and asked her how much longer before the doctor would be available, all the while keeping his biscuit-scented hand precariously close to Ulysses's mouth. Quick bursts of air escaped the dog's snout as it searched for an opening between his fingers. He left his hand there without flinching, even turning it to tantalize Ulysses into sniffing it in its entirety.

"I'm sure it will be just a few minutes," she said with an approving smile of his antagonistic taunt.

She reached her jewelry-laden hand into a jar on her desk and handed him some more treats. "Why don't you take these for your walk back."

"Thanks," he said, closing his fist around the offering. On the way back to his seat, he again brushed his hand past the Doberman before feeding some treats to the mutt, then the poodle, and beginning his trip back to Bailey.

Michael tried to rush the conversation. "He'll have his own opportunities in a few years. There must be something more than that."

"He recognizes you'll be leaving soon," his father said. "You won't be around to watch out for him anymore. That concerns him."

"I can assure you, Dad"—Michael made eye contact with him—"it concerns me even more." The words came out of his mouth straight and stiff, as if written on a placard.

Daniel returned to his seat and held the remaining treats in front of Bailey. She ate them slowly, one at a time, with her eyes trained on the Doberman. When she finished, she sat panting in his direction, laughing.

Everyone in the room had watched the scenario with satisfaction, with only Ulysses's owner revealing no sign that he understood Daniel's obnoxious mocking. Ulysses began chuffing and his owner struggled to restrain him.

"That pissed him off, all right," Daniel whispered to Michael.

Michael gave Daniel the approval he sought. "It sure did."

The receptionist poked her face out of the admitting window and called out, "Bailey Galler."

They all stood and marched toward the indicated examination room, where they were greeted by a man old enough to be a grandfather with a name that confirmed he had fulfilled his destiny of becoming a veterinarian.

"I'm Dr. Shepherd," he heralded them from the doorway with the overconfidence of a man who loved his work.

The last sound any of them heard from the outer room was a slow, deep growl coming from Ulysses, but it seeped from his stomach, not his throat.

The five of them crowded into the small room, with a stainless steel examination table separating the family from the veterinarian. Wall posters of skeletal dogs and cats went barely noticed as Michael, his brother, and his father fanned out against the wall like a police lineup, Bailey standing in front of them.

The music was gone but Michael continued to hear its meter dance in his head. He found the chorus but could not declare the lyrics of it and so he hummed it in his mind . . .

Mm-mm mmmm, mmmm mm-mm, mm-mm, yeah.

Once they exchanged introductions, he felt comfortable that Dr. Shepherd treasured every kind of animal, probably more than people. The doctor exhibited an immediate liking to Bailey and used her name more than necessary to get her used to hearing it from him. Dr. Shepherd impressed, as a master of the animal kingdom would.

"What kind of dog is Bailey?" he asked, clearly knowing the answer.

Michael watched the doctor lower his head to study her through wrinkled eyes that were obscured by the thick frames of his glasses. She had begun pacing back and forth around the small room, smelling the scent of uncountable dogs and cats and birds and iguanas and snakes and humans. All these conflicting odors seemingly confused yet delighted her. But as the doctor watched her, he seemed to observe something from her that did not confuse or delight him. Michael saw him make his diagnosis in the brief instant between the time he asked his question and the time Michael answered it.

"She's a Lab," he said.

"She's quite beautiful. How old is Bailey?" He kept his eyes on her, studying her, as he held his hand out to Michael, gesturing for the leash. His long-sleeved lab coat dripped off his skinny arms.

Michael was silenced. *There's something really wrong with Bailey*, he thought. He looked to his father with wide eyes, incredulous that his beloved dog could be susceptible to the evil that stalked his family. But there was no way for his father to know anything about the conceptions that tormented the streams of Michael's mind.

His father seemed to have interpreted Michael's expression as a call for help with the question and responded to the doctor, "She must be coming up on five years."

"And what brings you here today, Mr. Galler?" He took the leash from Michael and began leading Bailey around the cramped floor, his baggy pants camouflaging his careful steps.

Michael retreated toward a corner to give himself some breathing room, although he knew it appeared he was simply giving the doctor more room to put Bailey through her paces. He stood motionless in the corner, humming the song in his mind, while his father exchanged information with the doctor.

Mm-mm mmmm, mmmm mm-mm, mm-mm, yeah.

"She seems a bit lethargic at times," his father shared. "Not as active as she used to be. I think she may be walking with an uncertain limp, but not all the time."

"Yes, I can see that," responded the doctor as he continued to guide her around the examination room as if leading a majestic horse. "I noticed it when you brought Bailey in here." He reached gently under her and lifted her up onto the table; her paws clattered as she settled on the metallic surface. "Let's have a closer look," he said.

He first held her face in his hands and stared into her eyes as if examining them. He rubbed her behind the ears, gaining her trust, and then stood to her side to examine her hips. "She's very well tempered," he noted. "Michael, would you hold her steady while I examine her?"

Michael was numb, paralyzed by fear and disbelief of what he was about to find out. "Can you help, Daniel? I'd like to watch."

Daniel obliged—grasped the leash close to the collar with one hand and draped his other arm over her back.

Dr. Shepherd probed Bailey's hips and joints with his fingers. He looked like a blind man reading Braille, not looking at the surface he was touching, just feeling. At one point he pressed a little too firmly and Bailey yelped and turned her head back to the doctor, bared her teeth, and then began licking his hand. The doctor, having found what he was looking for, began working his hands all the way down to her hind paws.

"What are you looking for?" asked Michael's father.

"A common condition in this breed is hip dysplasia. It's when the bone doesn't have a good fit at the joint. Let me show you." He held up a fist as a prop.

Again with the fist, thought Michael.

The veterinarian wrapped his other hand around the tightly clenched fist as if holding a baseball. "This is the bone inserted into the joint—Bailey's hip. When the bone rotates, like this, it should stay firmly within the joint. Dysplasia is when the fit isn't so good." He opened the hand that was covering the fist, keeping his palm cupped. "Now when the bone rotates within the joint, there's more movement."

"Why is that bad?" asked Daniel.

"While examining Bailey, I felt scraping in the joint. When that happens you get a buildup of fluid, swelling."

"Arthritis," Michael's father said.

"Exactly."

Mm-mm mmmm, mmmm mm-mm, mm-mm, yeah.

Michael was so close to the chorus lyrics. The humming was replaced by nonsensical syllables, the way *fa-la-la* would be substituted in a holiday carol. It repeated continuously, and he didn't even want to know the words anymore; he just wanted it out of his head. It was like a record album playing one revolution and then continuously skipping back a groove and repeating it, and he could not lift the needle from his mind.

Now he felt like he was the needle, hovering above the black disc as it revolved beneath him, scraping his fingernails against it as if it were an endless blackboard. The room itself began to spin.

"I'll hold her now," he interjected.

"Sure," Daniel said, stepping back.

Michael assumed the same position, holding her for his balance, not for her comfort. Feeling steadier, he asked the doctor a question: "Will it spread?"

"Well, in the sense that it could occur in some of these other leg joints—here or here, for instance. But also, I can feel that the muscles have started to atrophy."

"What's that?" asked Daniel.

"Her muscles are wasting, or withering. With time," he said with regret, "she'll start to weaken."

Michael noticed the doctor had stopped using Bailey's name, as if now he didn't want to get emotionally involved with this patient. There could be only one reason for that.

"How do we cure it?" he asked, already assuming there was no cure.

"Well, we don't cure it, but we can treat it. I wouldn't prescribe an anti-inflammatory just yet. Let's give her some buffered aspirin for now, and if it worsens we can put her on carprofen."

The doctor pulled a book from a shelf and stroked through the pages until he found diagrams of two hips on facing pages: good hip, bad hip. Michael's father and brother crowded him as he pointed out the differences.

The doctor called it "arthritis," but Michael knew better. Cancer had invaded Bailey now and had set out to waste her away. He never set his eyes upon the diagrams. He did not want to see the doctor's drawings of the enemy. Those pictures were nothing but another disguise that Cancer used to deceive its victims—a mask used by a coward afraid to show his true face, like a little boy who broke windows and then ran when the lights came on—and it was Michael who was standing in the frame of every shattered window, searching in the darkness for the perpetrator of this broken mess.

Mm-mm mmmm, mmmm mm-mm, mm-mm, yeah.

He stopped searching for the words to the chorus because it occurred to him he had already been singing them. He realized it was the type of ballad where each verse expressed the writer's feelings of something lost, but the chorus was nothing more than the melancholic expression of the vocalist wailing a continuous melody as pianos and guitars wrapped his voice into a repetitive chant that shed its own tears.

Mm-mm mmmm, mmmm mm-mm, mm-mm, yeah.

The doctor had just confirmed that Cancer had entered into a contract with time for Bailey's life, and that left only one more question to ask.

It was Michael who asked it.

"How long?"

The vet looked into Michael's eyes as if they were being offered for him to see, and he appeared minutely disturbed by whatever thoughts accompanied them. "One, maybe two years."

Daniel didn't understand. "Can you die from arthritis?"

The doctor continued to stare at Michael as he answered. "No."

"Then what happens in two years?" Daniel asked, pursuing his own naiveté.

Bailey remained on the table, moving her head back and forth when each person spoke, as if lip-reading. But now she locked her gaze onto Michael.

The answer to Daniel's question was never spoken, yet the words hovered in the air like a helicopter looking for a place to land, rotors ready to cut down anything that got too close.

With all eyes piercing him, a feeling of unfathomable guilt overcame Michael. It had never occurred to him before this day that Bailey could be vulnerable to this curse. He could have tried to protect her from it, but now it was too late. It was inside her, growing and spreading. Just like he knew his father's arteries were continuing to harden within his chest. And he would be forced to watch her wane for the next couple of years, just like his father had witnessed his mother's erosion.

But with Bailey, the end would be different. Doctors would not enlist themselves to perform countless hours of surgery, therapy, and treatment. They would not spend tens of thousands of health care dollars to alleviate the parasite within her. Her condition would slowly and continuously decline until such a time when she could suffer no more, at which point she would arrive back onto this bitter table and be inoculated into a gentle and final sleep. And in its own way, this would be a heroic rescue of her life from the agony and humiliation that Cancer would ultimately have imposed upon her.

Michael briefly contemplated this unique solution. Until now, everyone who had encountered Cancer had taken only reactive measures. Doctors had repeatedly removed infected pieces of his mother's body. They had circumvented infected areas of his father's body. In each instance, the host had tried to eliminate the parasite in a war of attrition. But Cancer was too strong for the Galler family, or maybe too smart—a cure still unattainable.

Cancer had yet to breach the citadel Michael had constructed for his own body. But Bailey had now been penetrated, as she was too weak to defend herself, and once Cancer had invaded the body, death was a certainty.

Surprisingly, her future solution did not seem to bother Michael; it made sense to him. What did trouble him was that, ultimately, the decision of when to put Bailey down would belong to him. This thought terrified him, but he was able to shake it loose from his mind because the decision would not have to be made today. And when that day eventually did come, he would be ready for it. He didn't quite know how, but he would be ready for it.

"What happens in two years?" Daniel repeated.

Michael answered, but he twisted his response just enough to avoid answering the actual question. "For the next two years, we just try to keep her comfortable."

Dr. Shepherd reached to another shelf and fumbled among several plastic bottles of medication. Rolling the labels and finally finding what he was looking for, he turned back to the examination table. "This is just regular buffered aspirin. Take the bottle, but let me show you how to get her to swallow them." He pried open the childproof cap and shook out two tablets. After snapping it shut, he handed the bottle to Michael. "You could mix them into her food, but she'd probably find them and spit them out. With your thumb and forefinger, pry open her jaw like this."

Bailey struggled at first but quickly cooperated.

"Place the tablet way back on her tongue and then hold her mouth closed."

Bailey jerked her head twice in an attempt to free her jaw from the doctor's grasp. The foreign object on the back of her tongue was irritating her, and she did not know how to remove it. She twitched her head again, seemingly trying to push the tablet off to the side of her mouth, but it was too near to her throat. Finally, she swallowed out of reflex.

Dr. Shepherd gave the other tablet to Michael and everyone watched as he administered the aspirin. He pried open her mouth without difficulty and pushed it onto the back of her tongue. He clamped her mouth closed and looked into her eyes.

Bailey stared back, remaining perfectly still.

She would know she was here because of the pain that lived within her hips; the doctor had made that clear when he examined them, momentarily and unintentionally increasing the pain. But as she studied the faces of her family, Michael could see she was absorbing the enormous love that enveloped her and concluding that, whatever was taking place here now and whatever might take place here in the future, however uneasy it made her, it would be for her benefit. Even though he was holding her jaw securely in his hands, Bailey acknowledged that it was her life that was in Michael's hands, and she trusted him with it, so she swallowed.

The drive home was a silent one. Michael's father took a more scenic route along the coast, allowing the restful views to have their effect. The air was crisp and the low tide panted along the shoreline. Bailey lay still in the back seat, her head resting on Michael's lap. She didn't require any additional attention today, and she left each of the car's occupants to their own thoughts.

Jack kept his eyes on the road but could not help noticing that it was framed on his left by houses that encroached on the sea's doorstep. They moved past his view slowly enough for him to observe each structure individually but too quickly for him to remember any one of them specifically. Apart from a front porch and large picture windows soaking up the view, each house retained its own uniqueness of dormers and pitched roofs. As he studied them more intently, he noticed that their seaside perch was beginning to have its effects. Paint was peeling, roofs were weathered, gutters hung crookedly, and foundations were cracked. Each one was in a state of repair or disrepair. Some had new brick fronts to protect them from the debris thrown up from the ocean during winter storms that were coupled with high tides. Others were wrapped in vinyl siding, hiding the natural beauty of original cedar shingles that surely cowered underneath.

He ignored the vast blue expanse to his right.

Daniel sat in the front passenger seat and looked out his window at the seawall that protected the coast. It curved with the shoreline and its concave face sloped down to the beach. Below it, three jetties extended into the ocean like fingers pushed into sand. Beyond them, several hundred yards offshore, three breakwaters guarded the coastline, dismantling any wave big enough to test its mettle. He appreciated this system of giant rocks and poured concrete that defended the coastal town from the ever-present ocean. Yet he imagined himself sailing out beyond their protection, taming the rough ocean seas, challenged by the energy that lived within their deep, rolling undulations.

Michael sat in the back seat behind Daniel. Bailey's steady breath warmed his thigh as she appeared to sleep. He watched the ocean itself, captivated by its presence. He studied the waves as they rolled in from the horizon only to be dismantled by the offshore breakers. Just as one wave collapsed onto the rocky forearm, another appeared, seemingly destined to reach the shore and decimate it. Spying the entire coastline, he saw the white foam of cresting waves searching out unprotected areas of the shore. Having spent eons shifting sandbars, moving rocks, and churning up its own floor, the ocean waited patiently for the right combination of high tides, atmospheric pressure, and warm air fronts to create a sea so violent that it could hurdle the breakwater, roll over the jetties, punch the seawall, and throw itself and all of its refuse into the face of any building that dared to stand in its way.

For now, it lay dormant. However, one thing was evident: The ocean would go where it wanted to go, when it wanted to go there.

CHAPTER 11

Michael sat on his front lawn with the canvas bag by his side, remembering when Julie presented it to him.

It was a Saturday, the only day that seemed easy for him to spend time with her. They drove north up the coast to Rockport, staying on the roads that embraced the shore. Michael occasionally took a purposeful wrong turn to explore a quaint neighborhood in Swampscott, the Neck at Marblehead, or a view of the harbor in Gloucester. Once in Rockport, he parked his father's car and they stepped in and out of the rustic shops, admiring the paintings and other unique artistic pieces. They stopped for ice cream—Michael had frozen yogurt—and then came straight back to Boston using the most direct highway.

Back at Julie's apartment, they sank into the sofa pillows, letting the small television remain silent in the corner of the room. Julie rested her head on Michael's chest while caressing it lightly.

They talked very little, as if both were trying to fall asleep in this cuddled position. Eventually, Julie turned her head up and started kissing Michael. He was ready for her, and they shared long, moist kisses while their hands subtly roamed each other's body, testing and defining new boundaries.

Michael moved his hand onto Julie's breast and began massaging gently. She slowly moved her hand up to intercept, interlocking her fingers with his when their hands met.

They stopped kissing but kept their heads close, leaning on each other's forehead. Michael continued stroking her hair with his free hand, running his fingers back behind her ears while combing it away from her face, exposing the thin, supple lines of her jowls.

It was Julie who spoke first: "What are you thinking?"

The question was a difficult one to answer; the things he had been thinking were private thoughts kept within his own head, and by asking this question, Julie was trying to penetrate these deeply hidden places. He had been thinking about how his life was changing in so many ways and it was also being affected in so many ways. He was having difficulty discerning which were causes and which were effects.

"I'm thinking about us," he answered.

"What about us?"

"I'm thinking about how much my life is changing, how much it has changed since we met."

Julie turned her body and straddled Michael's thighs, facing him. "How has it changed?"

Michael continued looking at her, trying not to open up to her, but he weakened when she clasped his hand. "I think about you a lot. I want to spend more time with you, as much as I can."

Her eyes frowned and turned away. "You'll be leaving for college; that will make it difficult."

"I haven't worked that out yet." For the first time, it occurred to Michael that he could lose Julie. His heart began to beat a little harder and he was sure she could hear its echoes. He had lost his mother, had almost lost his father, and would soon lose Bailey. Now he might lose Julie as well? His eyes subtly widened in alarm and his breathing emitted an occasional shudder. He thought maybe she was considering taking the initiative and ending their relationship before they became too involved.

It was equally disquieting to him that he had not worked this out before now. He always had a plan to achieve what he set his mind to. But when he was with Julie he didn't seem to have the same control over his life; it seemed more that she was in control.

She returned her eyes to his and pouted her lips. Then she raised his hand between them and fondled his fingers while holding his palm inches from her breast. It was as if to say he could have her breast if he could give her something in return—something that would confirm for her that he was prepared to become emotionally involved with her, that he could commit more than his physical self.

His hand hung temptingly in the space between them as he searched his mind for something he could share. If he could only open up to her, she would find what she was looking for and they could continue moving forward. They would find ways to resolve the other issues that lay ahead of them. For now, Julie simply wanted to be let into his mind. She had been knocking on the door, ringing the bell, tapping on the window glass. If he did not open up, she would surely leave.

"Can I share something with you?" he asked. "It's kind of personal."

"Of course you can," she responded with ignited eyes.

"I've been having dreams."

"What kind of dreams? Nightmares?"

"No, they're not nightmares. And it's the same dream over and over, yet somehow it's a different dream."

"I don't understand."

Michael shifted his position under Julie's weight. Talking about this was difficult for him.

"You can tell me," she prompted. She leaned forward and kissed him on the forehead, fleetingly pressing her breast into his hand. "Tell me."

He sensed her growing eagerness to hear more. She thrived on these moments, and Michael was beginning to become engrossed in them himself. He was fascinated and intrigued by her and wanted so much to share his recurring dream with her. He also felt how warm her body was, how wet her kisses were, how soft her hair was, how smooth her skin was. He had become overwhelmed by her and did not want to risk losing her.

"The theme of the dream is always the same," he began, a cold chill enveloping his body. "I'm much younger, maybe seven years old, and I'm always looking for something."

"What are you looking for?" Julie listened intently.

"Little pieces of paper. Notes. And every time I read one it tells me where to find the next one. So, in the dream, I'm searching all over the house. In some dreams I might be searching the kitchen, sometimes the bathroom or the bedrooms, maybe the basement. In each dream I'm looking in different places, but I'm always looking for more notes."

"Why do you keep looking?"

"I want to get to the last note. I know it tells me where to find something good. Something I want or need. I believe if I follow all the instructions correctly, something good will happen."

"Does it?" Julie seemed very interested in this.

"I don't know," he said disappointedly. "I can never get the last note. I always wake up."

"How does it usually end?"

"It always ends exactly the same." Michael paused. It was difficult for him to discuss his mother.

Julie leaned forward again and they kissed. This time she moved Michael's hand to the side so she would not lean her breast into it. They spent several minutes kissing, and she never let go of his hand.

His body felt weakened; he was glad they were sitting. With Julie controlling the moment, his head felt lighter. All he could do was speak when she let him speak, touch what she let him touch. She slid down his thighs, closer to his crotch, and embraced him. They were like two matching pieces of a jigsaw puzzle lying side by side on a table, waiting to be pressed together.

Pulling away and bringing his hand back up between them, she asked him again, "How does it end?"

Michael reluctantly continued, "The last note I can read always tells me to look in my mother's hair."

"Her hair?"

"Yes, this part is always the same. I run into the kitchen and she's always there, just sitting there."

"Does she have the note?"

"It's stuck in her hair. All folded up."

"What does it say?"

"I don't know. I can't reach it. Well, I could reach it if I tried, but I can't move. I want to get it out of her hair but I just stand there, trying to move but unable to. I'm paralyzed."

Julie cocked her head, trying to interpret these strange images, or maybe trying to interpret how they were affecting him. "What do you think it means?"

He tried to dismiss it. "It's just a silly dream. It probably doesn't mean anything."

"*Everything* means *something*. What do you think this means?"

"I don't know," he replied. He started wishing he had never shared this with her.

Julie expressed her dissatisfaction with his lack of effort by starting to rise off his lap. Sure, he could tell about the dream, Michael thought, but the real sharing must be telling her what he thought about the dream.

He improved his grip on her hand and pulled her back onto him. He had come this far; he could go a little further. He made sure his hand returned to the space between them, loosening his grip so Julie could govern it again.

"Actually, I have given it some thought," he admitted.

She smiled, or maybe it was more of a grin, and resettled onto his lap.

He started to tell her but then hesitated and turned his face away. "I'm embarrassed. This is really stupid."

She pulled his chin back toward her with her free hand. Looking directly at him, she said firmly, "I want you to open up to me, Michael."

There was something about the way she used his name that seemed comfortable and secure, almost motherly. It warmed him; then he again felt a chill coming from somewhere in the room. He was like wax, evolving into a new shape when melted and cooled.

"When I see the paper hiding in her hair, it reminds me of the cancer that was hiding in her body. I want to take it out. I want to save her. But I can't."

Her throat pulsed with a hard swallow. "What about all the other notes?"

"It's like a wild goose chase. I feel like I was being misdirected all over the place when cancer was right in front of me the whole time. Maybe I could have stopped it if I wasn't looking in all the wrong places."

Her eyes remained transfixed on his, seemingly plotting to convert this opening into something more. Still holding his hand between their bodies, she started massaging his palm. Her fingers slid easily along the surface of his skin, lubricated by the sweat that seeped out of his lifelines. "There was nothing you could have done."

"I know. It's just a dream."

"Thank you for sharing it with me."

She released his hand and dropped hers to her side, leaving his hanging, defiant of gravity. Finally, it came to light on her breast without protest.

She remained sitting erect on his lap as he caressed her breast. He brought up his other hand to take advantage of its twin. They both kept their eyes open and watched each other's face as he explored the supple contours of her body, Julie's head swaying gently all the while.

He eventually moved up under her shirt and used his fingertips to independently explore. She appeared more impassioned than she did excited, and this empowered him.

This continued for several minutes and was intermingled with more passionate kissing. Finally, she stood up and stepped back with an exhausted sigh. "I have something for you," she said with a sultry gaze.

Michael felt like a blanket had been pulled off him on a winter morning as he watched her disappear into the bedroom and then return with a box she held with both hands. The wrapping had been perfectly prepared with straight seams and smooth creases that concealed any tape and was tied together with a red ribbon that blossomed into a bow.

He hadn't been expecting anything and unwrapped it guardedly. Julie snatched the paper he removed and folded it neatly several times, creating a pile that was difficult to identify as waste, though she appeared anxious to dispose of it. Then he pulled the lid off the box.

The small canvas bag looked familiar to him. "This is the bag you were using when we met."

"Yes, I thought you should have it. Although I changed the contents to things more suited for marathon training."

Julie always did her research. She seemed to always find out what was needed to accomplish something and then made sure she had it. If a recipe called for one-eighth of a teaspoon of ground nutmeg, she had a vessel of ground nutmeg in her kitchen. If Michael was running a marathon, then everything he needed would be in the bag she gave him.

Needless to say, it had been properly stocked.

Since the day he'd received this little treasure chest of running supplies, Michael had used all its items each time he ran, in a ritual that took on the manner of a religious ceremony. He drew open the bag's zipper and removed the training guide for first-time marathoners. Michael had already read the book several times. It included chapters on speedwork, mile age buildup, diet, and injury. The back pages contained a log for charting a runner's daily training mileage.

Today, he opened the tired pages easily to the log section, removed a pen from the bag, and wrote "8" on today's date, his scheduled distance.

Somehow, he felt that Julie had read the book before giving it to him, because all the key items mentioned in the book were also in the bag. In fact, one of the chapters suggested keeping a bag with all these essentials for the arduous task of training for a marathon. He reflected briefly on Julie's thoroughness before removing a water bottle he had filled before leaving the house and taking a long drink. The water was still cold, and it chilled his throat all the way into his stomach.

Sated, he reached into the bag and fumbled around for the nail clippers the way one would seek out the prize in a cereal box. He found and employed it on his toenails to prevent irritation against an adjoining toe, letting the clippings fall into the lawn with the clipped grass. When done, he tossed it back into the open bag, recognizing he'd have to search for it again the next time he used it.

With both hands, he pulled his right foot up to his face to inspect the small bandage on the ball of his foot. It was wrinkled and needed to be replaced. He peeled it off and examined the healing blister. Again, reaching into the bag, he removed some petroleum jelly and a fresh bandage. He applied the gel onto the blister as well as some other irritated parts of his foot to prevent additional blisters from forming. He redressed the healing blister, then pulled on his socks and running shoes. He always double-knotted the laces to prevent them from untying.

He swallowed two aspirin as a precaution against any of the normal aches and pains associated with a long run and chased them down with another mouthful of water.

Satisfied that he was well protected, he leaned back on his hands and took a deep breath, enjoying the pungent aroma of the freshly cut grass.

The sun heated his face as he stared into a thin sky, pondering what lay beyond the blue window that enveloped the planet. Even the earth maintained an atmosphere to protect itself from the harmful ultraviolet rays of the sun. This reminded him to apply sunscreen to his face.

He repacked the bag and zipped it closed. Each item within it was by itself insignificant, yet when accumulated in this one bag, its value was much more than the thirty dollars Julie must have spent stocking it. It contained everything he needed to prepare for the formidable task ahead of him. And the bag itself was representative of Julie. Just as it had all the necessary components tucked away into one complete package, she had everything his life had been missing and now she was supplanting herself within him, making him whole again.

As he started to think about her, a curious discomfort developed in his stomach. A place somewhere inside him had ached to see her all week long. He tried to identify the actual location of the strange new feeling, but it was like trying to point to the wind: He could point to the swaying trees, a rippling flag, or a leaf tumbling across a lawn, but the wind itself was unseen. As the weekend drew nearer it would become more pronounced, until finally they were together again. Then the feeling would subside, the way eating eliminates the pangs of hunger.

These new sensations confused yet excited him.

He placed the bag back inside the house, stretched for ten minutes on the lawn, and then started to run.

He used the first mile as a warm-up before settling into his usual pace. For the next several miles, he struggled to maintain his tempo. His breathing was erratic, his rhythm was off, and his stride felt awkward. He didn't feel the need to stop running; he just didn't feel comfortable.

He knew that not every workout would be better than its previous one—there would be good days and bad days—but what was important was to log miles. Every mile he ran brought him one mile closer to achieving his goal of completing a marathon and one mile farther away from Cancer.

He slowed his pace during the fifth mile, with hopes of finishing strong the last three miles, but he never regained momentum.

After one hour, as he reached the seventh mile, his mind drifted and random thoughts splashed around inside his head. He thought about how alone his runs had been without Bailey keeping pace at his side. He thought about his recurring dream and how he felt satisfied with his interpretation of it—although he still believed that one of these nights he would finally gain access to the final note and discover its secret.

He wanted to try to force this to happen if he could. The problem was he kept waking before gaining the ability to reach up and take the paper from his mother's hair. He'd recently started running at a quicker pace in an attempt to exhaust himself into a sleep so deep that it would be difficult to stir from. He envisioned himself someday in a perpetual sleep, forever standing in front of his mother, stubbornly refusing to wake up until the note rested firmly in his little hand.

He coasted in the last mile, conceding to a poor effort. It was not one of his better workouts, and he certainly would never have been able to run twenty-six miles on this day.

He loosened his laces and paced up and down the sidewalk with his hands on his hips. The air continued to rush in and out of his mouth and throat, seemingly slowed by a dryness that perpetuated an uncomfortable friction. His muscles ached and all he could think about was getting off his feet. The silhouette of a neighbor observed him from across the street, with detailed features hidden behind a screen door.

He lay down on the lawn with his arms spread wide, physically and mentally exhausted. He lay there longer than usual, giving himself an opportunity to recover from a distance that was less than a third of his goal.

It was here, in this bed of grass made damp from his sweat, that Michael realized the enormity of the task he had laid out for himself.

CHAPTER 12

The alarm clock jolted to life at 5:30 a.m. For the first five seconds, the crumpled mass of blankets did not move.

Then a long arm emerged from a hidden breach in the covers, pinpointed the snooze button without any awkward fumbling, pressed it, and scurried back to the warmth of the bed.

Ten minutes later, the alarm sounded again. This time Michael silenced it and threw his legs over the side of the bed, beginning this important day.

He reached down to the outlet and unplugged the clock, extinguishing the numbers to permanent darkness. He wrapped the cord around the unit and crammed it into one of the suitcases on the floor. He had now completely packed everything he was taking to college.

Beside his bed was the flotsam of his life: almost every article of clothing he owned, books, running gear, blankets, pillows, a reading lamp, and posters suitable for a dormitory wall.

He showered, drove ten miles into Boston to pick up Julie, and then returned to the house. By the time his father and brother had exhumed themselves from their beds, Julie had made a complete breakfast of freshly squeezed orange juice, toast, sliced grapefruit, and omelets that concealed diced pepper and onion.

Jack entered the kitchen with a crooked gait and sleep still in his eyes. The sight laid out before him was a portrait long since forgotten for this family. Fresh coffee was partnered with a hot breakfast on a table with full place settings on placemats. His eyes left the table quickly and panned the kitchen in its entirety, absorbing the sterility of the room: pans washed and put away, a spotless stove, and an empty sink. A newspaper was at the head of the table with the sports section moved to the front.

"I didn't think the paper would have been delivered this early," he said, taking in the entire scene.

"We stopped on the way back and picked one up," Michael answered with a nod in deference to Julie's thoughtfulness.

"This is terrific," Jack complimented Julie. "You really didn't have to go to all this trouble."

"My men deserve a hearty breakfast," she said. "We have a long day ahead of us."

My men, Jack thought. That was interesting phrasing. Julie had spent a lot of time with Michael over the summer. She had come out to the house and spent as much time here as Michael had spent going into the city. This gave Jack an opportunity to observe his son's relationship with his first meaningful girlfriend. He'd witnessed the traditional water fight while washing the car, Michael's arms around her during a scary television movie, and telepathic eyes exchanged over dinners. She had taken an interest in both Jack and Daniel as well, seemingly because she had observed how important Michael's family was to him. She was always thoughtful and polite, and it seemed to Jack that she made a purposeful effort of adding a female touch to their lives that was desperately lacking. She seemed to have grown an attachment not only to Michael but also to the whole family. Although he was jealous she provided Michael with the uniquely feminine tenderness he could not, he was glad Michael was receiving it. Maybe it wasn't such an odd statement after all. On second thought, Jack concluded, it was gratifying that she thought of them in this possessive way.

And they did have a long day ahead of them; they had to pack the car, drive to the college, fight the weekend traffic, unload everything, and deliver it to Michael's dorm room. All this would have to be accomplished while competing with hundreds of other families for parking spaces, moving carts, and dorm keys.

Jack offered a pleasant smile for her efforts, which Julie promptly returned.

Daniel's entrance was much less forgiving. He acknowledged that Julie checked so many of the right boxes and appreciated how she treated his brother and the family, but that was the problem: She seemed too perfect and he was envious, if not outright jealous, that someone else had acquired Michael's affections. He sat at the table and was about to prepare his toast with his usual pat of butter when a new thought entered his mind.

"Is there any jelly?" he asked no one in particular. But it was indirectly intended for Julie. They never kept jelly in the house. The thought of this perfect breakfast irritated him, and he wanted to see the look on her face when she realized something was missing.

"I wasn't sure if anyone would use it," Julie said, "but I picked some up anyway." She went to the refrigerator, removed a small jar of strawberry jelly, opened it, and placed it in front of Daniel with an extra knife. She spared him any confrontation by turning away and busying herself with something else.

His animus had backfired, as he now was obligated to eat his toast with jelly, which did not suit him.

The four of them sat at the table and completed breakfast, but it was Julie who, refreshingly, led the conversation. It had been a long time since a woman had been part of the family, and Jack continuously delighted in the female perspective Julie offered whenever she was around.

"Mr. Galler, this must be a big day for you, sending your first son to college."

"Why, yes. And his mother would be very proud of him."

"As I am sure you are."

"I've always been proud of him," he replied.

"You should also be proud of your own accomplishment," Julie continued. "You did a great job raising two sons by yourself."

It was a unique compliment. Uniquely Julie, as she was often able to compliment everyone in the room with one comment. Here she'd praised both Michael and Daniel as fine young men and at the same time commended Jack for his efforts in raising them. And she was right. It was the type of praise that normally would never be spoken and Jack was pleased to finally hear the words of recognition, regardless of who offered them. Today's news was filled with stories about children growing up and blaming their abnormal environment—divorced parents, an alcoholic father, having been the object of an uncle's sexual abnormality—for their deviance. Although society had come to accept all these excuses, Jack felt they too often neglected to recognize those who succeed in raising a loving family. So, when Julie recognized his efforts, a warm feeling swept through him. But with a modesty that was uniquely his own, he responded, "I'm not finished yet."

"Well, one son is down, and there's one more to go," she compromised, then looked at Daniel. "You're next, Daniel."

They all partook in packing the car, with Julie directing the order and placement of each item. When they finished, the trunk was fully loaded and half of the back seat was piled to the car's ceiling.

The trees had started giving up their leaves in preparation for the harshness of the New England winter. Like teardrops, they occasionally floated down out of the high branches, coerced by a brisk wind that gusted every few minutes. Bailey found a pile of leaves that collected into a corner by the house and played friskily among them, while the boys went back into the house to do one final search for left-behind items.

Julie took advantage of this moment alone with Jack.

"Mr. Galler, I have something for you. I thought it was the right thing to mark the occasion."

He was caught off guard when she handed him the envelope. It was long and thin, too flimsy to contain a card. He wondered what could possibly be the "right thing to mark the occasion." More curious than grateful, he stuck his thumb under the flap and tore open the seal. Out of the envelope, he withdrew what absolutely was the perfect item for this occasion.

As he held it out between both hands so he could read it, the two boys exited the house empty-handed.

"We have everything," said Michael. "What do you have there, Dad?"

"It's a decal with the name of your school. It's for the back window of the car." Jack looked at Julie. "Thank you, that was thoughtful. How did you get it?"

"I took a cab over to the bookstore," she said. "Wentworth isn't too far from the BU campus."

Perhaps too close for Jack's comfort. Michael had relinquished the opportunity to attend an Ivy League school, settling on the Wentworth Institute instead. There may have been a lot of reasons why he'd chosen it, but chief among them must have been staying close to Julie. Jack had spent the entire summer trying to persuade his son to consider the long-term implications of attending a university with a more elite name, but his efforts had proven unsuccessful. Instead, Michael had almost convinced him that if he took the right courses and studied hard, he would be successful regardless of the university named on the diploma.

Jack looked at Julie and said to her in the stern voice of a concerned father, "Take care of my son."

"That's why I'm here," she replied confidently.

Michael, not privy to this final exchange, shouted, "Let's pile in and get going!"

As they crowded around the four doors of the car, they realized it would be a tight fit to get everyone in.

"Daniel, you and Julie can squeeze into the back seat and I'll jump in front," offered Michael.

Jack looked at Daniel just in time to see his body bristle. "That's okay," he said, "I don't mind sitting in front with Dad."

"I'm bigger than you," Michael insisted. "I wouldn't fit in the back with Julie and my stuff."

"It'll be tight no matter who sits where," Daniel said. "Why don't I stay here? Dad, you may not get home until late, and Bailey can't wait that long to go out."

"Don't you want to see the campus?" asked Michael.

"You'll be there for four years; I'm sure I'll see it plenty of times," Daniel said. "You guys go ahead, I don't mind."

After a few more minutes of attempted persuasion, they all agreed with Daniel and the only thing left was for Michael to say goodbye to Bailey. He walked over to the leaf pile and led Bailey out of the mess. The stiffness had become more evident in her hind legs lately and she now scraped her hind toes when she walked, unable to lift her legs high enough to clear the ground. She had even started ignoring some of his calls for a walk in recent weeks, clearly dreading the painful traversing of the stairs.

Bailey sat in front of Michael with one leg out to the side, unable to tuck it comfortably underneath her. He kneeled down and rubbed her face, saying goodbye. Without diverting his eyes, he instructed Daniel, "Don't forget her pills."

"Two pills twice a day," Daniel replied, echoing Dr. Shepherd's more recent instructions.

Jack leaned into the back seat to apply the decal to the back window, then moved to the front seat to start the car. Michael and Julie climbed in, while Daniel raised a lazy hand farewell.

The street was now empty of activity except for the wind's continued assault on the trees. As they pulled out of the driveway, the large branches swayed above with a uniform rhythm, as if also waving goodbye.

It was late morning and the weekend traffic had already begun to flow like a swollen river after a heavy rain. The sun seemed larger than usual, melting any cloud that dared to float in from the Berkshires. The promise of good weather, coupled with the most popular moving day of the year, encouraged anybody with a car to make their way to or through the city. Every street, road, and avenue north of Boston attempted to squeeze cars through the harbor tunnel. Airport traffic at the tunnel's entrance applied additional pressure on the already-strained roads.

Radio traffic advisories reported a jackknifed tractor trailer on the Central Artery, compounding the stress onto every road within three miles of the city. The truck had already been righted but the spilled lumber was being collected slowly. Traffic on the other side of the highway was equally delayed by onlookers reacting as if they'd never seen wood before.

Jack tried every alternative route he knew to bypass the clogged areas. But every side street was equally congested with drivers who thought they were the only ones who knew the back streets. He abandoned the tunnel to make his way to the bridge and found no relief.

An hour and a half later, he squeezed out the other side of the city and made his way across the Back Bay to Huntington Avenue, home of Wentworth Institute of Technology.

The competition for space on anything paved continued with parking, followed by a long line for Michael's dormitory key. The stress was elevated when Michael was advised the school had canceled his room assignment. Another half hour later, this situation was resolved when it was discovered that Michael's assigned roommate was the one who had canceled his enrollment, due to an illness. Michael was advised he would eventually be assigned a new roommate, but in all likelihood, it would be no one's priority.

There were no carts available, so Jack and Michael carried the heavier items while Julie assisted with the smaller things. The elevators were slow and overcrowded so they decided to take the stairs to the fourth floor, trading one type of stress for another. The stairways and hallways were equally crowded with families, luggage, and carts.

Michael's room was small but had two windows overlooking the Muddy River in the Back Bay Fens. There were two beds, two dressers, and two desks, though there would be only one occupant. They unpacked everything and managed to stow it all away into a small closet and a sufficiently sized dresser. They left his unknown roommate's dresser empty, in the event an alternate was eventually found.

As twilight descended upon the city, Jack prepared for the equally stressful trip home through the traffic, this time alone. Julie would take a cab to her apartment later, after helping Michael put the finishing touches on his new residence.

As Jack stood in the doorway, ready to leave, he suddenly felt awkward. Although it was Michael who had left home for new adventures, it was Jack who was about to exit the scene.

"Well," he said hesitantly. "I'd better go."

Michael strode over and gave him a firm hug. "It's not a problem, Dad. I'm not that far from home."

But to Jack, that *was* the problem.

Sitting at the last traffic light before he could break free of the city street patterns, Jack closed his eyes for just a moment, shutting the continuously moving objects out of his sight. As he did, the city noise seemed to fade. It was the single most peaceful moment he had had all day. He could have easily fallen asleep, and may have for just an instant, but was quickly aroused by an angry horn behind him. He opened his eyes and saw the light had changed to green and there were no cars in front of him. He instinctively looked in the rearview mirror in reaction to the honk, and as he did his eyes settled on something that was new.

He hadn't noticed it before because it was mostly blocked by Michael's things, but now, with the back seat empty, the college decal was plainly visible to him—in fact, the words Wentworth Institute covered the full width of the rearview mirror. The spelling was reversed so that it could be read from outside the car, of course, but because Jack was looking at its reflected image in the rearview mirror, he could read it correctly.

Wentworth was a fine school with a good local reputation, but it was not as acclaimed as the Ivy League institutions Michael had passed up. Now Jack would be reminded of that every time he looked to see what was behind him.

The horn beeped again and he accelerated through the intersection and turned onto the two-lane Storrow Drive. He drove within the speed limit in the traveling lane, continuing to move his eyes back and forth from the road to the rearview mirror. The decal taunted him, reminding him that his son had settled for something less than he could have achieved. His heart was heavy with this knowledge, and he tried to understand Michael's reasoning for making the decision he had. He wasn't blind to the profound effect Julie had on his son, but he hadn't realized it was strong enough to make him alter his life in such an adverse way.

The heaviness within his heart deepened, creating a discomfort he had felt only once before. The seatbelt across his shoulder and chest contributed to the discomfort, so he loosened it and then released it entirely.

The car slowed and other cars accelerated past him as the weight of the day's exertion pressed against him. He was steering with only his right arm, his hand resting on top of the steering wheel. He hadn't perspired all day during all the moving and carrying of the heavy suitcases, but now he noticed a bead of sweat traveling down the side of his torso under his shirt. He writhed from the warmth of the cabin and cracked the window, which let in a crisp breeze but also invited in the sounds of the traffic. The muffled sounds of his car were amplified as he passed under the low overpasses that denied trucks passage on this drive by the river.

Impatient drivers moved around his now-crawling car in pursuit of their own destinations. His destination, however, was about to change.

The city of Boston was home to some of the finest institutions in the world in two very important categories. Today, Michael was taking advantage of one—education—and now Jack would take advantage of the other: health care.

At the end of Storrow Drive, Massachusetts General Hospital encroached on the river with a variety of buildings that seemed to have been built on top of each other. Their disparate architecture suggested that none of them had been built with any consideration for what was built before them, or any that might be built after them. Yet its footprint continued to grow, as if in competition with the diseases it continued to combat.

Jack parked near the emergency entrance and made his way to the front desk.

"I think I'm having a heart attack," he announced as he collapsed to the floor.

CHAPTER 13

The kitchen table swayed whenever she placed any weight on it; the legs had long been weak at the joints. Still, Tremont's mother continued to sit here daily and drink her coffee, smoke her cigarette, and nibble on her piece of toast. This had become the only nutrition her body knew, to the point where her stomach didn't even bother sending messages to her brain anymore requesting something more digestible.

She used to supplement the coffee with sugar and cream, but slowly, over the years, three sugars had become two, then one, then none, and cream had become no more a necessary household item than was a spoon to stir it with.

The apartment was quiet as she stared into the black abyss within the mug. The coffee had long since gone cold as the hours of her life had ticked away like seconds. She yearned for older days, when she could at least feel the numbness that had overcome her body. Today, even the cold, tingling sensation of the outside world rubbing up against her could no longer be felt.

She had not been high in about a week, partly because Barry had not shown his face and partly because her body had ostensibly shut itself down from its own addiction. She was sure it was temporary, like the moon temporarily eclipsing the sun when the light should still be there.

She had only two memories left stored in the hollow of her mind. The first was Barry's huge head hovering over her virgin face. With his eyes jammed shut, he injected his polluted semen into her body. Her own fear kept her from screaming for help, allowing Barry's hands to squeeze her buttocks instead of her throat. When he was finished, he pulled himself out of her, his penis covered with her blood, and placed his finger across her lips.

"Shhhhhhh," was all he said in a lengthened hiss that sounded like the air rushing out of the balloon that was her life. The fire in his eyes advised her that this was a permanent instruction.

Her second memory seemed more recent, even though it had happened two years ago. She remembered the day Tremont had invoked the courage to stand up to Barry, challenging his domination for a mere ten dollars. And it had worked. Barry had not laid a harmful hand on Tremont since that day. But plugging up that hole had intensified the pressure on her as an outlet. Barry's physical attacks had become accelerated and more frequent, and in turn she'd become less tolerant of Tremont, recycling the pain onto him. In the end, the abuse still ended on Tremont, just rerouted.

She cried a tearless cry, as if trying to drink water from a canteen that had long since been drained dry.

Barry's knock at the door roused her from her trance. She knew it was him because she recognized the unique sound of his fist hitting something. Although the door gave off a different resonance than her face, it was unmistakably Barry. She shook her head vigorously to become more alert.

She leaned on the table to lift herself, sensing it would not support her weight but not caring if it didn't. The coffee shook and spilled into the ashtray, dousing the cigarette. She unlocked the door, turned the handle enough to free the latch bolt from the jamb, and returned to her chair. Barry pushed open the door and closed it behind him.

"Where's Tremont?" he asked in the impatient tone that was his own.

"He'll be here."

"He'd better have all the money." It was a moot intimidation, because Tremont always had all the money. He never tried to cheat Barry; he knew there would be no profit in it. Barry had stopped hitting him, and the last thing Tremont would want to do was give him a reason to forget why.

Barry opened the refrigerator and reached in where a can of beer should have been but came up empty. "No beer? This fucking thing isn't even on!"

She stared vacantly at him.

It was the middle of the day and the room didn't need light, but Barry flipped a nearby switch continuously up and down. It had no effect on the bare bulb screwed into the ceiling.

"I gave you money to pay the bills. What did you do with it?"

She knew the wrong words were going to come out of her mouth, but she could not stop them. "I bought lottery tickets."

"You stupid bitch!" Barry swung his fist down onto the kitchen table. What was left of the cold coffee splashed into the air, soaking her down the front of her shirt. The package of cigarettes burst off the table, spitting up its contents. The table creaked at the joints, leaned away from her, and then crashed down to the floor on its buckled legs.

She jumped back off the chair, knocking it over as well. She didn't know where she got the energy but she stood as tall as she could, her wet shirt sticking to her braless breasts.

Barry was distracted as he watched her nipples harden from the cold coffee. A cruel smile formed on his face that scraped her spine. His voice calmed as his arousal became evident, but he seemed in no hurry to satisfy that urge—not yet, anyway.

He walked over to the closed sofa bed and removed a lumpy plastic bag from his pocket. He took out a compact mirror, a razor blade, and a two-inch straw and set them on the coffee table as if preparing to sit for a meal. He chopped and aligned the white crystal into four neat rows with the skill of a Japanese chef. He pushed the straw into his nostril, leaned over, and inhaled the first white line with a wet, sniveling snort.

His weight crushed the worn sofa cushions as he leaned back, allowing the drug to drip off his septum and onto his brain. He glared a sinister stare and she began to feel terribly uneasy as a crude smile formed on his face.

"Were there any winners?"

"None," she lied. It wasn't worth telling him she'd spent a hundred dollars to win twenty.

"Come here," he said in a voice that could have sounded inviting only to him.

"I . . . I can't. I have to clean up this mess."

"Do it later. Later in life, when you clean the rest of this dump. I want you to come here now." His tone became more serious and the smile melted away.

She walked over slowly, never taking her gaze off the floor, unable to meet his piercing eyes.

"Sit down."

She reluctantly obeyed.

Barry stared at her breasts, their shape enhanced by the clinging shirt. Her figure had returned after Tremont was born and she knew it remained enticing, even thinned as it was from malnutrition. He leaned forward, drew in another line, then leaned back to sniffle in every grain and handed her the straw.

Oddly, she had no interest. Her body was still in the eclipsed state it had inhabited all week. She wanted to decline but did not know how.

"I need a cigarette," she said and started to get up.

Barry grabbed her by the back of the shirt and pulled her back into the sofa. He kept a fistful of the shirt tightly in his hand, amplifying the effect of the wet shirt against her breasts.

"Have some," he demanded with the straw out in front of her.

"I'd rather not," she said, disbelieving that the words had actually come out of her mouth.

Barry cocked his head in puzzlement, clearly caught off guard from the challenge to his authority, even with the weakness with which it had been applied. He released her shirt and grabbed the hair on the back of her head. With his other hand holding the straw at the beginning of a line, he pushed her head toward the open end. "Take it," he commanded.

He easily forced her head down to the straw, but he could not compel her to ingest it. He released her and her head snapped back against the couch, where her chest heaved for breaths. He stood with the straw still in his hand and paced back and forth in the cramped room, which allowed only three steps before requiring a turn.

As Barry paced, he closed his eyes and pumped his hand into and out of a fist. She wasn't sure whether he was deciding to use it or whether he was simply contemplating where to employ it. She watched, terrified, as an erection sluggishly formed below his belt buckle.

He opened his eyes and squared himself to her. Her eyes widened while his thinned to an ominous squint.

He pointed a finger at her. "That shit is going in your nose."

He bent down to the table and pushed as much coke as he could into one end of the straw. He licked his finger clean and towered above her for a moment, presenting his power over her, before grabbing the back of her hair, pulling her head back, putting one end of the straw in his mouth, and blowing it into her nose as if blowing a trumpet.

Her nasal passage scalded from the invasion of coke and saliva. She began to gag and cough and unsuccessfully struggled to push Barry away from her. He was grabbing for her breasts when she unwillingly coughed up a string of mucus into his face.

Barry responded by punching her mouth.

He reached back and filled the straw again. This time he stuffed it into her nose, where it stuck like a dart. Then he bent over and blew into the straw as if her head were a stubborn party balloon, pushing the coke into her nasal passage and throat.

She kicked and screamed and coughed and cried.

Barry tore open her shirt, popping the buttons into the air, and began kissing and fondling her breasts.

She was too weak to push him off or prevent him from removing her pants. She kicked violently as he peeled them off her ankles and cast them aside.

He stood, unbuckled his belt, drew down his zipper, and climbed on top of her. He was about to plunge himself into her when she spoke a word that had never escaped her before.

"No," she said softly and meekly.

The surprise of her defiance only delayed his entry by seconds; he shoved himself into her and rocked violently in and out of the canal he'd long ago claimed as his own.

"No," she said again. "No, no, no!" She was screaming now at the top of her lungs. With every thrust of attack, a "no" was pushed out of her mouth. "No, no, no, no!" she yowled. She was saying no for each time she should have said it over these many years, not feeling the current pain but instead reliving all the collective pain she had suffered under him.

She started to feel his body tighten and she let out one long, continuous, wailing "Nooooooooooooo!" as if it would prevent Barry from polluting her womb once again.

Barry's entire body tensed and his groin exploded in a violent, enraged orgasm. As his body jerked from the muscle spasms, his head also exploded into a bloody mess.

Tremont stood over the two of them, smoke fuming out of the barrel of the gun he held in his hand. The blast silenced his mother's howls. Barry's body had gone completely limp, and peace immediately enveloped the room.

His mother's eyes clamped shut as a free hand worked its way to her closest ear as if trying to push away the concussive effects of the discharge. Failing, her eyes opened and lurched around in shocked confusion, trying unsuccessfully to decipher the situation she found herself in.

Tremont watched as she strained to push Barry off her, but he was too heavy and she was depleted of any measure of strength.

"Help me," she cheeped, totally oblivious that he just had.

He continued to stare down at her without speaking. After a long, disquieting moment, he lifted his eyes and surveyed the apartment. The kitchen was a broken mess of table, chair, cigarettes, and coffee. The floor was strewn with torn clothing and drug paraphernalia. His eyes resettled onto his naked mother and the depraved carcass on top of her. Her lip was bruised and bleeding, her teeth stained red. Pieces of Barry's head speckled her chest and commingled with the sweat seeping out of her pallid skin. Hanging out of her nose was a straw that slowly dripped blood like a maple tree being drained of sap.

He didn't see any of this as his mother's life; he saw it as his own. It was a prison that was unacceptable for any human being, no matter what evils descended upon their life. In his hand was the power to change it all. He had compressed his finger and three worlds had changed with a flash and a bang.

"Look at you," he finally said, calmly and effectively.

His voice had the deep intensity that had once emanated from Barry's vocal chords, and he could see this frightened her more than the words he spoke. Barry was dead, yet it was as if he'd been immediately reincarnated in Tremont's own frame.

His mother again tried to push Barry off, this time more urgently, but her efforts were hopeless.

Tremont raised the gun and pointed it at her.

They both remained wordless, surrounded by the ugliness that permeated the apartment and their lives. He wondered silently whether he wanted the bullet ejected from the chamber, and he would challenge his mother to answer that question.

He had entered the room to the cries of her repetitive "no!" He'd gone to the bedroom, located the gun, pressed it up against Barry's temple, and rescued her and himself from the seemingly eternal devil that had overwhelmed their lives. Now, standing there with a steady hand, he wanted to hear her say it one more time. He wanted her to tell him, *No. No, don't shoot. Things will be better now. We will make lives for ourselves.*

His eyes begged her to say it. She'd said it one hundred times just five minutes ago. *Just say it one more time*, he pleaded with a muted intensity.

But she was silent. Weakened and sapped of life, blood no longer dripping from the end of the straw. She closed her eyes and succumbed to a wasted life.

He fired the gun into the face of the woman he used to call his mother. The bullet went cleanly into her skull and the expression on her face never changed. Her face was the same in death as it was in life, confirming that for her there was no difference.

He sat down on the coffee table and stared at his parents, collapsed in a position reserved for lovers. But there was no love. There was no love anywhere in this room, least of all within him.

The source of all the hate in his life was now gone, but the hate itself still lived within him as a rolling boil ready to breach the lid. He still was not free, and if he did not think fast, all hope of ever becoming free would mutate into a prison yard.

There was only one way out. He would have to free himself the same way he'd freed his mother. This room was a practical hell, a place only for the dead. He withdrew the wad of money from his pocket and placed it next to the razor on the coffee table, completing the picture of drugs, money, guns, and violence. Who would blame him for what he was about to do next?

He placed the barrel of the gun into his mouth. It was still hot from its recent use and he could taste the gunpowder on his tongue. He heard only his steady breathing—no sirens, no shouts from outside. His breaths sounded labored, like he was drawing air from a scuba tank.

He looked down at the money: $800, folded at the heads of presidents whose names he did not yet know. It could be his money now, his inheritance. Money to start a new life. It wasn't much, but he also could inherit Barry's clients. And JT, Barry's supplier, would certainly work with him as long as he could guarantee continued demand.

He studied the scene in front of him and a different idea formed in his head. He removed the gun from his mouth and wiped it clean of his saliva and fingerprints. Next, he pressed it into Barry's hand and held it up to his head wound, then let it settle to a more natural resting place. He returned $600 to his pocket and pushed the balance onto the floor, where it scattered.

"This is how I found them," he would later say, a practiced truth in his eyes and a phony sorrow in his voice, as he cried and pleaded to go live with his grandmother.

CHAPTER 14

The white shoes with the rubber soles stepped as silently as the rubber wheels of the wheelchair they were pacing behind. The nurse rolled it into the hospital room later than she'd promised. Michael's father sat on the edge of the bed, fully dressed, with a small bag of clothes by his side, eager to leave the hospital.

As soon as the chair entered the room, his father leapt into it with an excessive anxiousness that had Michael concerned.

"Take it easy, Dad."

"It was only a mild heart attack," his father replied.

"If you say so. But the quadruple bypass that followed was major surgery."

"Maybe, but I'm still ready to go home," his father answered with the appetent tone that had earned him the affectionate nickname "The Impatient Inpatient" by the hospital staff.

His father was wrong about the heart attack being mild. According to his doctors, it had been a more severe warning of the threatening situation that had been redeveloping within his arteries. Doctors had recommended immediate surgery—another bypass operation. They'd removed a vein from his other leg and rerouted the flow of blood past four blockages around his heart. After two days in intensive care, followed by seven days in a semiprivate room, he was ready to be discharged.

Although Michael agreed with the doctor about this having been another warning, he better identified it as part of the ever-present threat that lived within his father and had pervaded the entire family. Now, with two bypass surgeries behind him and both legs having been stripped of their spare parts, he recognized that his father was another dangerous step closer to succumbing to the evil that stalked him. As a result, he was reticent about his father's eagerness to go home. He was equally uncomfortable watching him move so hastily, afraid he could disrupt the healing process or, worse, instigate another heart attack.

Daniel exhibited more optimism, recognizing the difference between the two surgeries. After the first bypass years earlier, their father had spent his recuperation in a depressed and lethargic state, only eventually regaining his emotional strength. Today, however, he was eager to return to work and grateful he had survived another flirtation with death, and Daniel cheered on his motivation to leave the hospital and begin rehabilitation.

Michael shook his head in astonishment at his father's vigor after everything he had been through. "I don't know how you do it, Dad."

"Do what?"

"He's a fighter," Daniel interjected, raising his fists. He started dancing around the room, boxing with an imaginary opponent—or maybe an invisible one—imitating an experienced pugilist.

"It's just that you've been through a lot," Michael said. "Most people would have given up, but you're still filled with"—he paused as he searched for the right word—"hope."

His father sat in the wheelchair with his feet propped up on the footrests and his hands on the wheels, ready to start rolling himself down the hallway. The nurse stood quietly behind him, only half listening to the conversation, waiting tolerantly for a comfortable break in the dialogue to start wheeling him to the exit.

"Adversity makes us stronger, Michael."

"Well, then, you must be the strongest person I know," Michael said. "If I had to go through the things you have, I think I would have put a bullet in my head."

"That's why it's important to take care of your body, which you're very conscious about doing," his father said. "In fact, significantly more so than most people. And I'm glad to see it, because they say that the problems I've had could be passed on. And I don't want you to be subjected to this."

Michael could not have agreed more. He felt lucky he'd recognized years ago that he could inherit this enemy he identified as Cancer and that he had dedicated his life to ensuring whatever lived within his father would not be passed on to him or his brother.

Daniel continued his boxing motions, seemingly evincing some kind of inner pleasure from his ability to bob, weave, and jab. He moved closer to Michael to demonstrate this newfound skill. "Don't you want to inherit Dad's ability to fight?" he asked, extending jabs that stopped inches from Michael's face.

"That's not what he's talking about. Now stop fooling around, before you hurt yourself."

Daniel bristled at his brother's dismissal. He increased his flurry of false punches to Michael's body and face, bouncing on his toes and circling him; then he squared off directly in front of him and threw out fists that inched closer and closer to his face, attempting to force Michael to flinch in acknowledgment. "It won't be me that gets hurt," he cautioned, his eyes simmering behind his clenched fists.

Michael stood calm and steadfast. He hadn't yet winced, although the bursts of air each time Daniel snapped his punch did cause him to blink. He was unsure what was bolstering this aggressive posture, but he supposed the whole family had been under a lot of stress since his father's admission to the hospital.

"Relax," he advised his brother.

Daniel faked one final flurry of punches before submitting—a right hand to Michael's kidney, a left hook to his jaw, and a jab to his face. But the jab hung out just an inch too far and collided squarely with the bridge of Michael's nose.

"I'm sorry! It was an accident!" Daniel exclaimed.

Michael was caught by surprise when he felt the solid thud. There was an instant of darkness that exploded into an abstraction of images that he recognized but could not identify. His ears rang and his eyes immediately welled up with tears, even though he felt certain he would not cry. He bent over and cupped his nose with both hands, trying to ward off the hollow sensation that deluged his sinuses.

Daniel apologized profusely during the awkward moments that followed, and when Michael started to raise himself from his bellied-over position, Daniel blanched, seemingly expecting to be punched back.

As soon as he had mentally controlled the pain, Michael stood erect but kept his hands over his nose and mouth the way one would to hold back a sneeze. It was now he who peered out over his hands at Daniel, waiting for the blood to flow out of his nose.

"Are you okay?" Daniel babbled. "I'm sorry. Are you all right?"

Michael maintained his silence, as if he'd heard a strange noise and was waiting patiently for it to repeat so that its source could be identified. But he was actually waiting to see if his body was strong enough to keep from bleeding. He felt challenged by the incident, and he willed himself, his body, not to be affected by this attack upon it. His concentration was intense as he felt for the wetness of the blood on his hands.

Their father had risen from the wheelchair and, alongside the nurse, was crowding Michael while Daniel stepped back out of reach.

Minutes passed as the nurse tried to instruct Michael to tilt his head back so she could inspect him and he ignored her and kept his nose covered, reluctant to release it and look at his hands for fear of what he might see. He was sure Daniel had struck him hard enough to break some blood vessels, maybe even break his nose altogether. But he didn't care if it was broken; he was only concerned with knowing if the punch had caused him to bleed. If there was blood leaking, it would indicate he was still vulnerable and susceptible to everything he feared. But if there was none, it would be a sign that all of his efforts over the years to strengthen and protect himself had resulted in some measure of success.

Jack looked sternly at Daniel and charged him with the task of getting some tissues. He returned from the bathroom with a wad of toilet paper and held it out to Michael as a peace offering.

Michael finally, slowly, pulled his hands away from his face. He studied them and found them clean. He touched in and around his nostrils feeling for wetness, then examined his fingertips. Nothing.

Now he obeyed the nurse, tilting his head back and allowing her to inspect his nose. "Is there any blood?" he asked.

"I'm checking to see if it's broken," she responded.

"I don't care if it's broken, just tell me if I'm bleeding."

"No . . . nothing . . . I don't see any blood. And it doesn't appear to be broken. But I think you should lie back on the bed for a few minutes."

"You're sure it's not bleeding? Check again!"

"Yes, I'm sure," she said, but checked again anyway.

As Michael looked out at his brother's outstretched hand, offering the tissues, he suddenly identified the images that had jolted his consciousness the instant his face was struck: It had been a series of images all morphed together but separately identifiable. Superimposed over the image of Daniel's striking fist had been the image of Dr. Prendergast's fist during her description of Jack's pumping heart, as well as the image of Dr. Shepherd's fist during his description of Bailey's arthritic hip. The fist had become an icon for Cancer, and the last person Michael wanted to see waving it in his face was his brother. He believed Daniel, that he had not intended to strike him, but there had still been some animosity in his actions, and that was what had caused the accident to occur.

He was suddenly overcome by an intense sense of nausea. The physical pain, the ignited emotions, and the sterile odors of the hospital, all stirred together, were settling into the bottom of his stomach like soup stock settling to the bottom of a kettle. He reached for the bathroom tissue and said to Daniel in the tone of a god issuing one last commandment, "Do not ever raise a fist to me again."

"Did it bleed?" Julie asked.

"No," Michael answered with a hidden pride that she would not have understood, even if she had noticed.

"Are you okay now?"

"Yeah, we left the hospital after about fifteen minutes and took my dad home. My aunt will stay with him for a week or so and he should be back at work in about a month."

"I'm glad you came here instead of going straight to your dorm."

"I have the car for a few weeks, so it was easy to get here. I just . . . wanted to see you."

"I'm glad you told me what happened."

Michael had found it easier to talk openly with Julie as time went on. He shared more and more of his feelings with her now but, fearful of exposing too much of himself, still stayed safely away from some of his deeper emotions regarding their relationship.

He was presently sitting comfortably on the sofa with his shoes kicked off while she prepared some cold drinks: water with ice for him, soda water and ice for herself. She returned with two napkins, placed them on the coffee table like coasters, and set the glasses on them. Then she asked the question that Michael had tried to avoid asking himself.

"Do you think he did it on purpose?"

This question went beyond a simple reiteration of the story; it reached below the surface to his emotions. Michael lifted his glass and took a long swallow. He returned it to the napkin, replacing it exactly on the wet ring already formed by the condensation.

"I want to believe it was an accident. He got a little excited and then . . . accidents happen."

Julie took a sip from her glass and then held it against the side of her face with eyes closed, enjoying the cold compress. Michael waited, hoping his answer would suffice, as he did not want to think about that possibility any further.

She opened her eyes and re-asked the question. "You *want* to believe it was an accident, but *do* you believe it was?"

While waiting for him to answer, she stirred her drink with her finger, slowly twirling the ice cubes around the glass. Then she pulled out her finger and placed it in her mouth to wipe the drips.

"What are you drinking?" he asked.

"Soda water." After observing Michael's doubtful expression, she confessed, "And vodka."

Michael looked at his own glass with sudden disinterest. Perhaps the vodka would unwind him. "Can I have some?"

"You don't drink alcohol."

"I need something to relax," he wheedled. "Maybe even numb the pain. The bridge of my nose still hurts."

"I'd be contributing to the delinquency of a minor," she jested.

"It's for medicinal purposes only," he countered with the same playfulness.

She grinned her familiar grin and took a big sip from her own glass but didn't seem to swallow. After staring at him for a few seconds that seemed like minutes, she leaned over to him and kissed him. Their lips formed an airtight seal, and the alcohol flowed freely between their mouths.

The unfamiliar taste of the alcohol burned the surfaces of Michael's mouth at first, and then it anesthetized them. The passion of the kiss was enhanced by the presence of the fluid being swished around by their tongues. Simultaneously, they both swallowed. Julie pulled back, took another sip from her glass, and this time swallowed it completely.

Then she asked the question yet again.

Michael stole her glass, took a long drink of the cocktail, and pushed it down his throat with a hard swallow.

Then he reflected on his answer while continuing to hold her glass.

"I really do believe it was an accident . . ."

"But . . ."

"But I think he's home right now thinking about what happened, and it feels good to him." Anticipating she would ask why it would feel good to Daniel, he continued, "I love my brother, and I know he loves me. But he feels like he's been living in my shadow, and now that I'm gone I think he's trying to find a way to break out and seek his own identity. Hitting me might have just been an outlet for his frustration, even if he didn't mean it."

"Did you want to hit him back?"

"No, the thought never entered my mind. I just wanted to be sure I didn't start bleeding all over the place."

"You're okay now?"

"Yeah, I'm fine," he answered, and took another sip of the drink.

They sat peacefully for a long moment, staring at each other. Julie then nestled closer to Michael and they shared the rest of the drink without talking.

When it was finished, she got up to make another one.

"Would you make me one too?" Michael asked.

"We'll share this one again," she answered, seemingly enjoying the act of sharing while somehow managing to commingle it with maintaining control. She returned holding a full glass with fresh ice. The need to conceal the contents had been eliminated, and there was now a twist of lime in the middle of the glass, not so much floating as it was pressed between the cubes.

"I have class tomorrow morning at eight o'clock," she said, "so you can't stay too late."

Michael felt a look of dejection kidnap his face. He quickly resettled himself on the sofa, erased the disheartened look from his face, and replaced it with one more serious, more intense.

"My first class isn't until ten," he said, setting himself up to negotiate for more time.

"What do you want to do?"

"Stay." He leaned over to kiss her.

Their lips met but Julie pushed him back, falling with him against the armrest, which creaked when it accepted both of their weight. She was now kissing him, having stolen the moment from him.

The kiss was long and slow. Time stopped and sounds disappeared, everything being drowned out by the intoxication that enveloped his body. Michael wanted to caress her hair but his hands were too heavy to lift, so much so that one of them drooped off the couch to the floor.

The moment was unlike anything Michael had experienced before. He felt as if his body had been infused with an indefinable passion. It was as if he had been injected with a foam that oozed into all the tight cracks and tiny spaces within his body. But as complete as the kiss made him feel, he felt as if the kiss itself was incomplete. That it was a prelude to something that was so much more overwhelming, like he'd been given a key and left with the sensation of inevitability that something else existed that the key belonged to.

Julie eased back, holding his numbed gaze. Her lips glistened like reflected light on a twinkling pond.

"Stay," she said. But her even tone left it unclear if she was repeating Michael's answer in consideration or if she was telling him to stay. It could even have been a question.

She swung her legs over the side of the couch, took up the drink, and drained half of it. Her throat pulsated as the swallows worked their way down. She returned the glass to the table.

Aping her actions, Michael sat up next to her, reached for the glass, and emptied it, leaving the ice and lime to compete for space at the bottom. His head felt like a leaky boat, taking on water almost too slowly to notice. He wasn't sure if it was rooted in Julie or the alcohol, but it was surely addling.

"Stay here," she said, rising with the glass.

Michael's eyes followed her down the hallway, where she turned into the kitchen. Her words echoed in his head as he tried to interpret the tone of her voice. He could not tell if he was to stay there on the couch momentarily or if she was permitting him to stay longer at her apartment.

Suddenly thirsty, he drank from the water glass that was still on the coffee table. It quenched his thirst but the taste was bland, void of the texture the vodka had held. He looked back down the hallway, suspicious of what Julie might be doing. No noises came from the kitchen or anywhere else in the apartment. He could see through the open bedroom door and spied shadows shifting along the walls like apparitions moving stealthily through a murky bog.

He sat alone on the couch, wondering what he should do. He knew what he wanted to do: He wanted to stay here with her. He wanted to spend the night here and hold her, touch every part of her body. He wanted her to hold him and caress him. He wanted to continue to explore the newfound intimacy that was taking over his life. But at this very moment in time, he didn't know what to do to get it.

He asked himself what Julie would want him to do and the answer came quickly. Michael could have anything he wanted from her, as long as he gave something in return. And the thing she wanted was always the same. She wanted more of him—more exposure of his thoughts and feelings and emotions. She wanted to be an important part of his life and she had succeeded in becoming that, but she wasn't aware how important she was. She needed to know Michael's true thoughts.

It was difficult for him every time they shared intimate moments, and he continued to struggle to give her what she needed. Each time he did open himself up, he felt vulnerable, like he was giving up pieces of himself. But each piece he lost was replaced by a piece of her, and this soothed him. It was as if she had discovered a dormant root within his mind and fertilized and cultivated it until it had grown into a deep, uncontrollable passion.

He stood confidently, knowing what he needed to do, and moved slowly down the hallway to seek her out. He ignored the kitchen—he knew she was no longer in there—and went straight to the bedroom. He stepped just through the doorway, turned his head, and saw her standing in the middle of the floor, waiting for him.

She was now wearing a white cotton chemise with eyelet straps that connected to the bodice with small satin ribbons. The hem curved above the knee, subtly exposing her thighs. Her hair was pinned up above her head, permitting stray wisps to float down to her shoulders. She fondled an earring with one hand.

"Michael," she whispered.

"Julie."

Michael stepped forward and grasped both of her hands, then stepped back to admire her. "You are so beautiful."

She stepped forward to close the space between them and they began kissing. For the first time, Michael felt her body weaken, like a turning key freeing a door from its jamb. Their bodies embraced in perfect symmetry.

His hands roamed down to her hips to see if she was wearing anything underneath and discovered no panty line. He sensed her shoulders sag disappointedly at his sexual adolescence; if she had been wearing panties they would have come off for him—there was no need to dip a toe in the water to test the temperature.

She pulled back but not away. "Are you ready for this?"

He caressed her back, finding it difficult to determine where the soft cotton chemise ended and her skin began. "Yes," he answered. "I'm ready."

"How do I know that? It's too important of a thing to get wrong."

"How can I make you know?"

"Michael, I want you inside me. I'm not afraid to tell you that. Do you want to be inside me?"

He stared into her unblinking eyes. Her pupils were fixed onto his and were as still as the headlights of a car. He returned her stare like a deer caught standing on a country road. "You know I do."

"You need to tell me."

"Julie, I want to be inside you." It was harder to say than he'd thought it would be.

"Then you can understand how I feel," she said in return.

Michael paused. The dialogue had somehow turned itself around, and he felt lost in it. He didn't understand how Julie felt, even though she'd just concluded that he did.

"You need to tell me," he said.

Julie explained it to him with ease. "You want to be inside me, to feel like you're a part of me, like our bodies are one and the same. And I'm ready right now to let that happen. I'm ready to open the most secret part of my body and let you in. But I want the same thing from you. I want to be inside you, to be a part of you. You're such a caring, intelligent, and honest person with so many unshared thoughts and feelings swirling around inside that head of yours. I want to be a part of you, your heart, your mind. Open up to *me*, Michael. Let me know you're ready for this."

Michael could not appreciate the stillness that existed in the room because his thumping heart beat back the silence. He looked down into Julie's eyes as she looked back longingly. Her tilted eyes made her look wanting as she waited for him to respond.

His headache became suddenly evident, though he was unclear on whether its source was the alcohol, the blow to his face, or even the emotional intensity of the moment. Here he had this unique woman right in front of him, ready to give herself to him in her entirety, and all he had to do was release the pressure that had been building up within his head. Just tell her exactly how he felt about her, about their relationship, about what she meant to him.

Michael's mouth opened and the words flowed out like champagne after the cork pops out. "Julie, you already are so much a part of what is me. And you know that you are, but you just need to hear me tell you. I love you, Julie. When I'm not with you I feel like a part of me is missing. Sometimes I feel this strange feeling inside, like I don't know where I end and you begin. You have to know that I can't ever lose you, because it would be like losing part of myself." He raised his hands and cupped her face in his palms. "Without you, I am without me."

The semblance of a tear rolled down Julie's face and Michael brushed it away with his thumb before it could leak into her smile.

"You *are* ready," she said.

They embraced tightly and fell to the bed. As Julie worked his belt buckle, Michael felt for the wetness between her legs. There was no hesitation from her, no shyness. He could place his hands anywhere he wanted to and there was no hurry.

She helped him undress, and after he pulled her nightgown over her head they lay naked together in a secure embrace. They kissed while feeling each other's body, and then Michael moved on top of her. She opened her legs and used her hand to guide him into her.

"We need a condom," Michael interrupted.

"I won't get pregnant." Her tone made clear that she had already taken a precaution, not that she felt she would beat the odds.

"That's not what I'm worried about."

"What are you worried about?"

It was an awkward moment to bring up protection, but he could not risk exposing himself to any sexually transmitted diseases. Still, it was a delicate subject at such an intimate moment, so he had to address it carefully.

"You're in the medical field; you must know it's better to be safe," he said.

"Would you rather be inside a piece of rubber or inside me?"

Michael smoothed her hair against the side of her head. "What I want and what's right are two different things."

"But this is our first time. Let's do it without the condom this time, and we can take that precaution after tonight."

Julie was still holding him in her hand and was massaging between her legs with his erection. Michael could feel how slippery her opening was, and it was all he could do to keep from allowing himself to slide all the way into her.

"Does this feel good?" she tempted.

Michael closed his eyes and imagined being inside her. "Yes."

"You won't be able to feel this with a condom."

Michael allowed himself to penetrate her about one-quarter of the way in and then quickly removed himself. Her muscles did not tighten but he could feel her smooth, wet vaginal walls surrounding him.

"Do you love me, Michael?"

"Yes," he whispered in her ear.

"Then make love to me. For real."

He pushed himself in halfway and stopped. Julie still did not tighten, but she took a deep breath and let it out slowly while he left himself there. Then, as if nothing mattered anymore except how much in love he was, he slipped all the way into her until their hips touched. Their bodies began to gyrate in unison and Michael could now feel her muscles locking onto him with every thrust. Each time he retreated, her hips rose up to meet him as if trying to swallow him.

They were like a single entity, their minds and bodies locked in a solitary, harmonious unit. Michael felt he was as much a part of her as she was a part of him. The rhythms of their bodies matched perfectly, as if they had done this thousands of times before. Michael felt himself on the edge of climaxing and moved his arms underneath her to hold her tighter. He slid his face to the side, nearly burying it in the pillow. Julie's body also began to tighten. Her arms and legs wrapped around his body. Their limbs clutched each other as if they were free-falling through the sky without parachutes and with nothing to hold on to but each other.

Then, as if smashing the ground, their bodies exploded in orgasm and went limp.

They lay silently for several minutes, unable to move, as if every bone in their bodies had been shattered. Michael turned his head out of the pillow to improve his breathing. It was the most perfect and complete moment he had ever experienced.

He pushed himself up to look in Julie's eyes and tell her exactly how he felt at this moment. He caught her broadened eyes and said, "I love you, Julie."

Julie's eyes stayed wide, wider than he had ever seen them. She was dismayed at the sight before her. "Oh, my!" she exclaimed.

"What is it?"

"Your face . . ."

Michael then saw the answer on the pillow next to her head: a large, dark smear where his face had pressed into it. He swiped under his nose and came up with the same result across the back of his hand.

Blood.

CHAPTER 15

The sun peeked above the horizon, but the caverns of the city cheated its inhabitants out of the beauty inherent in a sunrise. Only the glowing orange and red of the eastern sky was evidence of the glory taking place at the horizon line.

Tremont stared out at his own horizon of barrels and trash bags lining the neighborhood curb. Donning his thick city-issued leather gloves, he started his workday. He clutched a large tied plastic bag by the throat with each hand, turned to the open end of the truck, and tossed them in with ease. He disposed of the rest of the bags and then emptied the barrels, filling the bay of the truck with the discarded waste of people he didn't know. He reached around the passenger side of the truck for the lever and yanked it like a slot machine, and the hydraulics roared to life. The compression blade moved slowly down, closing the back end of the truck, then pushed the trash back into its belly, compacting it, before returning to its original position above the empty bay.

Tremont signaled the driver through the passenger side-view mirror. The truck lurched forward fifty feet to the next pile of refuse as Tremont trotted alongside. He could have jumped on for the ride, but the short runs kept him in shape. Although he had never tested himself, he believed he could comfortably run well over five miles. His arms and shoulders had become firm and sculpted from lifting the heavy barrels, bags, and boxes.

He had sprouted to six feet and one inch, Barry's genes finally taking effect, and he had the physique to accompany this height. All told, Tremont had grown into an imposing and intimidating figure, which was an asset to his primary source of income.

The truck rumbled down the streets of South Boston, disrupting the peace that existed only during these early morning hours. They visited each section of the city one day each week, following the same route and the same schedule. A supervisor could determine within fifteen minutes exactly where any of the city trucks would be making pickups on any given day.

But what a supervisor would not know was that this was the only truck in the fleet that also made deliveries.

The first stop was an easy one. Arnez, the driver, pulled in front of a locally owned coffee shop. He climbed down out of the truck, too heavy to jump, and went inside while Tremont cleared the sidewalk. When the hydraulics were engaged to sweep the trash into the body of the truck, a figure from a doorway of an adjacent building moved casually toward him. They both extended a hand, but no greeting ensued. Instead, Tremont took the money, confirmed the denomination, and then tendered a small plastic bag to the eager recipient. The figure retreated and disappeared.

Arnez returned with two cups of coffee and a wax-coated bag and walked to the rear of the truck, where he handed one of the coffees to Tremont. The coffee aroma was too weak to mask the stench wafting from the truck, but Arnez had proclaimed his preference for patronizing local shop owners instead of the national franchises that seemed to be spreading like a cancer.

They stood in front of the open end of the truck for several minutes while Arnez made small talk, attempting once again to befriend Tremont.

"Do you want me to jump out and help you today?" he asked.

"No, I want the workout," Tremont answered.

"It was a long weekend with the holiday, and it rained. Lots of extra weight. Maybe just today?"

"Just drive the truck, Arnez. You handle the front end and I'll handle the back." Tremont swallowed down his remaining coffee, signaling his impatience to get back to work.

Arnez was married with two kids and another on the way. He was overweight and overpaid and preferred not to leave the truck for anything other than coffee and lunch. Tremont supposed he would even use the drive-throughs if only the truck would fit under their awnings. The coffee was his effort to overcome his guilt for not participating in the more difficult element of the job.

"Okay, Tree. But you let me buy lunch today."

Tremont threw his empty cup into the gaping mouth of the truck and said in a deep, sardonic voice, "Let's go. We have a schedule to keep."

Arnez took his half-empty cup and the donut bag with him to the cabin and labored to climb back up into the driver's seat. He closed the door, shifted into gear, and pulled away from the curb.

Tremont would never thank Arnez for the coffee. He regarded him as harmless, but he purposely intimidated him. He never wanted Arnez poking his head around the back of the truck and discovering what really went on back there.

Tremont worked hard every day, which made his grandmother happy, even though she was oblivious to the real reason he held this job. The weekend rain had indeed added extra weight to the refuse. But it was a different kind of weight that burdened him today.

JT, his supplier, had recently approached him with an opportunity to increase volume. He was impressed with Tremont's unique distribution system and wanted to partner with him to increase supply concurrent with an increasing demand. He'd offered Tremont a true partnership, with one condition: Tremont had to come up with $15,000 to buy into the first shipment. Additional shipments would be paid for with profits.

Fifteen thousand dollars was a lot of money for an eighteen-year-old to attain. But for an eighteen-year-old drug dealer, the biggest problem was time. Tremont could come up with $3,000, maybe $4,000 now, but the rest would require increased business, which was difficult for a small-time dealer. Ironically, he needed a big score to make the big score.

JT had promised to be patient, but he'd never said for how long.

Tremont had struggled for days to figure out a way to come up with the money, but he always came back to thinking that he only knew how to do two things well: feed the truck and feed the habit.

The morning continued with Tremont doing just those two things: throwing the big bags into the truck and distributing the little bags to junkies throughout the city.

Arnez stayed happily in the cab, listening to the radio and munching on his snacks. He diligently checked his mirrors for Tremont's signal to advance the truck up to the next load, obeying promptly when he saw it. It was getting close to lunch now, and he was no doubt fantasizing about the smells of his hot-sandwich order.

Tremont was experiencing a different aroma. The rain had soaked into anything not plastic, exacerbating the weight and embittering the smell of the trash. The odor from the truck became more pungent and difficult to bear as he continuously added ingredients to the disgusting soup soaking within.

The last stop before lunch was the back of a small commercial building. Arnez carefully backed the truck into the narrow alley behind a sandwich shop, a convenience store, and a liquor store. The incessant beeping, warning the truck was in reverse, was like a signal for Tremont's customers, similar to an ice cream truck ringing its bell to attract children.

When he reached the end of the alley, behind the liquor store, Arnez stopped the truck and engaged the parking brake. The sandwich shop was in front of him, providing him with the real smells he would have only been imagining all morning.

The back door of the liquor store was obstructed by hundreds of folded cardboard boxes, evidence of a recent delivery. Tremont dispatched them quickly and engaged the compression blade. He took a broomstick stored on the side of the truck and used it to push in the larger boxes that extended out of the bay, protecting his hands. As the engine roared louder and the blade swept the boxes into the area behind, the shadow of a man oozed out of the shadows of the alley.

"Where were you yesterday, Tree?"

Tremont immediately recognized the roguish voice of Reggie Gaines and turned with the broomstick still in his hand. "It was a holiday, you stupid shit. The city doesn't work on holidays."

Tremont had no patience for Reggie. He never had money but always wanted something to feed his need. Barry had continuously warned Tremont about him but Tremont had given him a new start to gain a foothold following Barry's sudden retirement and his resulting promotion. Now he was regretting giving Reggie a foothold on credit.

He had recently found a phony bill in his money roll, and he suspected it had originated from Reggie. It was fortunate he'd identified it before passing it to JT, but now it was time to confirm his suspicion of the source.

Reggie was average height but half the average weight for his size. His dirty oversize pants were scrunched at the waist by an overtightened belt and his tattered work boots had no laces. It was evident he'd sensed Tremont's ire and was resolved to accelerate this transaction and move along.

As the blade completed its rotation, the motors supporting the hydraulics quieted. Tremont clapped the side of the truck with the broomstick and caught Arnez's attention in the passenger-side mirror. Arnez moved the truck forward to the back of the convenience store.

Tremont walked forward in the wake of the truck with Reggie in tow, then started tossing in half-filled green garbage bags. They weren't heavy and wobbled in midair as the weight shifted within the bag.

"What can you give me for fifty bucks?" Reggie held out a neatly folded bill that presented the fifty on its face.

Tremont took the bill, eyed it, and stuffed it in his pocket. "You get nothing." He returned to his pile of trash and continued tossing in bags.

"What are you talking about? You just took my money!"

Tremont stopped what he was doing and turned to Reggie. "Tell me how much money you just gave me, Reggie."

Reggie looked confused yet nervous. "I gave you fifty bucks. You even looked at it."

Tremont rested the broomstick on his shoulder like a baseball player anxiously waiting his turn at bat and glowered. "Tell me again how much money you gave me."

Reggie hesitated before answering. "Fifty." He shifted his weight to his other foot. "Fifty dollars."

"So, we're clear. You're telling me you gave me fifty dollars?"

The alley was suddenly quiet. Reggie looked left, then right. His foot started bouncing nervously. "C'mon, Tree. It was fifty. What's the matter? Why you fucking with me? It was fifty. You know, if there's some kind of problem, you know, just give it back to me. I'll go see Jimmy. Jimmy Papers. I'll buy from him instead." He wiped his nose with his sleeve and looked away from Tremont. "Fifty," he finished meekly.

"Nobody's seen Jimmy Papers for two weeks, Reggie. I'm the only one you can see. Don't you be cutting corners on me."

Reggie stood like a statue with a pigeon on his head. The "cutting corners" phrase had caught his attention. Tremont stood erect, knowing full well what Reggie was staring at. Tremont was as tall as Barry had been but was more defined. His shirt clung to his body, exposing his muscles as if they'd been etched into the material. He was sweating from the morning's exertion but his breathing was controlled. *I'm Barry now*, his presence stated. He was surely his father's son, but somehow . . . improved.

Tremont's fingers fidgeted on the broomstick, searching for a comfortable grip. Then he swung the stick.

He clapped the side of the truck twice, causing Reggie to wince hard. There was a grinding of gears, then the truck staggered forward to a row of three plastic barrels with lids loosely covering them and one tied rubbish bag. "Walk with me, Reggie."

Reggie obeyed as if he were sleepwalking.

Arnez stopped the truck right outside the kitchen door of the sandwich shop, which had been left open to vent the heat from the ovens. Tremont could see the steam rising off the grill as a cook flipped hamburgers and chopped shaved steak with a large stainless steel spatula.

Tremont dropped the first lid to the ground and emptied the barrel into the truck. It was filled with unbagged garbage—stale rolls, uneaten pizza crusts, and rotted vegetables mixed in with pizza boxes, wax paper, paper bags, and dirty crumpled napkins. He spread it all within the truck bay, then emptied the other two barrels.

Tremont removed Reggie's folded bill from his pocket and held it up with the fifty showing. "I know the names of only six presidents, Reggie: Washington, Lincoln, Hamilton, Jackson, Grant, and Franklin. If you can tell me which one is on this fifty-dollar bill, you can have it back."

The phony bill Tremont had discovered had one corner of four different fifty-dollar bills carefully spliced and taped onto a one-dollar bill with the corners removed. Looking at the corner quickly, he had easily seen the number fifty. But when he had unfolded it later that day, he had seen George Washington staring back at him. He could now feel the invisible tape under his thumb on the corner of this bill in his hand.

Reggie stared at the bill, shaking his leg uncontrollably. His pants slipped down and he pulled them up by the belt. "Look, Tree. I don't like this game. If there's a problem, a problem with the bill, we can fix it. I just bought cigarettes. I changed a hundred-dollar bill. We'll go back, we'll fix it."

"Ain't got time. Let's fix it here." He grabbed Reggie by his belt buckle and shirt collar, picked him up effortlessly, and launched him into the truck.

Reggie landed softly in the pile of garbage, but the shock of Tremont's quickness and strength left him stunned. By the time he could react, the compression blade had engaged and was closing off the back of the truck. He struggled to escape, but he could not get any leverage on the wet garbage. Just as he was about to be entombed in the truck, Tremont reached his hand in, grabbed Reggie's foot, and pulled it out of the truck. The blade came down onto the instep of Reggie's work boot and stopped—not because it was stuck but because Tremont had stopped it. There was enough pressure on Reggie's boot to keep him from dislodging it.

When the blade stopped and the engines quieted, Tremont heard Reggie's muffled voice screaming in horror.

"No! Don't! Tremont! It wasn't my bill! Don't do this!"

Tremont bent down and looked through the four-inch space that appeared to be held open by Reggie's foot. "You pay me real bills or I'll tear a piece of *you* off at the corner," he said into the truck.

Reggie was screaming with an unintelligible fear—and then, suddenly, money started flowing out of the opening like a slot machine paying off a jackpot, first wrinkled ones, fives, and tens and then any loose change Reggie managed to dig out of his pockets. Two more phony fifty-dollar bills followed as he bawled like a three-year-old, "Let me out! Let me out! Don't do this!"

Tremont had had enough amusement for one day; he moved to the side of the truck to reverse the blade. As he did, his eye caught the passenger-side mirror just in time to see the driver's side door close. Arnez had left the cab.

Tremont quickly cycled through which of three possible options to execute before the expiration of the three seconds it would take Arnez to lumber to the back of the truck. He could reverse the blade and have Arnez be witness to a screaming, enraged drug addict exiting the truck bay. He could leave the scene as it was, which would be equally difficult to explain. The third option, which was most likely unappealing to Reggie, seemed to be the most appealing to Tremont.

He leaned on the lever, engaging the hydraulics, and watched as the boot was squashed, snapping the sole, and then dragged into the back of the truck. The only detectable sound was the roaring engine as it employed the hydraulics.

Arnez appeared from around the corner of the truck and said loudly enough to compete with the engine, "WHAT'S THE HOLDUP? I'M STARVING."

Tremont kept the hydraulics engaged to mask any noise that might be yowling from within the truck. "I FOUND SOME MONEY," he yelled, motioning at the ground. "WHY DON'T YOU LEAVE THE TRUCK HERE AND GO AHEAD AND ORDER LUNCH. IT'S ON ME."

Arnez appeared more charmed by Tremont's unusual gesture of friendship than he was surprised at the sight of the money on the ground. He bent down, spreading his legs to give his large stomach a place to hang, and scooped up two tens, leaving the remainder for Tremont. "I'LL SEE YOU INSIDE," he said with an attempt at a smile.

Tremont kept his hand on the lever and watched Arnez until he turned the corner to make his way around front. Then, like a mad scientist about to unveil his latest monster creation, Tremont pushed up on the lever and reversed the blade, not knowing what to expect. The noise from the hydraulic engines amplified as the blade backed out of the deep end of the truck and lifted like a curtain rising at the start of a freak show.

Loose trash and garbage fell down into the bay, then Reggie fell in with a flop. He was writhing in pain, as Tremont had expected.

Reggie, a desperate look in his eyes, swung both his legs out, revealing one booted foot and one naked, intact foot. He pushed himself out of the truck and fell to the ground. Wet garbage stuck to his face and hair. His clothes were stained from head to toe.

"You're a sick fuck! Just stay the fuck away from me! You're a crazy motherfucker!" He stood up and tried to shake the soreness from being crushed with the garbage.

Tremont leaned into him. "Now you know what happened to Jimmy Papers."

Reggie's eyes widened in fear. He clutched his belt buckle to keep his pants up and started running backward until he was clear of the truck. Then he turned and ran, limping, out of the alley, dragging his bare foot behind him.

Tremont seized the remaining trash bag and tossed it into the truck, where it landed on the crushed boot Reggie had luckily wrestled himself out of. He leaned over and collected the bills strewn on the ground but left the loose change. He let out a deep sigh, knowing he needed so much more to make the deal with JT happen.

He threw the phony fifties into the truck, as he did not want to get caught passing them to someone else and suffer a similar, or worse, fate than Reggie. Then he went to join Arnez for lunch.

CHAPTER 16

It was time for Michael to start collecting the money.

He had completed the first semester of his second year at Wentworth and was home for the winter break, and what better place to ask for donations than from his neighbors who'd watched him grow up? He stepped outside the house he'd grown up in and walked directly across the street to see Old Lady Mim.

For as long as Michael could remember anything, Mim had been old. Even though he had aged nearly two decades in that time, which meant Mim had aged that many years as well, to him she'd always been an old woman.

He didn't expect to get a large donation from her; her husband had died during World War II, shortly after they were married, and she had been on a fixed income since then. But Michael was confident he would receive at least a token contribution from her, and this encouraged him to try her first.

As he approached Mim's house, he took note of a newspaper on the ground and retrieved it. He carried it up the three cement steps and pressed the doorbell with a chilled finger.

He knew he would only have to press it once, but it would take her several minutes to answer the door. He also knew she would be home; she did not own a car, and she was always home.

He stared into the oak door, unable to see through the glass pane unless he stood on his toes. Its purpose was to let in light rather than to provide a view for visitors.

Finally, he heard some rustling behind the door. He looked up and saw a head full of hair rollers bouncing behind the glass pane.

The door opened and there she stood, smiling, in her bathrobe and high heels at four o'clock on a Saturday afternoon. "Hi, Michael!" she said with the enthusiasm of an inmate receiving a visitor. "Come in. Come in."

"I'm sorry, I don't have a lot of time," he said, stepping into the foyer.

But she had already turned and walked through her living room and into her kitchen, leaving him standing alone with a wide-open door.

"You're letting out my heat!" she squawked from a place beyond view.

Michael closed the door, leaving himself trapped inside the musty smell of a house whose occupant hardly ever went outside. He placed the newspaper on a table next to her purse and walked into the kitchen. Mim was pouring boiling water into a single ceramic mug.

"Thank you for bringing in my paper," she said with her usual slur. She always wore a perfume of hard liquor, and today was no exception. Michael had always suspected it was scotch, though he'd never witnessed a bottle or the glass she drank from.

She stirred in a packet of powdered hot chocolate and handed him the mug.

"You know I'm always glad to help out," he said, taking the mug and submitting to a longer visit than he had intended. He recalled the many times he and Daniel had shoveled the snow off her walk, cut her lawn, or put out her trash, always without expecting compensation.

"Sit down and tell me how college life is," she said.

"It's been easier than I expected," he replied. "As long as you study enough hours, you can get good grades." He remained standing.

"I'm sure your girlfriend takes up a lot of your time."

"You know about her?"

"I see everything from my window," she said. "You've been dating her now for about a year?"

"A year and a half."

"Well, you'd best concentrate on your studies. Those college women will mess with your *head*." She emphasized the last word with a thicker slur.

"Julie's not like that, she's different."

"They're all different, Michael. That's what makes them all the same." The slur disappeared momentarily but then returned. "How's the cocoa?"

"It's good," he lied. "Aren't you having any?"

"I have a glass around here somewhere," she answered, half pretending to look. She exited the kitchen and moved into the living room.

"Then you must have seen me running a lot."

He let his words chase her into the next room, and then he followed.

Her living room was filled with antique furniture that must have been newly made when she'd bought it decades earlier. She was sitting in a wingback leather chair in front of a bay window but not looking out. The armrests revealed the wear that the other seats lacked.

"I've seen you running in the morning, the afternoon, even at night." She nodded at him. "In fact, I've missed you while you've been away at school. I used to time you. You were either getting slower or running farther."

Michael sipped the cocoa and prepared his sales pitch. "I've been running farther. I'm training for the Boston Marathon."

"My goodness! Isn't that far?"

"It's twenty-six miles." Michael was always surprised by how many people didn't know how far a marathon was. And the Boston Marathon, at over one hundred years old, was the oldest in the country. Surely Mim had been around for most, if not all, of them.

"That sounds far."

Michael pondered the fact that Mim probably had never traveled twenty-six miles from this house. He looked at the mantel and noticed the picture of her husband was missing although the American flag was still there, folded in a tight triangle in a glass case. His eyes wandered and he spotted the photo on the radiator cover. It was a black-and-white photograph of a twenty-something man in military uniform. A pair of stolid eyes peered out beneath the brim of the cap but not directly into the camera's lens. Anyone who didn't know Mim might have assumed it was her grandson. But it was her husband, forever trapped in his youth, while Mim showed the dreadful effects of aging.

For the first time, Michael felt he had something in common with Mim. They both owned no more than a photograph of the person who had loved them most. Special memories for both of them had long since faded away, diluted over time by new faces and new experiences. He thought of his own repeating dream of his mother and wondered what ghosts haunted Mim. He decided to sit down.

"It's very far," he agreed. "My longest run so far has been twelve miles. The marathon will be a big challenge for me."

"Are you going to win?" she asked with a smile.

"Truthfully, I can't even qualify to enter. The qualifying times are much too fast. My goal will be just to finish." He sipped from his mug.

"Then how will you enter?"

"The sponsors of the race provide racing numbers to over twenty different charities. The charities distribute them to potential runners who will raise money for the charity. Everybody wins because the charities raise a lot of money and runners like me get an opportunity to participate."

Mim got the hint immediately; she rose and, clopping across the hardwood floors in her high heels, fetched her purse. When she sat down, she asked Michael who he was representing.

"I have to raise fifteen hundred dollars for the American Cancer Society." He paused, then added with purpose, "But I'd like to raise a lot more for them."

Mim slowly turned and looked solemnly out the window in a learned repose, seemingly staring at something that was no longer there. A full minute of silence elapsed before, without taking her eyes off the imaginary spot beyond the window, she said, "I remember her."

Michael sat perfectly still, allowing the hot mug to warm his hands and allowing Mim to finish her thought.

"I remember her like it was yesterday," she continued. "Your mother was a wonderful woman." She had seemingly been prompted into this recollection by Michael's mention of the cancer society.

Michael sat frozen in the chair. He had an opportunity here to be refreshed of some memory of his mother and so he wanted Mim to continue. But she was staring longingly out the window, distracted.

"What are you looking at?" he asked.

"Her garden, across the street." She raised a crystal glass to her lips and took a sip of a golden liquid without showing a trace of a grimace. It was only at that moment that Michael realized she had been holding a glass at all. "Your mother spent so much of her time in that flower garden. It was a glorious display."

Michael peered out the window between the venetian blinds and saw a gnarly patch of land overgrown with tall weeds, flourishing from neglect. Mim looked out the same window and saw his mother in a garden of rainbows. He prodded her in controlled tones to hide his jealousy.

"You watched her?"

Mim hesitated before answering, as if she'd been caught looking in someone else's window. Then, as if realizing what Michael was searching for, she continued.

"She would come out of the garage in her shorts and with a baseball cap pulled down over her face, her hair always pulled back into a ponytail. She carried a small garden tool in one hand and an empty basket in the other. She would kneel in the garden and start pulling the weeds."

Mim paused and drank from her glass. She wasn't waiting or thinking. She was watching. She was watching Michael's mother with a glaze over her eyes, and he was sure even she didn't know if she was in the present or the past.

"But after a while," she said, "she couldn't keep up. They were growing faster than she could pull them. If she cleared one part of the garden, another would worsen. She used to bring me the tulips because she knew how much I loved them, but soon they stopped. The garden began to fail."

Michael's eyes darted back and forth from Mim to the garden, desperately trying to see what she saw. But all he saw was an old woman and a tangled garden, both suffering the ill effects of time and neglect.

"Do you see me there?" he asked her.

She looked in Michael's direction and for a moment it was unclear if she recognized him. She wasn't wearing her glasses, but he suspected she was drunk enough that a blur would have persisted regardless. She saw Michael, but the lines of his young face must have blended into the photograph she seemingly moved around the room from time to time, perhaps giving her the impression her husband was still living in the house.

Michael imagined her talking to the photograph, and after several glasses of alcohol the picture would likely talk back. Her husband would probably try to justify why he had to go overseas and protect this country and defend its freedom. They would talk deep into the night—Mim trapped inside her house and her husband trapped within the picture frame while everyone else enjoyed the freedom he spoke of. Michael saw it all vividly: Mim placing the photograph down on the floor and watching her husband maneuver through the minefield, then crying herself to sleep in the chair, only to wake in the morning in front of the toppled frame.

She tried to stand but failed and fell back into the chair. Michael almost stood to help her but relaxed when she raised her glass again.

"I must have been old enough to help her in the garden, but I don't remember," he said.

"She wouldn't let anyone help her in the garden."

"Why not?"

She paused and her eyes refocused on Michael. Then a realization seized her face. "You don't know, do you?"

"Know what?"

She faced the window again. "Sometimes I could hear her," she whispered.

Michael found it difficult to remain patient. He shifted stealthily on his seat and stared at Mim, sipping his cocoa whenever she sipped from her glass.

"The garden was where your mother used to go to be alone. It's where she cried."

Michael was stunned. He remained motionless, hoping Mim would continue and yet at the same time hoping she would not.

"She would fill the basket with weeds she pulled from the ground, but she couldn't stop them from returning and overrunning the garden. I used to think it was her tears that were watering them and allowing them to thrive."

"She spent a lot of time there?"

"About as much time as you spend running."

"I never, ever saw her cry."

"Of course not. She wouldn't want you to see her cry. She would want you to remember her smile. She had a smile so gorgeous that it compelled you to smile back. Surely you can remember that?"

But he could not, and that thought disturbed him more than imagining his mother sobbing in the garden. He still could remember nothing about her. The dream of her continued to haunt him, but all real memories of her always eluded him, and he felt cheated that Mim could have memories of her when he did not.

"Sometimes I think everybody waters their own weeds in one way or another," she added, staring into her glass; then she drained it with a shrug. "I guess time just ran out on her. So when is your race?"

"It's in the middle of April, just four months away."

"I'd like to help." She dug into her purse and removed two crisp, uncirculated bills. "I hope this will be enough."

This was what he'd come for, but Michael was suddenly disinterested in the money. Without bothering to check the amount, he stood, took the bills, and thanked her appropriately.

Mim also rose and walked him to the door, but she let him open it, which he did rather quickly.

As he was about to exit, she thanked him.

"Why are you thanking me?" he asked with surprise.

"For taking care of me all these years. The snow, the grass, the leaves. Your father did a great job of raising you kids."

Michael bowed his head humbly. "Thank you for your support."

And with that, visiting hours were over for this prisoner. He closed the door behind him and stood silently on Mim's stoop. He held his breath and stared across the street at the garden, or what was left of it. He tried to picture his mother working in it, but the stubborn image before him would not change.

Frustrated, he concentrated on finding an image within his memories of his mother smiling, but the closest he could get was the image in his dream: his mother sitting at the kitchen table with a piece of paper in her hair, waiting patiently for her son to grasp it. He promised himself that when he was done canvassing the neighborhood for donations, he would run fourteen miles. He would break his previous distance best and find a deeper sleep tonight in hopes of completing the dream.

He finally looked down at Mim's contribution, wondering how much more he needed to collect. He was startled to see two one hundred–dollar bills in his fingers.

He walked down to the sidewalk and turned back to look into her window. The blue sky, peppered with white clouds, reflected back at him. He knew she was there, sitting in the chair again, watching. He waved with the money still in his hand as a final gesture of thanks and then continued down the street to solicit the other neighbors.

CHAPTER 17

"Will you run a bath for me when I get back?"

"If you finish all twenty miles, I'll *give* you a bath."

Julie's response was representative of the sexuality that had begun to consume Michael. He was amid some form of sexual peak, and Julie's presence was like a flame, heating and exciting every hormone within his body right down to its atomic level. But as much as it was a physical effect, it was also an emotional one.

His love for her had saturated more than just his heart; it had also become entwined within his mind, coiling among his thoughts and memories. He was constantly thinking about her, and he possessed an insatiable need to always be with her.

But while she consumed him mentally and emotionally, his quest to successfully complete a marathon continued to consume him physically. He had acquired an obsession with logging miles and diligently maintained his weekly mileage schedule.

When he had started collecting money for his marathon entry he'd been running only twenty-five miles per week. Since then, he'd methodically increased his mileage to fifty miles per week. Each Saturday was reserved for his longest run of the week, and with one month remaining before the race, today he would peak at twenty miles. Wednesday was reserved for a mid-long run, which had peaked at twelve miles, and the rest of the week was filled with runs of five, six, or even eight miles.

As he spent long, lonely hours striding through the Boston streets, fighting off the blustery New England winter, he was always comforted by the knowledge that Julie was waiting for him at her apartment. When he was done, she would peel off his sweat-soaked clothes and wrap him in a large towel until he cooled down. Then, after a hot shower, they would crawl into her warm bed, where her massages would escalate into something more intimate. The emotional soothing associated with their relationship always erased the physical pain associated with his running.

"I can't believe I'm actually going to run twenty miles today."

"I remember when you couldn't even run six miles," Julie said. "Next month you'll have to run twenty miles as a warm-up to the six that you'll have left."

He tilted his head. "Do you think I'll be able to do it?"

She moved behind him and started massaging his shoulders, squeezing firmly at the crook of his neck. "That's the plan."

He closed his eyes and rocked his head to the rhythm of her hand movements. He was getting closer and closer to completing his goal, and his body was becoming stronger and more resilient with every workout. He was starting to feel invincible—which was, after all, exactly what he was pursuing. He would succeed where his mother had failed and where his father and Bailey were failing. He would not allow his body to be invaded and overcome by any alien presence, and he would continue to watch over his brother and protect him as well.

But it wasn't easy. With his eyelids drawn down across his pupils like blankets covering a pair of sleeping babies, he looked back in his mind to when he'd first escalated his training miles and his body had begun to change its shape. He looked further back, to the day when he'd dived across the finish line of a race that was only two miles long. And then he peered even deeper into his past, seeing himself as a small boy collapsing into the street after only a short sprint down the block. These visions were getting farther and farther away in his mind, almost as if he were running away from them. When he looked back, he felt like he was staring down into an abyss that held all his memories, and somewhere at the bottom, if there was a bottom, lay the memories of his mother. Suddenly, he wasn't looking down into the chasm but was *looking up into his mother's hair. He saw the piece of paper, still folded and embraced by her curls. His hands felt heavy but he tried to lift them anyway. For the first time, he was able to move closer to the note. He stood up on his toes with an extended arm and was just about to snatch the paper when something pulled back on his arm—*

"You were snoring," Julie said.

"I . . . I must have dozed off."

He started rubbing his temples with slow circles, keeping pace with Julie's hands as they burrowed into his shoulders.

The miles were accumulating, as if against him, and he was becoming overwhelmed by the mental and physical toll they were taking on him, even as his relationship with Julie continuously challenged his emotions and vied for his concentration. Meanwhile, his father's gait had become noticeably slower and Bailey had been reduced to slow, unsteady walks after being carried down the steps. Even Daniel's displays of ingratitude had become less inhibited. All this had caused his concentration to begin to wane, which was affecting his attention in class and ability to concentrate on his studying. Every aspect of his life was growing and amassing against him.

He rubbed his eyes, jamming the meat of his palms into his sagging sockets as if trying to push all the pressure from his head.

"I'm fine," he said with a sigh. "I just need to get through this."

He needed to get through the winter training, through the marathon, through his finals, through his second year of school. Once it was all over, he could rest. Warm summer breezes would take over the sky and he would have conquered one of the most devastating enemies he would ever have to concern himself with.

Just one more month was all he needed.

The sky was clear except for two large white clouds that sailed high above the planet. Michael stared at them as he lay on the ground, going through his stretching routine. Only by watching them carefully could he notice their shapes changing, slowly and subtly, as they floated across the sky the way great sailing ships used to traverse the vast oceans. One cloud was moving faster than the other and they seemed inevitably on a collision course.

He unzipped his equipment bag and continued going through his usual routine in preparation for his run. Starting with his log, he penciled the number 20 in a square that was four weeks before the number 26. He pondered both of those numbers, realizing how far he had come and how far he still had to go.

He stood and continued his exercises. He twisted his torso left and right, causing the buildings around him to rotate back and forth across his field of vision.

He hated this neighborhood. There was always a group of teenagers standing at the corner wearing beepers and cell phones like jewelry; residents walked with an uneasy pace; frequent, short-term visitors left their cars double-parked everywhere; and there were the occasional broken windows and stolen cars that reminded everyone it was important to make friends here.

But Julie had her reasons for living here and seemed unaffected by the same things that made Michael uncomfortable. Her demeanor exuded a unique confidence, as if she were protected in some unique way or simply untouchable.

He heard the speeding expressway traffic from several blocks away, but it was the noise of the slow-moving tires in front of him that caught his attention. The brakes squeaked as the car came to a cautious stop behind a car that was already double-parked. A strange choice, Michael thought, since there was an available parking space in front of the unattended car on the street. But when he leveled his eyes, he noticed this new car was different from the others on the block. This was a police car.

There were two uniformed occupants. The driver did not take his eyes off the car in front of him until he looked to his left and saw Michael on the sidewalk. Then he stepped out of the car with purpose. When the door opened, Michael heard the radio crackle, but it was silenced when the officer closed the car door behind him.

He was tall, middle-aged, with a look of experience occupying his clean-shaven face. He carried a small notebook in his left hand. His holster was on his right hip, a gun handle protruding out of its leather cradle. The number 61770 on his badge was the only indication of his identity.

"Is this your car that's improperly parked?" he asked Michael with a slight nod toward the black sports car with the American nameplate.

"No, sir." Michael spied the object in the officer's hand and realized it was likely a binder of unused traffic tickets. "I'm sure he'll be out in just a few minutes," he added.

"Do you know whose car it is?"

If he could prevent the officer from ticketing the vehicle, the good gesture might aid in protecting him in this neighborhood. And he'd rather have friends here than the alternative. "A friend of mine," he answered.

The officer turned to look at the car, and then he looked back at Michael with a hint of skepticism. "You'll have to move it off the street," he directed.

"I'm sure he'll be right out."

"Are you sure it belongs to a friend of yours?"

"Yes, sir." Michael had no idea who the car belonged to, but it was a casual exchange and an innocent lie. If he could stall long enough or convince the officer to be lenient, the car's owner would have to be grateful, and the only gratitude he required was for him and Julie to be left alone.

The officer studied Michael from his feet up to his eyes. Michael knew what he saw: a college boy dressed for a workout—a stark contrast to the group of kids on the corner that had dispersed when the officer stepped out of the car.

"Do you live here?" the officer asked.

"No, my girlfriend does. She works at the university hospital down the street." There was no need to mention she also attended Boston University across town.

"I drove by here fifteen minutes ago and that car was here. It needs to be moved or we'll have to tag and tow it." There was still some suspicion in the officer's tone.

"I don't think the keys are in it."

"Why don't you check."

Michael could not tell if the officer was testing him or if he merely wanted the car moved off the street. But he could take this a little further to save someone a fifty-dollar ticket and the cost and hassle of a tow. All he had to do was pretend to check for the keys and deny they were in the car. Then he could pretend to go inside and retrieve his "friend." The officer could then decide to issue the citation and call for a tow or leave.

Politely obliging the officer, Michael approached the driver's side door from behind the car. The officer kept pace on the passenger side and they both reached the front seat simultaneously. The driver's side window was rolled down and Michael poked his head into the car to see if the keys were in the ignition. There was an unpleasant smell in the car, but he did not keep his head in long enough to care. Although he could not see the keyhole from his angle, he saw no key chains dangling by the steering column. He withdrew his head and looked over the roof of the car to the officer.

"They're not there," he said.

The officer had also bent over to look into the passenger side, and as a result, Michael could only see his arm resting on the roof for balance and his hunched back as he took an extended look into the car. His shifting body position telegraphed that he was taking inventory of both the front and the back seats.

Standard procedure, Michael thought, or maybe he was looking for something specific.

Satisfied with his inspection, the officer stood and looked at Michael across the roof of the car. "There is a key in the ignition, son. I'll thank you to just move the car up into that space right there."

Michael fought back a yawn by biting his own teeth. He was exhausted and this officer's suspicions were starting to annoy him, even though they were warranted. All he had to do was get in the car, start it, move it up ten feet into the parking space by the curb, then exit and start his run. When he returned three hours later, the police and the car would be gone and he would have done his good deed for the day.

"No problem," he said, as he pulled open the door and slid easily behind the steering wheel. The officer thanked him and returned to his patrol car.

He felt for the key in the ignition and found it right where the officer said it was. There were no chains or rings, just the lone key. He twisted it forward and the engine came awake with a wroth grumble, then settled into a purring idle. He checked the rearview mirror and watched the patrol car pull away from behind him, then slowly pull up beside him. He looked across the passenger seat at the officer but the look was not returned. Once clear of Michael, the officer accelerated to the corner and was gone.

He put the car in gear and stealthily moved it up to the curb. He noticed the gang on the corner had returned and they were watching him carefully. One was talking into a cell phone.

The car was now perfectly aligned against the curb and Michael turned back the key, removed it out of habit, and then pushed it back into the ignition hole the way he had found it. The smell inside the car was stale and unpleasant, but it was familiar. It didn't seem like there was anything in the car that smelled but more as if the car itself had absorbed the pungent odor of something unpalatable over a lengthened period. He hesitated from exiting the car as he tried to identify the smell.

The odor seemed to be a mixture of smells the way chicken soup is a mixture of many ingredients that combine to form the unmistakable smell of chicken soup. However, this odor wasn't as pleasant. It was the combination of every foul smell there could be. It was the smell that would exist if you put everything you didn't want into a single place. It was the smell of garbage and trash.

He wondered for a moment what would cause the car to smell like this, considering there was no trash in the car. Then he lost interest and reached for the door handle.

He pushed the door open about three inches and felt resistance. Then it was pushed closed by an unseen force, trapping him in the car. When he turned his head to see who was there, his cheek bumped into a hard metal object that was pushing back against his face. He was unable to turn his head any farther. Then he heard a deep, rolling voice that made his eardrums quiver rather than vibrate.

"Problem?" said the voice.

"I hope not," Michael responded, succumbing to the realization he had a gun against his cheek.

The voice leaned up against Michael's ear, concealing the gun from anyone who might be watching. "You're trespassing."

Michael slowly raised both hands and gripped the steering wheel so they would be visible. After that movement, fear shut his body down, satisfied it was as close to the fetal position as it was likely to get. He squeezed the wheel tighter, which relaxed the rest of his body and allowed him to speak in a calm voice.

"This isn't what you think it is."

"You know what I'm thinking?"

"If you just let me out, I'll explain." Michael actually felt safer in the car—he suspected the voice wouldn't want to mess up the interior with his blood and brain matter—but he was getting claustrophobic in the tight space and raunchy smell. He needed to escape and breathe in some fresh air. And the window was no longer a source of clean air, as it was blocked by the massive torso belonging to the voice.

The smell of garbage radiating from the torso confirmed its ownership of the car like matched signatures.

The gun pushed deeper into the fleshy part of Michael's cheek, making it difficult for him to speak again. Ironically, he wanted the police to return, whereas a few moments earlier he'd wanted them to leave. He knew they would return in a few minutes to be sure the car had been moved off the street, so all he had to do was stall until then. But the seconds stubbornly did not advance.

He waited for the deep voice to speak again, but it was a different voice he heard next. It was a familiar and friendly voice.

"Hi, Tremont," Julie said as she approached the car.

The gun pulled away from Michael's face and the body pulled away from the open window, allowing in a gust of pure air. "Hey, Julie," Tremont answered politely.

"Is that Michael in your car?"

"It must be."

Michael reached for the door handle and turned his head, now free of the obstruction. He was about to call out and warn Julie about the gun, but he saw the man's hands were now empty. His eyes followed the arms upward in search of a face, but the man—Tremont—was too tall. He would have to leave the car to put a face on this new threat.

He exited the car and closed the door gently yet securely. Michael looked up at Tremont's face and saw a smile on a young man about his own age that belied the unfriendliness just expressed. The smile was for the benefit of Julie, though Michael saw through it. He saw in Tremont the embodiment of everything that was this neighborhood.

He was imposing, intense, and threatening—representative of everything that was foul, right down to his scent. But what shocked Michael most was that he was a friend of Julie's.

"You two know each other?" he asked Julie.

"Yes, Tremont lives in that apartment right there. What were you doing in his car?"

It was Tremont who answered, with false friendliness toward Michael, "He saved me a parking ticket. The police were just here, and I wasn't."

Michael was dismayed that Tremont had seen the whole episode yet had still felt obliged to threaten Michael for being in his vehicle. Suddenly, it occurred to Michael that a parking ticket might not be all he'd saved him from. It was now clear the officer had been interested in the *owner* of this car, not the negligent parking.

Michael, Julie, and Tremont stood together on the sidewalk next to the parked car. Michael took in the sight of the young man who'd threatened to expel a bullet into his face minutes earlier. He was about four inches taller than Michael, and his body was thicker and more defined. Tremont seemed constructed for short, powerful bursts of energy, while Michael's thin, lithe body was tooled for long, enduring tasks.

Michael clarified for Julie, "The car was parked in the street and I moved it."

"That was nice," she said.

"Yeah, thanks," said Tremont. "I owe you one."

As Tremont turned and started walking to the group on the corner, Michael wondered what it was, exactly, that Tremont owed him.

"I'm glad you came when you did," he said to Julie.

"Why?"

"He was pissed I was in his car. He put a gun in my face."

"He what?"

"Yeah. A gun."

"You saw it?"

"No, but I felt it."

"You must be mistaken; I know Tremont. He lives here with his grandmother and he's always been nice to me."

"You're kidding me. Look at him. I bet he's just another crackhead."

"No, he isn't," Julie insisted. "He has a job."

"Does he have a shower?" Michael retorted in frustration.

"Look, I just came outside to see you off. If you have a problem with Tremont, then stay out of his car and stay away from him. I'm going back inside to study. I have finals too, you know. Or hadn't you noticed?"

Julie turned and started walking away. She stopped at the gym bag that was still lying on the ground. "Are you done with this?" she huffed.

"Yes."

She picked it up and carried it inside.

Michael shadowed her to the door but did not follow her inside. He put his palms to his eyes again and began to rub. He just needed to get through this next month.

He started stretching again, keeping a watchful eye on the group on the corner as they waddled around Tremont. For a brief moment, Michael had wandered into a world he had always thought could be avoided. He knew this neighborhood was on the fringe of the darkest parts of the city, but he'd always believed the land mines were plainly visible. Today he'd learned that some were well concealed.

It was strange that Julie was blind to her environment; she was usually attentive and observant. It struck Michael as odd that she trusted Tremont. At some point he must have befriended her; perhaps Tremont saw in Julie the same caring and good nature that Michael was privy to. Thankfully, it would not be long before Julie graduated and could take her leave of this place.

Tremont started back toward Michael but stopped at his car, paused as their eyes connected, and then got in.

Michael approached the car.

He leaned toward the window, close enough to Tremont that he could smell the foulness again. "Was the gun necessary?"

"I'm just protecting what's mine," Tremont answered, looking startled to see Michael so close to him. "Just like you would."

"Just like I would," Michael concurred in his most protective voice.

CHAPTER 18

Michael was surrounded by at least thirty thousand other runners who shared his goal of running the distance from Hopkinton to Boston. Along the sides of the twenty-six-mile course were an additional five hundred thousand spectators and countless volunteers helping manage the production of the race—manning water stations, staffing first aid centers, controlling crowds, and officiating.

Yet Michael had never felt so alone.

He was alone with his inner thoughts and anxieties of whether he could or would finish this distance. He had properly prepared, from the moment he'd set the goal two years earlier to last evening's meal of carbohydrate-loaded pasta. Even so, ahead of him lay an unknown conclusion that would not be settled for another four hours.

His father, brother, and Julie would wait for him in a family gathering area on Boston Common, where he expected their congratulations on his achievement when he finished.

The race had started four minutes ago but Michael hadn't moved. He stood motionless in a sea of runners, waiting for the pack to thin to the point when he could start to walk, then cross the starting line, then begin to run. He didn't care that better runners were at the front, already approaching the conclusion of their first mile even though he hadn't yet started. He didn't care if he came in first or thirty thousandth; he only cared that he came in.

With no one moving, it was as if time itself stood still. Everyone bumped elbows trying to force themselves forward, but each runner was like a grain of sand waiting its turn to slip through the center of an hourglass. And Michael was a grain near the top, immobile while the grains below him squeezed through. He was briefly reminded of the feeling he had in his dream—urgently coveting the paper in his mother's hair but unable to move. He knew this obstruction would eventually dissipate, however, and he waited patiently.

Suddenly, there was movement. Michael was walking. The excitement began to build as each individual in the pack was somehow linked with every other to form a unique kinetic energy, the way raindrops somehow collect and form into raging rivers. And like a river, they all started to flow in a singular direction, picking up pace with every step.

"Here we go!" someone yelled from deep within the pack.

Michael looked down and saw the thick painted starting line pass beneath him and a chill overcame his body. With enough space to begin running, he took his first stride and vowed not to stop until he crossed a similarly painted line that read "Finish."

The beginning of the race was a downhill grade that fell three hundred feet over three and a half miles. It was a pleasant introduction that belied the difficulties to come. Upon reaching the center of the town of Ashland, the spectators thickened and Michael ran along the edge of the street to take in their cheers of encouragement.

He was wearing a thin sweatshirt that he now removed and discarded to the side of the course. The air's slight chill nipped at his unprotected arms at first, but the heat his body generated quickly pushed it away. The weather forecast was for rain and possible thunderstorms in the late afternoon, and

Michael quickened his pace to come in ahead of the storm. He turned his neck all the way around and caught sight of some ominous clouds coming in from the west that seemed to be chasing him from above.

As he turned his head back around to face the east, he took an awkward stride and accidentally stepped on the heel of the runner ahead of him, causing her to step out of her shoe. A bottleneck ensued as she retrieved her footwear and limped onto the sidewalk among the crowd to replace it. Michael heard some unpleasantries exchanged but blocked them out of his mind, pushing continuously forward and taking satisfaction that he had double-knotted his own shoes.

There were water stations every two miles and Michael forced himself to drink whether or not he felt the need. His running book had warned him that if he started to get thirsty, that meant he was already dehydrated and it could be too late to replenish what his body had already lost. Running through the row of outstretched arms, he would snatch a paper cup, purposely spill out half the water so it would not splash in his face when he raised it to his lips, take manageable gulps, and drop the cup to his feet, where it was immediately crushed under the trampling shoes of the endless herd.

The six-mile mark brought him into the heart of Framingham. He was feeling comfortable with his pace. He checked the digital clocks stationed throughout the course and tried to calculate his pace, but the clock had started long before Michael had, and he found the delay confusing to his calculations.

Resolving that his finishing time was completely unimportant, he put his eyes to the pavement and just continued to run. He didn't want to run too quickly quite yet, since he had no idea what to expect in the last six miles, but he still felt compelled to keep ahead of the storm. He did not want to be running in a downpour with soaked clothes and spongy shoes.

The fanfare along the course was intoxicating and motivating. It was Patriots' Day in Massachusetts; not all businesses took this Monday as a holiday, but most employees near the course sneaked out of their offices to watch, and turnout was high. They formed an endless line on both sides of the street, arms outstretched to offer an orange slice, a cup of water, or a paper towel. Empty hands trolled to be slapped in the tradition of sports camaraderie. Banners stretched across the road or hung from streetlights and telephone poles. Helicopters, ahead in the distance, hovered above the lead runners to provide live television coverage. Stereo speakers hung out of windows and blared motivational music.

It was the most exhilarating moment of Michael's life; he was pushed along by the collective emotion of the event the way a floating leaf is dragged along in the currents of a flourishing stream.

As he passed the ten-mile mark and ran into Natick Center, he thought he felt a raindrop.

"Let's go, we can't be late."

"The race isn't even an hour in, Dad. We have plenty of time."

"It's important he doesn't get there before we do, and I have no idea when he'll get there."

Jack and Daniel had watched the beginning of the race on television, knowing Michael would finish long after the winners and they would have ample time to get to Boston Common to meet him there. Seeing the prerace shows and parts of the race allowed them a better sense of everything Michael was experiencing. A camera truck transmitted an endless image of the lead pack spliced in with aerial shots of the river of runners flowing through the suburban streets toward downtown Boston. These visuals—thousands of heads bobbling like moonlight glittering on turbulent waters—were the most striking to Jack.

Daniel stroked Bailey's hindquarters. "Where do you think he is now?"

Jack stared at the screen, hypnotized by the televised images, contemplating how someone could be so alone among all those people. "I don't know, Daniel. He's out there. He's somewhere out there and trying his best to come in."

"Why didn't we meet him out on the course? I'm sure he would've liked to have seen us out there supporting him."

"He would have felt obligated to stop and spend a few minutes with us and he said he didn't want to stop for anything until it was over."

Daniel looked at his watch. "I figure he must be almost halfway by now. You're right, we should go."

Jack turned off the television and watched it fade to blackness. The runners' images had a ghostly effect just before disappearing.

The silence was broken by the ringing telephone.

Wellesley Center was a narrow street with expensive suburban boutiques on both sides. It was also the marathon's halfway point.

Michael started passing some runners who had begun to walk. Blisters, cramps, exhaustion, or simple lack of preparation had begun to weed out the weaker ones in the horde.

There was nothing Michael could do for them and this reinforced his sense of loneliness, so he just kept his eyes on the pavement ten yards ahead of him and pushed past them, moving forever forward.

The air was a fine mist that had come in ahead of the clouds. There was an occasional drizzle of rain that lasted no more than a few minutes at a time. His body and clothes were wet from sweating and the mist felt cool against his skin. A quiet rumble of thunder from behind warned him that it would not last.

He had been running for almost two hours—the average length of a feature film, the length of two of his classes, the time it would take to fly halfway across the country, or the length of most of his long training runs. But today he still had two additional hours to run. His breathing was rhythmic and unfettered and his heartbeat was steady and strong, but his body was beginning to feel the ill effects of the steady pounding of his feet—right, left, right, left, right, left, over and over again for the past two hours. His weight was repetitively transferred from one leg to the next. Each plant of his foot absorbed the load as his foot transferred it to his ankle, which transferred it to his calf, which transferred it to his knee, which transferred it to his quadricep, which transferred it to his hip. Then the other leg, then back again. Right, left, right, left, right.

He tried to refocus his concentration away from the pain by absorbing the sights and sounds of the event, but the pain continued to nag at him like a barking dog.

He unwrapped a nutrition bar from his pocket and let the wrapper fall to the ground. The runner next to him watched Michael and approved of the idea.

"Hey, let's do lunch!" he said to Michael while holding up his own bar.

Michael offered a friendly smile and picked up his pace. Suddenly, he wanted to be alone. He wanted to escape from this torrent of people and stop the pain and the pounding and the sweating and the bouncing and the bumping. He wanted to just stop running. But he could not stop; he had to keep running and finish the race and prove to himself that he was invulnerable.

At mile seventeen, he turned the corner of Washington Street onto Commonwealth Avenue and was stunned by the awesome sight before him. A long, bending incline rose up and out of sight, swelled with runners that struggled to conquer its peak. From his viewpoint at the bottom, they all seemed to be running toward the heavens, to a promised land of redemption. This was the first of the four Newton hills, which oscillated for the next four miles, and it was the first true test of what Michael hoped to accomplish.

He took his first steps on the incline and felt the dreadful effects of gravity trying to push him away. His motivation reborn, he attacked this mountain with a war cry.

As the sky opened to receive him, it released a heavy downpour, as if overburdened with the tears of all the runners ahead of him.

"Who was it?" Daniel asked.

"It was Julie."

Daniel waited for more information but had to prompt his father, who now seemed to be thinking about something in a far-off place.

"What did she want?"

"She doesn't need us to pick her up. She got delayed on campus and will meet us at the finish."

A unique silence engaged the two of them as they pondered what would keep Julie from joining them on Michael's most important day.

Daniel broke the silence. "We'd better get moving."

Upon opening the door, he felt a harsh wind slap his face, accompanied by a brittle rain.

"What an ugly day to run a marathon," he said.

All Michael could see was his feet—first the left one, then the right—taking turns in his minute field of vision. His head was too heavy to lift, so he stared down at the pavement and confirmed that his feet continued to move.

The cold rain was relentless, soaking into everything he wore. His shirt felt like a lead blanket a dentist would drape across a patient. His shoes were like sponges, squishing the water with every step. His cap protected his head, but the water streamed down his face and into his mouth, commingling with his runny nose and creating an unsavory taste. There was nothing dry available to wipe his face with and he searched the spectators for someone offering a dry towel but saw only an endless guardrail of umbrellas, keeping him in line.

He had reached the last major incline, which was the beginning of a 140-foot rise locally known as Heartbreak Hill. This was where the crowd was at its thickest, exposing an inner sadistic mentality, a desire to watch the agony on the faces of the runners as they fought with their bodies and their minds to overcome gravity.

Michael's head drooped down onto his chest; his stride had diminished to a shuffle. His arms continued to pump hard, as if he were running through a swampy muck. The physical exertion was unbearable and his mind was in a lonely zone where mere existence was a satisfactory state. Like a shark that required water to pass through its gills to survive, he had to keep moving; as long as he continued to move, he would continue to exist.

Everything told him to stop running—the pain, the hill, the distance, the weather. Yet he could not bring himself to cease the motion that had brought him this far. He lifted his head and saw the top of the hill ahead of him. That would be the twenty-one-mile mark. From there it would be five miles downhill to the finish line.

If only he could get to the top.

Boston Common was a joyous throng of runners who had completed the race ahead of Michael. Jack and Daniel wandered through the crowd looking for their predetermined meeting place. It was too early for Michael to have arrived, but it was important not to be late. The actual finish line was almost a mile away and occupied with dignitaries, media, and race officials, resulting in no opportunities for friends and families to watch the actual finish.

They passed a medical tent filled with professionals tending to cot-filled casualties. Intravenous solutions dripped into pale, sweaty arms, blood pressures were taken, blisters were treated, and massages were administered.

Daniel couldn't help but comment, "If these are the people who came in ahead of Michael, I can't imagine what he must be going through."

"This is where we wait," Jack said apprehensively.

"For Michael, or Julie?"

"Both."

"Who do you think will get here first?"

"I don't know. What's important is that they both get here."

Daniel narrowed his eyes with disdain. "Do you think she'll show at all?"

"Knowing Julie, she'll show."

"That's odd," Daniel said. "I would have said the opposite."

"What do you mean?"

"I would have said that knowing Julie, she won't show."

Suddenly, a rumble of thunder reconfirmed the rain, which began to fall from the sky with a heavier weight. Daniel huddled with his father under their single umbrella and wondered whether either Julie or Michael would show.

It seemed to Michael as if he had been running forever. He continued to lean into the hill and stare down at the ground, watching his feet take step after step after step. The pavement moved beneath him like a treadmill and at times it seemed like he was running continuously in the same spot.

The rain pelted his head, shoulders, and back like hundreds of bullies poking him with their fingers, telling him he didn't belong. He was sopping wet and felt he had gained twenty pounds. But he would not be discouraged. He would not stop, he would not rest, and he would not walk. He would only continue to run up Heartbreak Hill.

Suddenly, he felt like he was losing weight. He felt like a hot air balloon dropping ballast and rising more easily into the sky. His stride took more of the hill with every step and his back began to straighten. His head came up to see what could be causing this welcome relief.

He had reached the crest of the hill and the road had begun to level off. And just beyond the crest he could see the road beginning to fall away. He could have just as easily been summiting Mount Everest in the Himalayas instead of Heartbreak Hill in Massachusetts.

The top of the hill was teeming with students from Boston College, whose campus lay just beyond the summit. With plastic lawn bags repurposed into raincoats and beers in their hands, they cheered wildly for the weakened runners to conquer the peak in the cold, sloppy rain.

Michael was sure these spectators could not understand how each runner used this event to fight against whatever unique inner demons haunted them. Certainly, they would never be able to comprehend why a twenty-year-old man who had just completed his twenty-first mile in the lashing rain, who had just run the last four of those miles up and down steep grades, and who still had five more miles to go, was smiling broadly.

Complete joy overcame Michael as he passed over the summit and began jaunting down the gradual decline. He felt himself beaming and almost laughing as gravity suddenly became his friend, leaning on him from behind. At the bottom of the hill, he ran past the Boston College campus and then alongside the trolley tracks that would guide him into the heart of the city.

The twenty-two-mile marker confirmed he was in a new world. He had never run this far before, and each step he took extended that distance. And although he could not see the finish line he could feel it drawing him closer, the way Julie magnetically drew him closer to her. He was gripped by a fever, a tormenting obsession that was finally coming to a successful fruition.

But with every additional step he was continuously reminded of the pain in his legs and the physical drain on his entire body. The addition of the bitter rain and heavy clothing only added to the obstacles and burdens trying to stop him from succeeding.

The sky above him grumbled with a loud, rolling cackle of thunder that ended with a stiff, threatening crack.

In a sudden, fleeting moment, Michael understood his enemy as clearly as he understood himself. Cancer was a relentless assault on the body of an individual, taking its time to slowly and methodically wear its opponent down and erode him to nothing. Only then, when the infected individual admitted they could no longer go on, could Cancer claim its victory. But Michael had beaten Cancer at its own game. He had slowly and methodically prepared for this day with endlessly patient training. He'd built his body to withstand every assault, and there could be no greater symbol of the power he had over his enemy than the completion of one of the most difficult endurance tests that man could devise.

The distance would not stop him. Neither would the rain, nor the hills, nor the weight of his clothes, nor his squashy shoes, nor the sloppy roads, nor the irritation of wet fabric. Each time he thought about stopping, he ran faster. Mile twenty-three came and went and he began passing other runners with ease. He would look ahead and target a runner, then chase him until he passed him. Then he would pick another runner to conquer. Then another. Each of the other runners represented little tumors he was conquering and leaving behind: the man in the red hat, the woman in the blue shirt, the man with headphones.

He was untouchable. He ran past mile twenty-four and cruised into Kenmore Square, where a large banner bellowed "ONE MILE TO GO!"

His body had been completely drained, yet it continued to move. He grasped at a last cup of water and poured it over himself in a final cleansing of Cancer from his body.

He ran the length of Commonwealth Avenue to Hereford Street, and after two quick turns he was galloping down Boylston Street. Less than half a mile away, hanging across the breadth of the street, was a large blue banner with one word that epitomized his glory: FINISH.

"There it is!" Michael yelled joyously as his body continued to stride toward the finish line. He was running faster than any other runner around him and he had to maneuver between and around them.

His mind had been battling for hours with his body to slow down and even stop, but his body was much too strong and his mind was much too weak. In these last few yards, however, his body came into brief agreement with his mind, and in a last effort to stop the maddening toll on its entire system, Michael's calf muscles tightened around his bones as if two large hands had reached out of the pavement and grabbed him by the legs.

An unbearably sharp pain splintered up both of his legs as if they had been torn open at hidden seams. It felt like someone was ripping out the same veins the doctors had used to save his father's life. His legs refused to bend at his command and he had to find another way to propel himself across the finish line.

In an awkward hopping-and-jumping step, like a football player working to shed a tackler's grasp, Michael cast his body forward and landed with both feet solidly on the painted finish line.

He looked up into the crying sky, raised both arms toward the heavens, and, with what seemed like the last lungful of air he would ever expel, cried out, "I did it!"

CHAPTER 19

Michael stood in the alcove of Julie's apartment building, temporarily sheltered from the continuation of the hammering rain. The black nighttime sky was hidden by an even darker ceiling of clouds that seemed to absorb any light that tried to illuminate the immediate area. The street was quiet except for the raindrops dancing on the pavement, celebrating the destruction of a beautiful spring evening.

He thought about using the key she had given him, but he wasn't sure she was even home, so he pressed the doorbell and waited for her voice to leap pleasantly out of the speaker.

He was startled when the foyer door emitted only its inanimate buzzer, unlocking itself without a greeting.

He took a last look at the silent speaker and then let himself in.

His legs had stiffened in the hours since the race and the stairway was difficult to ascend. After reaching the third floor with the aid of the handrail, he knocked on Julie's door.

He stood at the insentient door, conflicted about how to proceed. He wanted to share his triumph with her and the exultation it had brought him, but he was also distressed that she hadn't appeared at the finish line to greet him.

As the door opened he was unsure which emotion would be dominant, but it became quickly evident when he spoke.

"Where were you?" he asked.

"Come in," she said, avoiding the question. "You must be exhausted, come in and sit down."

What he really wanted to do was stand right there and embrace her; he wanted her to melt into his body. But for the first time since he had known her, he sensed a coldness that recommended caution.

He moved toward the couch and sat slowly, grimacing from the soreness in his legs. There was room for two but she remained standing.

"Aren't you going to ask me if I made it?" he asked.

"I'm sure you made it," she said. "I knew all along you would."

"It was a very lonely experience," he shared. "I really needed you there."

Julie did not respond to Michael's openness; she seemed occupied with her own agenda. Oddly, she made no attempt to lead the conversation as she usually did. She allowed Michael to steer the dialogue. This at first gave him the sensation he had control, but he quickly saw it as a new way for her to govern him. He felt like he was still caught in the current of the race, running under his own power but staying on the course that was laid out for him.

"I can't believe you weren't there today," he said with a shimmer of resignation in his tone.

She was still standing and although she wasn't tall, she seemed to tower over him as he reclined in a stupor. "Michael, today was a very long day for me and we need to talk about it."

Her selfishness troubled him. He'd been up at five o'clock that morning to get to the start of the race on time, he had run for four hours—in a thunderstorm no less—then he'd waited two hours for her at the finish with his father and brother, then he'd driven home with them, and then he'd driven back into the city to her apartment, and here he was, still soaking wet, with every muscle in his body screaming to be touched by her, and she could only think of herself. This was supposed to be his day, and he wondered what kind of day could have possibly been longer than his.

He tried to stand but could not; he strained for a moment, then collapsed back into the sofa. It wasn't just the exhaustion of the day, he realized, but the nadir of the last two years of physical and mental depletion that had caught up to him. "I don't understand," he said.

"I've been accepted to graduate school," she said coolly.

This was the type of news that normally would be delivered as good news. But Michael had an eerie feeling that there was nothing good about this. It was as if he was steaming casually through the North Atlantic and someone had just barked, "Iceberg!" The alert of what was visible didn't bother him as much as what lay invisible below the surface.

"I didn't realize you had applied."

"That's because you've been focused on yourself and the things you were trying to accomplish."

This was true, but it still did not seem like a good enough excuse for her not to have told him. "So where were you today that you couldn't be with me?"

"A couple of the graduate school's professors had flown into town and it was a good opportunity for me to meet with them."

She let that sentence hang out in the air long enough for Michael to find the problem he was about to encounter. His mind was a blur and getting cloudier by the minute, but eventually an unearthly feeling registered with him. Somehow, he felt he was asking all the questions that Julie had expected he would ask, almost as if he were blind and she were guiding him down a crooked path.

"They flew in from where?"

"California," she answered without hesitation.

He stopped breathing, and he might not have ever started again if he hadn't needed air to speak. "California?"

Julie remained silent, as if letting the situation sink into his mind. She watched him as he projected his fate by evaluating thousands of scenarios each second, the way computerized chess programs search for the most effective move.

"You're leaving," he said flatly.

Another long pause, then: "I'm going to California, yes."

Michael's face went pale as the blood rushed out of it in search of a part of the body to heal. But the source of the pain could not be identified and it slowly returned. Or maybe it returned because it had concluded the injury was in his head.

"I think I need something to drink."

Tacitly acknowledging Michael's physical incapacitation, Julie went to the kitchen. She returned with one ice cube floating in a glass of tap water. When she handed it to him, the ice cracked from the change in temperature.

She sat down sideways on the sofa, against the armrest facing Michael, and drew her knees up to her chest, creating a barrier.

Michael drank slowly—at first to regain his poise but then to stall for time. He wanted to take her into the bedroom and he started to imagine himself inside her warm body, but the glass in his hand was warmer than what he was sensing from her.

He tried to ponder this sudden change in his life but found it difficult to think. Julie wasn't talking much, and leading the conversation was difficult for him.

"I'm sure it will be hard at first," he said, "but I know we can make it work somehow."

"Make what work?"

"Us."

She shook her head. "We'll be in two different worlds, Michael. You still have two more years of school left."

Up until today, twenty-six miles had been the longest distance conceivable for Michael in this world, but this new distance was the equivalent of traveling not within a single world but between worlds. This was an expanse that was incomprehensible to him.

"Then . . . then . . . then I'll come with you, I'll transfer." His mind was working faster now, but it was jumping too quickly to solutions without considering their impact. As soon as he spoke he thought of leaving his weakened father, his ailing dog, and his unprotected brother. He became further torn between his love for his family and his innate desire to prevent Julie from extricating herself from his life.

"You can't leave here," she countered, "your whole world is right here." She said this as if she'd already considered this scenario but only to prepare her response, not to consider it.

"Was it something I did?" He was grasping for hope now. "Or didn't do? Surely, it's something we can fix? I can change."

"No." She stood. "It's just time for me to move on."

"But you can't leave. I need you; you are so much a part of me. Every day I can feel you inside me." He thumped his forehead with the heel of his palm, indicating where he was feeling her most at this moment. "You can't take that away from me."

"There will always be a part of me inside of you, Michael."

For the first time it occurred to him that maybe this wasn't a good thing.

"I believed we would always be together," he said quietly.

"You have to understand that this has to happen. It *will* happen."

He had exhausted all possible moves and felt like a chess player who was only a few moves away from inevitable checkmate. He could either play out the remaining moves or tip over his king and resign, but the result would be the same.

He looked up at her with an apoplectic stare. His mouth opened but no more words would come out. A dull ache surfaced in his head; grimacing, he closed his eyes. He tried to replay the events that had brought him to this point in their relationship but his concentration had waned. He opened his eyes and offered a pitiful gaze, begging her to say something.

She obliged, but her words surprised him. "Surely, you must have seen this coming."

But he hadn't. He lived his whole life in prevention of what he believed to be any foreseeable event. He always planned appropriately and was always well prepared. But this situation had caught him completely by surprise. He had fallen so hard for her and allowed her to become so deeply rooted into him that it never once occurred to him what it would be like to be without her.

He closed his eyes again and bowed his head, disgusted with himself. He hadn't seen this coming and this infuriated him. He kept his eyes closed, partly to think more clearly and partly to squeeze back the tears that were compiling behind his eyelids.

They had been dating for two years but their lives were not in sync. She was two years older than Michael, but age was not the problem. The problem was that they had different timetables. Michael was planning to endure a lifetime and Julie was only planning ahead two years. It had always been there for him to see, but he'd allowed the passion he held for her to blind him to it.

He opened his eyes and wiped them clear of moisture with both palms. Stillness enveloped the two of them as Michael tried to regain control the only way he knew how: with silence.

They stared at each other with muted thoughts, interrupted only by Michael's continuous wiping of his eyes. Her silent gaze confirmed there would be no attempts of reconciliation on her part. His breathing became more labored and his body tensed as his shock turned to anger.

Although it was now somehow clearer that this breakup had always been inevitable and all the clues had been there for him to decipher, he still felt a gnawing sense that he wasn't yet seeing the whole picture.

He tried to stand again, to go over to her and hold her, but he was too stiff to rise off the sofa. He fell back, only to try again and fall back again; he was just too feeble.

A new feeling flooded his body. He had been in physical pain until now, but that was explainable from running the marathon. This strange new feeling was centered in his stomach, although it felt as if it was strongly rooted within his mind. It was a similar sensation to nausea but with no threat of vomiting. It abruptly occurred to him that if he and Julie were to break up, he would be devastated. He stopped struggling physically and tried to control himself emotionally.

For the next hour, Michael struggled to find the words that could save him. He tried every angle, every approach, every negotiation tactic, but he could not convince Julie to change course. His emotions were particularly fragile from the physical exhaustion, and at times he rambled with intermittent sobs to the point where only gibberish was spewing out of his mouth. But Julie remained steadfast in her decision, as if committed to it for some higher purpose.

In fact, as the conversation progressed it only got worse for Michael. Julie maintained it was best for them to terminate the relationship now, instead of dragging out their last few months together. Michael felt like he had fallen into quicksand and the more he struggled to free himself, the deeper he was sucked into the unforgiving pit.

With his anger building, his tears accumulating, and his sensibilities distorting, he finally felt compelled to leave. He was progressively losing control of his emotions and was fearful of the ultimate reaction this would produce.

With a formidable effort, he finally managed to rise and make his way to the door. He needed to be alone, he needed to lie down, he needed to plunge into an everlasting sleep where the world would remain placid and unmoving under his feet. Sleep seemed like the only solution to rescue him from the events of today and the effects that tomorrow would assuredly bring.

She followed him to the door, and when he abruptly turned to her, she was close enough for him to grasp. He wrapped his arms around her and squeezed her tightly, not wanting to ever release her. He held her inside the cocoon his body made for her, but he hadn't the strength to hold her eternally. Gradually, his shoulders drooped and Julie stepped back.

As she did he felt her slipping away, out of him, but not completely—something was left inside. She was like a syringe escaping after depositing some unknown contents.

If she'd expected him to see this coming, then she must have seen it coming herself. That made her much more prepared for this than he was. She knew every intimate detail about Michael and how he would react to any given circumstance. She'd made a distinct effort to learn about everything that was important to him, to the point where she had practically made him emotionally dependent on her. She knew Michael better than Michael knew himself.

She remained calm and assured while Michael became embroiled in doubt and confusion.

"Suddenly, I don't feel like I know you," he said wonderingly.

"You know me better than you think you do."

He wiped his runny nose on his sleeve, studied the room around them, and then made unrelenting eye contact with her. "You know this is going to hurt, don't you?"

"I know," she said earnestly. "I know."

Michael turned and grasped the doorknob, then rested his forehead against the door. "I love you," he said through restrained tears.

The words ejected out of him and seemed to sail across a gaping chasm. He waited momentarily for the echo of their return, but they were swallowed by the jaws of indifference.

He opened the door, stepped out, and closed it behind him.

He limped to the top of the stairwell and rested against the handrail. The look down made him dizzy and he waited momentarily while his body tried to steady itself. But once he was stabilized he continued to wait at the head of the stairs, hoping that Julie would come out after him, throw her arms around him, squeeze him tightly, and apologize—take him back. His eyes fixed on the doorknob, begging it to turn. But it only stared back at him like a single apathetic eye.

He'd run a marathon today; just hours earlier, he'd assumed he was at the strongest point in his life. But now he felt weak and vulnerable, and this troubled him.

He started slowly down the stairs, hampered by the same gripping sensation in his legs that he'd experienced during the last seconds of the race. He knew the pain in his legs would eventually subside, but he could not shake the inimitable fear that something new and unexplainable had firmly attached itself to him in an unknown place with barbed fingertips and the singular intent of taking residence.

Surely, you must have seen this coming.

The words reverberated within his mind. He *should* have seen this coming, but he hadn't. And if he hadn't seen this coming, how could he possibly expect to see what would come next?

CHAPTER 20

It was early Friday afternoon, the end of the month. Every waste-collection truck in the fleet would return to the city garage early because today was payday. Payday was the only day when each crew could finish their routes ninety minutes early, even though the volume of trash they were responsible for was unchanged. Oddly, supervisors never wondered why it took ninety minutes longer every other day of the month.

But this day had the additional enthusiasm of pay raises going into effect for city sanitation workers for the first time in two years. Although rumors had been circulating all week, no one knew for sure what percentage would be implemented or even if wrangling politicians had managed to have it revoked before the checks could be sealed in their envelopes.

Tremont balanced himself on the small platform at the back of the truck and held on firmly as Arnez sped back to the yard. He speculated Arnez was hurrying for several reasons: He wanted his paycheck, he wanted to know what the pay increase would be, he wanted to get one of the best parking spaces near the garage to limit his steps, and he needed to relieve his bladder from the many emptied two-liter cola bottles rolling around on the cabin floor.

They were the third truck into the yard. Arnez coasted into the last open space next to the building. Any other truck entering now would have to be driven around back.

Tremont jumped down off the platform, removed his gloves, and wedged them between the hydraulic lever and the truck. He chose not to sit up in the cab with Arnez during the rides back to the yard because limiting interaction with his driver decreased the chances he'd find out what Tremont did at the back end of the truck.

They met at the front of the truck and made their way into the garage.

"What do you think, Tree, nine percent? Ten percent?" Arnez asked excitedly.

"I think the percent doesn't matter," Tremont said. "What matters is how many dollars it is."

He normally didn't care about his paycheck; his primary source of income was selling cocaine. But today he felt himself a little more interested than he had expected because he was still trying to raise that $15,000. He had about $5,000 to go and any extra money he could acquire, no matter how small or what the source, would get him that much closer.

"What do mean?" Arnez waved a cheap calculator he was carrying just for today in the air. "You just take the percent and then convert it into dollars."

"Would you rather have ten percent of my salary or ten percent of yours?" Tremont shot back.

They both went silent as they each considered how much more Arnez made than Tremont, despite the fact that Tremont did all the heavy work.

Two more trucks raced into the yard and roared past them. One of them hesitated as the driver considered parking in a space where the truck surely would not fit. Then there was a grinding of gears and the driver continued around to the back of the building. It was a welcome distraction that ended the awkward conversation.

Inside the garage, six other workers reclined on assorted chairs and couches representing the spoils confiscated from the refuse piles of their routes. The furniture was covered with stained sheets that concealed an even worse condition of fabric. They awkwardly leaned on bent or broken legs. Various tables and footstools in similarly ragged condition added to the eclectic design in the area of the garage they all flippantly called Conference Room A.

Arnez took short, quick steps through the "conference room" area and straight into the bathroom, while Tremont bypassed an empty chair to lean against the wall.

It took fifteen more minutes for all the trucks to enter the yard and for Arnez to exit the bathroom. By that point twenty-five workers had filled the garage, most of whom were drinking cold beers pulled from an abandoned refrigerator that someone had coaxed back to life a year ago.

Arnez offered Tremont a beer, but he refused. It wasn't that he didn't want one—nothing would have felt better after a humid day of hard work—but he was under the legal drinking age, and Arnez giving a minor a drink could put his job at risk. Tremont was always careful not to jeopardize the job of the indolent sloth. His next driver might not be as inattentive and uninvolved. So he waved away the beer and instead lit a cigarette he removed from his own pocket.

An interesting feeling began to envelop Tremont as he waited with the others for paychecks to be distributed. For the first time in his short life he felt an attachment to the fate of other people by sharing equal enthusiasm for this anticipated adjustment. His coworkers had families and mortgages and responsibilities, and the threads from which their lives hung were dependent upon the amount of this approved raise. Tremont's life, although secured by different filaments, was also dependent on whatever additional money was yielded from this raise. This made him feel somehow linked within a broader network of threads, creating a web he had yet to recognize, though he lived each day flirting with the possibility that it was being constructed for the sole purpose of ensnaring him.

He began to realize this job provided a faint light that pierced the darkness that immured his life. It contained some hope that he could free himself from the unique gravitational pull of the desperate world he'd been raised in. Maybe with this raise he could stop selling drugs and focus on changing his life. He could learn to live off of his honest income, focus on succeeding in this job, and then pursue other better-paying jobs. Maybe if he put some honest money away he could eventually invest it in a legitimate business and use some of the skills he'd learned on the street to excel in the real business world.

He stood up straighter, no longer leaning against the wall. For this brief moment, his enthusiasm was equal to that of those around him. Society had given him a chance by giving him secure employment and his wage was honest pay for accountable work, with taxes deducted and payroll benefits provided. So now he would give society a chance to make good on its promise to reward those people who completed an honest day of hard work.

He walked across the "conference room," stood next to Arnez, and tossed him a friendly look, suggesting they were in this together, as colleagues.

The garage supervisor exited his office with a stack of envelopes. A thick, heavy mustache covered his mouth and seemed to prevent him from ever inflicting an expression on his face. Today was no different, and his impassive visage foretold nothing good nor bad about what changes had come about for this most recent pay period. Everyone else remained seated, seemingly fearful of crowding him.

The supervisor silently read the name on the front of the envelope at the top of the stack, then spotted the face of its owner and unceremoniously presented it to him, no differently than he would on any other payday. Tremont's name was the third presented. He reached out his hand to receive the envelope; the supervisor hesitated to once again inspect the hideous scar in the palm of Tremont's hand before relinquishing the envelope and moving on.

Tremont did not open it. Instead, he stood by Arnez and waited for him to receive his.

The room was filled with the sound of spirited conversation and tearing paper as everyone ripped open their envelopes. Arnez finally got his and eagerly tore it apart.

The noise abated and Tremont could tell by people's reactions that there had, indeed, been a raise. But their faces telegraphed ambiguity regarding how large it was.

Only Arnez had a calculator, and while some tried to work it out in their heads, most looked to Arnez as he poked at the device.

Tremont was the only one who had not yet opened his check. He held it by his side against the deep bulge of bills at the bottom of his pocket and waited for Arnez to announce the change.

Arnez stabbed at the calculator again and again. When he was sure of the result, he stopped and looked up. "Two percent," he announced dejectedly.

Someone stole the calculator out of Arnez's hand while the rest of the group began to grumble like hungry cattle. The useless envelopes were crumpled up and discarded onto the floor in disgust.

Tremont remained impassive and took the last draw of his cigarette. He was currently making eight dollars an hour. This raise provided him with an additional sixteen cents each hour he worked, or less than two dollars per day.

He needed more.

He felt adrift on a sea that offered no wind to his sails. This society offered no reasonable way for him to be propelled through life, and he berated himself for even considering its trust.

Maybe it would work for people like Arnez, because after twenty years of his self-imposed gluttonous behavior, he'd end up collecting a disability check while secretly driving a cab for additional income. Tremont would have no part of this.

He dropped his cigarette butt onto the concrete floor and extinguished it with his foot. He folded the unopened paycheck and shoved it into his pocket, where it came to rest on top of a wad of money totaling several hundred dollars. The check would be given to his grandmother, who would be proud he'd gotten a raise. The cash would be used to buy more drugs from JT.

His exit went unnoticed, as it usually did. He would return on Monday and start the week anew, staying true to his original course.

If his life was indeed attached to something, it surely was not this.

CHAPTER 21

Michael sat alone in his dormitory room. The wooden desk chair wobbled and creaked whenever he adjusted his weight upon it. It had supported the weight of many students before him as they had studied for endless hours in preparation for final exams, but Michael sensed its useful life was finally coming to an end.

His elbows were propped up on the desk and his head was nestled in the cradle made by the palms of his hands as he lamented over how far behind he had fallen in his classes. It had happened so gradually he hadn't even noticed until his professors started announcing exam dates, and now he was realizing how difficult it was to recover.

He stared down into an open textbook but an icy glaze over his eyes prevented any of the knowledge from seeping into his mind. The only thoughts capable of occupying him were thoughts of Julie. It was as if she had taken residence inside his head and spread herself within his brain, leaving few places in which to store the important information necessary to pass his final exams.

He reached for the phone again and dialed her number. It rang four times, like it always did, before the voice message clicked in. He listened to her voice announce she was unavailable and then suggest that the caller leave a message.

He knew she would not answer. After the breakup, he'd called her frequently, wanting to reconcile. The more he'd tried, the more she'd rejected him. And the more she'd rejected him, the greater his obsession had grown. She'd finally begun screening her calls, but this hadn't stopped him from trying to contact her. He would sometimes call simply to hear her speak, even if it was a recorded version. She changed her greeting frequently, as if to taunt him with new releases of her voice, and her greetings grew ever longer, too, coercing him to yearn for her even more.

She was gone, but she was somehow still with him in a way he could not explain. He thought about things they'd done together, the places they'd gone, or the conversations they'd had. When he closed his eyes, he could feel her there with him and see her in his mind. The images were clear and vivid, and he forced himself to think about her so he could continue to have her in his life. But each of his attempts to think about only her forced other memories out of his mind. Thoughts of her consumed his mind like a wildfire consuming a dried-out forest. Her presence jumped from synapse to synapse the way flames would leap from tree to tree. No part of his brain was a safe haven.

He waited for the voice message to beep, signaling his turn to speak, and then he terminated the call.

He tried to return his focus to studying but it was no use. His relationship with Julie and his training for the marathon had sapped him of most of his mental and physical energy, and now the breakup had crippled whatever attentive abilities he'd had remaining. His concentration had waned to the point where sitting at his desk had become only a formality and the images from the books lay inert on the page.

Loneliness overtook him.

He'd been spending all his time in his dormitory room surrounded by his books but making no progress. He pretended, even for himself, that he was studying. But the reality was that as his final exams got closer and closer, his ability to pass them was retreating beyond reclamation.

He'd distanced himself from everyone else, including his own family. He avoided his father and brother by lying about how much he was studying and telling them he would not see them until after exams had concluded.

The more he stayed in his room, deprived of sensory input from the outside world, the more he was left to fester over the thoughts and memories of her that were lodged in his mind. He'd become an inmate in his room, just as those unshakable thoughts were incarcerated within him.

He got up from his desk, switched off the light, and dropped onto his thin mattress. The sun had already slumped below the horizon, leaving only subtle streaks of twilight to illuminate the room in eerie shades of gray. The lack of color made it easier to keep his eyes open while sleep continued to elude him.

He continued to think of Julie. She had not come after him the day he left her apartment and she hadn't followed up with phone calls to check on him. It was Michael who had continued to chase her with an uncontrollable obsession.

He stared at the phone and willed it to ring. He was able to momentarily focus all the power within his mind while lasering it into the telephone with squinted eyes and clenched teeth. If he had the power of a single wish, he would use it to simply cause the phone to ring. And when he answered, it would be to speak to the one person in the world he loved the most.

He was startled when the telephone actually lurched to life. It rang once, then again while Michael hesitated to answer it. He cleared his throat and tested his voice to be sure he didn't sound morose. Then he raised the receiver and said hello in his most hopeful tone.

"Hello, Michael."

The voice on the other end of the line was the most confident and reassuring voice Michael had ever heard.

"Hello, Dad."

"I just called to see how you were holding up."

Michael wasn't sure exactly what he meant. He could have been asking about his studying or about the impact of the breakup with Julie. He kept his answer equally vague. "I'm hanging in there."

"I'm sure you'll do your best. Just try to stay focused on your exams for now; you can resolve the other issues when the semester is completed."

"I know, Dad. It's just not easy."

He felt an unusual distance separating him from his father. What made it unusual was that at the same time, he'd never felt closer to him. It was like measuring the distance around the planet; it could be all the distance in the world or, if he looked the other way, his father could very well have been standing right behind him.

"Is everything all right?" his father asked.

"Everything's fine," he lied. "I've been spending all my time studying; I take my first exam next week."

There was a pause that reminded Michael of the great distances communications need to travel in space before they can be received.

"Well, you know I'm right here for you if you need me for anything."

"Thanks, Dad. You've always been there for me."

There was another extended silence. Michael broke this one.

"Can I ask you something, Dad?" He asked this question as if he were tapping his father on the shoulder from behind, confirming his real proximity.

"Anything at all."

Michael hesitated, trying to find the best words to ask a delicate question. "How did you feel when you lost Mom?"

His father started with a pause, then a sigh, then another pause while Michael waited patiently. "I was prepared for it; I knew she was dying. But when it happened . . . I felt so many different things: pain, loss, anger, hate. A lot of hate. I felt like some kind of enemy had stolen her from me for no reason, but at the same time I didn't feel anything at all. There was a numbness."

Another extended silence followed as his father waited for a response.

"How long before it all stopped?"

More extended silence—then, "It never really stopped. But you and Daniel soothed it."

Michael didn't like what he had to look forward to. He considered the feelings that were now part of him, the same feelings his father had just described, and could not accept that he could suffer these volatile emotions forever. All he could think about was Julie, and it was these thoughts that caused him the pain. If only he could remember his mother; perhaps that would soothe his wounds.

"Do you ever think about her?" he asked.

"She's with me every day," his father said. "And she's with you, too."

"But I . . . I can't remember her," he reluctantly admitted. In fact, he could not remember anything related to his mother. All he could think about was Julie during every waking moment, and although she was slowly devouring all his other memories, he had an eerie sensation that one part of him remained a haven where a single memory unrelated to Julie had found asylum.

"Surely you can remember *something*," his father said. "She had a smile that was impossible to forget."

"I'm sorry, I guess I was just too young." Michael could hear the guilt in his own voice.

"I know it's tough being without Julie," his father consoled him, "but you're young. You'll meet someone else who will make you forget about her."

Michael wanted to move off the subject but could not. It was part of his obsession. "I trained for what seemed like forever and I ran a marathon. I thought that would make me strong enough to conquer anything. But I don't feel like I can overcome this. She may be just as harmful removed from my life as I now see she may have been when she was part of my life."

"Not everything is physical," Jack responded in a fatherly tone. "Now, start filling your mind with studying so you can do well on your exams."

"All I've been doing is studying," Michael deceived again.

"Well, if finishing the marathon should have taught you anything, it's that as long as you prepare for something, you can achieve it."

They finished the conversation with some idle banter and then Michael was alone again. He lay back on the bed and realized the last remaining wisps of twilight had vanished from the sky, leaving his room totally dark.

Not everything is physical. Was it possible he had overlooked something in his quest to avoid Cancer? Panic rose within him.

His pillow was thick but soft, and his head sank deeply into it. He closed his eyes again and tried to relax, but all he saw behind his eyelids was Julie.

He needed sleep. The kind of deep eternal sleep that science fiction writers provide space travelers so they can overcome vast distances. He hoped that when he woke, he too would be light-years away—from Julie, from his exams, and from all the inner turmoil that currently corroded his mind.

He suddenly felt something brittle in his hand. When he raised it to his face, he saw it was a folded piece of paper. When he opened it, the message instructed him to look in his toy chest. He sprinted through the house to his bedroom. The rectangular wooden box was against the wall and under the window. He lifted the lid and found another piece of paper. He read the location of the next note, and then he scurried into another room . . .

CHAPTER 22

Michael was now holding a fistful of small pieces of paper in his little hand. He had diligently collected them from around the house, and now, as he'd expected, their instructions had led him to his mother, who sat poised in the kitchen. She towered over his diminutive body like a friendly giant ready to raise him up in her hand. If only she would raise him up, so he could reach that last, mocking note poking out of her hair.

He took one step forward and held out the collected pieces of paper, almost as an offering. His mother continued to stare away, offering only her profile, outlined by a thin line of light. He took another step forward and made a mental measurement of his arm and the distance to the note. If he took just one more step he could reach it.

He tried to slide his foot forward, but it was obstructed. He looked down at the floor and saw nothing impeding his progress. He tried to push the foot forward again, but it would not move. He tried the other foot with the same result. It felt as if something was holding on to him, but he could not tell what or from where. He tried to raise his arms but they, too, were being gripped by some unknown entity. He inspected his body to see what had him in its grasp but saw only his own form.

He struggled as if trapped in a straightjacket but could not break free from the invisible mass surrounding him. He tried to leap toward his mother in a last, desperate attempt to reach her, and in that moment it occurred to him why he could not see what was gripping him: Whatever it was, it was holding him firmly from within.

"Time is up."

He looked up at the stillness of his mother's lips and wondered where the voice was emanating from.

"Pass in your papers, time is up."

Michael held the collected, crumpled papers tighter in defiance of the anonymous command as his mother's portrait began to slip away into a dark tunnel. He was too far away to reach her shrinking image as it collapsed into itself like a dying star. He wanted desperately to chase her down into the void, but he was at the mercy of the unknown presence within him that seemed now to control his every movement—

Michael's head jerked up off of his chest and he was awake. He was sitting in a classroom filled with other students whose concentration seemed much more intense than his own. The professor was pacing down the aisle, collecting the test papers off the desks as she passed. She kept a curious eye on Michael, as if she had been observing him in particular and for longer than just the length of the exam.

She came toward him wearing an expression that telegraphed a sympathetic attentiveness normally reserved for a child in distress. She paused by his side with the stack of exams bundled in her arm and looked down at his desk. He guarded his exam with his arms so she could not see it.

"Time is up," she repeated to him specifically.

Michael slowly uncovered the test paper, let his arms fall to his side in a defeated pose, and stared down at his own exam—not because he wanted to but because it was the only thing he could look at without moving his head.

The professor curiously inspected the visible answers on Michael's test paper without attempting to collect it and then looked down at him disapprovingly. Although the top page of the five-page packet was filled with writing, it did not promote the appearance of a completed exam. His name was written in the upper left corner and answers to the first two questions had been attempted, but there were also several doodles in the margin, and the lack of a crease along the left edge confirmed that it had not even been folded open. Someone else's name was written repeatedly along the bottom of the page.

He was unwilling to look up to meet the professor's eyes, fearful of displaying his embarrassment and revealing the intense shame he felt for failing the exam. He continued to stare down at his desk—pretending the paper wasn't there, pretending he wasn't there, pretending thoughts of Julie were not overpowering him. He wished the professor would just take the test paper already and end this disgraceful moment, but she did not.

Instead, she bent at the knees and spoke to the side of Michael's turned face at eye level. "Is everything all right, Michael?" she asked with a breath so soft it would not have flickered a candle flame.

Her kind voice would have been comforting to anyone who secretly wanted to be comforted, but Michael retained a singular focus that was uninterrupted by the professor's concern. And if there was any doubt as to what he was focused on, its name was spelled out obsessively along the bottom of his test paper.

"I wasn't as prepared as I would have liked to be," he answered without looking up. He continued to stare at the written name: *Julie, Julie, Julie . . .*

"Why don't you stay and we'll talk about it," she said.

The test paper occupied the desk in front of him like a piece of unavoidable evidence in an important trial. He stared at it with eyes that bobbed off-center within their sockets like the air bubbles in a carpenter's level, indicating that whatever they measured was tangibly unbalanced. He flipped the paper over to hide the distraction and then pushed his chair back to distance himself from it.

"I have someplace important to be," he said.

"Let's still talk after class," she proposed. "We'll keep it brief." She smiled affably and—ignoring Michael's test paper like a penny on the pavement—stood to continue retrieving the other exams.

After picking up the last exam, exclusive of Michael's, she returned to the front of the room to dismiss the class. "Your exams will be graded and your final grades will be posted by the end of the week," she announced. "Enjoy your summer, and I'm sure I'll see some of you in my other classes next year."

Chairs were simultaneously pushed back from their desks as everyone stood. The scrapes and squeaks from the chair legs rubbing against the hardwood floors sounded like the stirrings of a pack of dogs disturbed from sleep. There was some subdued confusion as the students filled the aisles and formed smaller groups to discuss the exam and share their answers for the more difficult questions. Some of them stopped up at the professor's desk like politicians trying to win last-minute votes.

Slowly, they filed out into the hallway until every last one of them was gone.

Including Michael.

He normally would take the subway but the exam had run later than expected. The taxi dropped him one block from Julie's apartment.

From there he walked stealthily toward the foot of her street. Extending his head around the corner building, he studied the neighborhood, which was eerily quiet for this time of afternoon.

The idleness was guarded by several rows of pigeons sitting like gargoyles on the parapet of Julie's building. They ignored a lone tern circling high above them as it considered an unobtrusive perch to light on.

Michael moved slowly toward a mailbox as if about to mail a letter but then continued past it to a telephone pole. He leaned against the pole briefly, then walked carefully to the next pole, hesitated, then moved to the next one, as if they were first-down markers on a football field and he was driving for the end zone.

He was careful not to attract attention because he did not want to be seen; he just wanted to see *her*. She was due back from work at the hospital any moment, and all he wanted to do was watch her and drink in her beauty—satisfy his thirst for her. He felt like a junkie who needed a quick fix, and as the anticipation escalated, the churning agitation in his stomach returned.

From the third pole, he slid over between two buildings. The space was small but he could fit in it comfortably and still have a clear view of the street and all of its activity. His brown shirt and pants camouflaged him against the dirty brown bricks, and not by chance—he had done this before.

He stood completely still against the wall and stared fixedly down the length of the sidewalk, which was framed by her building on the left and parked cars against the fence on the right. Four disengaged youths were gathered at the end of the sidewalk, standing like candlepins at the end of a bowling alley. Graffiti defaced a nearby stairwell in an unintelligible font, and across the street the wind had blown orphaned papers against a chain-link fence where they had become entangled in some tall, wispy weeds. This was not a good neighborhood for lurking about, but this was the only remaining course of action he had if he wanted to see her.

Not wanting to attract attention with additional movement, he looked down at his wrist instead of raising his watch to his face to check the time. He had a few minutes to spare.

The waiting was always the hardest part. Sometimes he stood for hours with all the stillness of the queen's royal guard, only his blinking eyes differentiating him from an inanimate statue. It was an unrelenting anticipation that turned time into a stagnant foe, with each passing second no different from the one that preceded it, until she finally pierced his field of vision and injected into him a sated relief.

She always came quickly around the corner at the other end of the street, sauntered toward him, then turned into the alcove of her apartment building well before she reached his hiding spot and vanished. This brief glimpse of her filled him with an ease that dispatched his fervid emotions into temporary remission and wrapped him in a cocoon of hope. It was a fleeting stasis that calmed him and mollified the daily torment that invariably occupied him. Sometimes, the thought of extending it into eternity was a welcoming one.

But the feeling never lasted long. His mind had become an open and untreatable wound, festering with his desire and need to be with Julie.

His attention was suddenly diverted when the flight of pigeons simultaneously leaped off the apartment building. The continuous slapping of their wings attested to the effort they expelled to maintain flight. They circled the area with no leader and no apparent destination and then returned to their original roost. Like rowdy spectators congregating in bleacher seats, they waddled impatiently along the edge of the building high above the street as the solitary tern floated gracefully down out of a stream of ocean air that had blown in from the harbor and alit on a lamppost opposite them.

Michael checked his watch again and then trained his eyes on the distant corner of the street. *Soon*, he almost said aloud.

A black sports car came from behind the direction he was looking and passed him. Immediately recognizing it as Tremont's car, Michael instinctively tucked himself a little more tightly into his hiding place, slouched over, and pushed his hands into his pockets to conceal any part of himself he could.

The car's brake lights lit up like fiery eyes. Michael was unsure if he had been seen but didn't want to lose the opportunity to see Julie stride around the corner, so he stayed squeezed against the building and continued his covert campaign.

The car came to a stop on the street near Tremont's apartment entrance, which was also near Julie's. Tremont had continued his habit of double-parking, indifferent to past law enforcement efforts. The brake lights flicked off, but the door did not open.

Michael continued to look at the car and then look to the corner to watch for Julie and then look back at the car again. One last glance at his watch confirmed Julie would turn the corner at any moment, and he hoped Tremont would either enter the building or drive away before she appeared. But the car sat as idly as Michael stood within his little enclave.

The group standing on the corner acknowledged Tremont's presence but did not approach the car. One of them ended a call and shoved his phone into the front pocket of his sagging jeans.

There was a momentary stillness, as if a stage had been set, actors had taken their places, and a curtain was about to be raised. Michael continued to observe the scene as if he were watching a poker game and trying to determine who the patsy was.

Then the most unexpected thing happened—something that confirmed he was not only in the game but was the designated mark: The car's passenger door opened, and Julie stepped out onto the street.

Michael's jaw tightened and he fell back against the wall. He blinked repetitively, wishing each new image would now be absent of Julie, but she continued to occupy his view with unrelenting ruthlessness.

The pit of his stomach began to stir like a witch's concoction, the foulest of ingredients combined within a gurgling pot. It had already been simmering for almost two months, ever since their breakup—not having Julie in his life, not having a woman in his life, not having someone to share his inner feelings with, not having the warmth of her naked body next to his. But seeing her now with Tremont was like having a pound of salt spilled into the boiling morass, causing it to swell up and seethe over the brim.

He jumped up to improve his view, but it was only a temporary fix. He jumped again and again, providing himself with a strobe-like series of images that smoothed out like a reel of film. He could see her clearly once she stood up straight, but he continued to hop and bounce with an anxious and overwrought tension he could not control. He wanted desperately to start running as fast as he could, but he couldn't decide if he wanted to run toward her or away from her. His stomach tightened like a wet, twisted towel and he bent forward.

He tried to keep from vomiting at first, wanting to control his physical reaction. He squashed his eyes shut to push back the pain and regain some focus, but images of Julie continued to be telegraphed behind his eyelids. He then succumbed to the inevitable and purposely tried to eject the evilness from within his stomach, but he could only produce a dry, heaving gasp. As he continued to lean over his shoes, it occurred to him that the affliction did not reside in his stomach but somewhere else entirely, and his physical health had somehow become resolutely yoked to it.

He swallowed hard and the nausea abated. He straightened and watched as Julie walked around to the driver's side door and began talking to Tremont through the open window. She stood with a relaxed and flirtatious pose that taunted Michael further. He couldn't tell what she was saying, but he noted a light laughter that heightened his ire.

Without consciously deciding to do so, he stepped out onto the sidewalk and marched toward her. He was like a railroad car being pulled helplessly along by an engine that had no concern for what it was dragging behind it.

As he got closer, Julie's image grew until she filled his entire view, in much the same way as his mind had become overrun with her. When she turned toward the entryway of her apartment, Michael was in her face.

They both asked the same question at the same time: "What are you doing?"

There was silence as they both waited for each other to respond, but Michael had less patience and repeated the question: "What are you doing, Julie?"

"What do you mean?"

The thought of her being with another man incensed him, but the thought of Julie with Tremont specifically created a seething rage of indignation that purged whatever remaining sensibilities he'd previously maintained. Between heavy breaths, he gestured toward the car and asked the question a different way: "What are you doing with *him*?"

She leaned her body slowly back and then took a backward step to catch up to it. There was no apology in her expression or tone when she answered, "He gave me a ride."

For an instant, Michael was relieved it was only a ride—but the relief was short-lived, because he really had no idea if she was telling the whole truth or even part of it. And even if it was just a ride, he didn't want her involved with someone of Tremont's ilk in any capacity. He was intensely confused as he tried to read Julie but received no data. Her expression was taut and unaffected, while he could feel that his own was anguished and befuddled.

It had been too long since he had been this close to her, and while the perfect lines of her face were exactly as he saw them every day in his mind, he could now smell the fragrance that was uniquely her. It was exactly as he remembered it. He suddenly realized this was the first time in a long time he had been able to be with her, and he did not want to squander the opportunity to have a meaningful dialogue with her. So, although the jealousy still raged within him, he managed to dislodge it from the forefront of his emotions, relax his breathing, and attempt a smile as he asked, "Can we talk?"

"If you think you need to," she said.

"Of course I think I need to," he said, surprised. "I think *we* need to."

"I've already told you everything I need to tell you."

"But I've done everything you asked me to do," he pleaded. "I've opened up to you, I've shared my innermost feelings with you, I let you inside of me just like you wanted. I don't understand why we're not together; help me to understand."

Her face remained impassive. "Sometimes you have to just accept things the way they are. Fighting it only makes it worse."

There was something odd to Michael in the way she said that, almost sinister.

"But this is too much. You're always with me and I can't stop thinking about you. I can't get you out of my mind." He put both hands up to his ears and momentarily closed his eyes. Then his tone became more urgent. "It hurts," he said. "*Please*, make it stop."

"Have you tried getting some help?"

The question sobered him and he dropped his hands. "I don't need help, I need you." He raised his palms halfway out to her, signaling her to take them into hers. Their eyes connected but Julie's face was too heavy for him to hold her gaze. His eyes drooped simultaneously with his hands, and his shoulders also fell away.

"You're right, Michael," she said. "This has to stop. You can't keep coming around here."

He lifted his guilty eyes.

"Yes, I know you've been watching me. I've seen you in that little nook down the street, and I've seen you on campus and at work."

Michael's mind was racing, trying to reach for a conclusion that seemed beyond his grasp.

"You knew I'd be here today?" he asked.

"Yeah," she said as if it were obvious.

Michael looked away, down at the ground, and tried to think. He felt foolish and somewhat childish, while Julie seemed strangely more mature. It was the first time he'd felt weakened by having her in his life. Something deep within him told him she had been through this before—that she had broken many hearts and would destroy a legion more, like an incurable disease.

Something else about this scene made him uncomfortable, but he could not determine what it was.

"You knew I'd be here," he repeated aloud but to himself. He looked over at Tremont's car, which still idled almost next to them on the street, but he couldn't see inside because there was another parked car between them. His mind sifted feverishly through the sequence of events as he tried to calculate the situation.

"Did he offer you a ride, or did you ask him for one?" he asked.

Julie was caught off guard by this question. "What difference does it make?"

"You knew I'd be here. You asked him to give you a ride because you wanted me to see you with him."

"You're just being paranoid."

"Am I? I think you baited me . . . maybe even from the beginning."

Michael's mind was now afire with new feelings of hate that were emerging within him, and the mixture of fervent love and outright hatred only intensified the confusion that raged within his mind. He had never hated anyone before—had never even been exposed to real hate—and now he was not only experiencing it for the first time but was experiencing it toward the person he loved the most.

He took a step forward, but he wasn't sure whether it was the love or the hatred that compelled him to do so. As the space between them closed, he found the strength to raise both arms and reach for her, but he was unsure what part of her to grab. He saw her small hands, her firm shoulders, and her delicate face. He also saw her throat.

Julie took another subtle step back but Michael steadily pursued, still unsure of which emotion was controlling him, until she was within reach.

He took hold of both her shoulders, immobilizing her. "Why are you doing this to me?" he asked.

Julie did nothing more than stare back into his eyes. He scanned her face in search of hope or some other answer to the pain he was suffering and gripped her tighter in an attempt to squeeze a response from her, but she would not give up as much as a wince.

It was then that Michael felt a similar sensation in the crook of his own neck—large fingers pushing into his collarbone, causing him to lean to one side and weaken his grip on Julie. It wasn't until he heard a deep baritone voice stream into his ear, however, that he understood his problems existed both in front of and behind him.

"Problem?" asked the invisible voice.

Tremont eased his grip enough to allow Michael a half turn. When Michael lifted his eyes and saw Tremont glaring back at him, he released Julie but without apology.

"What are you doing?" Michael asked, unafraid that anything worse could happen to him. He swung his arm around and swept Tremont's hand away. "This is between her and me."

Tremont's nostrils flared and his chest expanded as he took in a deep breath. "I'm looking out for her," he said.

Michael was insanely offended by the idea that Julie was Tremont's to protect. He secured a more guarded position between the two and widened his stance to improve his balance. "*I* can take care of her," he asserted.

Tremont poked a contemptuous finger into Michael's chest. "You can't even take care of yourself. How are you going to take care of someone else?" He left his finger hanging in the space between them, stoking the flames that burned within Michael.

"What do you mean by that?" Michael snapped back.

"You're falling apart," Tremont said. "You look worse than some of the junkies standing on that corner."

Michael looked past Julie to the group on the corner. They were a band of slovenly drug users who wasted away both their lives and their bodies. He was offended to have been compared to them when he'd spent his whole life treating his body with care and respect. But Tremont was somehow right. Something had gotten inside him and destroyed his desire and ability to care for himself. He was exhausted and weak, and something was continuing to erode his will even further.

He was insulted and speechless. He looked back at Julie, who just stared listlessly at him. He shifted his weight onto his other leg and began uncontrollably shaking the free one, causing the loose change in his pocket to rattle with the same urgency. He glanced at Tremont but was instantly drawn back to Julie. He studied her with a painfully different view that he had never experienced before. Her perfect face shone brightly, like a full moon, but for the first time he realized that she, also like the moon, had a dark side that was kept from him due to some type of macabre rotational lock, continuously circling him with focused and deceitful purposes.

He took an instinctive step backward, partly to remove himself from the space between Julie and Tremont, partly to step away from Julie, partly to step away from Tremont, and partly as an attempt to step away from himself. He didn't understand what was happening to him or what the cause of it was. He was frightened but did not know what it was that scared him, and that scared him even more. He felt an incredible discomfort, but its source was diminutive Julie, not the imposing Tremont. He didn't want to be here anymore, and he concluded that coming here today had been an incredibly grave mistake. He needed to turn away but felt that something was unfinished, and he didn't know whether to try to conclude it now or leave it for another day. He felt compelled to run away but felt equally compelled to stay, and he was also torn by the divergent feelings of love and hate still roiling within him. All of this turmoil entangled within him and his head began to ache again, and then the nausea returned.

He took yet another step back but did not take his eyes off Julie. "This isn't over yet," he said to her firmly.

"No," she replied, "but almost."

Michael turned in disgust and began to escape down the sidewalk, but walking wasn't getting him away fast enough. He increased his pace and kept his eyes on the far corner. He just wanted to get far enough to turn onto a different street so that Julie and Tremont, no doubt now amused at his cowardly parry, would no longer be able to see him.

He had an overbearing urge to run but did not want to do so until after he was out of their sight; he knew they were watching him and felt as if he might suffer some type of wrathful rebuke, the way harness racers are penalized when their horse breaks stride, if he did. Each slow step he took, however, did not take him away quickly enough. Faster and faster he strode, lengthening his steps and swinging his arms, until he could not take the relative stillness anymore and broke into a slow jog.

When he finally reached the corner, he turned it at a sharp angle and continued to run.

He had not run a single step since the marathon and he found it difficult to maintain an even pace. His breathing was labored and his legs immediately began cramping, defiantly alerting him that his body was no longer in peak physical condition. He wanted to at least be able to run the several miles back to his dormitory, but every new step he took made it less likely he could take another until finally he submitted to his inability to go any farther and came to a dead stop.

He stood still on the sidewalk, not understanding what was happening to him, feeling that he had been banished to a mental and physical wasteland. He began to walk a slow death march, avoiding eye contact with anybody who crossed his path. He felt an incredibly unique pain that he could not diagnose. It was everywhere, yet it was nowhere specific. All he wanted to do was eject every drop of the evilness out of his body. He wanted to run but couldn't. He wanted to stop thinking about Julie but couldn't. He wanted to make the pain go away but couldn't.

He again felt like he was trapped in the flow of a dominating river, but he was no longer swimming within it so much as he was being helplessly carried downstream, where he would eventually reach the vastness of the ocean and be swept away into oblivion. But because what had happened to him had been undetectably slow and methodical, he hadn't noticed that the current had now intensified and the turbulence had become more agitated, much the way the Niagara River behaves just before it spills its flotsam off the edge of the horizon.

CHAPTER 23

Daniel stood in front of the closed door of his father's study and wondered whether he should enter. He had looked for Michael in every other room in the house, hoping he would find him in conversation with one of the many visitors, but Michael had become so completely withdrawn that he could now only be found in dark and lonely places. Due to even more recent circumstances, this was the last place Michael should be.

There was no light coming from under the door and the light switch was pointing down at the floor, but Daniel knew he was in there. Without knocking, he opened the door and leaned into the quiet darkness.

"Michael?"

There was no answer, but he heard the rattle of Bailey's dog tags when she lifted her head. If Bailey was in there, then so was Michael. Daniel flipped on the light and stepped in, closing the door behind him.

Michael was sitting on the sofa, staring through the window across the room. He seemed to be looking deep into the nighttime sky, to a place that existed out beyond the stars. Bailey was up on the sofa with him, and when she confirmed it was Daniel who had entered the room she replaced her head on Michael's lap and let out a deep and saddened sigh. Michael, who did not react when the light came on, was gently rubbing his hand back and forth across her failed hips.

"Are you alright?" Daniel asked.

More staring and rubbing.

Daniel sat down in the desk chair and observed his brother. He looked so utterly exhausted and forlorn, like an abandoned tractor rusting away on a forgotten farm. But it wasn't Michael's physical decline that bothered Daniel most; it was his complete mental decay. He prodded gently, "There are people here. I know it's hard, but you need to see them."

"Tell me," Michael directed while continuing to stare blankly out the window.

Daniel thought for a moment. "Tell you what?"

"Tell me about when you found him."

He stirred on the chair. "There's really nothing to tell that I haven't already talked about."

This time Michael looked directly at him with inclement eyes. "Tell me what you saw."

He leaned forward, about to put his hand on Michael's knee, but reached up to Bailey's head instead and scratched behind her ears. "How did she get up there?" he asked in avoidance of Michael's subject.

"I lifted her. Now tell me."

Daniel leaned back into the chair, and its supporting spring released a creaking groan. He looked over at the bookcase to avoid Michael's scrutinizing gaze and studied the arrangement of the books. The shelves were overflowing with several hundred novels his father had read that were jammed haphazardly wherever they could be squeezed in. Scores more were stacked precariously on their sides on the top shelf, building several towers up to the ceiling. His father refused to buy a bigger bookcase, always convinced he could squeeze in just one more book or stack one more above without toppling the piles.

Suddenly, Daniel realized he was still holding a book in his hand. A bookmark was stowed between the last two pages. He began fidgeting with it, without completely freeing it.

He sensed Michael's continued stare but wasn't comfortable telling him everything he wanted to hear; he wasn't sure how his brother would receive the information in his current state. Michael was sicker than Daniel had ever seen him, and although he partly understood what had caused it, he could not fully comprehend how it had affected his brother so substantially.

He continued to stall by standing up at the bookcase, searching for a place to fit the book. He studied the bottom shelf, then tried wedging the tome into a few places on the second and third shelf. Finally, he abandoned the shelves and tried to balance it somewhere on the stacks above—but the damn book just wouldn't fit. It was the second time today he had tried and he sat back down, rejected but not yet defeated.

As he gripped the book, he began to realize that he had been deeply affected by what he had found and he needed to talk about it for his own sake. He felt a sudden urge to tell someone all the details, which he hadn't shared with anyone else. And although he was concerned about the lucidity of Michael's mind and didn't think he would handle it very well, Michael was still his brother, so by default it should fall to his ears.

"Are you sure, Michael?"

"I said to tell me, didn't I?"

Daniel paused to establish his composure. He turned his head away from his brother to stare at nothing in particular and then, cautiously, began.

"As you already know, it was a school day. When I woke up, I heard voices . . . I thought people were in the house.

But I knew that couldn't be right, because it was too early in the morning." Daniel adjusted himself several times on the chair but found that no position offered comfort. "The voices were coming from across the hall in Dad's bedroom. I listened for a few minutes and realized it was just his radio alarm, and that's when I got a weird feeling that something just wasn't right."

He watched Michael as he stared, unaffected, at some minute speck of space that existed somewhere out beyond the window. His brother seemed unconcerned with this part of the story and listened with a detached air that even he seemed oblivious to.

"I got up to see if he had left for work." With the book still in his hand, he walked over to the window at the same cautious pace he had walked to his father's bedroom several days earlier. "I walked across the hall and saw him from the doorway, still lying in the bed. He was already late for work, so I called out, 'Dad?' I said it softly at first because I was reluctant to wake him. I don't know why, because it was time for him to get up, but I still remember that it felt odd disturbing him. I called him again but this time a little louder—'*Dad?*'"

Daniel was now also staring out the window, barely seeing the ghostly forms of the many parked cars or the trees or the houses. Their nighttime images had no more mass as objects than the shadows they cast in the daylight. What he did see was the solid mass of his father's body, lying completely still under the crumpled blanket. The image was as real to him now as when he'd seen it several days earlier.

"*Dad?*" he called again, as if it were happening for the first time. "*Dad?*" His voice grew louder as it began to crumble. "I went to the bedside and turned off the radio and called to him one last time." Daniel spoke very softly now, amid emerging tears. "I shook him once but he never moved . . . that's when I called you."

Daniel was now sobbing quietly, with his head sunk into his chest. He reached up with his empty hand and rubbed his palm all around his face, rubbing away the tears with large, forceful swipes. Then he turned back around to face his brother, expecting that he too had begun to cry.

But Michael just continued to stare listlessly, rubbing Bailey's hindquarters as if she were now attached to him and her pain was his own.

It had been four days since their father had died, and as far as Daniel could tell, Michael still had not shed a single tear. He was now the depiction of an emotional wasteland, drifting in and out of a semi-catatonic state. But although Michael's outer shell had not cracked open and gushed forth tears, Daniel had no doubt that his brother was struggling to fight off a terrible and unforgiving grief, and this alarmed him with equal measure.

For there had been something very wrong with Michael even before their father was lost to a final heart attack. Something unique and undeterminable had possessed him so completely that now, without his father, without the one person who would have been capable of coddling him into security, he would be beyond repair. Ironically, the one time Michael should surely be seeing a doctor or seeking some other form of professional help, he was simply sitting and ignoring its very suggestion.

"Tell me what you saw," Michael said.

"What do you mean?"

"You were looking right at him; tell me what you saw."

Daniel was unsure how to answer the question to Michael's satisfaction but tried anyway. "I saw the bed, the blanket, the clock radio. A book . . . this book . . . was nestled up by his head and pillow. He must have fallen asleep right when he finished it; I'd like to think he died in his sleep."

He looked down to confirm the book was still in his hands.

He looked back up and saw that Michael was now staring directly at him with haggard, shrinking eyes, which only reconfirmed his concern for his brother's well-being. When the eyes were sure they had Daniel's complete attention, Michael asked the one question he must have really been trying to ask the entire time.

"Did you see his face?"

It was such an odd question to Daniel. He pondered its importance to Michael while simultaneously searching his memory to see if he could recall any such image.

The two brothers stared intently at each other across the vacuous space of the room. Michael waited for a response to his question while Daniel waited for a proper response, if there was such a thing, to the death of their father. But Michael seemed no longer able to control his actions or emotions. It wasn't so much that he was out of control but that something else seemed to be in control. It may have started with Julie ending their relationship, but with the death of their father it had now metastasized into a more onerous and virulent form. And as Daniel continued to stare at his anguished brother, he could not help but equate that same tormented expression with the one that had been on his father's face when he found him dead. It was this very expression that Michael now sought a description of. This could not have been more evident than if the two faces were superimposed.

It was at this singular moment that Daniel finally found his place, his raison d'être. For all of his eighteen years, his older brother had protected him from any and all dangers, known and unknown. And although Daniel had long maintained a private resentment toward his unsolicited guardian, he now realized his behavior had been foolish and unjustified. He regretted all the brash antics and gratuitous challenges with which he had tested his brother's love. Michael had only been trying to insulate him from the things in this world that he, Daniel, was too young to understand on his own. And even though he hadn't understood what they were then and perhaps still did not understand completely what they were now, he recognized that they must have existed—at the very least, in Michael's mind.

And because of all these years of protection, Daniel now felt completely healthy, safe, and unencumbered from anything that might hinder him in life. Even now, without parents, he did not feel like a defenseless child but rather a secure and hopeful man. And it was clear to him that he was now the strong one and his role was to protect his older brother, who was no longer capable of taking care of himself, let alone what remained of the rest of the family.

Michael's question still hung in the air between them. He wanted a description of his father's face as Daniel had found him. But nothing good could come from Daniel explaining what death looked like to a person who himself had that same look occupying his face. The only thing left to do was shield his brother from this fixation.

"I didn't see his face," he said. "He was lying on his stomach."

A look of disappointment overtook Michael's face, but Daniel could not tell if it was because he was caught in a lie or because Michael truly wanted to understand something about what had taken his father away from him and now felt he had lost that opportunity. Regardless, Daniel was now going to do what he thought was best for Michael in the same way that Michael had historically enforced his idealism on Daniel. He would start by shielding Michael from anything that would accelerate a further decline, and once his brother was stabilized, or once the family unit was stabilized, he would find a way to rescue him from the deepening abyss he had sunk into.

He watched as Michael continued to stroke Bailey's hindquarters. His hand never wavered from the metronomic pace he employed—back and forth, back and forth, back and forth, soothing Bailey into a similar hypnotic trance. Her eyes were open slits as she lay across Michael's lap in a paralyzed heap.

"Do you remember Mom?" Michael asked. "Do you remember *her* face?"

Daniel was taken aback by this new question. They had never really spoken about their mother with one another before. There were times when they had sat across the dinner table from their father and he had shared his own fond memories of her, but Michael and Daniel had never spoken of her when they were alone, just the two of them. So now he was unsure how to proceed, because this moment was more delicate than any other they might have previously shared. He had been very young, of course, when their mother died, even younger than Michael, but he still had some vague memories of her tucked away in his childhood vault. And he wasn't encouraged that although Michael had seemingly changed the subject, he was somehow stuck on the faces of the dead. Still, he saw less harm in talking about his mother to Michael because at least the memories he was asking about were from when she was alive.

"I have a few memories," he replied cautiously, "but they're faint."

"Can you tell me one?" Michael challenged him.

"Well, the one I remember most, the one that really sticks out in my mind, is her smile. I can see it now, just as well as if she were standing here." He smiled broadly to himself in an almost exact genetic duplication of his mother's delightful expression, but Michael appeared not to recognize it as anything other than an expression that belonged to his brother.

"How do you remember it so clearly?" he demanded.

"It's really strange," Daniel said. "I remember it distinctly. I remember she came into my room one night and woke me up. I asked her what was wrong and she simply stood over me with that wide, genuine smile that just seemed to beam out how much she loved me. She adjusted my blanket, kissed me, and said goodnight. It was like she woke me up just to give me that memory, like it was a gift she purposely made sure I would keep forever." He reflected a moment. "Yeah, it was like a gift."

After a brief, uncomfortable pause, Daniel turned the conversation back to Michael.

"How about you?"

Michael winced as if accosted by the question, then answered tersely, "I was older than you, so of course I have a lot of clear memories." Then he redirected his attention back to Bailey.

Bailey opened her eyes wider and turned her pupils to the edge of their sockets to stare up at Michael. Their eyes seemed to have an unattached link, the way wireless phones magically make a connection across vast distances.

More staring and rubbing.

Daniel had now lost his connection with his brother in the abrupt way those same cellular phones detach when one party goes into a tunnel and becomes insulated from the outside world. He opened his mouth to speak but no words came out, because he had no idea what to say.

This was going to be difficult. Not the next five minutes, or the rest of today, or the next day, but the next several *years* would be difficult as the two of them attempted to move on with their lives without any parental guidance. And before they could do that, they first had to get through their grief about their father's passing. Daniel knew he would overcome it; he was not certain Michael would. It was hitting him abnormally hard, especially on the heels of the depressive state he had already developed subsequent to his breakup with Julie.

Daniel felt it would be best to leave Michael alone for now. He, Daniel, would tend to the many family members and friends who had come by the house to pay their respects. And when they were gone, he would immediately turn his focus to tending to his brother.

He stood up to leave, but the stubborn book was still in his hand. He measured its dimensions with his eyes—length by width by height. Then he studied the shelves again, looking for a space big enough to hold it. Suddenly, he saw a short book on the second shelf that didn't fill the full height of the space it stood in. He tried to wedge the book he was holding into the space above it, but the combination was about four inches too tall.

His dejection over this failed attempt didn't last long, because he spied another short book on the fourth shelf, this one seemingly even smaller than the one he had just tried to crowd. He again tried to squeeze his father's last book into the space above it but came up one inch short. There was simply no room left in this shrine of unrelated stories, and they were somehow collectively conspiring as a single entity to keep out any other book from infiltrating their private sanctum.

Daniel finally abandoned the book—on the floor, as if laying down his sword in unconditional surrender—and retreated toward the door. With his hand on the doorknob, he said to Michael, "I'll be out here if you need me," and was completely surprised when he received a response.

"You need to put the two together," Michael said.

"What?"

"You need to put the two smaller books together."

Daniel didn't understand at first because he didn't believe Michael had been paying any attention to him. He turned back to the bookcase and looked at the two smaller books he had tried to mate separately with the larger book, and as he did he saw what Michael was talking about. He pulled the shorter of the two small books from the fourth shelf and placed it in the space above the other short book, where it fit snugly. Then he picked up the book from the floor, removed the bookmark, and squeezed it into the space previously occupied by the shorter book. It was absolutely the last book that could have possibly been placed on those shelves.

Daniel stared at the new configuration, not disappointed that he hadn't figured out that solution but rather excited to discover that Michael's mind was still capable of analyzing a situation and calculating a solution. But when he turned to his brother and witnessed the same staring and rubbing as before, he became less convinced this was a good thing.

And it was this same grave image that convinced Daniel he had recently made a mistake a thousand times more terrible than sharing his feelings with his brother, and that the consequences of that mistake could be a thousand times worse.

The door closed and Michael was alone again. Daniel had left the light on, so Michael no longer enjoyed the friendly darkness. His eyes ached from the brightness but he simply absorbed the pain in the same manner he sponged up all the pain currently assaulting him.

He continued to rub the fur on Bailey's hindquarters, first brushing it forward against the grain and then smoothing it down until his hand returned to her hips. He was very gentle; even with amiable strokes he could feel the brittleness of her bones, and he didn't want to aggravate her pain. If she adjusted her position even slightly, he would feel her cowering joints creaking like corroded hinges.

Her hips had deteriorated beyond whatever comfort Michael could provide. She could not walk without extreme pain and she spent most of every day in a single corner within the house. She had to be carried down the stairs to get her outside to relieve herself, and something as necessary as squatting in the grass had become a painful and humiliating experience, reducing what was already a less than dignifying pose to a complete act of debasement. Sometimes, sadly, she even defecated on her own legs.

She had even less control over her bladder, and leakage had begun appearing around the house. No one ever disciplined her for these transgressions, of course; it was understood that it was not for lack of obedience. Whenever someone began wiping up her urine Bailey would fawn nearby, expressing her shame.

It wasn't until these last few days since Michael had returned home from school that he had become witness to the extent of her decline. She was simply wasting away, without any clue as to what was attacking her.

But Michael knew.

He stopped caressing her and rested his palm directly over her hip. Just beneath his hand, beneath her fur, beneath her skin, and beneath the entanglement of muscles and veins, Cancer was alive and consuming Bailey from within—and Michael was powerless to stop it. All he could do was sit idly by with his hand tenderly on her assailant, afraid that if he squeezed too hard in an attempt to crush it, he would only cause his beloved pet more pain. He was indeed helpless to save her.

Just as he had been helpless to save his father.

He had done everything he could to help keep his father healthy over these many years, but he had not had the power to prevent the fist of Cancer from squeezing his father's heart until the blood could no longer be pumped through its chambers. Maybe he had prevailed in delaying Cancer's victory, but he'd been unsuccessful in stopping what was apparently inevitable. And if he had been unsuccessful at stopping his father from being consumed, then surely he could not prevent the weaker Bailey from becoming its prey.

The weight of his failure had now been piled atop the existing collection of guilt, fear, and confusion that had been burgeoning above him and turning his mind into nothing more than a decaying compost heap. But even as a rotting mass can generate heat, so did a fire burn within Michael. Although he had become a portrait of physical exhaustion in recent months, his weakened state contained a writhing, overpowering hatred. He hated how his mother had been taken from him at such an early age, he hated how his father had been robbed of a fulfilling life, and he hated how Bailey had been stripped of her dignity and youthfulness. But what he hated most was the very thing that had caused all this to happen. He hated Cancer, and he hated it in all its forms.

The room was perfectly still and silent, making it exactly the type of space that Michael sought out these days. His sullen eyes surveyed the room—the overburdened bookcase, the cluttered desk, and the squeaky chair. Only the movement of Bailey's steady breathing disturbed the placid surroundings. Her body gently rose and fell like ocean swells lolling along far out at sea as he continued to rub her with loving strokes.

Suddenly, she lifted her head to listen to something that had her attention. Michael did his best to listen as well but could only hear the faint voices of guests from behind the door. She struggled to stand; Michael helped her by lifting her and placing her on the floor. She tried to compose herself in the middle of the room, but a tremor hindered her progress. He leaned forward to caress her again but felt her entire body trembling beneath the fur in what seemed like a cold shiver. He would have accepted a chill and her disability as the cause of this unrelenting quiver except that the room was seasonally warm and it was her entire body that was trembling, not just her legs. He recognized it as the same type of shaking she had suffered as a puppy during ominous rainstorms with long, rumbling thunder. He resolved that what she was experiencing now was an unidentifiable fear of something only her heightened senses could detect.

He knelt and hugged her, hoping to gently squeeze her into calmness, but he was unsuccessful. Bailey began to emit short, feeble whines as her ears perked up and her eyes searched for an invisible enemy. She struggled to free herself from Michael's grasp until he released her, then she crawled under the desk like a frightened turtle retreating into its shell.

Michael returned to the sofa, where he watched Bailey tremble under the desk. She stared back at him with afflicted eyes, practically begging him to help her. As he sat helpless, agonized by her distress, her expression seemed to slowly change to a more chastising gesture, as if to ask the question of him, *Why don't you know?*

But he did not know.

He held his head in his hands and tried to concentrate, but there was too much pressure behind his eyes. He felt as if something had been eating away at his mind, leaving an emptying chamber within his skull that seemed destined to collapse into itself.

Sitting there, holding his head, he came to a bitter, wretched conclusion: He was not well.

He was immediately overcome by a harsh panic as he began to suspect that maybe Cancer had actually found a way inside him despite all his efforts to keep it out. He contemplated the frightening notion that Cancer had been so incredibly smart as to bypass attempting to overcome Michael from a physical perspective and focus its attack on his mental capacity.

There was no doubt his recent traumas, culminating with the loss of his father but catalyzed by his attachment to and separation from Julie, had put him in a dangerously depressive state. And although Cancer could be capable of developing tumors within his mother, hardening arteries within his father, and swelling skeletal joints within Bailey, Michael could not be convinced it was capable of coercing Julie into terminating their relationship. Even if each of Cancer's victories with his mother, father, and Bailey had been nothing more than an overall plot to peel away his mind, he could not make a connection to Julie. And without finding an association between Julie and Cancer, Michael remained hopeful he could overcome whatever was ailing him.

His head was still in his hands. He began to rub his temples; after a few seconds of this his fingers slipped into the caverns that sheltered his eyes, which he then rubbed even harder. He could not imagine being more physically or mentally exhausted, and when his arms lost the strength to continue to hold up his head, they flopped down to his lap. His head fell back next, pulling his lifeless body with it, until he slumped into a useless, moribund heap on the sofa. Only Bailey's repressed whimpers indicated any life at all existed within the room. But she, too, was just another layer that would soon be peeled away.

As his mind wandered in search of the ultimate answer to his suffering, Michael found that all roads led to one inevitable and devastating conclusion: Cancer had come to penetrate him after all.

As he began to accept this fate, he braced himself against an irrepressible, extended wail.

But it never came.

He waited for it like a blindfolded prisoner awaiting his execution, but still it never came. He tried to force the tears from his ducts by making crying facial gestures and whimpering; still, it would not come. He focused on all the sad things that had happened to him in his life, on all the terrible things that had happened to other people he knew and even people he did not know—yet still he could not cry. He dug his fingernails into his arm until the skin tore off under the pressure, and still no tears would liberate themselves from his eyes.

He looked down at Bailey under the desk and saw her staring back at him. Her glossy eyes and soft whimpers confirmed that she had no difficulty crying for her situation. Yet still she glared back at Michael with that disturbing expression that continued to ask, *Why don't you know?*

And still he did not know.

All he knew at this moment was that the most terrible and lamentable events had presented themselves into his life, and where any one of them would have enveloped a normal person in a surge of tears, in him even their aggregation could not cause so much as two hydrogen atoms to commingle with a single atom of oxygen to form the suggestion of a watery tear.

If he could not cry, that could mean he was either already emotionally dead and Cancer had defeated him or that he had complete control of his emotions and was therefore beating Cancer. His mind continued to tangle with paranoid theories and conjectures until he somehow convinced himself that tears were indeed the blood of emotions and that crying would signify his defeat as he'd once thought bleeding would. With his focus renewed to prevent crying at all cost, he moved to exit the darkened morass he had floundered in these past few hours. Or was it days, or even weeks? Time no longer existed; only his emotional state propelled him forward along an indefinable continuum.

He forced himself to stand and move toward the door. He took one final look at Bailey, who now rested her head on her front paws and released a deepened sigh. There might not be anything he could do for her now, he thought, but maybe he could still do something for himself. It was as if the tide had swept him far out to sea, and now, in his most weakened and exhausted state, he was beginning the swim back to shore.

However, the trip would be overshadowed with the awareness that a single diminutive wave, to say nothing of a tidal surge, could roll over him and wash him under for good.

The door opened and Michael glided through it. He floated through the hallway without feeling his footsteps, passing several doorways without so much as providing a glance at the many people—and there were a lot of them—who had come to pay their respects to the Galler family. He wasn't being rude; he merely needed to make it to the kitchen so he could rest and collect himself from the hallway journey, the way the frail and elderly are singularly focused on getting from point to point.

He recognized so many faces. As their voices blended into a gentle murmur around him, he realized how difficult it must be for Daniel to singlehandedly keep track of all these people who had come to honor their father's memory. There could very well be people here that Daniel did not even yet know had arrived, although they all seemed comfortably tended to. He felt suddenly proud of the maturity his younger brother was deploying during this difficult time, even as he himself suffered the embarrassment of his lack of control. He had abandoned his brother at a horrible time, and this crime was no less repulsive than had his father forsaken the two of them when he lost his wife. But sadly, Michael felt too weak to suffer the guilt anymore. Not that he didn't know he was guilty, just that punishing himself for it seemed no different than condemning a serial killer to consecutive life sentences;

what impact could additional consequences have against the weight he was already carrying?

He looked down at the floor and measured his steps against the floorboards, each one bringing him closer to the safest place in the house. *Just make it to the kitchen*, he continued to think with every deliberate step. Once he could harbor himself at the kitchen table, comfortably out of the secluded darkness that had become his institution, he could then begin to integrate back into a more socialized environment. *Just make it to the kitchen and everything will be all right.*

As he approached the kitchen doorway, two people he probably knew but did not readily recognize stepped aside, giving him a clear view to a sight that could not have been more unexpected—though somehow, it was this complete lack of probability that made her presence so absolute. Julie sat with perfect posture, her hair was brushed with precision, and she wore an impeccably pressed black blouse. Her lips were glossed over and her eye shadow was flawlessly applied. It was the sort of elegance any woman could achieve, but it was the type of perfection that only Julie could craft.

No one engaged her in conversation, Michael noted; in fact, people seemed to be standing clear of her the way they might keep a safe distance from a crime scene.

The kitchen was more crowded than the other rooms because that was where the food was. There were multiple platters of cold cuts and bread, bowls of potato salad and coleslaw, jars of mayonnaise and mustard, and trays of lasagna and tossed salad. The countertops were overburdened and the table abounded with a buffet fit for a feudal lord. All of this bounty had been provided by the people who'd come to call on the Galler family, and as these neighbors and family members heated, chopped, sliced, and stirred, as well as washed, wiped, cleaned, and put away, they generated a frenetic energy. It seemed they were all abiding by the single rule that if you came into the kitchen, you worked.

Julie, however, sat as motionless as a crocodile with eyes floating patiently above the water line. But it was not this insolent failure to help that offended Michael most; it was the fact that she was sitting in his mother's chair—a chair that was reserved for a venerable matriarch, not the loathsome, manipulative wretch that was Julie—and was doing so wearing a look of worthiness.

Their eyes made instant contact. He received no solace from her presence; rather, her attendance provoked him. She made no gesture toward him but simply let her presence absorb into him, until suddenly and finally, in a fait accompli, Michael was fully saturated with everything that was Julie. His hatred toward her now equaled the hatred he had toward Cancer to the point where it was impossible to discern between the two.

Her presence polluted the scene, and he could think of nothing other than extricating her from that chair, from this house, and from his life.

As he seethed with a barely containable anger, he restrained himself from acting aggressively in this public forum. "Why are you here?" he demanded with a shudder.

Julie sat at ease, her crossed leg revealing a knee covered with black stockings. "To offer my condolences," was all she tendered.

"Get up," he demanded, still fighting back his rage.

She obliged without pushing back the chair, rising in a fluid, polished motion to a statuesque pose that enflamed Michael's longing for her. She was dressed exclusively in black, which should have been suitable for this occasion except that on Julie it was more suggestive of a threatening cloud than compassionate mourning.

He leaned in close to the side of her head, careful not to touch her scented hair, and whispered clearly and concisely into her ear, "The only people here today are family and friends. You had an opportunity to be both and you chose neither. You need to leave."

She seemed unaffected by Michael's strong words. Smiling delicately to shelter her facade in view of the kitchen audience, she returned Michael's stare with her eyes slanted inward in her typical disturbing fashion. Her head tilted and her lips parted. "Michael—"

"Now. Please."

A look of fulfillment occupied her face, as if she had now done all that she had come to do. Her eyes looked over Michael's shoulder to the doorway, communicating that he stood between her and her exit. She could have easily stepped around him, but nothing about Julie had ever signified she would alter her course for anyone. She reached up and touched the side of his head—too quickly for him to avoid it—and held her palm against his skull. Although she had never done this to him before, it felt eerily familiar to him, as if she had been attached to his head all along.

"Goodbye, Michael," she said while extracting her hand. She walked gracefully through the kitchen doorway and vanished down the stairwell.

Michael slumped into the seat she'd just vacated and watched the doorway with a careful eye for her return. The hallway had cleared and Michael could see all the way down to his father's study. Bailey was standing awkwardly in the doorway. She stared back at him with the same chastising look she'd delivered earlier. Then she turned and staggered out of sight.

He lifted his elbows to the table to build a cradle for his head, but there was no room to place them among the platters of food. He could not remember when he had last eaten, yet nothing in front of him was particularly appetizing. He was still too overcome with Julie's presence. He had not seen or talked to her in several weeks, and that made her visit all the more unexpected and all the more devastating. If she had intended to do the one thing that could hurt Michael the most, she had achieved it.

That thought lingered with him longer than he expected it to. He wondered why anyone would deliberately want to hurt him. But as he pondered this thought further, one last question began to burn in his mind—and for someone in as highly a combustible condition as Michael was at this moment, it was not good for anything to be burning too closely to him, least of all within him.

He bolted upright and raced out of the kitchen and down the stairwell after her. At the bottom of the stairs, he swung open the door, passed through it, leaped down the last few brick steps, and found himself on the sidewalk staring directly into Julie's face.

His breathing grew loud and heavy as the pressure built within him. The pain of Julie's return was now commingling with the pain of his father's departure, creating the type of lethal combination that would cause scientists to run screaming from a lab.

He let fly a torrent of emotion.

"For weeks and weeks I've tried to call you and see you and talk to you and be with you. You ignored me and shunned me like I was some kind of plague or disease. I was going crazy trying to be with you, but you kept pushing me away and making it worse. I couldn't think straight, I couldn't sleep, all I could think about was you, you, *you*!" Michael's eyes darkened and spittle spewed out of his mouth as he lost complete control. "Of all the days, why did you have to pick this one? Why today? Why now?"

He paused to catch his breath but his chest heaved even harder. Then he asked the burning question: "How did you know?"

She stood steadfast. Her very presence now poisoned him.

"How did you know my father died?" he repeated.

Julie remained silent and averted her eyes over Michael's shoulder. Michael did not want to look away from her but she was definitely looking at something specific—some*one.* She gestured her head in the same direction.

He turned his head all the way around while leaving his shoulders square to Julie. Only when he saw his brother standing there did he turn his whole body around to face him. "Daniel?"

"I'm sorry, Michael," he said slowly. "I didn't understand."

Michael turned back to Julie. "What's going on?" But he knew he would get nothing from her, so he turned back to Daniel.

"She called me. She was asking about you, how you were doing. That's when I told her Dad had died." Daniel bowed his head. "I'm sorry, I didn't understand. I do now, but it's too late."

Michael turned back to Julie. "You called *him* to see how *I* was doing? No, you're not that simple. It's always something more with you. You knew *before* you called him, that's *why* you called him. There's just something inherently evil in the way you do things. I didn't see it at first. You came into my life out of nowhere and just became so much a part of me and now I can't get you out of me. It's you that's killing me, and I can't stand it anymore. You got into my head and then just kept spreading and spreading, and now I feel you everywhere and it's nothing but pain. You're like . . . like . . . like a . . ."

Michael's mind was like a jigsaw puzzle coming together with the last pieces left. The fewer the remaining pieces, the easier it was to determine where they fit. And now the total picture came into view, and when he saw it he fell to his knees in complete defeat and uttered a single word: "Cancer."

His mind snapped simultaneously with the realization of what had actually caused it to snap; Cancer was in him.

He began to mumble softly to himself, "It was you all along . . . I didn't see it coming . . . I was so stupid . . . It's in me . . ."

He looked up and glared at his enemy. Cancer had finally shown its face, and it was Julie.

From behind him, he heard Daniel's cautious voice asking, "Michael, what are you talking about? Are you . . . all right?"

Michael was now the only thing between Cancer and his younger brother. He felt submissive on his knees, which was no useful position from which to protect Daniel, so he lifted up one leg and then forced himself to stand. He improved his position between Julie and Daniel and, the rage having resumed building, began to breathe heavily again. His head lowered but his menacing eyes rose toward her. "Stay away from my brother."

Daniel stepped forward. "Michael—"

"Stay back, Daniel!"

"I'd better leave," Julie said, breaking her silence. She looked past Michael to Daniel. "I'll check back with you later."

Witnessing Julie—Cancer—reaching out for his younger brother was too much for Michael. "LEAVE HIM ALONE!"

He charged at Julie and clutched her throat with both hands. His momentum knocked them both over and he landed on top of her at the edge of the curb. His hands jarred loose and he grappled to find her neck again, searching relentlessly while he howled at the sky in a psychotic frenzy. Julie struggled beneath him but could not get herself free from his weight. Michael's left hand found Julie's neck again and then his right hand mated with it and together they squeezed Julie's windpipe closed. The sudden, total control over Julie liberated him, at the expense of his own self-control. All his energy drained into his clenching fingers. He had to end the very thing that had been attacking his family. He had to terminate the disease that now crawled freely within him.

He had to prevent Cancer from ever getting close to his brother.

As soon as Michael and Julie toppled over, Daniel rushed forward and reached for his brother's shirt, to no effect. Daniel then found a more secure hold, with a forearm around Michael's neck, and began prying him off. Progress was slow at first as Michael struggled to stay on top of Julie, but finally, with one giant tug, Daniel broke him free and the two of them tumbled over backward like cockroaches.

"Let go!" Michael yelled and flailed, trying to shake his brother loose. But Daniel held him tightly in a bear hug from behind, his legs wrapped around his body.

Michael rolled and tried to throw his elbows backward, struggling to jar himself loose. Even though his face was unobstructed, he felt smothered in Daniel's tangled grip. He was already mentally smothered by Julie and internally smothered by Cancer, and now his brother had finalized his confinement from the outside. He screamed and gasped helplessly, "Let me go! Let me go, she's in me! It's in me!"

They thrashed and rolled across the lawn while Michael continued to rant and Daniel kept calling Michael's name, trying to calm him. At the edge of the garden Michael managed to stand, but Daniel still would not release him. They both continued to struggle until they toppled over again, into the thicket of the garden.

When they hit the ground this time, Daniel lost his grip. Michael swung his arms wildly and his legs kicked in a mad flurry, trying desperately to remain free. As he continued to thrash about, however, he became entangled in the garden's long, wiry weeds like a spider's prey. The more he struggled, the more the knotted garden gripped him, until the tangled mess subdued him completely. A straightjacket could not have contained him more tightly.

His strength fully depleted, Michael lay still except for his large, heaving breaths, each of which pulled in dirt and leaves. He gagged and coughed and tried once more to break free from the snarled mess. When he failed again, he simply went limp. He didn't just give up trying to break free; he gave up on everything. He gave up on Julie and he gave up on keeping Cancer out of him. He gave up on life. And as soon as his mind and his body succumbed to this defeat, he was able to do the one thing that had eluded him through this whole ordeal.

He cried.

He cried and he cried and he cried. He cried like he had on the day he was born, wailing and whining and wheezing with tears pouring down his face. He cried for the loss of his mother that had been building within him for over twelve years; he cried for the loss of his father that had been building within him all weekend.

But most of all, he cried because Cancer was in him.

CHAPTER 24

Tremont always found sanctuary in his car. It was an American sports car born in the 1950s and had evolved into a sleek roadster in the years since, yet it wasn't timid about sacrificing a little aerodynamics to flex a few fiberglass muscles. The gears slipped easily through to fourth, but because Tremont rarely left the city streets, the fifth gear engaged with a sticky resistance as he pulled into the passing lane on the Massachusetts Turnpike.

No sooner had he accelerated beyond the Back Bay than he had to stop to pay a toll. He fumbled for his wallet while downshifting, reading the lane signs, and interpreting traffic signals. Multicolored signs and flashing traffic lights disoriented him as he assessed his payment options. Ultimately, he elbowed into a line of cars snaking into a cash lane. He slowly advanced while cars with transponders whizzed through dedicated express lanes and continued on their way with barely a pause.

Having paid the toll, he cycled back through the gears, urged the car into fifth, and once again accelerated into the passing lane—but after only another five miles he found himself braking for another tollbooth, this one governing the convoluted intersection of the state's two busiest highways.

Cars, trucks, and utility vehicles all merged and then dispersed via a web of ramps and bridges. To the left were points west and to the right was the most exclusive and expensive suburb in the metropolitan area. Tremont went to the right.

He worked his way into a long cash lane by cutting off a tractor trailer, not making eye contact as he did. Every few seconds his car lurched forward in the frustration of first gear while Mercedeses, BMWs, and Range Rovers greased through the prepaid tollbooths on the way to their elaborate and comfortable homes.

It's all about being ready with the money, he thought as he inched his car forward again.

Tremont exited the highway and followed the first main road until it forked, chose an arbitrary direction, and followed the new road deeper into secluded, wooded neighborhoods. He quickly noticed that unlike the flattened topography of cities, these roads followed the contour of the land as they undulated through the knolls. Out in these neighborhoods, roads were an encroachment kept in line by old stone walls and rock outcroppings, as opposed to cities, where it was trees that intruded on sidewalks or stood on display in concrete planters. He continued past lush green parks and manicured athletic fields with teenagers chasing soccer balls and small children guarding outfields with oversize baseball mitts. He passed watersheds and ponds with verdant reeds and braces of mulling ducks.

About every half mile he came to a wandering side street with an amiable name like Edgebrook Road or Laurel Lake Lane—each one a reminder of how far he had driven from the unassuming city names of Mason Street and Courthouse Way. Each name evoked an image of prestige that was confirmed by large houses fortifying wide swaths carved out of the tree line. Three-car garages, cedar shingles, and slate roofs characterized their opulence, and the multiple gables and bay windows that swelled out from their sides overlooked meticulously landscaped lawns beautified with seasonal flower beds and perfectly nurtured shrubs.

He'd heard of these upscale towns with their untouchable real estate prices; he was here because he wanted to see for himself where money lived. Driving down these streets, he was not only impressed by the enormity of the houses and their obviously exorbitant price tags but also by what he knew must be the sky-high ancillary costs of their maintenance and furnishings. It took a lot of money for people to live here and, considering the quantity of these imposing homes, it was evident that a great number of people managed to accumulate that kind of money. As he strayed through these streets, he wondered what he, too, could do to get the money he needed. JT continued to pressure him to become his partner, but Tremont would need a windfall of money to do that. All he had managed to do so far was work harder and harder to chisel away at the sum, and the more he delayed, the higher the price of entry became.

Most of the side streets in this neighborhood looped him back to the main road, but some were cul-de-sacs with tidy turnarounds that escorted him out. He tolerated countless stares by homeowners watering flower beds or playing ball with their children, their eyes following his poorly muffled sports car with its oversize wheels and flashy pinstripes until it was well out of sight.

As he continued past the street signs, the names seemed to compete for the most pretentious designation, to the point where they were no longer even called "streets" but were replaced with monikers like Drive, Place, and Glenn—until, ultimately, he came upon the most ostentatious neighborhood of them all.

The entrance was buttressed by large granite blocks assembled into a grandiose wall that swept up to meet tall white pillars that guarded admittance. Set into the wall was an iron plaque identifying the audacious Supreme Court. Tremont passed slowly between the columns, not so much respecting the speed limit as he was awed by the architecture of the homes that emerged into view. Gated driveways led up to gracious Georgian homes with multiple chimneys and distinctive detail collaring windows and supporting overhangs. Each house he passed was even more dramatic than the one before, looking as elegant as the day it was built and suffering no ill effects of weather or age. The road, absent of sidewalks, eased up a gentle grade and bent to the left, where tall maples extended their branches over the street and shaded out the sun.

Just ahead, one of the driveway gates was open and a table was set up in the entryway. A white tablecloth rippled in a gentle breeze and an adolescent boy sat behind a homemade placard advertising lemonade. Tremont passed the table, swung around in a tight turn, and pulled alongside the lemonade stand.

"How's business?" he asked in his perfected ominous voice.

"Slow," came the squeaky reply.

"It's not exactly a high-traffic area," Tremont observed.

"My dad says I have to stay in the driveway," the kid said. "You want some lemonade? I have brownies, too."

Tremont was at first amused by the little kid sitting at his diminutive lemonade stand. But this was a boy of privilege, one who would one day be sitting at a college desk before graduating on to a corporate office, while he, Tremont, was consigned to a life of abusive parents, hauling refuse, and dealing illegal drugs. Resentment began to simmer inside him as this advantaged little shit tried to peddle flavored water to him, as if Tremont was somehow obligated to support his cute effort.

Like a cat batting a mouse prior to protracting its claws, Tremont began to toy with him.

"Is it homemade?" he asked.

The kid nodded. "I made the lemonade, but my mom made the brownies."

"Real lemons?"

"No, just powder and water," he answered without apology.

"Give me a lemonade and a brownie."

The boy dipped a long wooden spoon into a pitcher and stirred. Then he filled a paper cup and handed it to Tremont with a crumbled brownie.

Tremont pushed the brownie into his mouth and washed it down with the full contents of the cup in a single swallow.

The boy eyed Tremont suspiciously, seemingly grateful that the table was between them. "You're not from around here," he said hesitantly.

"No."

"Are you lost?"

"Sometimes," Tremont answered, handing him back the cup with his long reach. "How about another?" The boy refilled the cup and handed it across the table with another brownie. Tremont pulled them into the car and repeated his spirited consumption.

He continued to measure the small boy. He was young, but short even for his apparent age. His puffy cheeks magnified a mole that would likely keep him from dating when he reached his middle teens, but he still had some maturity about him. The lemonade stand was probably not his own idea for making money but rather an obtuse scheme of his father's, meant to teach him the lessons of running a corporation. A bowl on the table with a few crumpled bills represented the futility of this endeavor.

"One more," Tremont instructed. He extended the empty cup out the window again but this time not as far. The boy had to reach across the table to get it, and a little farther to return it.

"I sell stuff too," Tremont said.

"Really?" the boy responded cautiously. "What do you sell?"

"I guess you could say I sell candy. But I don't wait for people to come to me, I go to them."

The boy was skeptical but intrigued. He turned around to look back at his house and, seemingly finding safety in its presence, turned back to Tremont. "What kind of candy?"

"The kind that makes you feel good. The way this cold lemonade makes you feel good." Tremont swallowed down the new cup and let out a sated sigh.

The boy seemed captivated by Tremont's antics. He began apprehensively rubbing his cheek as if trying to erase the mole as Tremont, exaggerating his smooth mannerisms, lit a cigarette and vented the first draw of smoke out the window. He could see the boy beginning to emulate his relaxed posture and lazy eyes, eager to test a mimicked persona.

"Is it drugs?" the boy asked in a deeper, unrehearsed tone.

"You're a smart kid," Tremont said. "How much money did the smart kid make today?"

The boy was embarrassed, but he picked up the bowl anyway. A sudden breeze tried to lift out a dollar but he grabbed it before it escaped.

Tremont held up a messy roll of bills as big as his fist. "One week," he flaunted. Then he took another draw on his cigarette, making it look easy and harmless.

The boy's eyes widened, but quickly retracted into a relaxed state that imitated Tremont's easy expression. He turned and looked back up the empty driveway again, this time perhaps finding comfort not so much in the presence of his house but in the fact that the authority of a parent was not around while he flirted with the dangers introduced by this stranger. He turned back around quickly, as if he didn't want to have his eyes off Tremont for too long. His manner projected a combination of caution and excitement, and he seemed to be attempting to emit an aura of maturity that Tremont might find appealing.

Still holding his paltry cash register, he reminded Tremont, "You owe me six dollars."

"Sure. Do you have change for a hundred?" Tremont asked through an insulting grin.

The boy dejectedly looked down into his bowl. "No."

"Then it looks like we have a problem."

"So, what do we do?"

"You're the smart kid, figure it out."

The boy was silent while his eyes lurched from side to side, indicating a thought process at work. It was clear he knew he was being tested but wasn't sure what the test was.

Tremont flicked his spent cigarette out the window and released an impatient rev of the engine.

The boy looked down at his stupid lemonade stand. "Maybe it doesn't have to be money," he finally said.

"Now you're thinking, little man. So, if not money, then what?"

"Why don't you show me what you have?" he braved.

Tremont started to reach into his pocket but was stopped by a loud, commanding voice making its way down the driveway in the form of the boy's name.

"William!"

The boy turned abruptly and snapped back to his former persona, confirmed by his high-pitched response. "Yes?"

"William," his father repeated for effect as he arrived at the table. "What's going on here?" He didn't wait for his son to answer but rather bent down to spy into the car, evincing that Tremont's appearance confirmed the suspicions he'd garnered from the window while watching the transaction take longer than it should have. "Did you pay him yet?"

"We were just working that out," Tremont answered.

"I don't know what you had in mind, but you'd better take it someplace else."

Tremont had no interest in engaging the protective parent; he was focused only on the money, and there was nothing to be gained by staying around. He winked at William and passed six dollars out the window, but it was the father who took it.

The father then attempted to lean closer, but the table was in his way, so his son was able to hear him say to Tremont, softly yet firmly, "I don't know what kind of person you think you are, messing with little kids, but don't come around here again."

They both knew the threat was idle. Tremont's size alone was intimidating enough, let alone the gun in his waistband. But there was no reason for Tremont to pursue the situation any further. The whole incident was a stupid, ineffective solution to his cash shortage. He smiled derisively at William's father and then sped off, leaving a patch of rubber on the street the way a dog would urinate on a bush.

The incident did confirm one thing for him: He was not beneath any action to get what he needed. If he was willing to sell drugs to children, then surely there was nothing too illegal, too reprehensible, or too vile that he would not do for money.

And that's what kind of person Tremont thought he was.

CHAPTER 25

The receptionist sneaked a flirty smile whenever Michael looked in her direction, but Michael largely ignored this. Each time, she returned her eyes to the textbook in front of her, taking an occasional note or highlighting a particular passage.

But Michael sat in the waiting room with a singular focus. He teetered on the edge of his seat, staring at the blemishes on the linoleum floor. It wasn't that he was ignoring the world around him; rather, he was barely aware it existed. He had never held Bailey's leash as tightly as he did now, even though she lay perfectly still on the floor at his feet. He continued to grip the slackened leash like a sustaining lifeline. Even though the other people in the waiting room were tending to their own pets, he could feel their accusing eyes upon him, as if they knew why he was here. He frequently looked to the receptionist, hoping for her to call his turn so he could avoid the penetrating stares of this room, but in the continued theme of his confliction he also hoped she would not call him, because the next room would bring him closer to the terrible act he had to perform.

He wound the leash an additional turn around his hand to confirm it was securely attached, then looked to the receptionist again. She looked up from her book and started to smile but settled for a more mechanical look instead. "I'm sure it will be just a few more minutes," she said politely. Then she smiled anyway, until Michael turned away.

The side door opened and the veterinarian escorted out a mother with her adolescent daughter. The mother was carrying a birdcage and her daughter's eyes were affixed to the parakeet inside, which was laboring to keep its balance on a creaky swing. Without taking her eyes off the bird, the daughter asked the veterinarian, "Is Joshua going to be all right?"

The doctor feigned a smile. "Of course she is. It's perfectly normal for a female bird to lay an egg. The only surprise for you is that he is a she."

With the bird's false gender imprinted on her mind, she asked, "So there's nothing wrong with him?"

"The only thing wrong is that you have misnamed her."

The little girl's face drew a confused look, which was quickly erased by a threatening tear. She was crushed that Joshua could no longer be named Joshua simply because the vet had told her so. She looked up to her mother and asked in a way that refused to accept the notion that because her special friend was not what she had expected, it would require a different name, "Do I have to change his name, Mom?"

The mother spent a glare toward the tactless doctor as she continued to the exit. "Of course not, sweetie."

"Yay, Joshua!" the little girl cheered as the door closed behind her animated departure.

The veterinarian moved, unaffected, to the receptionist and asked for the next file, then took it out of the room without acknowledging any of her other clients.

Moments later, the intercom buzzed and her voice followed: "All set, Kerrie."

The receptionist stepped around the counter first and then adjusted her skirt in a further attempt to gain Michael's attention. She kept the yellow highlighter in her hand, seemingly as a symbol for Michael that she was studying—that she strived to be something more than what he might have assumed of a receptionist.

Still ignoring her interest, he stood and gave Bailey a delicate pull, petitioning her to stand, which she attempted but failed. He bent down to lift her.

"Let me help," the receptionist offered, stepping forward. She extended her hand to Bailey's nose and whispered, "Hello, Bailey."

Although her manner was genuinely kind, she seemed to be magnifying her charm for Michael's benefit. She slid her arms underneath Bailey and lifted her while cooing into her ear. Neither Bailey nor Michael offered an objection, and she carried Bailey into the windowless examination room and carefully placed her on the metal table in a standing position. She then turned to Michael one last time and offered an amiable smile. He conveyed a conventional thank-you—the idea of responding flirtatiously did not interest him—and returned his attention to Bailey.

There was nothing left for her to do but return to her station.

"Where's Dr. Shepherd?" Michael asked the veterinarian.

"He's retired, driving around in a golf cart these days," she said. "I'm his daughter, Dr. Shepherd-Lowe."

She seemed to carry that hyphenated appendage like excessive luggage—likely one of many concessions in her life that probably included taking over her father's veterinarian practice. She picked up Bailey's file and spread it open in her hands, leading with an oversize diamond engagement ring and a simple, uninteresting wedding band that fit together to form another compromise.

The examination room appeared more sanitary to Michael than it had in the past, but as he continued to regard the familiar table, posters, and cabinets, he realized it wasn't much different than he remembered it. He concluded it was Dr. Shepherd-Lowe herself that seemed to enhance its sterility.

"I see we've had her on carprofen for quite a while," she said while looking at the file and ignoring Bailey. "How has she been responding?"

"It's not really helping, but you should check her yourself."

She put down the file and proceeded to examine Bailey in a very textbook fashion, as if posing for close-up photographs for a manual on symptom-assessment procedure. She quickly checked Bailey's eyes and teeth and then moved directly to her legs. She evaluated her paws, pasterns, hocks, knees, and hips in a brusque manner that ultimately solicited an unwelcome squeal.

The doctor's disinterest in her work was glaring, and Michael's discomfort grew with each poke and prod. What he needed was the gentle compassion provided by Dr. Shepherd himself, who had always tended directly to the animals and treated them as members of the family when discussing conditions with their owners. Standing beside Bailey, stroking the length of her body with one hand, Michael reeled in the remaining slack of the leash with the other. His whitening fist struggled beneath the coiling nylon as the inevitable task before him drew closer.

"It doesn't seem to be helping much anymore," the veterinarian said. "I can give you more—"

"*Her*," Michael interjected.

"Excuse me?"

"*Her*. You can give *her* more medication, not me."

"Of course . . . that's what I meant," she responded with a startled look.

But the examination and talk of medication were irrelevant to Michael. He had his own agenda for this appointment, and although this doctor's demeanor did not suit his emotional needs, he felt sure she would be more than effective at carrying out the chilling task at hand.

Bailey turned to him and nuzzled her face into the nook of his arm to get his attention. She then pulled away, slipped out her tongue, and began to pant. She was exhibiting the discomfort of the room and it was as if she was trying to show Michael she would abide by him—take more pills, subject herself to more painful examinations, or even receive more injections—the way a child becomes more obedient when intuiting the penance may be more unpleasant than the chore.

"We can continue to do what we're doing, making her as comfortable as possible. I can also give her a shot of cortisone to alleviate the pain."

Bailey was having difficulty maintaining her stance on her rickety legs, but Michael knew it would be more painful for her to try to sit or lie down on the narrow table. He clutched her mane with his free hand but did not stroke it; he merely gripped it, as he did the leash with the other hand. He was reaching out with all he could to hold on to Bailey, but he could not hold on to the words that escaped out of his mouth.

"I don't think there is anything more I can do for her."

The doctor paused and stepped back to lean against a cabinet. Behind her were various renderings of cats and dogs. The animals had been undressed of their fur and skin and stood in a cooperating profile with their eyeballs bulging out from their skulls and matted muscles. They all stared at Michael like an appalled jury.

"I see," she said, acknowledging Michael's purpose. "Have you thought this through?"

"More than you know," Michael said, both of his hands squeezing their contents of fur and nylon.

"What are you suggesting?" she asked as if she needed to hear him say it.

Michael closed his eyes and took the kind of yawning breath that deep-sea divers use before descending beneath the ocean's surface. His body wavered and he seemed to drift away. "Sleep," he said.

"You want to put her down?"

He swallowed hard, still floating in the murky darkness of his mind. "Yes."

"Have you discussed this with your parents?"

His eyes opened abruptly and advanced out of their caves like attacking eels. His parents were gone and could not be a part of this decision, but he settled on an answer he knew to be unquestionably true: "My parents would approve."

The intensity in his eyes forced her to look away. She looked at Bailey first but found no relief in her meek and humble pose, and then she looked down at the file and likely found the comfort of a credit card number.

"Alright," she said, putting down the folder. She approached Bailey, lifted her from underneath, and carried her like a stack of firewood to a back door, trailing the unwinding leash from Michael's hand like an umbilical cord. All the eyes on the posters followed her across the room, but only Michael protested aloud.

"What are you doing?" he asked.

"This is the kind of thing I do at the end of the day."

This was unacceptable to Michael. He would not allow Bailey to be placed on some kind of backroom death row, to be fed her death through the bars of a crate and slump into finality under the hand of this uncaring provider of care. He would hold her until the final knock of her heart, leaving her secure with the knowledge she was loved for as long as she could draw breath.

"I want you to do it now."

"It's not something we recommend doing with the family present." Her tone suggested it was more difficult for her to deal with the emotions of the family than it was for the family to witness the event.

"Well, it's not fair to Bailey."

At the mention of her name, Bailey began to struggle to get free, her drooping legs twitching as they searched for solid ground.

The veterinarian moved Bailey over the table, where the dog's paws scratched at the metal in search of secure footings. Slowly, Dr. Shepherd-Lowe allowed Bailey's weight to settle into a prone position, and then she placed her hand on Bailey's ribs to settle her breathing. It was the gentlest maneuver she had employed since Michael's arrival.

"Okay," she said. "But there is one last thing. How would you like her handled . . . after?" She hesitated. "Would you like her buried or cremated?"

It was something he hadn't considered, and he wondered if it really mattered. He stood closer to Bailey and put his hand on the familiar curves of her hindquarters. Her eyes offered a unique serenity, like a soft red sun as it settles blissfully into the horizon's pillow. But her hips continued to tremble as if disconnected from the rest of her tranquility. It was Cancer—lurking beneath her, trying to finish what it had started—but Michael was going to beat it to its endgame, and if he could do that then he could have some form of control over his enemy. As Michael moved his gaze back and forth between the calmness of Bailey's eyes and the disturbance of her hips, it occurred to him that the trembling was not Bailey. It was Cancer, and Cancer was afraid.

"Do you have a blanket?" he asked.

Dr. Shepherd-Lowe turned and grabbed a wilted towel from a hook and handed it to him. He draped it over Bailey's body and smoothed out the wrinkles, but it was too small to cover her legs. Her chest heaved rhythmically, keeping time with her panting, but it was her hind legs that continued to shudder at a different meter, reminding him that Cancer would not quit.

Without looking up, he answered, "Let's burn the body."

A notation was made in the file and it was closed and placed on the countertop. Dr. Shepherd-Lowe assembled a syringe with a long, protruding needle that looked oddly comfortable in her hand. She removed a stethoscope from a drawer and placed it in her ears, then stepped closer to the examination table without hesitation. There was no reluctance in her actions, just precision.

She now stood over Bailey, staring at Michael like an executioner awaiting the decree of the court.

Michael felt like he was on a roller coaster that had slowly cranked itself to the top of the track and was about to plummet over the other side. He rewound the leash and fixed his grip on Bailey's mane. The posters continued to stare at him with seething eyes.

The only eyes that spared him were Bailey's. She lay on the table with her back to the doctor and her legs pointing at Michael, but her eyes continued to look into a bare corner of the room. Her tongue came out of her mouth several times, and when Michael moved his hand in front of her mouth she began licking it. She lifted her head and cleaned his entire hand before resting back down on the table.

Stroking her head, Michael said to the doctor, "It's alright, go ahead."

The doctor cleared the fur in Bailey's front leg and plunged the needle into a vein, squeezing in the poison with measured speed. Bailey winced at first but then settled when the doctor placed the working end of the stethoscope over her heart.

Then they waited.

Michael watched as Bailey's breathing slowed and then her eyelids blinked, drooped, and collapsed as the doctor kept a vigilant ear over her heart. She lay so incredibly peacefully on the flat table that envy began to crawl into Michael's mind. He had the sudden and incurable urge to run—to run fast and far from this place, from this act, from himself and what had become of him. He wanted to run out of the building, out of the towns and cities, to places where fields stretched across the landscape and flowers challenged each other in a competitive bloom. A place where birds chirped and swooped overhead in playful acrobatics while the sun warmed their wings. A place where he, too, could lie down and be cajoled into a pleasant, eternal sleep.

As he watched the doctor's attention become more acute to the sounds of Bailey's fading heart, his guilt over murdering his dog began to subside into the comfort of knowing he had rescued her from the grips of her tormentor.

Bailey's jaw loosened and her mouth fell open. She lay still for elongated seconds until the doctor finally reported, "She's gone."

Michael stood frozen, one hand grasping her lifeless mane and the other clutching the useless leash. The doctor disconnected the clip from Bailey's collar and the metal end slid down Bailey's body until it clunked on the table, jolting Michael out of his daze. He heard the soothing hum of the ventilation system and saw his hand still clutching her fur. Then he saw the pool of urine that had leaked out between her legs and he abruptly released his hand.

As soon as he did, he found himself standing alone and disconnected from one of the last things that gave him purpose in life.

For reasons he could not understand, he thanked the doctor before bending over, kissing Bailey's face, and then walking out of the examination room.

He found himself back in the waiting room, the target of disapproving eyes that had seen him enter with the dog but not walk out with her. The empty clip of the leash dangled from his hand like an empty noose as the nylon continued to strangle the blood out of his misshapen hand.

It suddenly occurred to him that in a sweet and clever solution, he had turned death on itself; now he wondered how he could use this strategy to eradicate the evilness that lived within him.

The last thing he heard before fleeing the clinic came from the intercom.

"All set, Kerrie."

Michael ran down the sidewalk, dodging children holding hands with their parents and dogs attached to owners. He turned into the parking lot and, evading cars pulling in and pulling out, found his father's car—his car now—and jumped into its protective shell. He sped home, breezing through stop signs and ignoring traffic signals, until he arrived to the safety of the driveway.

He sat silently there for a while, but even the driveway was not enough protection from the watchful, accusing eyes of the world. He scurried into the house and up to his bedroom, where he slammed the door shut and flopped onto his unmade bed.

"What have I done?" he cried into his pillow.

He tried to think of Bailey, but all memories of her had already been erased from his mind. He tried to concentrate on images of her as a puppy or even something more recent but could not. His mother's image had long since disappeared, and even images of his father had now faded.

He hated Cancer and all the suffering it had caused. He was so alone, and the loneliness created a pain that he could not relieve, so much so that it no longer made sense to live another day as long as Cancer lived within him. He raised himself from his bed, taking the blanket with him. He threw it over himself so it covered his head and shoulders, went to his bureau and took his jackknife, and then raced out of his bedroom down to the bathroom, where he kneeled at the toilet.

His belly erupted, ejecting phlegm and bile and whatever undigested nibbles he had managed to feed himself that day. Aim seemed unimportant, and he splashed the toilet seat and sullied his face and hands with his vomit. The ache from his stomach did not eject with it, however.

Sitting on the floor, wiping his face with his sleeve, he saw only one viable end to the assault. He pushed his shirtsleeves up to his elbows, pushed himself over to the bathtub, and began running the cold water. He shivered as he thrust his forearms into the chilly flow, letting the water sap the feeling from them. With urgent, unsteady hands, he unfolded the knife, held it over his wrist, and prepared to drain himself of the wretched poison that had lived within him and his family too long.

It would take a steady slice along the vein to carry out the solution that had worked so well for Bailey, but both of Michael's hands were shaking so hard with fear and chill that they were knocking together. His enraged heart thumped within him and adrenaline surged through his body, pushing the veins out from his wrist. He could see the purple pulsating lines beneath his skin telling him it made sense to release the pressure. Slice the vein and the pressure within his entire body would be released and washed down the drain, leaving him with the final sleep he so desired.

His head began to knock, which blended with the muffled rushing of the water, but then he heard someone calling his name from a far-off place, as if calling him back from the void he resided in.

"Michael?" It came from behind the bathroom door, followed by more knocking. "Michael?"

The knife fell out of his hand and splashed into the tub.

"Yes?" he answered between heavy breaths.

"Are you all right?"

He wasn't all right. He stared into the water and saw his distorted reflection. He was a living, breathing mess.

Suddenly, he realized that even if what he was about to do was a viable solution for him, it was not an answer that would keep Daniel protected. Michael had vowed to guard him, and ending his life now would remove Daniel's protection from Cancer—from Julie, from all its horrible forms. He could hold on to the pain a little longer, until he could find another way.

"Yes, I'm . . . it was something I ate," he called hoarsely. "I'll be fine."

"Well hurry up, I need the bathroom."

Michael heard Daniel step away from the door but then return. "Have you seen Bailey?"

CHAPTER 26

Michael now moved with the uncontrollable attachment of a shadow that could only move when the thing that guided him moved. And like a shadow, he could only be detached and free when the light was extinguished. He found comfort in the darkness because it was only without the light that a shadow could not exist. And as each day passed with Cancer swelling uncontrollably within him, with memories of his mother and father and Bailey now consumed, his desire to cease existing began to govern him more powerfully. Fighting death with suicide began to make sense as it only could to someone in such a sad, depressive state.

The only thing that kept him from surrendering to its pull was the fact that he could not leave his brother exposed and unguarded.

He needed a plan, a single plan that would accomplish the trifecta of ending his misery, imprisoning Cancer, and providing a means for Daniel to live unfettered by the imperceptible evils that would seek to destroy him. And it was only in dark and lonely places, places free of distraction, that he was able to assemble the disassembled pieces of his dilemma and develop a plan with the very tool that Cancer sought to destroy: his mind.

It brought him to the only place left for him to go. He sat motionless in a comfortable chair and waited for Cancer to arrive.

He went there without hesitation and without fear, for he no longer feared what he had become or what would become of him. He had long ago learned to sit in this frozen silence, blocking out the scratchy sounds of people and things and chasing away the light. Time wafted by like driftwood on the open ocean, appearing and then disappearing among the bobbing waves. He assumed that sleep crept into these stationary hours, but he was never certain of that because the white and black of everything had melted into gray, forever dissolving its edges.

He stared for hours at the back of the door with the patience of an astronomer and did not even blink when he heard jingling keys scratching at the lock. He watched from the inside as the confused bolt twisted back and forth until it finally realized it had been unlocked at the start.

The door moved slowly open and Cancer entered its lair with a startled eye and a cautious step.

"What are you doing here?" Julie asked.

Michael just stared at her, studying her in a way he had never done before. His initial snapshot of her face when the door opened was a fresh, revitalized portrait, but that image was instantly erased and supplanted with a bemused expression that struggled to restore itself.

She stepped in slowly but left the door open. "What are you doing here?" she repeated.

Michael looked away from her to acknowledge the presence of her computer and printer at the desk, wrapped with a dust cover. A ream of paper and a box of envelopes were perched nearby. Pencils and pens poked their heads out of a university-branded beer mug while a stapler, tape dispenser, and calculator sat at their respective stations. He returned his eyes to her and answered, "It's the only place I have left."

"What makes you think so?"

The numbness that had draped itself over him kept him insulated against her insolence, which now dissipated around him like a wave washing up on an uncaring shoreline before retreating back to the sea. He looked away from her again and inventoried the neatly stacked magazines on the coffee table next to a candle and a ceramic dish. Square coasters were stacked with all their corners in perfect alignment. His eyes returned to her as he held up her one and only mistake. "This makes me think so."

"You still have my key."

"Yes."

"So, are you here to choke me again, or worse?"

"No, that time has passed," he professed.

She stepped farther into the apartment with more confidence than trust but still left the door open. She gave him a wide berth on her way to the kitchen, where she placed her book bag on the counter, took a glass from a cabinet, and filled it with water from the refrigerator. Her pause in the doorway of the kitchen left it unclear who the drink was for until she took a long sip.

"What, then?" she asked.

Michael was in control now for the first time, or rather for the first time something other than Julie was controlling him. His eyes continued their tour of the apartment, pausing at each individual wall hanging, each lamp, each shelved book, and each potted plant. Not a single curio escaped his inspection before he once again returned his stare to Julie, this time with accusing eyes.

"You're not packed."

"What are you talking about?"

"California, remember? You're not packed."

She hesitated and looked around the apartment to see all the things that Michael saw. Then she slowly stepped over to the sofa, sat down across from him, and removed a coaster from the stack for her use. Her movements seemed unusual for her, individually choreographed and executed without regard for any underlying composition. Disregarding his question like a spider ignoring its own web, she looked pitifully across at Michael until compelled to relieve the silence.

"Don't do this to yourself, Michael."

"I didn't do this, you did."

She leaned forward. "This should have ended a long time ago."

"You were never going to California, were you?"

"Does it really matter?"

"No," he answered. "Not anymore."

He stood up slowly, using the armrests for support. His clothing slithered down his body in search of something to latch onto lest it fall all the way to the floor. His jersey dripped down from his shoulders, where it melted into his waistband, while his pants clutched his hips and leaned on his shoes.

"It didn't have to be this way," she continued.

"What other way is there? It happened to my mother, it happened to my father, and it happened to Bailey. Now it's happening to me. Every day I lose a little more of myself, and soon . . ."

There was simply no escaping the gravity of Julie. She continued to suck on his emotions like a baby on a nipple, and he halted himself to retain what little strength he had.

"I have to go," he finished.

She stood quickly. "No, wait—"

"*Stop!* Just stop."

The jolt snapped the room into a suspended silence. They were both standing now, but Michael's eyes had closed. In his mind he was running, toiling, slogging up the never-ending incline of Heartbreak Hill. But what he remembered now was how easy it became once he cleared the peak, how he glided down the other side and cruised the last five miles to the finish line, five miles that existed in a distance territory he had never before entered. Only now did it occur to him that the whole marathon had been easy. It was getting there that had been the hard part—the daily training, the time sacrifices, the loneliness, the first twenty miles.

He opened his eyes and found himself beyond Heartbreak Hill, beyond the hardest part. What he had to do now was still hard, but he knew he could do it.

"It will all be over soon," he said, and started for the door.

"What about my key?"

"I don't need it anymore." He loathed to hand it directly to her and placed it on the coffee table, then resumed his trajectory toward the exit, intent on slipping straight through.

"Michael!"

He stopped.

"Why *did* you come here?"

He turned and looked at her. "My brother," he said with coldness in his eyes that emanated from his heart. "To be certain you stay away from my brother."

"What do you mean?"

He looked around the room at her possessions one last time and said, "You should have gone to California."

Then he floated through the doorway like an apparition, satisfied he had done what he came to do.

CHAPTER 27

The long summer days had stolen darkness from the night, leaving Michael fewer hours to hide. These compressed hours of darkness squeezed him into a tighter corner of existence that he could not escape. He had no one to talk to and no place left to go, with the exception of the one place that continued to hold the promise of sanctuary; the loss of his father had allowed him to trade away that furtive alley for the shelter of the family car, which was now in his sole possession. He would park the car inconspicuously on Julie's street and peer over the steering wheel as if his eyes were the only part of him still capable of registering input. The seat beneath him, molded to his father's shape, made him feel secure among the smells that were remnants of his father's smells. After everything that had happened to him, and after all the efforts of his preparation, the only thing left for him to do was wait.

The waiting was easy, for his enemy had taught him to be patient. It had taught him that planting even the smallest kernel in the proper place could produce significant results, if only it were saturated with patience. And as Cancer continued to slowly intensify within him, his depleted mind could only accept that its consummation would soon be complete. He sat with melancholic ease and blended into his surroundings the way his defeat would soon blend into a victory that only he would understand.

The bitter glare of a streetlight shone down on the car. It also spotlighted a dead tree that protruded out of the sidewalk, its leafless branches reaching out in a tangled silhouette. Its thick limbs separated into smaller boughs and then to twigs that resembled veins penciled against the purple sky. At its base, blackness consumed a hollow carved into its trunk. Disease and rot had gnawed through the wood, stealing up the inside until the lifeblood was no longer fed up from the roots. Yet, even as its skeleton relented to decay and its roots softened underfoot, this ghostly tree continued to stand its post.

Michael sat quietly in the company of this ethereal tree with Cancer inside him, churning through his mind in search of the one place it had not yet invaded and consumed. And Michael did feel as if there was such a place within his mind—a place that contained some impenetrable thought or memory, unrelated to Julie, that even he could not discover. But once Cancer unearthed it, he knew, it would be ingested like all the others. It was inescapable, and containing Cancer before his total demise was now his only hope of protecting his brother.

He was suddenly aware of a faint clinking noise behind him and checked his rearview mirror to capture an approaching figure with one arm outstretched. The sound persisted as the figure meandered toward him on the sidewalk at an erratic yet controlled pace. Just as the figure reached the back of the car, the jingling and the person stopped.

Michael sat stiff in his seat as the darkened figure lingered by the trunk of his car. Ten seconds . . . twenty seconds . . . thirty seconds . . . Michael's breathing slowed.

Forty seconds . . . fifty seconds . . . one minute . . .

The figure stooped down out of sight and Michael's breathing stopped completely.

Another ten seconds . . . then twenty . . . then the clinking started again and the figure emerged and continued past the passenger side window. As it moved ahead of him, Michael saw more clearly an elderly woman pulled along by a ragged dog. One of her hands held out the leash and the other coddled a detestable lump contained safely within a plastic bag.

His breathing returned to him.

A tired breeze from the open window feathered against his face as he watched them saunter up the street and disappear around the corner.

Another night.

He was parked a few car lengths back from the forsaken tree.

The evening was calm and silent until a car moved down the street at a moderate speed. At the end of the street, the brake lights blinked in obeisance of a stop sign, then released as the car eased left and accelerated away.

The air was quiet again until another vehicle broke the stillness to travel this street, comply with the silent command to stop, and proceed on its way.

The cars continued to come, pause, and go, like his nights, until the time between them could no longer be discerned and they swept by him like the big hand of a clock sweeping by the little hand with a nudge toward midnight.

Another night.

A car raced past him to the end of the street. It jolted in a downshift but did not stop, and then it leaned around the corner and raced away. Blue lights immediately awoke from under cover and gave chase.

He found he was not the only one lurking in the shadows.

Another night.

An old man carrying a laden shopping bag walked toward him with one heavy shoe clumping on the ground. The clumping continued toward Michael until it mindlessly passed him and continued on its way. Once past the car, the noise waned in a metronomic *thunk* that teased him with sleep.

Thunk . . . shuffle . . . thunk . . . shuffle . . . thunk . . . shuffle . . . thunk . . .

Another night, perhaps.

He was enclosed in the car like a mummy, with only the open window keeping his sarcophagus from going stale. It was more silent than it had ever been. No cars drove past him and no silhouettes traveled the sidewalk. Not even a breeze was available to stir loose a piece of litter or ruffle a leaf. The streetlamp was now not functioning and Julie's building veiled a thin crescent moon, causing the light to diffuse and bestow a softened glow on everything it touched.

He checked his mirrors and found they were angled to keep his reflection agreeably absent.

The macadam of the street looked like a river whose gentle flow could not be discerned. He felt weakened on its bank, as if he could spill in and be swept away without ever caring. He would crumple in a slow-motion fall and lean into the water with hardly a splash. He would loosen out of his clothes and then float away with the weight of a sprig riding along the surface, unable to control its final destination.

It was these relaxing thoughts that told him he finally and desperately needed to sleep. He needed to collapse in exhaustion, throw down his eyelids, and let his mind submit to endless hibernation.

He began to engage in all the final physical preparations for sleep: He allowed his arms to fall limply into his lap and his eyelids to draw down and close out the world. He relaxed the muscles of his neck and his chin sank into his open collar, where it softly rose and fell with each fragile breath. The weight of each body part settled to its lowest comfortable position, and at long last he began to feel the sensation of a deep and overwhelming sleep looming above him.

Until he heard the voice.

"You need some help," it said.

Deep, dark, and familiar, the voice said this in a tone that indicated help would be shortly provided.

For the second time in his life, Michael felt the hardened steel of a gun barrel pushing against his head. Before he could open his eyes, he suffered a scorching burn that could only be the flash of the gun.

There was an instant of sharp pain behind his left ear that accelerated with the speed of lightning toward his face; then nothingness; then an unusual clarity. As if the bullet had jolted a storage bin and dislodged his memories, Michael started experiencing vivid scenes from his life.

He saw himself diligently studying for an exam with books piled high in front of him. He felt the fingers of a hand crawling through his hair and the fingers of another hand crawling up his sensitive thigh. He turned his head and Julie's mouth attached to him and her tongue reached deep into his mouth. Then he saw himself lying on the infield grass of an outdoor track and looking up into a promising sky while she bound his arms and legs with tape. Then he saw himself on a long training run that took him down neighborhood streets and through vibrant parks until he was physically exhausted and leaning over his throbbing knees in front of Julie's apartment. After drinking in a refreshing winter air, he lifted his weakened body to see Julie standing before him with a sated smile.

As soon as Michael grasped the emotion of a scene, a new memory was inserted in its place, bullying the last one aside. They came in no particular order, not chronological but random and disjointed, as if the bullet were only pushing forward the images that lay in its path—like a rodent crossing through a garden that would not notice that the seeds had been planted in nice, neat rows.

The images continued, with some lasting longer than others, but they were clearly memories of specific moments in his life. He sat alone in his campus cafeteria, eating a salad. He glanced at his watch and saw that the minute hand had leaned over the top of the hour, and then he made a phone call; after several impatient rings, she answered, and her voice began streaming through his ear into the spaces beyond.

Next, he was in a department store, slowly walking through colorful, scented aisles. A basket of lilac bath soaps moved suddenly from the store shelf to Julie's lap, sitting atop carefully separated wrapping paper. She raised it up and coaxed him to enjoy what was her favorite fragrance. He inhaled the wonderful smell as if inhaling all of her. Then the image changed to him standing as a small boy before the open door of a closet.

Standing as a small boy.

This was the first image that represented a time before Julie, one he knew could not evolve into Julie. It stayed with him as he looked up into a closet among coats and jackets. He seemed to know he was looking for his mother's raincoat, and he found it hanging between two heavy winter coats. He reached into the pocket and found a small piece of paper that he unfolded and read.

Look in the car cupholder.

He ran outside to the car, and sure enough there was another note in the cupholder that directed him to the car's glove box.

As the bullet carved through his brain with his memories racing ahead of it, he could not understand why images of his dream were appearing among his actual memories. But before he could resolve it, the image changed once more. He was older again, on a date with Julie; he began kissing her, and then she began touching him in places no one else had touched.

Continuous images of her streamed past him—countless episodes of fondling and intercourse, the breakup, "It's just time for me to move on."

But she didn't move on. The images kept coming in a relentless barrage of him stalking her day after day and her unexpected condolence visit when his father had died. There was no image or memory remaining that did not contain Julie, as she had completely overrun his mind. Julie, Julie, and more Julie.

But then the image of himself as a small boy standing in front of his mother emerged. He was looking up into her hair, where his eyes were locked on the piece of folded paper lodged into one of the many swirls. She would not turn her head to acknowledge he was there. She kept listening to his aunt, who was seated across the kitchen table with a coffee mug in front of her. Michael could only continue to stare at the neatly folded paper.

He expected to wake up, as he had so many times before, or that this last image would change, as it was only part of the mosaic that signaled his life was ending. But his mother just continued to sit there and the note in her hair taunted him further. He slowly raised his hand to reach for the note, trying not to disturb this one last opportunity or scare the image away. The closer his hand advanced toward her head, the more he feared his mother would crumble into a pile of worthless shards.

Finally, standing on the very tips of his toes and vigilant not to unsettle even a single strand of his mother's hair, his tiny fingers embraced the sacred note. He pulled it down, hastily retreated to his heels, and took a guarded step back. At long last, after so many futile attempts, he had captured it, and as he began to unfold it he was giddy with the excitement of a sailor unfurling a spinnaker.

But his excitement was immediately replaced with confusion. This image represented the finality of his recurring dream, yet it appeared among the iterations of his memories being paraded through his mind.

And then, as if the sun had broken over the horizon and cast its light on everything beneath it, he understood. This was not a dream after all; it was a memory, one planted so deep within his subconscious that it had taken a bullet to dislodge it from its synaptic tomb.

And suddenly he remembered everything. He remembered how, when he was young, his mother had played this game with him whenever his aunt had visited. She'd called it Treasure Hunt, and she had hidden simple notes containing directional clues all around the house to occupy the boys' time. The last note would always reveal the location of the treasure, be it a piece of candy in a pocket, a cookie under a pillow, or coins under a sofa cushion.

All these years he had believed and accepted he had no memories of his mother. But now, as he advanced toward death, he understood that he did in fact have one single precious memory of her that had simply been buried deeper than he'd been capable of reaching. It was apparently so deep that even Cancer had been unable to locate it. Now that it was unearthed, both Michael and Cancer raced to it, to have it and to own it—but Michael reached it first. Now he needed only to read the note and follow its instruction to receive his final reward.

As he stood poised to set his eyes upon the message and look to his mother for approval, to savor what would be his only and lasting memory of her and receive whatever it was she would offer him, the bullet pierced through the back of his left eye on its exit from his mind, blinding him from his prize.

He clutched the final note in his hand with all his conjured strength, trying to hang on to both worlds, afraid that if he let it go he would lose his prize—afraid that Cancer was right behind this memory, pushing to sweep in and steal its final unoccupied space and finish him. Even though he so terribly wanted it to be over—in fact invited the bullet as a welcome solution to his torment—he suddenly refused to give up until he could grasp his prize. And as long as he could hold on to the note, there would be hope he could still obtain it.

With blood leaking out of the side and front of his head, his wilted body slouched forward into the cradle of the steering wheel, where he fell into a deep and endless sleep. A sweet, sweet, sweet, wonderful sleep.

CHAPTER 28

The bandages enveloped the left side of Michael's dormant face. They draped across his nose and wrapped around the entire top of his head, where blood had seeped through and dried into a blackened, flaky crust. A thick breathing tube went into his mouth and two thinner tubes disappeared through the gauze and under the bulge of his nose. Only his right eye remained exposed and undisturbed.

Daniel watched his older brother lie motionless in what appeared to be a peaceful sleep. It had been a long time since he had seen Michael's body this serene and he gained some small comfort from this, even though the circumstances that had made it possible were utterly tragic. He had been sitting vigil at the hospital bedside long enough for his heart rate to mimic the heart monitor's little blips and for his breathing to emulate the pace of the wheezing apparatus that kept his brother's lungs filled with oxygen. He stared incessantly at the uncovered eye, waiting for it to open or blink or twitch, even though the doctors had assured him it never would. The only movement Michael was now capable of was the rhythmic rise and fall of his mechanically inflated chest.

Daniel sat for hours, filled with a silent, steely anger that hindered his ability to decipher the steps that had brought his brother from a vibrant, intelligent boy to the comatose patient that now lay before him. He vowed to ensure that whoever was responsible for harming his brother in this violent manner would pay a regrettable price. But the more he studied the circumstances, the further he felt from solving it. It was a set of dots he simply could not connect. He felt as helpless to solve it as if standing under a full moon without any knowledge of its invisible forces, while trying to explain why the tide was retreating away from him. And this impotence to explain it enraged him even more.

A myriad of doctors, nurses, and technicians had taken their turn to monitor machines, assess bandages, change saline solutions, and sometimes do nothing more than offer emotional support to Daniel. But there was one vocation that still had not made its appearance, and its absence compounded his anger. So, when two detectives finally entered through the doorway in their dowdy suits, he reacted with abrupt censure.

"You took long enough to get here," he snapped, maintaining his lock on Michael's eye.

"You must be the brother."

"I'm Daniel." His gaze stayed on Michael.

"Danny, my name is Detective Benjamin Larin, and this is Detective Jonathan Naishe."

Daniel looked up at last, but not before placing his hand on Michael's arm to compensate for uncoupling the link to his eye. "Daniel," he corrected. "Not Danny."

Larin acknowledged his words with a nod. "Daniel," he repeated for effect, "I recognize this is a difficult time, but I'm sure you realize it's important we talk to you as quickly as we can." He stepped slowly nearer to the bed and leaned toward Michael, looking intently at the dressings on his face. At first Daniel assumed he was examining the wound from a professional perspective, but he stared for too long without really passing his eyes across the damage.

"What do the doctors say?" he asked.

The question sounded genuine to Daniel, but he could not help answering with terse frustration. "He's in a coma. He's going to die."

The blunt, terminal answer left little margin for any reasonable or compassionate follow-up question.

Silent for a moment, Larin walked around to Daniel's side of the bed to sit in the other chair in the room. This required Daniel to turn away from his brother to keep the detective in sight.

"How are you holding up?" Larin asked.

Daniel's visual attention was now on Detective Larin but his physical attention was still on his brother. One of his fingers began caressing Michael's arm as he settled on a trite, "I'll be fine."

"Are your parents here?"

"They both passed away, my dad only recently. My aunt is here, but she's been in and out."

The other detective, Naishe, had now moved toward the bed and was standing directly over Michael, using his index finger to test various bullet trajectories around Michael's bandaged head. When he bent over for an even closer look, Daniel released a deliberate cough as a signal for the detective to respect Michael's space. Naishe stood a little straighter but continued his inspection.

"I'm sorry," Larin said. "I'm sorry this happened to your brother. Can I get you anything, a glass of water?"

"Let's just get to it, Ben," Naishe interrupted. "Danny, we're going to ask you some questions—"

"Easy, Jon." Larin's eyes darted to his partner. "This is tough on *Daniel*. Why don't you get a glass of water?"

Naishe was in and out of the bathroom in seconds and gestured the paper cup toward Larin.

"No," Larin said. "It's for you." Then he turned back to Daniel and in an easy, permissive manner asked, "Do you mind if we ask you some questions?"

Daniel recognized this difficult conversation as a necessary element of his brother's situation; he even recognized it was as difficult for the interviewer as it was for the interviewee. He also preferred Larin's measured style to Naishe's loose aggression, so he would cooperate with Larin.

He took a deep breath to settle in. "I don't mind at all, thank you."

"Do you know what your brother was doing in the city?"

"No, not really."

Naishe jumped in again—"Just ask him, Ben."

"Relax, Jon. Give us a chance."

Daniel felt obligated to add more. "I really didn't know what he was doing at all lately. He'd come home late at night or not at all, and I hardly saw him during the day. And if I did, well, he just wasn't himself."

"How do you mean?"

"He lacked focus." Daniel paused. "Or was overly focused. It was hard to tell which."

"What does that mean?" Naishe enjoined impatiently.

Larin spoke to Daniel but looked directly at his partner as he said, "I know exactly what you mean."

That exchange seemingly exhausted Naishe's patience. "How long has your brother been involved with drugs?" he demanded.

Daniel jolted up in defiance but kept his hand on Michael. "That's a wild accusation."

"What was he doing in that part of the city?" Naishe pressed. "There's nothing there but drug pushers and drug users. Come on, Danny, he was making a buy and it went badly. Just save us a lot of investigative work."

"My brother would be the last person to put anything harmful into his body, and he has nothing to do with drugs. And you would know that if you paused to find out a little more about him. But if you don't believe me, do a blood test—that is, if you're capable of finding any of the blood that poured out of his head." Daniel turned back to Larin in dismissal of Naishe and calmed his tone. "His old girlfriend lived in the city. But I really don't know why he was there; they broke up a while ago and there was no chance of them getting back together."

There was a long pause, finally interrupted by Larin.

"Jon, why don't you give us a few minutes alone."

Naishe put the cup of water down and huffed out of the room.

When he was gone, Daniel asked, "How long has your partner been an asshole?"

"Two years."

The quick, precise response erased Daniel's obvious sarcasm and now he was curious. "How long have you known him?"

"Ten years."

Daniel turned back to his comatose brother and then looked to the doorway through which Naishe had exited. It occurred to him that bad things seemed to have a way of happening to everybody. "What happened?"

"A friend of his—a very good friend—lost a daughter to drugs. She fell in with the wrong crowd, took some things she shouldn't have taken. Then she fell headfirst off a fraternity balcony."

"That's sad, but it's not an excuse." Daniel frowned. "He shouldn't treat people like that."

"Anytime he's involved in what he thinks is a drug-related case he gets a little too zealous. I don't want to make excuses for him, but different people react to tragedy differently."

Michael's lifeless presence suddenly became abundantly obvious as the tragedy at hand. Daniel studied him and reflected on how his brother had reacted to the tragedies that troubled him, casting him into an irreversible emotional spiral. When he turned back to the detective he saw that Larin was also looking at Michael but with an expression that seemed to indicate that Michael himself was the tragedy.

For a brief moment Daniel weighed how he would now be affected by this most recent event. Contemplating the chain reaction that tragedy had once again set in motion, he picked up the cup of water Naishe had left and drank from it. He didn't realize how thirsty he was until his tongue touched the bottom of the small cup in search of any last drops. Then he slouched back in his chair and turned away from his brother to the detective, who resumed his questioning.

"You have some information you think might be helpful?" he prompted.

Daniel blinked. "How did you know?"

"You were too anxious for us to get here—even a bit angry when we walked in. We were at the crime scene; that's why we couldn't be here any sooner. You should know we are taking this very seriously."

"Then I'm sorry," Daniel said, "but my brother is all I have left."

"I understand." Larin paused to ponder a secret thought and then added, "I lost my wife many years ago, and my daughter and I were very close; she was all I had left." He tried to smile but it failed him.

At this admission, Daniel relaxed and studied Larin's face. His skin was coarse, with deep lines carved in all the places a wide smile would penetrate except they seemed healed over from disuse, like footpaths on an abandoned trail. His eyes were alert and intense and dominated his face below meaty eyelids that stretched like tired sails. He was like a weathered little boat—weary and yet eager to leave port each morning for the day's catch.

"Like I said before," Daniel said, "he wasn't acting himself lately, so I don't really know if this is useful . . . but no one else could have done this to him."

"Anything you can tell us is useful."

"I didn't see him much anymore, and we talked even less. He came home early one morning when I was waking up and he looked like he hadn't slept in days. He told me he had been going to Julie's apartment, trying to see her and talk to her, and there was a guy who was threatening him . . . had even put a gun in his face. When I told him to just stop going over there, he said it was out of his control—it had to be that guy who did this to him."

Larin drew to attention. "What do you mean, it was 'out of his control'?"

"Those were his words," Daniel said with a shrug. "His girlfriend broke up with him and he was distraught." He was about to describe the night Michael attacked and tried to strangle Julie but decided it was better not to shine any tainted light on him, especially while he was lying right there in the room. "It hurt him really badly," he finished.

"I don't suppose he told you this guy's name?" Larin asked.

"Actually, he did." Daniel's jaw clenched. "He said his name was Tremont."

"Tremont?" Larin took out a small notepad and a stubby pencil and wrote the name down. "Was there a last name?"

"No. He just told me the first name, and it was strange to me that he shared even that, since I didn't ask him."

"Why was that strange to you?"

Daniel shrugged again. "People usually don't say names when it's not important to the story they're telling."

"What makes you say that?"

Daniel paused, not sure if he should push aside the thicket and step on Larin's abandoned trail—but he decided to go ahead. "It's like when you just told the story about your daughter falling off a balcony. You didn't mention her name."

Larin's thick eyelids recoiled like window shades snapping open. "I didn't say that was my daughter." He looked like he was about to deny the story belonged to him but seemingly saw no point to it. "How did you guess?"

"You said she *was* all you had left. Who else could you have been talking about?" With a nod toward Naishe's exit he added, "You're his 'very good friend,' right?"

Detective Larin looked uncomfortable at having been exposed. "You're very perceptive," he said, clearly trying to draw the attention away from himself. "Maybe you should be the detective."

Daniel remained focused on his brother. "So, you think it means something?"

"Maybe he really felt threatened—thought he might be in danger. Maybe he told you as insurance in case anything bad really ended up happening to him."

Daniel considered that idea but wasn't convinced it explained his brother's behavior. He looked at Michael again, his mind resting peacefully beneath the gauze. "Maybe," he said, almost absentmindedly, "but I don't think Michael is that simple."

"Well, if you think of something else, you be sure to share it with us."

"Of course."

"We'll go have a talk with"—Larin looked at his notebook—"Tremont." He stood to leave but hesitated at the foot of the bed for a last look at Michael. Again he stared for an unusually long time, but this time Daniel observed the heavy eyes and understood. The detective stared at the helpless, lifeless body as if from the distant side of a canyon he could not cross. The bandages hid his daughter's face and the machines spoke to him with an emotionless whisper that faded into stark silence. For probably not the last time, he likely cursed the person who made his daughter do things she would not have otherwise done.

"The other name?" the detective asked.

"Who?"

"The girlfriend. You said she lived there."

"Julie. Julie Myers."

He penciled it into his notebook and put it away. "Look after your brother."

Daniel gave a slight nod. "He's holding on to something, and I won't lose him until he lets it go."

The detective took in one last look of the bandages, the bloodstains, the tubes, and the machines. "He's holding on very tightly. Whoever is responsible for this will get what they deserve."

"I'm sure of it," Daniel responded.

Larin broke his abstraction with Michael and sailed out of the room full of purpose.

Daniel replaced his hand on his brother's arm and felt the awkward absence of even the slightest response. He passed his eyes over the length of the white blanket that covered Michael's body like a fresh mantle of snow. Although unharmed, Michael's body had died, and the blanket was a shortened shroud that soon would be drawn up over him.

His head protruded out of the top of the blanket and sank into two soft pillows, but the pale remnant of his right eye was sunk even farther into his face. The bloody bandages and plastic tubes could not distract Daniel from observing the unwavering eyelash and wondering what thoughts echoed endlessly behind it. The lifeless body and mechanically operated lungs confirmed that the only part of Michael's body now capable of activity was the very part that was pierced. He would not recover—and yet still he did not die. If his mind knew that death was its final remaining course and still had not yet succumbed, Daniel thought, then some incalculable strength was resisting with some purpose that could have meaning only to him.

Daniel was alone now. No mother, no father, no Bailey, and only a small window of time before he lost his only brother. But somehow, with all his guardians gone, he felt like he would be safe. All that was left for him to do was wait for his brother to pass and curse the person who did this to him.

He leaned forward to continue staring at Michael's hopeful eye and said softly, "Not until you know I am safe. But from what?"

CHAPTER 29

Tremont lay stretched out on a foreign bed and yearned to be back in the haven of his grandmother's apartment. For his entire life he had slept only on a sofa bed—a mattress and cushions doubled over in a daytime disguise that was unfolded and revealed only at night. His mother's had been a broken contraption that he wrestled with daily; his grandmother's glided effortlessly into and out of its shell to suit his needs. Both shared the same maniacal construction of metal bars that pressed uncomfortably across his back, but he still preferred either of them to the bed he currently occupied. For although this was an actual bed, the horizontal bars that had once pushed him out early in the morning were now supplanted by vertical bars that pressed him into the confines of a tiny jail cell.

He stared at the ceiling with his hands behind his head and replayed the knotted events that had put him there. The police cruiser's arrival to his street-corner perch had been nothing new to him, nor had the officer's questions. What had been different was the first question they'd asked him—and as soon as he'd heard it, he'd resigned himself to the fact that, for the first time in his adult life, he would not be able to control what would happen next.

"Would you face the wall and spread your arms and legs?"

His first attorney attempted to convince him the search was legal because the victim's brother had indicated he possessed a weapon; the police had a right to search him prior to questioning for their safety, he had said. When the ballistics test established that the bullet recovered at the crime scene had been discharged from the gun found in his waistband, he'd discharged that attorney.

When his second attorney had tried to convince him he needed a better alibi, one that could be convincingly verified to show he had not had the opportunity to commit the crime, he'd instead sought out a better attorney.

When his next, and last, attorney had directed her focus to what the district attorney's office lacked instead of what they possessed, he'd felt significantly more confident that his interests were being protected. This attorney had acknowledged that the facts related to both his opportunity to commit the crime and means to carry it out were inescapable. But she'd also recognized that what was delaying the commonwealth from actually filing charges was a continued failure to discern what had motivated him to try to murder a seemingly benign college student.

Tremont knew this was a secret that would ultimately astonish no one, but an understanding of the deeper origin would be of constructive interest to those wishing to mete out punishment. It was information he had been tightly withholding until the full weight of its value could be exploited for his gain—and today was that day.

The cell served its purpose to confine him, but it also allowed him to focus his thoughts without distraction. Even though he was behind bars, jail connoted a sense of hope to him in terms of his fate not yet being set, as opposed to a prison, which would sanction a finality he hoped to minimize. He had learned to deal, and that had become his greatest skill. But instead of dealing for money, his mission was now to deal for time, and if it was indeed true that time was money, he should prove to be very successful.

A guard appeared at his cell and rapped his club softly, but firmly, against the bars to get his attention. "They're ready for you."

Tremont rose in a single, fluid motion, stepped toward the bars, and submitted his hands through an opening. He stood four inches taller and two inches wider on each side than the guard. He glared down at his captor's thin face, but he could not make eye contact because the guard kept his eyes on his business.

The handcuffs promptly snapped closed to a tight fit. Only then was the door unlocked and opened for Tremont to step out, and as soon as he did his upper arm was grasped from behind. Tremont tested his guide by attempting a subtle turn, but the grip immediately tightened and adroitly forced his body frontward.

"You know the way," the guard affirmed.

They walked the length of the short corridor, past several other cells, then through a heavy door, down a much longer corridor with many doors, and into another corridor that ended at a door framing a single pane of glass. The door was painted the same flat beige as the rest of the hallway and casings; even the metal hinges and doorknob had not escaped the overly aggressive paintbrush responsible. The entire trip was made without Tremont glimpsing another prisoner or any natural light.

The guard reached forward with his club and rapped once on the windowpane with the same soft-yet-solid knock as before. Detective Larin's face sailed into the window frame and promptly opened the door for Tremont to pass through, which he did.

The room was square and bare except for an awkward rectangular table and two sets of chairs arranged on opposing sides. There was a pitcher of water and glasses but only a single can of soda. A tape recorder was noticeably absent. The walls were otherwise barren, devoid even of windows or mirrors, and if not for the corner floor grate resonating the faint hum of ventilation, no other noise would have been capable of entering or leaving the room.

Tremont's attorney sat next to an empty chair on his side of the table with a briefcase at her feet; an anxious assistant district attorney sat erect next to an empty chair on the opposite flank.

Tremont reached for the chair closest to him with both hands, as they were inexorably linked, dragged it backward, and slid down into it. Detective Larin walked to the other side of the table but propped himself against the wall with a patient pose.

The assistant DA claimed the soda can by snapping it open and pouring its entirety into a glass with a practiced hand; the others watched the foam rise like a river cresting against its banks and then melt away, leaving the soda fizzling safely below the rim. He raised it to his taut lips and took a mouthful before starting the meeting.

"Mr. Williams, I trust you understand the importance of this conference," he said. "There is indisputable evidence that proves you shot Michael Galler with the intent to murder him. But your attorney believes you have information that would interest us to the point where we might be willing to reduce the sentencing you would otherwise receive at trial. Although we make no promises as to what the value of that information would be—as we haven't yet heard what you have to say—we have, in effect, come to an agreement with Ms. Timberland, here, to modify those penalties to something less severe. That assumes, of course, that we like what we hear." He turned to Tremont's attorney. "Ms. Timberland, do you have the completed document?"

Tremont's attorney reached down to her pristine briefcase, retrieved from it a single manila file folder, and placed the folder on the table in front of her. The folder looked as if it had been pulled freshly from a new box, with no creases or folds or writing. Additionally, there was nothing to indicate there was anything even in it, as it lay completely flat on the table.

Before speaking, Ms. Timberland reached down again and pulled out a second folder, identical to the first. She placed that folder on top of the other, then protectively rested her hands on them.

Detective Larin stood back from the theatrics but observed intently.

Tremont studied Ms. Timberland, who sat upright in her crisp navy blue suit. She had a thin, shapeless frame and closely cropped hair, which created not so much a boyish effect but an air of efficiency. The fact that she had just pulled out the files in two separate motions belied that characterization, but since Tremont knew what was in both folders, he understood the intent.

"On behalf of Mr. Williams," Ms. Timberland said, "I'd like to thank the office of the district attorney for giving us the opportunity to shed additional light on these tragic events." She opened the first folder, removed a single sheet of paper, and handed it to the assistant district attorney, then returned the empty folder to the briefcase, leaving the other one alone on the table, amplifying its curious effect. "You'll find it properly executed," she added.

The ADA looked down his nose for the signatures and, without lifting his eyes from the page, he spoke to Tremont again. "No doubt your attorney has explained to you that any information you share with us today is for the purpose of plea bargaining only. But we're not obligated to negotiate a lesser plea if we determine the information has no value." His eyes went back to the top of the page and he squinted at the print as if searching for a specific clause. When it appeared he found it, his nose wrinkled, somehow indicating he hated, yet understood, its necessity. "You are, however, afforded some protection in that we can't use anything you tell us against you if we deem it unworthy of a plea bargain. In other words, for today only, you have free rein to tell us anything you want without the risk of incriminating yourself. In effect, Mr. Williams"—his eyes lifted off the page and narrowed directly at Tremont—"this piece of paper says that you are *queen for a day*."

Tremont started to grin with acknowledgment of his current, albeit transitory, control. However, something in the detective's overhanging and rutted brow suggested arrogance would not be a wise attitude in this forum, so Tremont discarded the smirk and affected a more collaborative approach.

"Is he still alive?" he asked.

Larin leaned forward and placed his hand on the DA's shoulder to halt him from responding.

"I'd call it alive," Larin said, "but I wouldn't call it living."

"That's actually an important question," the ADA continued in a more legal fashion. "If Michael Galler dies, the charges will change from attempted murder to murder in the first degree. That means little hope of seeing the outside world again, and I wouldn't call *that* living either. Additionally, our interest in what you have to say will be significantly diminished. And seeing as the thread by which his life hangs is stretched exhaustively thin, I suggest not wasting any more time."

"We're ready to proceed," Ms. Timberland interjected, dovetailing her fingers and resetting her hands on the remaining folder.

At last, Detective Larin took his assigned seat and squared off with Tremont. "Did you shoot Michael Galler?"

Tremont looked at his attorney, who nodded affirmatively that it was safe to answer the question truthfully.

"Yes," he answered.

"Why?"

"Why does anybody do anything? For money."

"He owed you money? For drugs?"

Tremont furrowed his brow, astonished that they were so far from the truth. "It didn't have anything to do with him or drugs."

"You tried to kill him, but it didn't have anything to do with him? Then why?"

"Like I said, for the money."

Larin gritted his teeth. He looked tired but not necessarily sleepy. It was more the kind of fatigue associated with a long journey not yet complete. "Tell us about the money," he said.

Tremont looked down at the folder next to him and then up at his attorney, but she merely guided him to continue.

"It was five thousand dollars," he went on. "I was paid five thousand dollars to do it."

Larin's eyes widened at the unanticipated answer and then he leaned all the way back in his chair and found himself exchanging a confused stare with the ADA, as if collaboratively pondering which of many questions to ask next.

It was the ADA who leaned forward first to confirm what they were hearing. "There was someone else involved?"

Tremont nodded and yielded to Ms. Timberland, who was ready to speak now.

"Does this change things?" she asked with muted smugness.

"It could," replied the ADA in a tone that suggested it would. "Given that a person who arranges for someone's murder suffers the same consequences as the person who actually committed the act, this could interest us a great deal."

"Not so fast," Larin jumped in. "We know you threatened him recently, and that's not indicative of a hired gun." He turned to the ADA. "He's conning us."

"Where did you hear that?" Tremont retorted.

"The brother told us you pointed a gun in the victim's face and threatened him."

"That was months ago, way before . . ." Tremont looked to his attorney for help, but she offered none. It seemed she was pleased with the progress of the interview and saw no need to facilitate his testimony.

"Before what?" Larin pressed.

Tremont relented. "Before he started stalking her. He was always there, standing out in the dark or just sitting in his car." He looked impatiently at the file sitting uselessly on the table, anxious to disclose its contents—until it occurred to him that its mere anonymous presence was having an effect. He'd seen the ADA look at it several times since its appearance on the table.

He reflected back on a conversation he'd had with his attorney a couple of days earlier:

When do we give it to them? he had asked her.

When they ask for it.

How can they ask for something they don't know exists?

Trust me, she had said assuredly. *They always ask for it.*

He'd been wearing handcuffs when they had that exchange and he was wearing them again during this interview. The metal pinched his wrists, a throbbing reminder that he had been snared for one of the most serious crimes he could have committed and they most certainly would not let him go. He finally recognized he had no choice but to rely on his attorney, if not everyone in this room, to pilot him through this complicated situation. He'd grown up in a world where trust lasted only as long as a puff of breath on a windy day. But his past experiences with agents of the commonwealth had taught him that truth could exist. When he'd become an orphan, they'd promised him a safe and secure home, which he'd received with his grandmother. When he'd needed work, they'd found him a job. On paydays he was given a check in the amount he was promised, and when he presented it to a bank it never failed to be honored. They lived by a set of documented rules that could not and would not be broken, simply because the rules said they couldn't be. Now he sat in a private room in the bowels of the legal system with his life controlled by people whose perpetual role was to protect other people, and the only way for him to receive the most advantageous outcome was to overcome the indelible core of distrust that proliferated within him. He would start by having faith in his attorney to direct the course of events.

He was pleased with her businesslike efficiency. He'd learned she did not have a reputation for winning at trial, and for two simple reasons: Her typical client was inescapably guilty of a violent crime, and she rarely went to trial.

The day they'd met, she'd told him that in the face of the facts as she understood them, her focus would not be to get him released but to minimize his incarceration. *I don't get my clients off*, he recalled her saying to him. *I get them good sentences*. That was when he'd provided her with the contents of the second folder.

Larin removed a small spiral notebook from his sport coat and turned immediately to a page with the corner folded back.

"You said he was stalking someone? Was it Julie Myers?"

"Yes."

"And Julie Myers paid you five thousand dollars to kill Michael Galler?"

"Who else?" he responded with a sardonic raising of his brow.

"Did he ever threaten her directly?"

"Not that I know of. He just showed up there and waited."

"Waited for what?"

"Only he would know that."

Ms. Timberland did not move, she did not tilt her head, and she did not blink. She simply waited stiffly, like a blackjack dealer waiting to reveal the inevitable hit card but not until the player requested it.

"That's an interesting story but a story nonetheless." Larin pushed back his chair, feigning disinterest, and stood back at his post behind the ADA. "I've heard better," he added to no one in particular while his fists dove deep into his pockets.

The ADA was not so quick to react; his eyes toggled back and forth between Tremont, Ms. Timberland, and the file, considering this new information. Then he smiled with an odd aura of knowledge.

"Do you have proof?" he asked at last.

Tremont now understood why Ms. Timberland had waited. As he answered affirmatively to the question, she slowly slid the folder across the table, where it came to rest in front of the ADA with significantly more credibility—and garnering significantly more interest—than if she had just handed it to him at the beginning of the meeting.

The ADA regarded it for a moment; then his hand reached forward, but it was the glass of soda that it came to rest on. He lifted it and took a long swallow. While the glass was tilted back and mostly blocking his face, his eyes leaned out of their sockets to continue inspecting the nondescript folder. Finally, seemingly satisfied he had not appeared over-anxious, he replaced the glass and flipped open the file without lifting it off the table.

A transparent plastic bag protecting a single sheet of paper was inside the folder. The paper had two wide, meticulous creases, suggesting it had once been carefully folded into thirds around something thick, but now it lay flat open and empty in the plastic bag with nothing written on the visible side. The edge of an envelope protruded out from behind the paper, and the ADA turned the bag over to see it fully. A nondescript letter *T* was handwritten on the envelope in blue ink. The ADA touched the *T* uselessly with his finger, then jiggled the bag to shimmy the envelope out of the way, revealing the typewritten text of the note.

The room went eerily silent; even the ventilation fan seemingly paused to take a breath while the ADA's eyes followed the words across the page.

He read them again. Then once again. Then he raised it up and handed it to Larin as he brought his attention back to Tremont.

"Where did you get this?"

Tremont leaned back in his chair. "I found it in my car. It was put there for me."

Larin, still holding the note, read it aloud: "'There is twenty-five hundred dollars more if you kill Michael Galler.'" He turned it over, looking for something more, but there was nothing but the curious wide creases from being previously folded. "Was this all there was?"

"There was twenty-five hundred in cash with it."

"And the 'twenty-five hundred more'?"

"You didn't give me time to collect it."

Again, there was silence. Larin returned his attention back to the contents of the plastic bag; he studied the ink of the lone handwritten character on the envelope, he inspected the typeface of the computer printout and the ink used to print it, he tried to feel through the plastic for the texture of the paper. At last, he looked up, but with a different inquisitiveness that had not previously been part of his interview. "Do you honestly think you would have seen the balance of this money?"

Tremont's intense eyes narrowed as he leaned forward with an otherwise expressionless face. "Anyone who would pay me to kill someone is already convinced I would do what it takes to get paid the balance."

"Interesting," Larin replied. "That was my thinking exactly."

The ADA took back the plastic bag from Larin, returned it to the folder, and closed it. "So instead of getting an unwelcome visit from your client," he said to Ms. Timberland, "she's going to get an unwelcome visit from us. Either way, she loses." Then he spoke the only words Ms. Timberland now needed to hear: "I think we can work something out."

Detective Larin was much more acerbic. "So," he said to Tremont, "five thousand dollars is the going rate today for a person's life?"

"I would have done it for less," Tremont answered snidely.

"Apparently," Larin said, "you have."

CHAPTER 30

Michael had finally attained the blissful sleep he so desperately sought. He lay isolated within his comatose body, shrouded by a stillness that lurked over him. The darkness was a perpetual black with no hint of dimension or boundary—so much so that light might never have existed at all—while the silence was impenetrable, vacuous, and numbing. It was a newfound peace that supplanted his suffering with an ethereal calmness he simply floated within.

It was in this state that he experienced the extraordinary absence of everything, from the individual parts of his body to the elements of the world they would normally touch. His feet no more searched to alight on the earth than did gravity seek to draw him down.

Yet within his body, within his shell of skin and bones, he was not alone. A single memory remained patiently concealed while Michael lay nuzzled up against it, guarding it with the dormant ferocity of a sleeping pit bull at its master's feet. Not only was it the final memory he held that remained untouched by Julie; it was also a memory of the person he'd previously thought all recognition of had been swept away. He now understood it had only waited persistently for his arrival so she could finally present her gift to him. It was as if each time Cancer threatened its deletion, the memory had withdrawn into safer reaches of Michael's mind, until finally there were no remaining places for it to go. The memory's conclusion had remained locked away and the means to release it had dangled beyond his reach until Tremont's bullet had jolted loose the key and dropped it into his hand. The final note was now firmly in his grasp, and the end would not escape him this time.

But this was not the occupant Michael was concerned with. Somewhere else, if not everywhere else, Cancer continued its smoldering march through his mind—hunting relentlessly, like a rat in a maze, for the one elusive morsel that would be its final prize.

He had no cognition of how long he had been comatose, as the hours and days in this motionless state had no more significance than did millennia. But like the end of an hour, the end of a day, or the end of a millennium, he was sure this time was also coming to an end. The balance of his memories had already dissolved away like an arctic iceberg with no control of its southerly drift; all that remained was a diminutive wedge of ice that the warm waters of Cancer continued to assail. He was interned in a confined and diminishing space with only his enemy and his prize—a fact that gave Michael an extreme sense of urgency.

Cancer was here, and with an equal obsession to claim that same memory Michael was compelled to experience.

But Michael held the only key. The note he'd scavenged one afternoon as a little boy, and that he'd subsequently pursued for years within what he'd thought was a repetitive dream, was suddenly illuminated by an undeterminable source.

Look up at me to receive your treasure, the note said.

Curiously, the words had become readily available to him. He had not so much read them off the paper as he'd suddenly remembered their simple message, which he had read so many years before. But as soon as he'd recalled and understood them, they'd melted away as if succumbing to the notion that they had been part of the water all along.

Now, with no more memories behind him and Cancer racing forward to steal even pieces of this final one as they became available, Michael's only option was to continue his advance through the uncharted parts of his mind before being overrun by Cancer.

In accordance with the instruction of the note, and just as he remembered, little Michael raised his eyes up slowly toward his mother. The peculiar light persisted, and her profile was softly outlined. He remembered the sense of sheer insignificance that only a child could intuit as he gazed up at the woman who gave him life, and he waited expectantly for the well-earned reward of his efforts to reach her.

His mother sat poised and stoical, her face turned slightly away—but now, as if sensing the moment was finally right, she turned toward Michael with deliberate ease until their eyes connected.

Michael's were wide and anxious, while his mother's were buoyant and hopeful.

"Yes?" she asked inquisitively. She knew exactly why he was here, yet she still played along demurely, as if acting out her part in a play, a play she'd assembled herself, having written and placed the notes that had brought him to her.

Hearing the gentle tone of her voice, Michael was dumbfounded; immediately after remembering it he tried to replay it again from his memory, only to find that it too had now dissolved away.

He had recalled the words from the note; he had remembered the timbre of her voice. All that was left for him now was to remember her face.

It flashed before him and held his eyes with astonishment, as if it had suddenly occupied the entire sky. It was radiant and unguarded. A pleasant glow emanated from behind her yet somehow illuminated her entirely. Her lines were distinctive yet without sharpness. Casual curves allowed each feature to blend seamlessly into the next. Her forehead was open and full; her eyes, big and round, framed a wide yet delicate nose that pulled gently on the corners of her mouth, lifting them up into her cheeks and culminating in petite, graceful hollows. The expression it wrote was simple and now familiar to him from the waning months of her illness, and he knew it belied an emotion that could have manufactured in her a smile just as easily as a tear.

Michael could only stare up helplessly at her while the note clung to the edge of his fingertips like a pawn ticket he was anxious to redeem for what he had so long ago stored away.

His mother, as if sensing his paralysis, reached down and took the note. She read it for effect and looked back at him. Then she took his two little hands into her own and looked into his eyes until the moment was right for her to give him his prize. She leaned in closely, blocking out the remaining landscape. Slowly and deliberately, her mouth curled up into an overflowing smile that ignited her entire face.

The smile was perfect, and it reached into his heart and held it like a fledgling sparrow. He remembered it as the same smile that allowed strangers to feel comfortable in her presence; it was the same smile she had surely shared the day his father fell in love with her, and it was the same smile she had gleamed often before ultimately being humbled by Cancer. This was the smile that everyone spoke about whenever they spoke about his mother. The smile they remembered so clearly and wondered why Michael, strangely, could not.

As she continued to smile broadly down on him, Michael observed that it was not the smile that made her beautiful; it was her beauty. It represented hope and trust and love and embodied everything that was beautiful about being alive.

But there was no token. No coins, no chocolate, no cookie. As Michael saw it on that distant day, there was no "treasure."

He had stared, disaffected, at her while she fought off the waning throes of her disease to smile lovingly at him. He had waited for his treasure, which he believed was never received. He had sulked for days, vowing never to play "that stupid game" again—and he never had.

Today, as he sat perched on the edge of the end, contemplating how naive and wasteful a small child could be, he realized that his treasure was nothing more than the portrait of his mother smiling, and he had squandered it away by casting it high into the attic of his mind. Only now, while rummaging through the remaining artifacts of his life, did he realize its true value. As Cancer weakened the light in his mother's eyes, she had managed to give Michael the one thing a young child would need to carry him through his years: a hopeful memory of a loving parent. Dying, she'd wanted him to have this memory of her face, of the smile that she knew she alone owned—but somehow, he'd managed to selfishly misplace it until it was too late.

At the very moment Michael realized what a terrible mistake he had made, his mother began to pull away. But rather than release Michael's hands she clasped them tighter and pulled him with her, guiding him.

It was unclear to Michael now whether he was still recalling the memory, having new thoughts, or experiencing something altogether different. He felt as if he were being pulled by his mother in front of him and pushed by Cancer from behind. He was caught between the two, with no control of his body—but his mother's grasp persisted until she drew him into her, hugging him tightly, covering him, and protecting him.

All other sensation began to slip away as he folded into his mother's embrace.

He wanted to reach up to her but he had no use of his arms.

He wanted to look up to her but he had no sight.

He wanted to cry out to her but he had no voice.

He wanted to run but he had no motion.

And at last, he wanted to live—but he had no life.

CHAPTER 31

The first time Daniel sat at his father's desk, he could only stare at the daunting task in front of him. Laid out before him was the disorder of his father's files, bills, and other documents necessary to govern the household, and he could not fathom what to touch first or what to do with it if he did.

On his second attempt he arrived armed with a large stack of file folders, a box of paper clips, a stapler, and a sandwich big enough to last him the entire afternoon.

Although the desk had served its purpose as a place where his father managed his administrative affairs, it had not avoided the additional function of haphazard storage facility. But if the consequence for organizing the safety, growth, and education of two young boys in a motherless home was some measure of disorganization of the papers to do it, Daniel thought, the mess that was splayed before him was completely excusable.

Unfortunately, his task was additionally compounded by the pile of unopened mail that had amassed since his father died. These envelopes contained bank statements, medical bills, health insurance benefit statements, and no doubt countless late notices, cancellation warnings, and collection agency threats for a multitude of utilities and other expenses.

It wasn't that the funds were unavailable to satisfy the obligations but rather that no one had tended to them since his father died. So Daniel proceeded to dedicate his nights and weekends to assembling the clerical pieces of his father's life into a more ordered, functional, and up-to-date system.

He began by simply lifting and moving items, a careful separation of categories. He made notes of all the account types, company names, and existing folder labels. Stray pens and pencils were disinterred and returned to drawers, while abandoned paper clips were swept up and discarded as if rancid from disuse. As he labeled fresh folders and filled them with related papers, neater and more relevant stacks began to take shape, while the wastebasket filled with emptied envelopes, duplicate statements, second notices, and junk mail.

It was an intimidating mess, but his task was to bring it all to order—to confirm all expenses were paid up and all accounts were reconciled. The undertaking required extended hours of intense concentration, but Daniel was in ample supply of those. As a recent high school graduate and the lone survivor of his family, his home distractions had been all but eliminated.

During these long hours he experienced a unique vacancy at home. His mother had long since been removed, his father recently taken, Bailey spirited away—and Michael, finally and more tragically, erased from the stage. With the warm breath of life removed, it was more evident to Daniel now that the entire house contained only props—just "things," like tables, chairs, lamps, dishes, and beds, that had no real material weight when balanced against the intangible love that had once permeated what would have otherwise been vapid spaces. As he wandered through his days among the austere rooms, Daniel felt himself indeed alone.

But he did not feel unprotected or unsafe, and he found that unusual for his circumstances. He appreciated that his father's prudent life insurance purchases, combined with a modest accumulation of home equity, would provide him with reasonable financial security. He was as healthy as he imagined himself capable of being, with no physical ailments or fatigue and no unusual emotional distress, given all recent events. He felt capable and mature and prepared for his situation.

With the shelter of his brother and father removed, he'd become suddenly more aware of light shining directly upon him, and his own presence had begun to feel important to him. For the better part of his life he had looked only up—up to the example of his father and up at the protective wing of his brother. But today he looked out—out at a horizon that was both concealing and promising of his future. He stared fixedly in his mind at the vast ocean of possibilities and knew that what awaited him over the edge would be filled with nothing but glorious wonder. But before his journey could begin, he would have to navigate his harbor's exit.

He sat in his father's desk chair with the hope of accomplishing the final arduous task of a balanced checkbook. The desktop was now bare except for the most recent bank statement, the checkbook, and a calculator. Over the course of many weeks, every piece of paper had been touched, reviewed, addressed, followed up on, and then discarded or filed. Every file had been placed in a drawer or a box, and every box had been dismissed to the basement. He had spent hours poring over statements and learning about payment terms, interest penalties, and late charges. He'd engaged in uncountable customer service calls, getting lost in endless recorded menu loops until he'd found patterns he could take advantage of to get the correct person to assist him:

"I'll transfer you now."

"Before you do, can you tell me the number you're transferring me to, in case we get disconnected?" he'd learned to interject before his call was released.

He'd also learned to manipulate the service representatives to act outside of their normal protocols by listening carefully to their scripts and finding holes he could slip into:

"I don't have the authority to take that action."

"Can you transfer me to the person who has that authority?"

He'd dodged their call-ending traps and refused to allow them to escape his inquiries merely to meet their call-production quotas. He'd pressed until he got the adjustment he wanted, the extension he needed, or a clear explanation relating to the question he'd asked.

He wasn't so much being relentless as he was being smart.

And now, with all documents properly filed and all accounts finally in order, he was feeling confident he could get the checkbook balanced to the penny and instead of looking backward with angst would be able to look toward the future with promise.

But long before he could draw the double underline of financial affirmation, the telephone rang and pierced the quiet he had become accustomed to. He found the noise jarring in the empty house, not so much because of its simple ringing but because in the last few weeks the phone had gone from an active intrusion to a dormant background contrivance used only for his outgoing purposes. After his father's passing, the phone had jumped briskly with condolence calls that had died away with the concluding funeral arrangements. After Michael was shot, the phone had rung with calls from law enforcement agents sharing information about

Tremont's arrest and the surfacing of evidence from Tremont suggesting Julie's involvement. After Michael died, the phone calls from those same authorities had persisted, these ones sharing forensic test results linking the envelope and ink and the paper and printing to items in Julie Myers's apartment, and then confirming her arrest and detention.

There had then come exasperating calls from media outlets, probing for information or trying to jab at an emotion to leverage into a headline. But they too had faded away as victims of other calamities had volunteered themselves into the spotlight.

Eventually, the telephone had become just another quiet prop in a house emptied of its cast.

Daniel lifted the receiver and waited for a response.

The voice was female and solicitous. "Is Michael there?"

The question stopped Daniel for a breath before he answered vaguely, if not truthfully. "He's not here. Can I help you?"

"Only if you can help me reach him."

"I'm his brother, maybe I can help you. Who is this, please?"

"Lisa, from the American Cancer Society. Michael pledged money to us this year to earn a racing number for the Boston Marathon. A lot of runners do that when they aren't able to officially qualify."

"Yes," Daniel responded hesitantly, "I helped him with some of his fundraising."

"Well, after the race I was in touch with him to make arrangements to send us the money. There was a delay, and then I lost the ability to reach him. It's been a while and I thought, why not try one last time."

Lisa paused, signaling an opening to assist, but Daniel was caught off guard having to explain an intimate tragedy to a stranger. He pushed the checkbook aside to give the phone call more of his attention, but his mind was still filled with numbers, and words struggled unsuccessfully to get to the surface.

"Do you know how I can reach him?" she prompted.

The words just would not come skillfully to Daniel's lips, and he finally concluded it was best to just release them, even if he tripped over them. "Michael died," he managed. He then provided more to spare her the awkward curiosity. "He got sick . . . he had an accident. Well, a little bit of both, but he's gone."

"Oh . . . I'm so sorry. I didn't know, but that explains it."

"And I'm sorry—sorry to say that means I won't be able to help you."

"I understand," she said. Then she added a bit uncomfortably, yet politely, "I apologize if I come across a little cold, but I'm sure you realize the money is for a good cause. Your brother worked hard for the donations, and if you came across the money I trust you would get it to us, like the contributors intended?"

Daniel's eyes glimpsed the ending balance of the bank statement near him, flush with the proceeds of his father's life insurance payment, and dismissed the natural reaction to be offended. "Don't worry, Lisa. I'll make sure it gets to you."

Hanging up, he lamented his brother's loss yet again. He had spent so many hours thinking about Michael, sometimes independently of his father and mother and other times collectively. Even thoughts of Bailey continued to tug at him. He cried on occasion but less frequently now, as he forced himself to right his ship and be emotionally strong.

He understood why his mother and father had died, and he forgave Michael for stealing Bailey away. Yet the deep hours of the night held him captive with his failure to comprehend how Michael had gotten so terribly sick and why Julie would not just let him go. The district attorney's office had successfully made the case to a grand jury that out of fear from Michael's relentless stalking of her she had taken matters into her own hands using the only tools she had: a capable neighbor, $2,500 in cash, and an anonymous note of instruction.

Daniel had detested Julie from the instant he'd met her but had never been able to decipher what it was about her that so unsettled him. Only since Michael's death, and with endless solemn thought, had he recognized how her little manipulations had intensified until they'd scorched Michael like the solar eye of a magnifying glass trained on an unsuspecting bug.

Time would pass, Tremont and Julie would be convicted of their ghastly actions, and they would spend scores of years locked away in a prison. He was comforted by this. But mostly he was comforted to know that he had been able to so quickly lead the police to Tremont, which had led them ultimately to Julie. And the more he internalized the whole affair and visualized the degradation of his brother's emotions, the more he realized that Michael's death had merely been the inevitable result of his illness and that Julie's imprisonment was far more warranted for causing the death of his mind than it was for the death of his body. He had no doubt that even Michael would agree.

Coinciding with that last thought, a sudden and brutal pain traveled through Daniel's body like a bolt of lightning that searched to end him but found him well grounded instead. It was as if his heart had stopped in the middle of a beat and every other organ had simultaneously failed in collaboration. It must have been the same feeling his mother felt when her disease arrested her body, or what his father must have felt when his heart squeezed closed, or what Bailey must have felt when her infrastructure groaned with every movement.

No sooner had the pain arrived in Daniel and dominated his entire being, if only for an instant, than it was dispersed and discarded, as if successfully defended.

But there was still something else. A curious and very terrible thought had initiated the attack—an attack so severe that, even though it had passed, its effect was to seemingly open a hole in his stomach as he further considered its possibilities. It was a single thought that made so much sense to him upon falling into his head that his attempts to dismiss it were thwarted by the awful feeling that accompanied it.

Daniel tried to replay the analysis that had caused the thought to materialize, and although he could not replicate it with the same clarity, the attempt made the notion even stronger, intensifying the coupled physical reaction. He worked it like a jigsaw puzzle, and no matter how many times he disassembled it, the pieces always fit back together the same way.

He stood and began to pace erratically—first within the room, then among all the rooms—as an irrepressible anger began to leak into him. It was an undirected anger, not because he did not know where to direct it but because there were too many directions in which to aim it. And he did not want to disperse it but rather to concentrate it on the one place, the one person, that was the root of this new thought.

The more he visualized the collision of Julie's apparent scheme with Tremont's utility, the more he pictured Michael standing in the middle like a traffic cop.

He found himself back in his father's office, staring down at the telephone, knowing that proof resided on the other end of an easy phone call. He saw his left hand lift the receiver and his right hand jab at the numbers, sending shrill, erratic tones into his ear. He heard his voice request the listing of the American Cancer Society, then saw his fingers stabbing harder and longer at the numbers again, tones mashed together until they were replaced by a steady ringing.

"Is Lisa there?" he asked when connected.

"She's on another line," said an unfamiliar voice. "Is it something I can help you with?"

"I'll hold."

There was a click as he was put on hold, and then his ear filled with a string concerto that tried to sound gay but came across as a seething screech that struggled to an awkward crescendo.

Two minutes passed before the foreign voice returned to the line.

"She's still on the phone; would you like to leave a message?"

"I'll hold."

The music returned, replaced by a mournful saxophone that pacified Daniel. He was glad for the uninterrupted moments that followed. He used them to negotiate with himself over the consequences of this pursuit, using the unconvincing argument that it was better not to know what he was about to know—but he would not let this idea die. Too much had already died around him, and there was nothing left to grasp but this one idea. If false, it could be unceremoniously disposed of, but if true—

"This is Lisa."

"Hi, it's Daniel Galler again. We spoke earlier."

"Hi again."

"I want to try and help you, but I'm not sure what to look for. You never told me how much money Michael raised."

"Just a second."

Daniel heard the tapping of a keyboard.

"We only ask the runners to raise fifteen hundred dollars, but many of them raise more, and of course some raise less. Here it is . . . Michael Galler . . . twenty-five hundred dollars."

The cavity in Daniel's stomach ripped wider, as if it were about to swallow him whole. He could barely hold the phone against his ear as his hand shook uncontrollably.

"Hello?" Lisa said.

"What did you say?"

"I said Michael claimed to have raised two thousand five hundred dollars, but as I told you earlier, we never received it."

Daniel tried to swallow to clear his mouth and speak but a pasty dryness was bonding it closed. He coughed to clear his throat, and it could have equally been a gag.

It was all he could do to force one final sentence out of his mouth before dropping the phone into the cradle: "I know where the money went."

The extent of Michael's horror was so suddenly realized that it took Daniel more than an hour to rise out of the chair. His first stop was the bathroom, where he forced himself to vomit what his body was reluctantly holding on to. He then went to the kitchen, drew a tall glass of water, and swallowed it down to wet his throat, as well as to fill the hole that still gaped in his gut.

He returned to his father's chair and, staring morosely into the center of the room, tried to bring all the pieces together.

His mind continuously wandered off on improbable tangents that always seemed rooted in the one inescapable fact that Michael had become terribly ill. But it was not so improbable to consider that he'd had access to the same three tools Julie did, and he could have used them in a way that would have solved all his problems. His actions, as incomprehensible as they were to Daniel, could have been perfected by his intelligence as equally as they could have been flawed by his illness. Nothing else could explain his foresight in disclosing the story of Tremont's threat to Daniel. He'd done so, and specifically mentioned Tremont's name, for the exclusive purpose of planting the information in Daniel so he would replay it to the police at the appropriate time—a time choreographed by Michael himself.

Hours continued to sweep by as Daniel slowly and bitterly accepted Michael's fate. It was an acceptance not fueled by reluctant defeat but by understanding. He understood his brother completely because he loved him completely, and he knew that nothing would have happened to Michael unless Michael had wanted it to happen—indeed, had planned it to happen.

He wept well into the late evening hours and it felt healthy to him, even if it was unpleasant and painful. It relieved the pressure that stretched over him and he took it like a nasty medicine, fully comprehending that it was making him feel better—if not today or tomorrow, then sometime soon for sure.

When his eyes weren't buried into his palms or forearms, he stared blurrily into random spaces, but he never saw the thing his eyes were aimed at. He saw what his mind had neglected to see over the last few months: that Michael's spiraling depression had sunk him into a place he could not return from, and that when he'd finally concluded that he had spilled into an abyss he could not escape, he'd hastened the journey to the bottom and made sure he took down with him the person responsible for his demise. And he'd done it with the only three tools available to him: a capable neighbor, an anonymous note of instruction, and $2,500 in cash.

The explanation confounded Daniel and he struggled to give the thing a name. Something he could blame and direct his anger at. Something he could avenge or hate. Until now they had called it murder; he now saw it to be suicide. And yet neither was exactly correct. It was not a single event but rather a succession of events that were part of a larger entity. He resolved that a thing so evil neither needed a name nor should have one, for to call it something specific would be to focus on it and feed it. A name would give it life.

The renewed ache Daniel experienced now was not quite an extension of his grief but rather a refinement of it. He now recognized it was not simply Michael's death he mourned; it was his complete destruction. And when something was destroyed, one could choose to rebuild it or decide that it should never be built again. But irrelevant to those two options, a third and more important perspective defined what was at the root of all Daniel was beginning to feel—that the thing responsible for the destruction should never be allowed to destroy again.

Once again, he had no doubt that Michael would agree—in fact, had agreed.

All that was left for Daniel to do was to confirm that Michael had succeeded.

CHAPTER 32

The formality may not have been necessary, but in an effort to show respect for an important municipal building, Daniel donned his only suit and made his best attempt at a Windsor knot. He positioned himself in front of the mirror and felt the echoes of a family wedding or some other formal ceremony when his father would stand behind him, knees bent, and craft a knot on Daniel's neck in a flourish of swoops. Today, he watched his own hands flit about his collar and could only imagine his father's hands guiding in shadow.

He made numerous tries to achieve a presentable knot and the correct length but each time ended with a sloppy clump and a tail that either fell too short or hung down to his crotch like the cravat of a circus clown.

He ripped it completely out of his collar and began anew, making a slight adjustment after every failed effort until finally the tie fell close enough to his belt buckle and some semblance of a bulky triangle guarded his throat. He wrapped himself in his jacket and, with no one to tell him how handsome he looked, smiled at his reflection—pleased not only with his ability to assemble himself into the suit but also with his decision to wear it.

He left the house as the sheen of morning dew began to fade, walked past the dreary garden and the vacant driveway, and marched to a bus stop that would link him to train service into the city. The family car remained impounded by the police, but he held no interest in ever seeing it or thinking about it again anyway. The banality of public transportation suited him just fine and brought him to within one city block of his destination.

The county jailhouse was a relatively new building and could have easily been mistaken for river-view condominiums if not for its guarded stance, noticeably back from the sidewalk, and the vertical bars on its windows. It had an architectural profile that seemed to invite you in but not all the way inside, the way a stadium affirms you are only an observer, not a participant. In all, the design was a study in contradictions that seemingly endeavored to justify its presence on a piece of prime real estate, because its function certainly could not.

Daniel walked up the wide horizontal steps and entered through tall vertical pillars as if slipping freely between the bars of a jail cell. Upon arrival at the front desk, he dutifully submitted his name with identification, signed a guest log, received a visitor's pass, and stepped back against the wall to wait.

The lobby was wide and open, with a high ceiling and sparse furnishings that somehow suggested it was a respite against something, but Daniel felt no sense of relief as he stood within it. He watched foot traffic pass to the security desk, past bag screeners, into metal detectors, and through sealed doors beyond. Others came in reverse, emerging into the lobby and exiting quickly. Even though there were no mulling or gathering groups, Daniel maintained that this space offered a relief against some indeterminable thing, though he could not discern how he had come to that conclusion without having experienced the very feeling he accused it of creating.

The attire of everyone who passed through the lobby was consistently formal. There were uniforms that identified guards and police officers and suits he could only surmise contained attorneys, prosecutors, and other public officials. He trusted that his own suit would grant him enough deference to overcome what diminished importance his youth might otherwise lend him.

After twenty minutes of careful observation, a familiar face came floating across the lobby with a uniformed escort in tow. Detective Larin tacked left and right to avoid the streams of people but maintained a clear and steady course toward Daniel until he arrived in front of him.

"Thank you for meeting me here," Daniel greeted him.

"This place can be intimidating for some, if not all," Larin said kindly. "I thought a friendly face would help. Are you sure you want to go through with this?"

"It's a conversation I need to have."

"Then come with us."

Daniel tucked himself single file between Larin and their guard escort and followed with measured steps. They pushed through a turnstile and through the metal detectors and then beyond the sealed doors, where they stopped at a security checkpoint manned by another guard seated behind a sliding window pushed fully open.

The guard sat fully attentive in the confined space, which was smaller than a toll booth and had no noticeable ventilation other than the window open to the hallway and a small plastic fan, clamped to the window, that whirred quietly into his chest. His moustache was small and smartly trimmed and his tie was neatly assembled and locked into place with a tie clip. His shirt was pressed with crisp creases that defined his shoulders and traced down his sleeves like singular pinstripes.

The fan made nary a ripple in his shirt, and if he was warm, as the fan's presence suggested, he certainly did not reveal it.

Larin and their escort stood aside while the guard behind the window spoke to Daniel about the myriad of safety instructions with which he would have to comply during his visit to the facility. As Daniel listened intently to the long list of guidelines and responded reverently to the guard's questions, he began to feel the awkward pinch of his tie and the warmth of his suit jacket creeping in on him. Starting to lament having worn the ensemble, he loosened the tie just enough to release the tension. As soon as he did that, the guard reached up and turned the fan in his direction.

"Thanks," Daniel said, appreciative of the gesture.

"It's good to see you cared how to dress," the guard replied.

Daniel acknowledged the compliment with a modest nod and moved closer to the fan to make full use of its whispered breeze.

When the interview was complete, Daniel found himself more pleased than annoyed at the excessive levels of security and detailed instructions. He had taken note of the workings of the facility since entering the building—the cameras and monitors, door locks and identification badges, hallways with long sightlines, and walls without windows to the world—and not as a casual observer; it was as if he were acknowledging the strength of a vault to which he was about to give custody of something of great value.

They were buzzed through a heavy set of doors to another hallway that led them deeper into the bowels of the building. As the layers of security sealed behind him, Daniel began to taste a dreadful isolation with every breath of the fusty air. The guard who led him was not enough to ward off this intensifying sense of lonesomeness, and he turned around to confirm Detective Larin was still following.

Larin flashed a comforting smile, indicating he had sailed these waters before.

It was then that the guard stopped in front of a nondescript door. “This is the room,” he said.

“Thank you,” said Larin. “I can take him from here.”

Daniel watched the guard retrace the length of the hallway, at the end of which a door buzzed opened and swallowed him. It closed with a soft click that was followed by a loud clack, confirming the lock had engaged. Only silence remained, and Daniel could not imagine being any more isolated than where he was now—and yet one more door remained for him to pass through.

Larin checked his watch and nodded with apparent satisfaction. “It will be a few minutes before they’re ready. Go inside and make yourself comfortable. Take as long as you want and just come out when you’re finished.”

“Thank you,” Daniel said sincerely. “You’ve been a big help.”

Larin’s face hollowed. “If I knew what you were hoping for, I might have been able to do more.”

“I’m not quite sure myself”—Daniel shrugged—“but if it comes to me, I’ll know it.”

There was nothing left for Larin to do but open the door and gesture him in. “I’ll be right out here if you need anything.”

Daniel stood alone in the small square room. The walls were a pastel green that reminded him of the first blades of grass of a newly seeded lawn as they began to peek thinly above the soil. A metal table was positioned against the wall with a single chair blankly facing a large windowpane fixed into the wall. A telephone handset hung by its neck within easy reach.

The room had no other distinguishing features, and it was the glass that dominated, the way a screen dominates the features of a cinema. Daniel stared through it into an exact replica of the room he occupied. He saw a tabletop, a chair facing him, a phone mounted opposite the one in his room, and a door beyond. It was as if he were looking into a surreal reflection that echoed everything back except himself. He stared fixedly at the image like it was a mirror that ignored his presence and even prohibited his attendance, as if he were able only to observe and take note of what should be someone else's scene. It made him feel consigned to the role of witness—but to what, he had no idea.

He stepped up to the glass and placed his hand flat against it. He moved it around and sampled the surface but felt no texture or temperature or imperfections because it was not an object to him; it was a boundary. He had come as far as he could. He hadn't stepped in an elevator or traveled a flight of stairs since entering the building, yet he felt he had reached its depths. Beyond the glass was an even deeper level of seclusion, but it was one that he could not reach—nor wanted to. It was an isolation reserved for those who no longer deserved to feel the warmth of the sun. Beyond the glass was a chair, and in a few minutes the chair would be occupied by the person responsible for his brother's demise.

His body temperature slowly rose and he felt the wet gumminess of his undershirt pasted to his upper chest. With the need for formality fulfilled, and given the repute of the person he was about to meet, he allowed himself the comfort of removing the bane of his outfit. He ripped apart the tie with both hands, canceling his morning effort of lashing it together, and rolled it up into his jacket pocket. He then placed the jacket over the back of the chair and unbuttoned his collar.

Only then did he sit.

He stared into the glass and waited. He stared at the exactness of the two rooms and insisted there was a difference. He stared at the absence of his reflection and asked himself what he was there to observe. He stared at the empty chair and waited for her to fill it.

Then a heavy hand pushed open the door and guided her in. The hand then pulled the door tightly closed behind her.

Daniel did not react. He did not gesture; he did not move. He studied her in a way he had never done before. He studied her behind the glass as he would study a specimen under a microscope, like a lesion just removed from his body that he needed to examine to determine whether or not it was benign. Although the glass dampened the sound between the two rooms, the silence amplified the subtleties of her presence. She stood in an ill-fitting jumpsuit that hung loosely around her body. Only her waist was cinched tight and made her look separately diminutive both above it and below, as she failed to fill both halves. The flaccid outfit implied a slouch, and only because Daniel knew her could he tell she was maneuvering to appear fully erect. Her eyes emitted subtle surprise upon acknowledging it was he who had come to visit her, followed by a long, pensive look as if instinctively trying to penetrate the glass and force a reaction.

Getting none, she sidled up to the chair and settled in.

In order for them to communicate, they both had to lift the handset, yet neither would be the first to reach for it.

They sat like stubborn children for a moment, then Daniel, unfazed, lifted the receiver. He knew it was inevitable she would follow, but she would also undoubtedly be the first to speak—and for that he would mark the victory.

As he predicted, she did lift the handset after him, after which she smiled falsely and broke the silence. "You're the last person I expected to see in here," she said.

"That's interesting," Daniel replied with mock congeniality, "I was thinking the same thing."

"About you being here?"

"No, about *you* being here."

She hesitated to absorb his meaning, as if not expecting him to speak words with meaning—then: "I didn't do this."

"What didn't you do?"

"The things they say I did."

"They say you're responsible for my brother's death . . . is that wrong?"

"You know what I mean."

"And you know what I mean."

She leaned back in the chair, again in an apparent effort to absorb his meaning. Her eyes betrayed a clumsy disorientation, as if she was not used to someone volleying with her, let alone winning consecutive points while doing so.

She spoke more slowly now, measuring her speech: "I didn't have anything to do with your brother's death."

"Is it safe to say that Michael is dead because of you?" Daniel asked.

"How would I know?" she asked with a conjured innocence.

"Because nobody knew my brother better than you."

"And whose fault is that?"

"Yours, of course."

She quieted, signaling her conclusion that Daniel was in no way an ally to her predicament. She had searched for some type of verbal handle to grasp and thereby control the conversation, but Daniel had swatted away her politesse with an effective ease that he suspected she'd never experienced before.

Finally, she seemingly restrained her instinct to lead and relinquished the serve to him. She switched the phone to her other ear and asked, "Why did you come here?"

"There is something about you that repels people from you yet somehow still inevitably draws them to you," he said. "I find myself somehow temporarily drawn to you."

"Temporarily?"

"I don't plan on staying here long."

"Well, neither do I."

"But you will," he said, keeping his tone neutral. "The evidence against you is dense. You'll be here for a very long time."

"I didn't give Tremont any note and I didn't give him any money. I had no part in Michael's death."

"Would Michael be alive today if he'd never met you?"

"He . . . I . . . we . . ." She fumbled for the correct pronoun until she finally stumbled upon it. "You . . . you're twisting it."

"No, I'm untwisting it."

He was impervious to her attempts to manipulate the conversation; her efforts merely bounced off the glass. He felt a peculiar confidence that he could joust with her and come away unscathed—because he was well protected or because she had been disarmed, or maybe a little bit of both. He was, nonetheless, compelled to continue testing this premise.

"All I did was break up with him," she continued with a perturbed and elevated tone.

"No, you broke his heart and then you broke his mind."

"You can't hold me responsible for . . ."

She stopped herself and steadied her manner. Her mouth opened to take a breath and continue her response, but then her eyebrows tilted downward and her mouth pursed.

Daniel waited for her to finish her sentence, only to realize her mind had moved on to something else, something more calculating. At first he thought she was finally going to acknowledge responsibility for destroying Michael, but then he detected something more discomfiting in her posture. Had he pressed too far? He eased his chair backward, now unsure if the glass was adequate protection against whatever she was attempting to engage him in.

The silence continued. He resisted the urge to break it. He sensed his time to be an observer had arrived. He kept the phone tight against his ear and remained steadfast in his seat. His eyes blinked at natural intervals, unaffected by the darkening stare coming through the glass.

"You don't care that it was Tremont who really murdered your brother," she said at last. "That's not why you're here."

Daniel remained silent and steady.

"What is this about?" she continued, more thinking out loud than expecting an answer.

Again, he did not dare move. He knew full well she was like a shark trolling the reefs, feeling for even the slightest tremor in the water—a signal there was something nearby worth poking, prodding, devouring.

"You don't think there is a connection between me and what Tremont did," she said pensively. "The police do, but you don't." She stared into Daniel with a ferocious intensity, looking for some kind of tell that would betray him. "Now why is that?"

Her eyes darted back and forth, up and down, across Daniel's face, to his hands, and back again. She tried to settle a gaze directly on his face but failed with each attempt, continuously diverting away and then trying to connect again, until finally her eyes snapped squarely into the center of the glass just long enough to spit out her accusation: "You know something."

Daniel stared blankly back at her, betraying neither a confirmation nor a denial.

Julie apparently absorbed this lack of response as total confirmation because she leaned toward the glass and repeated the charge with an elevated voice: "You know something . . . you know something they don't."

Daniel felt no compulsion to respond, even as her tone became more urgent.

"What do you know? Tell me what you know!"

She stood up and leaned as far forward as she could. This seemingly made the glass barrier more painfully evident to her and escalated her frustration. She moved the earpiece away from her ear so she could speak more directly into the mouthpiece.

"You know something that can get me out of here. Why are you just sitting there? Talk to me, tell me!"

She wasn't looking at him anymore but was now studying the window frame, as if looking for a crack, a space, an opening to freedom. Her head rotated around the room, up to the ceiling and down to the floor. She spun around and spied the door. She got up and approached it, then returned to the window. The realization of her entrapment, Daniel surmised, had begun to take root.

He, meanwhile, clutched the handset and continued to just stare directly back at her. He was unaffected by her urgency and felt neither an inclination nor an obligation to respond to her. As he watched her spiral into an abyss of anger, he found himself confronted with the simple and poignant realization that this was exactly what Michael had sought: for her to be entombed in a place where she could harm no one else and for Daniel to be free and safe from her. And even though Daniel could not condone Michael's actions and would rather have had the opportunity to save his brother from himself, he did find some solace in the end result.

Comforted by the truth and a complete understanding of the sequence of events that had led to Julie's confinement, Daniel was left with only the single urge to walk away. His whole life was still ahead of him, and he, thanks to the sacrifices of his father and his brother, was both safe and secure. He needed only to leave this room and release himself into his waiting future.

But when he raised himself up, Julie's face snapped in his direction.

"What are you doing?" she snarled. "Where do you think you're going?"

Anger continued to occupy her face, but on her it looked like a mask of evil. She paced in front of the window, keeping the phone as a tether, as if fearful to move too far from the glass and lose connection with Daniel.

"You know I didn't do this," she said. "Why do you want me to be in here? What did I ever do to you? Don't leave me here! *Help me!*" She screamed these last two words into the mouthpiece.

Daniel continued to ignore her pleas. He showed no emotion; he was determined to give her nothing from which to feed. He placed the handset down on the table and removed his tie from his jacket pocket, then draped it around his neck and began to tie it in a casual, disaffected manner.

"Don't you ignore me," Julie shouted, loud enough that he could still hear her voice coming through the earpiece on the table. "Pay attention to me! I . . . I . . . I will get you! I'll get out of here, I'll find you, and *I'll get you!*"

Daniel merely stared back into her. Michael had seen to it she would never get to him. He knew it would be a very, very long time before she was ever released, if ever at all, and he also knew that where he was going now, she would never be able to find him.

He effortlessly crossed the long end of the tie over the short end, tucked it up through the loop in front of his neck, then pulled it firmly down in front.

In the face of his impudence, Julie's fury escalated. She dropped the handset with a clatter and began yelling directly into the glass. She discharged pleas and commands, insults and accusations. Her eyes were ignited with rabid flames, her face became fully flushed, and the veins in her neck pulsated with uncontrollable rage as spittle ejected onto the glass. Right before Daniel's eyes, she transformed into the evil thing he'd always known her to be.

While she continued her vitriolic assault, his hands continued the unwavering motions of reassembling his tie. Her taunts had no effect as his hands expertly maneuvered the ends across, under, up, and through the materializing knot. He threaded the end firmly through the top and slid the knot up to his neck while gently tugging at the bottom. Both the knot and length were absolutely precise, and he knew so without the benefit of a mirror.

Julie grabbed the handset again and shouted loud enough for Daniel to hear, "Your brother was *weak*." Her eyes burned into him from behind the glass. "His *mind* was weak."

Daniel absorbed her harshness with immunity. But this time he provided her a reaction she clearly hadn't expected. A thin, contemptuous smile formed on his face, and he made no attempt to conceal it. It was Michael's mind, after all, that had solved for a way to trap and dispose of her. If his mind had indeed been weak, then hers was weaker still for getting ensnared by him.

"Don't you laugh at me!" She stood up against the glass and pounded tenaciously at it. "Do not laugh at me!"

Ignoring the tears that formed in the corners of her eyes, she fell into a rambling diatribe. But to Daniel her sounds were no longer words, just the barking of a harmless animal. She was like a caged and frightened creature, roaring, like animals are wont to do, for attention.

As he pushed his arms into his jacket sleeves and watched the continued spectacle beyond the glass, he regarded the black numbers stamped above her left breast and observed that she no longer had a name, just an identification. In fact, it was even less than an identifier; it was simply an oblique reference to an entity that occupied a jumpsuit in a jail cell somewhere within the criminal justice system. And it was then that the difference between the two seemingly identical rooms finally revealed itself to him. The woman before him barely existed, and where she did exist was isolated behind an impenetrable frame with boundaries and limits, while the area in which Daniel stood contained all the rest of infinite space. The difference between the two rooms could not have been greater.

In a last act of desperation, she reached out to attack him directly.

"You're alone now—no mother, no father, no brother. Even your stupid dog. They're all gone and you're all alone."

Daniel calmly picked up the handset and raised it to his mouth. "No," he said coolly. "You are."

He placed the phone back in its cradle and broke her with the only weapon he needed: the same glorious and enduring smile that had once lived on his mother's face.

Daniel opened the door only wide enough to step out and then closed it quickly, before the muffled yells and slaps on the glass could clearly register to Detective Larin.

"Is everything all right?" Larin asked.

"As it should be," Daniel replied.

"And her?" Larin asked, subtly acknowledging that he had observed her final pleas for attention.

Daniel looked back at the closed door. "I guess you could say she's not happy with her situation."

"What hap—"

"Can we go?"

Although now out of the small room, Daniel still felt the captivity of the building squeezing around him. The structure had an amazing ability to perform its confining function, and he could not wait to escape its grip. He found himself already moving quickly up the hallway ahead of Detective Larin.

Sweat returned to his chest and around his back as he strode forward. When he discovered that the faster he walked the more of a breeze he could create for himself, he picked up his pace. He bounded down the corridors and through doors and security checkpoints as quickly as Larin provided access, and it felt as if the world was slowly opening up to him.

As he approached the final door to the lobby, he began to feel the imminent release that waited for him on the other side, like the surfacing of a deep-sea diver ready to pierce his head into the wide-open plane of the ocean. When the door opened ahead of him, he scooted through it and past the security desk to the lobby, where he found himself finally enjoying the atmosphere of respite he'd so accurately identified when he first arrived.

He let out a long, tremendous sigh.

He was now, finally and forever, free.

CHAPTER 33

Daniel walked out of his home for the last time. Nothing remained there any longer that provided a connection to his past worth lingering for. He had graduated high school, the prosecutors had finalized their cases against Tremont and Julie, and his family was gone forever. With no more strings attached to him, it was time to move on. He felt he had lived the first part of his life as an unremarkable caterpillar and was now emerging from the restraint of his cocoon as a different entity altogether: reborn, vibrant, and free to fly away.

He took nothing tangible with him except bathroom sundries and the clothes he could carry in a duffel bag slung over his shoulder. Everything from the house he truly needed was carried in his mind: the deepest thoughts of his mother nurturing him as a small child, his father raising him to be a man, his brother shielding him from harm, and Bailey frolicking about. All these happy memories danced safely within him, enjoying a separate life of their own.

As for everything else in the house, he had charged his aunt with allotting furniture to extended family or selling items as she saw fit. Window treatments, clothes, books, and kitchen accessories had been boxed and distributed to a variety of local charities. The realtor's sign planted on the lawn advertised his intentions for the house itself.

Standing tall on the top step, he surveyed the street with sentimental affection. It was a modest neighborhood of self-maintained lawns and sparse shrubbery with an occasional window box that clung to a sill under the burden of a late-spring bloom. The road was lined with mature oaks that linked their extended branches and swayed in subtle agreement.

He stepped down to the walkway and regarded the sign. It was a thick post stuck deep in the ground with a placard hanging from a rigid yardarm. "For Sale," it beckoned to passersby.

He imagined his mother and father standing in the same spot more than twenty years earlier—newly wed, with little money in their pockets and big dreams in their eyes—withdrawing a similar sign out of the ground and asserting their ownership. The house would not have looked much different then than it did today. The cedar shingles likely looked a little more tired today and the peeling paint retreated farther from the window frames than before, but it was nothing the eagerness of a new owner could not happily restore.

The surrounding landscape was a different matter. The west side of the house had once been just a long stretch of lawn that extended the full length of the driveway and around to the garage in back. His mother had painstakingly carved out the sod, turned and screened the earth, and created a realm so rich in color that it had become a welcome oasis in an otherwise monotonous quarter. The sun-soaked front had erupted with daffodils, daisies, geraniums, irises, and zinnias, and a following sea of black-eyed Susans. A small bed of tulips had plumed just outside the shaded back, where the pastel florets of impatiens and begonias had populated the soft, cool spaces.

She had built and cared for a beautiful expanse shared by worms, bugs, and birds that had all lived in a harmonious civilization she'd conceived out of a barren tract. She'd fertilized, mulched, watered, pruned, and deadheaded, and the garden had thrived. She had loved getting down into the soil and cultivating life—had even loved the very soil itself.

But at some point, the soil had stopped loving her back. It had begun to sprout persistent and undesirable plants that had choked away the world she had built.

Daniel was now standing at the garden's edge without knowing when he had actually moved toward it. It was like a miniature jungle of countless weed varieties that swarmed over themselves and created a single entity. Tall, wiry vines grew up out of the endless tangle and leaned over the top of each other in long arcs that buried themselves back into the tumult. Large, leafy stalks pushed their way through impossible spaces and unfurled themselves to steal the sunshine. The diverse colors of individual flora had been replaced by a common green, mottled only by shadows that blended into a dense morass.

He stared out over it as if it were an unconquered kingdom while a calm breeze washed through it. He heard it tremble with hidden whispers, as if it were collectively alive and sensing his thoughts.

What he thought was that he could not transfer this terrible blight to a new owner—that it had to be eradicated. He thought of the lawnmower sitting idle in the garage, ready to come alive and gnash through the thicket from beginning to end. He thought of the furiously rotating blades chopping down this nasty growth and spitting the scrappy refuse to the side.

But weeds have stubborn roots a lawnmower cannot reach. So instead, he took hold of a tall, sinewy stalk and, with the firmest jerk he could muster, tried to yank it from the ground. But it snapped cleanly above the dirt and left its foothold intact, ready to return in little time. He made a second similar attempt with a different kind of weed and obtained the same result. It was a defense system protecting them all against just this kind of anger and aggression. They were stubborn, clever roots, indeed.

Another breeze whistled through the brush and the weeds jiggled with amusement.

But Daniel would not be swayed. He dropped his duffel bag on the walkway and reached for another tall weed, only this time he coaxed it with a sturdy, uninterrupted pressure. When the weed did not budge he tugged it more firmly, not showing any hint of the rage it deserved, knowing another quick yank would only fail him again. He gradually increased the pressure until soon he felt the weed begin to dislodge.

When it finally pulled free from the ground, it stole a large clump of dirt with it. Daniel slapped at it and the soil loosened and fell back into the hole.

He cast the weed aside and removed another in the same manner, then another, and another. He quickly learned the right pressure to apply and started grabbing two and three at a time, followed by fistfuls. With firm steady pulls he released them from the ground, shook off the dirt, and lobbed them to the side.

As he worked his way deeper into the garden, a path of clean earth began to materialize behind him. He grasped and pulled and grasped and pulled until he found he had carved his way to the middle of what had once been an impassable barricade.

Not satisfied with his pace, he went to the garage and returned with a rake, a shovel, a pair of crusty leather gloves, and a box of large plastic bags. He began anew from the front of the plot and started digging out anything and everything that claimed residence in his mother's garden.

He pulled, exhumed, and piled in the hot afternoon sun. Some plants came out easier than others; when he encountered more obstinate ones, he popped them out with the shovel. He raked them into a pile and pushed them into a bag until the plastic stretched thin. Hard sticks tried to escape by piercing through the plastic, but Daniel snapped them and thrust them back in.

The bag was tied and moved to the curb, and a fresh one was snapped open.

The farther he slashed his way along the driveway, the greater the variety of wild vegetation he discovered. A biologist might have studied all their unique properties and assigned them botanical names, but to Daniel they simply shared the same monotonous green color, the collective yearning to choke out more desirable life, and the simple connotation of "weed."

While the sun marched across the sky, Daniel marched on through the garden. He filled and hoisted bag after bag and carried them to the curb, where they accumulated in a lumpy row. A long dirt swath appeared out of the wasteland, littered only with his forward-pointing footprints, reminiscent of Sherman's unyielding March to the Sea.

Red.

From the corner of his eye he thought he saw the glint of a color that did not belong amid the incessant and tiresome green. At first look he failed to locate anything out of the ordinary so he dropped to his knees to better peer through the tangle of his workspace.

He stared into the shadowed spaces in the hopes of spying the object again. When he did not, he removed his gloves and poked at the gaps in the weeds, continuously adjusting the angle of his sight. Still, nothing.

Wondering if he had really seen anything at all, he fully extended his arm and swept aside a curtain of tiny leaflets—and revealed the most unexpected thing.

Hair rollers jostled in the window above Daniel's sightline and Old Lady Mim—standing in a bathrobe on high heels and wearing a wide smile—opened the door.

"You should have done that years ago," she squawked at him.

Daniel turned around for Mim's view of the cleared garden and was astounded to realize the difference from this vantage point. How had it gotten so out of control?

He turned back to her and could only nod with resigned agreement.

"I was hoping you would stop by before you left," she said.

"I wanted to sooner, but things got so crazy—there was so much to do, so much to understand, so much to accept."

"Well . . . here you are," she said.

"I found something, something I want you to have."

Mim cocked her head in curiosity.

Daniel raised a single red tulip and presented it to her. "I found it growing in the garden. I remember my mother used to bring them to you, so I thought you should have it."

The smile fell from Mim's face, but the happiness did not. Her nostrils flared and her face flushed out a rare color, as if something more than blood had suddenly cascaded through her. She gazed warmly back at Daniel, ignoring the flower.

"They're beautiful, aren't they?" she asked him.

"Tulips?" he said, looking down at it.

"Memories," she replied.

An awkward silence settled between the declining old woman and the rising young man. They were separated by so many years and experiences yet suddenly connected by this little flower.

She turned away and walked back toward her kitchen with the tulip. "I have a cold drink waiting for you," she said over her shoulder.

Daniel stood, dumbfounded, in the doorway.

"You're letting out my heat!" she called back in a tone that suggested she was saying it to him for the thousandth time.

He closed the door and walked in hesitantly, then turned into the living room to wait.

From the threshold, his eyes lurked around the lonesomeness of the empty furniture with sun-faded fabric and dishes of pink, Depression-era glass sitting on linen doilies. The fireplace mantel had two silver candleholders with thin ivory candles and virgin wicks. To the left was a folded American flag and in the center was a photograph of her young husband in military dress.

Daniel stepped forward and stood eye to eye with the soldier. He could have just as easily been looking into a mirror. They were about the same age, had the same intensity in their eyes—the same understanding of what it meant to protect—and were both wrapped in a solid frame.

"It's right for you, this thing you're doing," Mim said from behind him.

Daniel turned and saw she was placing a large cup of iced tea on a table next to him. Separately, she placed a vase that now held the flower.

"I know," he responded. "It feels right."

"When do you leave?"

"Today. I report for boot camp on Monday."

Mim reached up and placed a hand on each side of his face, the way a mother would to a son, but the words that came out sounded more like those a wife would speak to a husband: "I'll miss you."

He smelled a harsh trace of alcohol on her breath and observed a wet haze across her eyes that made him think she was reliving a similar scene from long ago, but he chose not to interrupt it, as it worked for both of them.

The photograph looked on.

After a moment, Daniel took her hands and guided them down away from his face and smiled. "I should go," he said gently.

When he turned to leave, his eyes again caught the stare of her husband, which froze him. The picture was a compelling visage of black and white and shades of gray that never changed. For scores of years this photograph had stared ceaselessly back at Mim, without the ability to speak to or hear her, when both had so much to say. Daniel felt compelled to oblige them both.

"Would you tell me about him?" he asked.

Mim's face was thunderstruck with joy. "I'd love to."

They sat across from each other until the sky began to fade. Daniel drank from his plastic cup while Mim sipped from an old-fashioned glass and talked about her husband—how they met, their courtship, his quirks, and other funny stories that had meaning only to her. They'd had only a short life together but one that had stayed with Mim for many more years, making it seem longer and more meaningful than Daniel suspected it had actually been.

Her husband was gone and it was only the intangible entity of love that survived, having grown larger and stronger in the only place that could keep it alive: her mind.

BOOK CLUB DISCUSSION QUESTIONS

1. Have people close to you been diagnosed with cancer? How have their diagnoses impacted your life?
2. What are your greatest fears, and do they show up anywhere in this story?
3. What role do naming conventions play throughout the story's development?
4. Describe and discuss the stages of Michael's relationship with Julie, then do the same from Julie's point of view.
5. What are your perceptions of the antagonist in the story? How do they differ from other readers' perceptions?
6. What major goals have you set for yourself, and how has your dedicated pursuit of them impacted your overall well-being?
7. Describe the moments and places in the story where genuine hope exists.
8. What moments in the story pulled on your emotions the most?
9. Was Daniel justified in his final actions? Would you have handled the situation differently?
10. In what ways would Michael's life have been different had he not met Julie? How would it likely have been the same?

11. Compare and contrast Michael's environment to Tremont's. How would their lives have been different if their places were reversed? How would they have been the same? Are their lives a function of nature or nurture?
12. Was Julie everything Michael believed her to be?

ACKNOWLEDGMENTS

Writing a story, like running a marathon, is a very protracted and solitary ordeal. Although you may do it alone, and the sacrifices are yours, it does not happen without the support of those who help propel you through to, and across, the finish.

Thank you to Gary Vura, for reading the original first chapter I had written and then asking me the most critical question and the one that set me on a true course: "What is the inciting incident?"

Thank you to Krissa Lagos, my copyeditor, for taking the time and making the effort to truly comprehend the complexities of the characters. She suggested edits that, at times, proved she knew who they were better than I did.

Thank you to Brooke Warner and all the colleagues at SparkPress for creating a viable avenue for this story to be published.

Thank you to my wife for . . . (I will leave it there because I have page limitations).

Thank you to my father for taking the marginal tools he was provided and building the strong bonds of a family that live deep in the hearts of my characters. We do not put you in the Fatherhood Hall of Fame; we name it after you. This book is my gift to you.

There are others I am grateful to, and if you think you are one of them, you are.

ABOUT THE AUTHOR

Nick Canessa Photography

Steven M. Rubin was raised in Winthrop, Massachusetts, played college football at the University of Pennsylvania, and spent his career developing, negotiating, and implementing employee benefit strategies for large employers. He has completed the New York Marathon, the 100th running of the famed Boston Marathon, and the Marine Corps Marathon. Although a heart attack ended his third marathon at the halfway mark, he returned five years later to successfully finish what he started. After raising three children with his wife, Kerrie, he now lives in Weston, Connecticut.

For more about Steven and *The Unraveling of Michael Galler*, visit www.stevenmrubin.com.